Daydreams

JOANN DURGIN

This book is a work of fiction. Names, characters, places and events either are products of the author's imagination or are used fictitiously. Any resemblance to actual events or persons living or dead is purely coincidental.

ISBN 978-0-9912252-6-2

Daydreams is © 2012 by JoAnn Durgin. All rights reserved, including the right to reproduce in whole or in part in any form or medium.

All Scripture contained within is from the New American Standard Bible.

Text set in Garamond
Printed and Bound in the USA
COVER DESIGN BY Dino Piccinini

Praise for JoAnn Durgin and *The Lewis Legacy Series*

"I love JoAnn Durgin! Her stories and characters are fresh and engaging, and her writing is among the strongest I've seen. I love her unique style and tone. Her stories are right up my alley, offering a fun, romantic getaway."

- Janice Hanna Thompson, author of the *Weddings by Bella* series

"Keep your eye on JoAnn Durgin—a fresh voice in Christian fiction who writes from the heart, straight to the soul."

- Julie Lessman, award-winning author of
***The Daughters of Boston* and *Winds of Change* series**

"With characters that dance off the pages and into your heart, JoAnn Durgin's books overflow with humor, faith and oh-so-sweet romance!"

- Dora Hiers, author of *Heart Racing,*
***God-Gacing Romance*, White Rose Publishing**

"It's evident author JoAnn Durgin loves her characters—and readers can't help but fall in love with them, too, as they tackle real life problems with faith and Durgin's trademark sense of humor."

- Beth K. Vogt, author of *Wish You Were Here*

"JoAnn Durgin writes fun, fiesty, and inspiring contemporary Christian romance."

- Becky Wade, author of *My Stubborn Heart*

"JoAnn Durgin is an inspirational romance writer with a pen that overflows with witty dialogue, creating stories both edgy and fun. Her delightful tales make a reader want to keep flipping pages long after the lights should be out!"

- Elaine Marie Cooper,
author of *The Road to Deer Run,*
The Promise of Deer Run, The Legacy of Deer Run

From the Author

Dear Readers and Friends,

Thank you for coming along on this fourth adventure with my TeamWork Missions crew, led by "Papa Bear" Sam Lewis and his wife, Lexa. Since the beginning of ***The Lewis Legacy Series***, Amy Jacobsen has been one of the faithful volunteers. Now, it's her time to shine in ***Daydreams***. While not specifically a Christmas book, the events begin in early December 2002 and end in mid-February 2003. As you share in Amy's journey, you'll take a carriage ride in New York City's Central Park, attend a wedding and reunion with other beloved TeamWork members, and discover adventure and romance from Manhattan to Texas and back.

One of the aspects of Amy's character I most appreciate is her trusting heart and willing spirit. She's also a passionate and tireless defender of the sanctity of life, and this book holds a very timely message for us all during this most special season of the year as we celebrate the birth of our precious Savior.

You can always count on my lively characters to keep you entertained. It's also my hope you'll find something unique and special in ***Daydreams*** and all my stories through the themes of redemption, forgiveness, and our Father's boundless grace. As a Christian author, I pray life lessons will be learned and spiritual truths will be revealed that you can apply to your own lives and relationships.

Special thanks to Eleni Varnavas, Hotel Concierge at The Driskill, prominently featured in ***Daydreams***. Unlike most of my settings, this charming hotel is an historic landmark in downtown Austin, Texas. I visited The Driskill in late September this year and Eleni was most gracious in answering my many questions both in person and later via e-mail.

For all my faithful readers, I thank you most sincerely for your prayers and encouragement. For my family, as always, I am so honored by the many ways you make sacrifices for me in order to help make this writing journey a reality. *You* are my heroes.

Now, may I present ***Daydreams***.

Blessings,

JoAnn Durgin
Matthew 5:16

Hebrews 11:1

Now faith is the assurance of things hoped for,
the conviction of things not seen.

Matthew 19:14

But Jesus said, "Let the children alone,
and do not hinder them from coming to Me;
for the kingdom of heaven belongs to such as these."

Revelation 3:20

Behold, I stand at the door and knock:
if anyone hears My voice and opens the door,
I will come in to him, and will dine with him, and he with Me.

Chapter 1

Tuesday, December 3, 2002 – Early Evening

AMY JACOBSEN'S BREATHING slowed to a crawl. *Could that be . . . ?* Swiveling on the counter stool at the upscale Manhattan eatery, she tilted her head toward the large picture window of Café Eduardo to get a better view. Holiday shoppers crowded the sidewalk as the tall, dark-haired man made his way toward the entrance.

"Landon Warnick." The name escaped her lips without conscious thought.

Tuning out the clink of glassware, piped-in holiday jazz and animated conversation all around her, Amy observed with unabashed interest as he held open the front door and ushered two austere businessmen inside. She'd seen his photo on the masthead of his magazine and splashed across the society pages enough times to recognize the founder and editor in chief of *New York Scene.* The majority of men in her industry who'd reached Landon's status were well past fifty with paunchy middles, deeply-grooved faces and more hair on their chins than their heads. Stereotypical or not, unfair or not, most smoked or drank like fiends. None of them looked like *this.* Ever the literary groupie, Amy mentally catapulted the well-respected figure to the top position on her list of "Publishers I'd Like to Meet Someday."

Today might be that day.

Closing the door against the onslaught of blustery, early December temperatures, Landon peeled off his gloves and greeted a man by the door with a hearty handshake and matching smile. No doubt, the publisher knew half of Manhattan, or the other way around. In person, he appeared younger and more personable than she'd imagined. All he needed was a baby to kiss and he'd be a worthy political candidate—towering over most men and seemingly in complete control of his world. The erratic rhythm of Amy's pulse testified to his good looks. Hardly what she'd term a pretty boy—in spite of his impeccable clothing and slightly long-but-stylish haircut—he radiated a rugged masculinity in the way he moved, his posture and the set of those broad shoulders.

When Landon removed his black overcoat—revealing a dark suit, white dress shirt and pale blue tie—it was impossible to ignore the dozens of women turning their heads in his direction. A disgustingly thin, bubbly blonde hostess bounced forward and greeted the group with a cloakroom attendant in tow. After gathering their coats, the attendant hurried off as the hostess marched them past the small crowd already waiting for tables. *All that and clout to spare.*

Lost in thought, she turned back to the front. She startled when the bartender placed a napkin beneath her half-Coke, half-Diet Coke and slid it across the bar.

Resting his elbows on the highly-polished wood, he lifted velvety-brown eyes—fringed with insanely long lashes—to hers. New York City had enough cute, suave bartenders to fill Yankee Stadium, but she didn't want or need one flirting with her. "Afraid he's taken, sweetheart."

Her father was the only man allowed to use that endearment, but she hadn't heard it from him in over four years. A wave of nostalgia swept through her. Swallowing a sharp retort, she raised her chin. "I don't know what you mean." Glancing at the clock on the wall, she willed Mitch to be on time for once. Too bad this was the only semi-warm place to wait for her brother or an available table, whichever came first. Next week, *she'd* choose the restaurant.

A low chuckle escaped as the bartender wiped a dry cloth over the bar, buffing it to a high shine. "Landon Warnick. He's always a hit with the ladies. Gets them all stirred up, but that guy's married to his work."

"Excuse me?" *Stirred up?* "I only have the highest regard for Mr. Warnick as a writer, editor and publisher."

His laugh was hearty. "Sure. That must be it. His journalistic credentials." When he anchored a lemon wedge on the side of her glass, it earned him a little extra tip for remembering that minor but important detail before he endangered it with a suggestive wink and a bet-you-can't-resist-me smile. "Can I get you anything else?"

Feeling awkward under his brazen scrutiny and embarrassed she'd been caught staring, Amy tucked a few strands of hair behind one ear, avoiding those flirtatious eyes. Surely the bartender didn't believe her fascination with the handsome publisher would translate into a date—or more—with *him.* Sad though it might be, it probably worked with some women.

"This is all I need, thank you." The half-and-half was perfection, but she'd hug that compliment to herself. No sense in giving him undue encouragement.

The bartender lowered his stubbled chin and surveyed her with puppy dog eyes, his smile revealing a deep dimple in his right cheek. "Name's Marco, at your service. Are you sure there's nothing else you—"

Okay, enough of this. "As a matter of fact," she said, lowering her glass, "maybe I do need something." She hoped it came across as firm and businesslike.

Hearing a grunt, she turned as Mitch dropped into the vacant seat beside her. "Hi, sweetie. Glad you could make it." She gave him a peck on the cheek and pasted on a smile that begged him to play along.

"Want anything from the bar, sir?" Marco tugged on the towel draped over his shoulder and swirled it inside a freshly-washed glass. Judging by his wink, he didn't buy the idea she and Mitch shared anything other than genetics. Their matching dark hair and gray-green eyes gave them away every time.

"Club soda with lime, please. Don't let me interrupt. Go ahead, love bunny. Tell"—Mitch peered at the bartender's nametag—"Marco what you need. I'm curious to hear the answer myself."

Might as well make this good. "It's tomorrow night, but it'd be great if you could come," she said, resisting the urge to laugh at the incredulity in her brother's expression. After twenty-seven years, he shouldn't be surprised she'd taken his bait.

Serving Mitch his drink, Marco propped one elbow on the bar and leaned close. "Sure thing. Where to, sweetheart? If it's an AA meeting, I know a lot of the counselors."

Mitch turned aside and coughed as Amy met Marco's gaze. "Actually, it's Wednesday Bible study and prayer meeting at my church. Want to come?" *Yep, that should do it.* She avoided looking at her brother. He'd seen her in action before and she'd hear about it later. As expected, Marco ducked his head, mumbled something under his breath and wasted no time disappearing around the corner.

"You're a wicked one," Mitch said, making an annoying clicking sound with his tongue. "Using your faith to turn away men. You can't help yourself, can you?" As he raised his glass halfway to his lips, his grin was wry. "Is this your method of missionary dating, luring unsuspecting men to church under the guise of something or other?"

"Of course not. Don't be smug. That would be disingenuous."

"What's that mean?" He shot her a look before draining his club soda. "I'm a stockbroker, not an expert on the English language."

"You know very well what it means or you should return that fancy Ivy League degree and demand your money back. I gave Marco the opportunity to go, and I'd love it if he'd take me up on the offer. On the other hand, if he's not interested, it's a surefire way to send a guy sprinting in the opposite direction. You saw what happened. He couldn't get away fast enough. I guess that's what I get for waiting in the bar—in the restaurant *you* picked, by the way—but it's not like I'm going to find a man by strutting around Manhattan wearing a T-shirt that reads, 'I'm a Bible-believing girl—Only Christians need apply' emblazoned across my chest." She frowned. "Not that I'm looking in the first place."

"First of all, you never strut," Mitch said. "Maybe you should try the T-shirt idea, though. It'd be interesting to see the kind of response you'd get, although that slogan's a whole lot more provocative than you realize. I'm afraid I'd need to summon the Chastity Patrol to protect your honor."

She blew out an exasperated sigh. "Give me a break, Mitch. Contrary to what you believe, I can take care of myself, thank you very much. The right man will come along in God's timing, if it's meant to happen. I'm in no hurry." Drumming her fingers on the bar, she made a mental note to get a manicure—maybe splurge on a pedicure—before the wedding in Louisiana next weekend.

"I'd pay good money to see Amy in love. It'd smooth out your rough edges, soften you up." Mitch met her gaze. "Seriously, it'd be nice to see you smile and enjoy life more. You work too hard and play too little."

"Speak for yourself. It's not like I'm sitting home alone, pondering my single status. As a matter of fact, I haven't been home one night this week."

"Then I guess I shouldn't remind you it's only Tuesday."

The corners of her mouth quirked. "You know what I mean. I stay busy and have plenty of friends." She waited as Marco replaced Mitch's drink. *Why am I so defensive?* Plenty of time remained on her biological clock and she wasn't anywhere near the desperation stage.

"Snobs," Mitch said with another fake cough.

"Are you calling *me* a snob? And what's with the coughing? Are you catching a cold?" She pressed her hand across his forehead.

"No, Florence Nightingale. The company you keep. *They're* snobs."

"Enough of that," she said, withdrawing her hand. "Find a man who can challenge me and then we'll talk."

"I imagine most men run in the opposite direction like Marco and don't know what to make of you. The difference with you is you *mean* what you say. You'd love nothing more than for this guy to go to Bible study with you and maybe find Jesus."

"A girl can hope."

Mitch stared her down. "I know you'd never purposely pull a holier-than-thou, sanctimonious attitude, but have you ever considered you might come across that way?"

Amy swallowed a sharp comeback. At least she *tried* to help others, even if her efforts—or her words—were sometimes misconstrued. Inside, she cringed, not wanting to admit there might be a sliver of truth in what Mitch said.

Chapter 2

RETURNING HER CELL phone to her purse, Amy stole a quick glance Mitch's way. The tiny lines surrounding his eyes and tautness on either side of his mouth tugged at her heart. No matter what else was happening, Tuesday night belonged to Mitch. Ever since their dad died, it was a comfort knowing he was only a phone call and a few city blocks away.

Only thirteen months separated them, but tonight he looked five years her senior. The events of the last year had taken their toll on his handsome features. Losing a number of colleagues on 9/11, including his closest friend, Brad, devastated him. His solace in dealing with the grief had been to throw himself into his work, erecting an impenetrable shell to harbor his fragile emotions. She hated that he floundered spiritually, questioning why a sovereign God hadn't stopped the tragic events that fractured so many families.

She'd given Mitch time to heal but wondered how long it would take for him to work through his pain. Like a noose, it held him in a stranglehold. Problem was, he bottled everything up inside, whereas she preferred to face life head-on and force confrontations, no matter the consequences. Hard to believe she was shy as a child. Mitch was going through the motions of life, but he wasn't living. Losing their father had left the first huge, gaping hole in their lives. If only their dad could be here, he'd offer soothing words and impart them in the gentle, compassionate way that endeared him to the members of his longtime congregation. For now, she'd continue to pray Mitch would eventually find his way back home.

"Maybe I should be worried you'd actually accept a ride from a stranger if Marco decided to take you up on your offer," he said. "Although the odds of that happening aren't looking good in your favor."

His words startled Amy from her reverie. "I'm sorry. What?"

"Your trusting nature is admirable, but not all people have your best interests at heart." He pinned her with his intense gaze.

She squirmed in her seat. "I hadn't thought of that."

"That's why you need me," he said. "For self-protection, among other things."

"I'll always need you." After brushing dark hair from Mitch's forehead, she tweaked the small cleft in his chin. He smirked at the affectionate gesture, but leaned into it instead of pulling away like usual. "You're not getting enough sleep," she said. "Should I be worried?"

"Been spending time at Felicity's." His eyes met hers. "Don't start with me, Amy. It's a big house with lots of things to keep up and fix. I owe it to Brad. I can't let him down."

Taking a quick breath, she hoped she wouldn't regret her words. "Felicity isn't your responsibility. If she wants to invest in the stock market, then you're the guy to call, but she can afford the professionals for home repairs." Although his devotion to Brad's widow was admirable, she prayed he wasn't mistaking friendship for deep affection or anything more. Thank goodness Felicity didn't have a child to pull on Mitch's vulnerable heartstrings. While strong in many ways, he surrendered his heart too easily. The one time Felicity joined them for dinner, she'd clung to him like a lifeline. While not wanting to be insensitive to the woman—and although her brother's generosity and caring spirit were wonderful qualities—Amy hated to see him hurt over a sense of misguided loyalty.

Mitch's lips pressed together and his cheeks flushed with faint color. "I like working with my hands and fixing things. It's good to wear jeans and a T-shirt and sling a hammer every now and then. Gives me a sense of satisfaction I don't get sitting behind a desk."

"Good to hear it. I'll let you know the next time a TeamWork mission or local project comes around. We can always use more volunteers."

He gave her a look that said it wouldn't happen anytime soon.

She made sure she had his eye contact. "Some things you can't fix no matter how hard you try. You need to accept it and move on. I thought your training at Harvard Med—"

"Yeah, well, we don't need to talk about that. Old news."

Ah, that wound's still raw, too. Her heart swelled. She adored her older brother, always had. Unlike the relationship she shared with their younger sister, Celeste, Mitch understood her. If it was within her power, she'd do anything to ease his heartache.

"Have *you* taken that lesson to heart, Maddy?"

Mitch's rarely used childhood nickname for her brought unexpected tears to her eyes. "Yes, as a matter of fact."

"When?" He didn't bat an eyelash.

Turning her head, she inhaled a deep breath and released it slowly. "When Celeste broke her leg in three places and I couldn't do anything except hold her hand while we waited for the paramedics. When I got Mom's call about Dad's stroke and then found her crying on the kitchen floor last Christmas, still missing him like it was yesterday." Her words choked in her throat. Moisture pooled in Mitch's eyes, mirroring hers. "When I saw a homeless man being carried away on a stretcher last week, his poor old dog wailing as the ambulance drove off; and then when I heard a woman berating a child in public yesterday because the little boy was hungry and asked for something to eat."

"I get your point," he said. "You're one of the few people I know who can come up with ten reasons for anything at the drop of a hat."

Amy leaned closer, making certain she had her brother's eye contact. "There are so many things that could break my heart on a daily basis if I let them. People will let you down, but I've learned that God *never* fails. We can't always protect the ones we love, but we have to trust God knows what He's doing. Without that trust, where's the hope?" She prayed he understood her dual meaning.

"I know. Give me a little more time."

"All you need."

~

Landon shifted in the chair, forcing his attention back to his guests. His plan couldn't have worked out better if he'd scripted it. When his assistant, Dona, had departed his office after telling him his presence was required at this wine and dine of potential advertisers, he'd pulled out Mitch Jacobsen's business card. *Might as well make this more than a working dinner.* With his hand on the phone to call his new acquaintance and see where he might be meeting Amy tonight, a little niggling inside had stopped him. Landon's gaze slid once more to where Mitch sat with the lovely woman as he exchanged pre-pitch small talk while attempting—and failing miserably—to keep his eyes away from the stunning, dark-haired woman. This had to be Amy, but her photo in *Habits* hadn't done her justice. Normally, he preferred a table at Café Eduardo away from the bar, but tonight it proved to great advantage.

Amy possessed a natural effervescence he found incredibly attractive, her smile the most infectious he'd seen in a lifetime of Tuesdays. Shoulder-length, straight dark hair swept her narrow shoulders. In her stylish but nondescript "uniform" of the professional career woman—straight gray skirt with crisp white blouse and jacket—the glimpse of long, toned legs got his heart pumping to the point of distraction and stirred feelings he'd pushed aside for a long time. He'd maintained a hands off policy for years, all the more reason to appreciate a beautiful woman like Amy. Although difficult to guess her age from this distance, he estimated she must be four or five years his junior.

The twosome closely resembled one another, but they also shared an ease of familiarity and camaraderie. Not only were they siblings, these two were close friends. That thought brought a quick, unexpected rise of envy. His dinner companions were engaged in an animated, ongoing political discussion while he half listened. Amy and Mitch were now huddled close, exchanging a more serious, involved dialogue.

When he'd met Mitch three weeks ago at a Knicks game, he'd immediately liked him. Waiting in the concessions line next to each other, he'd made a random comment about coming straight from work, still dressed in his suit pants and dress shirt. When Mitch introduced himself, something about him seemed oddly familiar. Listening to the cadence of the man's voice and observing his mannerisms, it took him a few minutes to understand the reason.

"Sorry for staring," Landon finally said, "but you look and sound an awful lot like Eric Carlisle, the movie actor. Anyone ever tell you that?"

Mitch chuckled. "All the time. My mom happens to be Eric's daughter. Live theater was actually his first love. After twenty years in Hollywood, he traded it all in for Broadway and meatier character roles. Grandpa earned a shelf of Tony Awards and performed up until the night before he died. Not many of us have that luxury, but he knew how blessed he was."

Family loyalty was getting harder to come by these days, and—after hearing Mitch's appreciation for his famous grandfather—he liked him even more. They'd discussed New York sports teams and the stock market and, for once, he didn't grumble about the wait to buy a soft pretzel and a beer. After exchanging business cards, they parted ways but met again when a mutual Wall Street acquaintance had invited them both to the same charity event.

Mitch caught his attention when he mentioned his sister Amy worked for Juliet Hargrove at *Habits*. Juliet had never been fond of him—a sentiment he returned—but they shared a healthy respect for one another. Still, every time he ran into the *Habits* senior editor, she never failed to get in a dig about the whole Lenora Granaud debacle, an unfortunate miscommunication. Juliet would hate him if he "stole" another one of her promising staffers. She'd also never forgiven his unfortunate remark claiming her magazine sounded like the preferred reading material of high-end drug dealers. He'd checked out the latest issue of *Habits* and read Amy's article about a current art restoration project at The Met. The best editors were usually writers-at-heart, and her writing voice was engaging and intelligent with a hint of playfulness to make the driest subject fascinating. Much like the woman herself, from all appearances.

Lord, let me meet Amy tonight and I'll owe you a lifetime of Sundays.

~

"You look like you could use a good meal," Mitch said.

Amy hid her smile. Payback for the Felicity comment, although he couldn't know how it secretly thrilled her. "You'd understand if you had to squeeze into a skinny bridesmaid's dress in less than two weeks."

He chuckled. "That statement's wrong on so many levels. The TeamWork wedding, right? Ken and Barbie?"

Balling her damp napkin, Amy tossed it at him. "Stop that. Kevin and Rebekah. You know better than to insult my TeamWork friends."

"I'm sure they're all wonderful people and not a snob in the bunch," Mitch said, draining his second glass of club soda—or was it his third?

"One of these days you'll meet them and find out for yourself."

"Don't hold your breath." His attention riveted to the hostess—this one tall and blonde, lithe and cat-eyed—as she stepped into the bar and purred Mitch's name.

Please. No woman's natural voice sounded that deep and sultry. Amy tried not to roll her eyes as she caught the gleam in his eye. *Are men really that gullible?* Retrieving a couple of dollars from her purse, she left them on the bar. "Come on, Mitch the Itch. Our table's finally ready."

"I'm right behind you." He smirked and replaced her money before pushing the bills back in her hand. She half expected it and knew not to protest, especially since his job paid five times more than hers.

As they threaded their way among the tables, Mitch flirted with the Nordic-looking hostess, no doubt intent on collecting a new phone number before evening's end. Whatever he said brought a rush of color to the woman's lovely, fair complexion. Based on his behavior, he must not be as committed to Brad's widow as she presumed. That observation brought more satisfaction than it should.

"So, what's happening in the exciting world of magazine publishing this week?" Waiting by her chair, Mitch helped her scoot closer to the table. The way he thanked the hostess, you'd think she possessed an advanced degree in the art of menu distribution.

"Apparently I have a new assignment but not a clue what it is."

"Daydreaming again?" he asked, dropping into the chair opposite her.

"Always, Romeo. I'm thinking of forming a support group."

He shook his head and made an annoying *tsk tsk* sound. "Better pay attention or that dream job of yours at *Habits* will morph into one at *Unemployment Weekly*. Considering your magazine caters to the upwardly mobile urban professional, it sounds almost . . . seedy."

"It's all about publishing a magazine you can't live without, something you crave because you can't get enough." Even as she said the words, Amy cringed, detesting the worldliness of it all.

"Then why not migrate to a magazine with things that matter and you're passionate about? Life's too short to waste on anything less than what you really want."

She tamped down her irritation. *You should talk*. "It's not easy to find a job—much less keep one—in publishing these days, and migrating is something birds do. It was a boring meeting, that's all. If you want the truth, I got distracted making my mental to-do list for the trip to Baton Rouge."

Mitch looked up from his study of the menu. When he smiled, it eased the lines across his forehead. "Being with your friends at the wedding will give you a chance to relax. You could use the break."

"That's what *you* think. Weddings aren't relaxing until after the ceremony, and we both got Dad's strong work ethic, you know." Her eyes widened. "Here's a thought: why don't you come with me? I know it's late notice, but you can be my date. We'd have fun." With Mitch as her escort, she'd feel less of a tagalong since most of her TeamWork friends were pairing off these days.

"Sorry. Can't this time."

"I'm sure Felicity could spare you for one weekend."

His eyes met hers over the top of the menu. "I'll pretend that statement doesn't make you sound petulant and me a kept man."

After placing their dinner orders, she gave him a bright smile. "Your turn. Tell me what's happening on Wall Street. Any new hot stocks or insider trading tips?" She knew he hated it when she posed that particular question in a room crowded with Wall Street types. "Lighten up. It's not like the stockbroker police are lurking around the corner, waiting to handcuff and haul you off to minimum security prison."

"Very funny."

Her lips twitched. "At least if that *did* happen, you'd finally get some decent rest and improve your puny backhand."

"Puny nothing. I'll schedule a match and beat you with one hand behind my back."

"You're on."

Hearing laughter at the next table, Amy peered over his shoulder and locked eyes with . . . . *Oh my.*

Chapter 3

DURING A BREAK in the discussion a few minutes later, Landon stole another glance at Amy. Judging by her expression when she looked his way, she recognized him. In a good way. This was one very focused woman, but he liked that about her, along with the genuine smile and the honesty in her expressive face. Even her nervous habit of tucking hair behind one ear was endearing.

Although he wasn't looking for a serious relationship, a steady companion might be nice. For the last decade—after earning his graduate degree in journalism at Columbia—his sole focus had been on establishing his presence in the publishing world and making a success of *New York Scene*, leaving precious little time for much of a personal life. He knew his mom and Dona meant well, but their increasingly overt suggestions to find a lifetime mate were beginning to needle him. The last year, his social life consisted of charity gigs or perfunctory business dinners. He usually arrived and departed alone, but that didn't stop the roving photographers from snapping his photo with any available female in close proximity. Those events provided ample opportunity to meet beautiful women, but most were pampered and self-indulgent, focused on snagging a man to maintain their lifestyle. His dry cleaners regularly brought back an envelope along with his clothes—crammed full of notes and phone numbers—none he requested, none he returned. Then there was that inane magazine article naming him as one of New York's most eligible bachelors. Yeah, right. No thanks.

Perhaps he was getting older and facing his mortality, but faith mattered and he needed a woman who would share that part of his life. While many ladies professed to be "spiritually-enlightened," their lifestyle didn't back up their words. Of course, it would help if he'd get back into church on a semi-regular basis again. *Time to reassess priorities.* The last time he attended a church singles event, he was swarmed by Bible-thumping spinsters who lived with mama, wore sensible shoes and focused their conversation on pets or food preparation. Then there were the overly clingy types who bordered on desperation and tried way too hard. He'd seen Amy's name on the roster for a few of the TeamWork inner-city projects and he'd made a few discreet inquiries. From what he knew, she was a woman of strong faith and active in a number of Manhattan charities, especially those benefitting children.

You're working, so act like it. His thoughts brought back to the present, Landon started to ease the magazine into the discussion, presenting the magazine in a way to make his guests believe they'd come up with the idea to advertise, all without bombarding them with numbers and statistics. Advertising revenues were the lifeblood of *New York Scene*, and now wasn't the time for humility or reticence. Time to employ his advertising director's motto: *Speak up and talk it up.*

A few minutes later, during a momentary lull in the conversation, he kept his eye trained on Mitch, willing the other man to look his way. When he did, Landon quirked a brow and angled his head toward Amy. Mitch's barely perceptible nod accompanied by a small, knowing smile pleased him. Good thing the guy was sharp and intuitive.

Game on. Let the adventure begin.

~

"What was that?" Straightening in her chair, Amy forced her attention back to her brother. She hadn't heard a word he'd said. Worse yet, Mitch knew it.

"Focus please." Faint irritation laced his tone. "Look, I know stocks and bonds might not be the most exciting vocation to you, but it's what I do. Rudeness aside, when you ask a question, at least pretend to pay attention."

"I want to hear all about it and you can tell me in a minute, but this is important." Leaning across the table, she lowered her voice. "Don't look now, but Landon Warnick's at the table right behind us." Deeply engrossed in their conversation, she hadn't even noticed him. Celeste often teased her, saying the world could crumble around her and she'd be oblivious.

"Really?" Mitch's quick intake of breath and feigned shock almost made her laugh. "Who's that? Some hunky soap opera actor?" He turned in his chair, not being very subtle. "Let me guess: this Warrick person's the youngest, tallest one, with a bright blue tie and a head of hair most men over thirty would envy? Looks your type, but the real question is, can he keep up with you?"

"*Warnick*, and don't be ridiculous. Besides, since when have I ever had a type? Never mind. Don't answer that. He's the founder, editor in chief and publisher of *New York Scene.* The man's brilliant and he's written some of the most hard-hitting and insightful articles I've ever read."

Mitch pointed his finger at her. "And there you go. *That's* your type since you're a card-carrying literary geek. You sound like the guy's PR person with that little spiel. Let me guess—he writes thought-provoking articles about things that matter?"

He could read her so well and understood her better than anyone. "Exactly. From what I know, he's as ethical as they come, at least in his professional life." The man's photo graced the society pages on a semi-regular basis, always with a gorgeous woman nearby. She'd also seen a recent magazine cover article naming him as one of New York's most eligible bachelors. Ah, well, no point in dwelling on the man's personal life.

"Then it sounds like you definitely need to meet Mr. Publisher. Give me a minute, and I'll be happy to arrange something." Mitch started to his feet, but dropped back into his chair when she gripped his arm and stared him down.

"Humor me, Amy. It's the least I can do for my little sister. Actually, it'll do us both good."

"I'll 'little' you." She leaned slightly to the left to gain a better vantage point. "Have you been working out? You seem . . . broader, not to mention I detect solid muscle."

Male pride creased Mitch's lips and relaxed his features. *Better.* "Thanks for noticing. I've been working out some and all the work at Felic—" He stopped and grunted. "I'm encouraged by the fact you seem interested in this guy. Here's a thought: how about I ask Lover Boy Marco to mix a getting-to-know-you drink and have it delivered to Mr. Warnick's table compliments of the lovely young journalist the next table over?"

Amy pinned him with a warning look. "Not on your life, and please don't tell me you're insinuating the man drinks."

"No," he said slowly, as though addressing a child. "I'm suggesting we get Marco to whip up some kind of love potion." He chuckled. "Since this guy shares your passion for words, it'd be a marriage made in Heaven. I can see it now: the two of you sitting across the breakfast counter—glasses perched on your respective literary noses—writing or editing away, sharing granola with fruit, anecdotes and bemused smiles. If you eventually get around to having a little Warnick, the uncommonly verbal tyke would be babbling away in a nearby port-a-crib while classical music plays in the background."

She couldn't help but laugh. "I didn't know there was such a thing as a 'literary nose,' and now who sounds like a snob?"

"Look, it's obvious you'd like an introduction to this Warnick guy. Being such a powerful force in the publishing world, maybe he's exactly the man to contain your sarcasm. Or at least match it word-for-word. You two could sit around and challenge one another. Indulge in lots of . . . I don't know . . . word pl—"

"Watch it." Amy narrowed her eyes.

"Sorry." He cleared his throat. "If this guy's ethical, then I'm sure he's not disingen—what was that word again?"

"The word is insincere, Mitch. Still, the idea's not totally without merit. The man's a master with words." From a few feet away, she could tell Landon's eyes were as blue as some of the ladies at her magazine said. She'd heard the talk in the lunch room . . . and the rumors. Still, she knew better than to listen to idle gossip. If the man got around town as much as purported, he'd never have time to sleep or helm such a high-quality publication. Perhaps Mitch was right. Not that she was interested in pursuing anything serious or long-term, but a few hours spent in this man's company would be time well-served.

"Okay, that's it." Tossing his napkin on the table, Mitch started to scoot back in his chair. "If you want an invitation to the prom, Amy, allow me to arrange it. Sit back, relax, be quiet, listen and let me take care of you."

She grasped his arm again, squeezing tight. "Stay in your chair. It's not like I can waltz over there and ask out a man like that, especially when he's with dinner companions. Not that I'd want to. It enables the masculinity of a man to let *him* do the asking, the seeking, the pursuing, the wooing."

"Where'd you get that? Some kind of mid-century finishing school handbook? I think he'd probably welcome the interruption from his dinner with the stuffed shirts over there. Besides, you're a whole lot prettier." Mitch took a sip of his water. Lowering his glass, his eyes lit. "Here's an idea: why don't you invite Mr. Publisher to Bible study tomorrow night? That could be your opening line. I doubt he's heard that one before." Reaching into his pocket, he pulled out his cell phone. "If you'll excuse me, I need to take this." He rose from his chair. "I'll be back in a few."

"Give Felicity my regards," she called after him. Not surprisingly, he didn't acknowledge the comment.

Settling back in her chair, Amy nodded at a couple of copyeditors and a photographer she'd met at a holiday party last year. Servers moved among the tables with deft skill, carrying steaming plates of food. Her eyes gravitated to Landon. An animated conversationalist, he moved his hands a lot. She would have imagined him to be more serious, but the sound of his laughter was rich and hearty without being overbearing or annoying. A nearby acquaintance caught her eye and raised his glass in a salute. After returning the gesture, she retrieved her cell phone again to occupy her time and keep her eyes away from the man the next table over.

A few minutes later, Mitch returned to his chair. His brows rose when she shifted to the right. "Maybe I should move? Heaven forbid I should block your view."

Amy shrugged, feigning nonchalance, knowing her brother could see straight through her act. "Your prerogative. How's Felicity?" She bit her tongue not to ask for the woman's list of current needs.

"Sends you her best regards."

To her relief, Mitch launched into a story about his latest work adventures while they waited for their dinners. He always managed the impossible: making the stock market enthralling. Her heart swelled when she heard him laugh. Amy told him about her latest conversation with Celeste, and they discussed plans to visit their mom in Pennsylvania for Christmas. Mitch asked for gift ideas and she did the same. As usual, he said he didn't need anything and not to bother. Maybe she could ask Felicity. As long as the widow didn't suggest power tools, they might be valid ideas.

When the servers brought their food, Amy frowned. "This isn't what we ordered." At the same time, food was delivered to the table behind them. She caught the mischievous look on Mitch's face. "Don't tell me." Ever since they were kids, he was transparent and she'd learned the hard way never to trust him with her secrets. "Mitchell, what did you do?" It came out more of a hiss.

"Exactly what you hoped I'd do, Amelia. Getting you a date to the prom." The smug smile creasing his lips was as telltale as a verbal admission. He raised both hands. "Okay, confession time. I met Landon at a Knicks game a few weeks ago. Decent guy. You two would be a great match and in popular demand at dinner parties all over Manhattan."

"You what? And you let me sit here making a fool of myself by going on and on about him." She leaned across the table. "Where's your sense of loyalty? Not to mention scruples."

"Flew straight out the window, I guess. Calling on my inner Eric Carlisle and all. Made my night, though. Highly entertaining."

Her low growl escaped. "I'll either hug you—or kill you—later."

"Always looking out for your best interests." Mitch inclined his head to the table behind them. "Don't look now, but I predict Landon will be coming over here in five . . . four . . . three . . ."

Chapter 4

SURE ENOUGH, LANDON rose from his chair. The closer he came, the faster Amy's pulse raced, the higher her chin raised. Six-foot-three was her best estimate.

"Excuse me, did either of you order a salad?"

If he'd said liver and Harvard beets—her two least favorite foods—she'd gladly claim them or anything else the man offered. Never had she been so affected by a man with such a powerful attraction right from the start. *Down, girl.*

"It's a Cobbler salad and that would be my sister's," Mitch said.

"*Cobb* salad." Amy hoped she wouldn't stumble over her words and sound the inarticulate fool. "Thank you for bringing it over. That's very kind of you." She darted a glance at Landon's table where the waiters served his guests at the same time as another server set Mitch's plate in front of him. The aroma of sizzling steak wafted toward her and the loaded baked potato almost made her groan. After this wedding, she'd pig out for an entire week and eat every fattening food she'd denied herself the last couple of months. With only one fitting for her gown, she couldn't risk anything.

Landon lowered her salad to the table. "In that case, your dinner is served."

Speaking of loaded. "Thank you, Mr. Warnick." Amy concentrated on smoothing her napkin on her lap but not before she caught Mitch's approving wink.

"It's Landon." Those blue eyes lit with undeniable interest when she glanced up at him.

She extended her hand, not knowing what else to do. "Amy Jacobsen, junior flunkie at *Habits.*"

Landon took her hand in his—a firm, warm and not-too-tight grip. *Nice.* "Juliet holds her staff to the highest standards. I doubt you're a flunkie in any sense of the word."

"Junior editor then," Amy said. "To humor you."

"Better." His lips curled.

"I believe you've met my brother, Mitch Jacobsen."

Turning to Mitch, Landon shook his proffered hand and smiled. "Nice to see you again."

"I admire the innovative, progressive direction you're taking with *New York Scene*. It's becoming the standard of measure," she said, ignoring Mitch's smirk.

Landon's expression was one of pride mixed with appreciation. "Thanks. It's a riskier format, but it's a direction I felt compelled to take."

"Your piece on inner-city youth programs and educational incentives was insightful, and the ideas you proposed were solid. I only hope the article was read by the people who're in a position to actually *do* something to bring about the needed changes."

The spark in Landon's eyes intensified. "That was one of my primary objectives in writing it, so I hope you're right. Still too early to tell." Leaning close, he lowered his voice as Amy struggled to control her breathing. "Maybe you could come join me at my table, be my secret weapon to convince these potential advertisers." He nodded at his dinner companions. "I'm not sure how well I'm doing on my own."

"Tell them about the Brooklyn special needs teacher you featured in the magazine last month," she said. "There's also the single mom of five who spearheaded the school campaign for fresh produce and shut down the vending machines. Or how about—"

"As you can tell, my sister's never read *New York Scene*," Mitch said, frowning when she kicked his shin beneath the table with the pointy toe of her pump.

A broad smile creased Landon's handsome face. "I'd better return to my table if I hope to convince these guys to buy some ad space. In spite of the mix-up with the food, it's very nice to meet you, Amy. Please give Juliet my best." He nodded to Mitch. "Enjoy your dinners." As he turned to leave, Landon's eyes met hers and lingered for few seconds.

Unless her imagination was livelier than ever—that gaze meant something. *Either that or long-term food deprivation is doing weird things to my mind.* It was all Amy could do not to stare as he returned to his table.

"Don't be so obvious. You're embarrassing me," Mitch said. "And close your mouth or you might drool. I wouldn't believe it if I hadn't witnessed that little exchange. You're smitten."

"Zip it. And who says smitten?"

"Probably the same ones who say wooing. Should I ask the waiter for a bib?"

"Not necessary." She picked up her fork. "I need to eat my rabbit food now so I can fit into that bridesmaid dress next weekend. Can you please pray for our meal?"

Mitch chuckled. "Clue number one my sister's smitten? For a girl who never babbles," he said, leaning forward and lowering his voice, "you babbled. Big time. And why do I have to be the one to pray? Because it enables my masculinity?"

With that comment, Amy closed her eyes and launched into a short prayer, knowing Mitch wouldn't be so inclined. He'd all but abandoned prayer, both public and private, in the past year. She swallowed her sigh. *Lord, hold him close.*

"At least the little meet-and-greet went well, don't you think?" Mitch busied himself cutting his steak, but paused when he caught her watching. "Now you're positively salivating. Here, have a bite." Stabbing a generous section of meat, he transferred it to her plate. "A few bites of steak won't undo all your hard work."

"Okay, but only because you're forcing me."

"You really do look great," he said. "Sorry about the needing a good meal comment. That was payback."

"I know. Sorry if I said anything unkind about Felicity."

"You didn't. Not really. However"—he paused to chew another bite—"as your sworn protector, I feel compelled to say, smart as you are, you can sometimes be incredibly naïve."

"I'm not naïve. Just . . . realistic," she said.

He put down his knife. "The servers are expected to correct their mistakes, Amy. Surely you realize Landon didn't come over here because he wanted to impress the restaurant manager?"

"A perceptive journalist gathers all the pertinent facts while a better one always ensures those facts are made known."

"What's that mean?" Mitch gave her a blank look. "You're doing that annoying 'writer speak' thing again."

"She gives her reader the pertinent information needed to make a proper evaluation of the facts."

"And the pertinent information in this case would be . . . ?" An exasperated sigh escaped his lips. "We're starting to go in circles here. Speak English, please. It *is* your mother tongue, last time I checked."

"Landon knows my name and how to reach me, should he care to do so."

"Well, why didn't you say so in the first place? More importantly, would you care for him to do so?" His tone mimicked hers.

She made him wait while she took her first bite of salad. "You know the answer to that one as well as I do."

"Say it already. For a woman who works with words for a living, you can be annoyingly obtuse. Admit you want to do more than talk shop with this guy."

She shrugged. "Fine. You have your way of saying it, and I have mine."

Mitch motioned to her salad. "Keep eating. You need to keep up your strength, and I'm not talking about the wedding." He laughed when she crossed her eyes and plopped a bite of steak in her mouth, chewing in an exaggerated manner, savoring it.

A loud, anguished cry from across the room startled her, making her jump and turn wide eyes on Mitch.

"Someone, help us!" It came out a sputtering, prolonged wail followed by, "Jack, honey, hang on! Stay with me. Please God, don't let him die."

"Amy, call 9-1-1. *Now.*" Shrugging out of his suit coat, Mitch bolted from his chair and across the restaurant.

With Landon right behind him.

Chapter 5

AMY'S FINGERS FUMBLED on the cell phone as she dialed 9-1-1. When pandemonium broke out around her, she put a hand over one ear and ducked under the table to relay the basic facts to the emergency operator. She heard the servers canvassing the room, attempting to calm other patrons. Mitch's authoritative voice rose above the rest. Completing the call, Amy frowned as a noisy group departed a table near where Mitch knelt beside Jack, adding to the confusion and commotion. *Where's your sensitivity, people?* Rolling his sleeves, Mitch performed a quick assessment while asking Jack's wife practiced questions. Her quiet sobs were muffled as an older woman enveloped her in an embrace, smoothing her hair. Landon crouched beside Mitch, and they talked together in low tones with the restaurant manager.

Amy bristled when she heard the older woman ask Mitch if he was a doctor, her tone skeptical and borderline accusatory. *How* dare *she?* Without a clear view of her brother, she strained to hear his answer. "I used to be." If it weren't for his quick thinking, Jack might not survive. No doctors or nurses had rushed forward, only Mitch. She admired how he didn't hesitate. With him, it was instinctual, his passion. Her brother's training and innate instincts had kicked in. What he'd been trained to do until a tragic misstep in his Boston residency decimated what promised to be a brilliant medical career.

At Ground Zero on 9/11 for thirty-six hours straight, he'd worked tirelessly until police officers finally ordered him from the scene. When Amy learned his best friend perished in the South Tower, she feared for her brother. It took her four stressful hours to travel a few city blocks. Once there, she stayed by Mitch's side for three long days and nights—watching his fitful sleep, feeding him, praying for him and rocking him when his tears finally came. Their mother, still shell-shocked from their dad's death two years earlier, offered to come. Seeing Mitch's grief firsthand would only bring the widow further heartache, so Amy insisted she stay home and away from the chaotic scene. True to his nature, Mitch returned not long after to that horrific, gaping hole where the majestic towers once stood, wanting to do something—anything—to help. In a strange, cathartic way, being on-site helped him work through the pain.

"We need to clear a path for the paramedics," a man instructed with a calm confidence.

Stirred from her thoughts, Amy knew it was Landon. As if on cue, sirens blared in the distance, growing louder by the second. Jack's wife stepped back, her eyes never leaving her husband.

Amy heard her brother counting under his breath and knew he was performing CPR. An eerie, hushed silence pervaded the room. His wife leaned heavily against Landon, clutching the front of his shirt, bunching it with shaking fingers. With a sad expression, his features drawn, he moved his arm around the woman.

Standing on the peripheral of the circle gathered around where Mitch worked on Jack, Amy shifted, riveted but not wanting to stare. Darting a glance toward Landon's table, she saw his two dinner companions watching the scene with wide eyes. Lowering her head, she whispered a prayer. *Lord, if it's Your will, spare Jack's life tonight. Thank you for Mitch and his expertise. Let him be Your instrument.*

A soft cry caught her attention. Amy took a quick survey of the immediate area. There it was again. *Doesn't anyone else hear that?* "Where are you?" she murmured. Hearing it again, she slowly turned to her right. A little girl of about five with dark curls stood by herself in the middle of the dining area, clutching a black teddy bear. Dressed impeccably in red patent leather Mary Janes, a red and green plaid Christmas hair bow and an outfit that likely cost more than her monthly salary, the child buried her face in the bear, her small shoulders shaking with muffled sobs. *Oh, Father, she's so frightened.* Amy moved toward the child and leaned down, eye level. "Are your mommy and daddy here, sweetie?"

Rubbing one eye with a curled fist, the girl sniffled and brown eyes the color of melted chocolate met hers. "My grandpa fell down." When she wiped the back of her hand over her damp cheek and pointed in Jack's direction, Amy's heart skidded to a halt. Swallowing hard, she gave her a smile she hoped was reassuring and struggled to find the calm in her voice. "What's your name?"

"Ellie."

"That's a very pretty name. I'm Amy." She motioned to Jack's wife, still leaning against Landon. "Is that your grandmother over there? The blonde lady in the blue dress?"

Ellie nodded, moving her thumb into her mouth. Tears glistened on her long, dark lashes. They both looked up when EMTs rushed into the dining area, carrying a stretcher and equipment. The child whimpered when the team huddled around Mitch and her grandfather. Inching closer, Amy stretched her arm around Ellie. Although Jack was conscious, the urgency in Mitch's tone as he briefed the emergency personnel clued her in his condition was serious. Surely someone must be looking for Ellie? Now that medical help had arrived on the scene, she needed to take the child back to her grandmother.

Amy turned to the little girl, her heart aching at the sadness in those brown eyes. "Would you like me to take you to your grandmother?" When no answer came, she offered her hand. "It's okay, Ellie. You're not alone."

Biting her trembling lower lip, Ellie grasped her hand. Amy held on tight as they walked together. The youngster squeezed her hand harder the closer they moved to her grandmother. Spying them, the woman's lips downturned. "Ellie! There you are. Where did you run off to, child? Your poor grandfather had a heart attack, thinking you'd been kidnapped."

Amy swallowed her shock at the woman's tone—harsh and bordering on scornful. No wonder the girl was frightened. Was she implying Ellie *caused* Jack's collapse? Saddling a child with a guilt trip for the rest of her life was unconscionable. Biting her tongue not to say something ill-advised, Amy glanced at Mitch. He shook his head and gave a slight shrug. How she hated there was nothing they could do.

"Your grandfather's being taken to the hospital," the woman said, the lines on her face tight, eyes unyielding. "I'm sending you back to the penthouse with Nelson. Ingrid will get your coat and take you to the car. Now, don't be a nuisance and climb straight into bed when you get home." She waved her hand in dismissal as though swatting at a pesky, annoying insect. The blank look on Ellie's precious face, the glaze over her eyes, was haunting. *And when she gets home, who will comfort this child? She's not only frightened, she's alone.* The lack of affection in the woman's voice was appalling. *Where are Ellie's parents?*

Amy met the woman's sharp gaze. "Ellie was frightened when her grandfather fell. She meant no harm."

"I'll be the judge of that," her grandmother said, her eyes narrowed. "If you don't want to be slapped with kidnapping charges, young lady, I suggest you go on your way."

Mitch put an arm around her shoulders and stepped aside, pulling her with him. "Shh. I know," he said, giving her a quick hug. "You tried. Thanks for helping."

Shaking, Amy managed a mute nod as the EMTs carried Jack from the dining area.

Feeling as though she was on the outside peering in, she watched the events with a heavy heart. Ellie's grandmother departed with the EMTs while the woman Amy assumed was Ingrid corralled the little girl in a none-too-gentle manner and marched her out of the dining area. Amy closed her eyes. *Father, be with Ellie. Give this child the comfort only You can give. Let her feel Your presence. Be with her grandmother, too, and soften her heart, if not her tongue.*

Amy wiped away a tear. Her lids fluttered open and her gaze locked with Landon's. In those blue eyes flickered an unspoken understanding.

"Looks like our job here is done." Rolling down his sleeves, Mitch fastened the engraved, gold cuff links Mom gave him after Dad died. Finishing his task, he nodded to Landon. "Thanks for your help."

"Glad I could help, but you did all the work," Landon said. "I'm impressed. Jack's blessed you were here tonight. Thanks for your quick work." Amy's heart jumped. "Blessed" was a conscious word choice. Before she could ponder it further, Landon turned to her. "I'm thankful you picked up on what was happening with the little girl and brought her back. A lot of people would have stood on the sidelines, not wanting to get involved."

"I was lost once, so I know what it's like," she said, wiping away another tear. "She was scared when her grandfather fell, and I wanted her to know she's not alone."

Mitch rotated his shoulders and directed a tired grin at Landon. "I'd say Mrs. Jack was thankful you were here tonight."

Glancing down at his rumpled shirt, Landon shrugged with a sheepish grin. On such a confident, self-made man, it was as charming as it was unexpected. Within seconds, his smile sobered as he adjusted his tie clip. "Convincing potential advertisers to buy ad space has pretty much lost all relevance, at least for tonight. But," he said, heaving a deep sigh, "for the second time this evening, I'd better get back to my table before my companions think I've abandoned them." He ran his hand over his hair. "What an evening. Nice to see you again, Mitch." His gaze found hers again. "I hope our paths will cross again soon, Amy. Good night."

"Night." As he walked away, she watched, not bothering to be subtle. Much could be learned from a man's gait and the way he carried himself. With his broad shoulders squared, Landon moved with a purposeful stride.

She darted a quick glance at Mitch as they made their way back to their table. "I'm proud of you."

He nodded without speaking. When she reached for his hand, he squeezed, and a new peace settled in her heart.

Chapter 6

Manhattan Editorial Offices – New York Scene Magazine

"LANDON, WE HAVE a problem." True to form, Dona burst into his office without knocking. Not that he minded. She usually had good reason. Good thing she sounded harried, not panicked.

He marked his place on the galley for the next issue of the magazine. "What's that?"

"June Larish called a few minutes ago. Ted's surgery is scheduled for next Friday, but that's the same day you're leaving Los Angeles to fly to Baton Rouge for Kevin's wedding."

Unfortunate timing. Diagnosed a month ago with an aggressive form of lung cancer, his executive editor had been his most stalwart colleague during the growing pains of the magazine's infancy. No way would he miss being at the hospital, especially since the couple's only son was stationed overseas and their daughter-in-law and five grandkids lived out West. As far as he knew, the couple had no other close relatives living nearby.

"What time is his surgery?" he asked.

"Eleven."

Sitting back in his chair, he pondered his options. His eyes met Dona's. "I need to be there."

"I know, love."

He suppressed his grin as Dona scooted into the chair opposite his desk. She'd been to London a few years ago and adopted the British endearment. He'd grown accustomed to it, even liked it. Retrieving her glasses from the bejeweled chain around her neck, she positioned them and poised her pen above her trusty notepad.

"My meetings in LA will be done by late afternoon on Thursday. See if you can book me on a flight back to New York leaving LA sometime after six p.m. At least I've got the time advantage coming back East. I'll need you to reschedule the flight to Baton Rouge for Saturday late morning. If you would, please call the inn and tell them I'll arrive a day later. I'll call Kevin and tell him not to expect me until Saturday."

Dona nodded, jotting notes. "I'll call the rental car companies in LA and Baton Rouge and reschedule all the airport shuttles. Shall I have them pick you up here or at the townhouse on Saturday morning for your flight to Baton Rouge?"

"Home. This is why you have my undying loyalty." He gave her a tired smile and massaged his forehead. "One other thing: send some flowers to June and Ted with a card from the editorial staff saying we're thinking of them and praying for his surgery. I'll call Ted later and let him know I'll be at the hospital with June on Friday morning."

"That'll mean a lot to him. You're a good man." Dona made another quick note. "So, I take it Madelyn's not available for your trip to Baton Rouge?"

"Not this time, unfortunately. I wouldn't hesitate to take her otherwise. I'm headed to Austin for a few days after the wedding, so I'll pick her up there and fly her back to New York."

Dona rose from the chair. "That's what I figured. I'll go take care of those calls now, print out the confirmations and put them in a folder for you. I'll also send them to you via e-mail. Now, don't forget to call the groom and let him know you'll be late but you'll make it to the church on time." Crossing the room, one step in front of the other as though a bridesmaid in a wedding, Dona softly hummed the wedding march. Pausing at the threshold, she gave him a sly grin. "One of these days, I'll be humming that for *your* wedding, love."

Next to his mother, Dona had been his greatest source of encouragement through all the ups and downs of the magazine. As much as anything, she brought life and laughter to his workday. She could also recall the name of every guest in the history of *New York Scene* and relay the magazine's up-to-the-minute stats at any given moment. He couldn't *buy* such efficiency and thanked the Lord every day for finding Dona in a Columbia University faculty office. In one of the best snap decisions he'd ever made, he managed to coax her into leaving the staid world of academia for the unpredictability and challenges of magazine publishing. Sending her a huge bouquet of red roses and promising her everything short of his firstborn hadn't hurt, either. Firstborn *what* was quickly becoming the question. The way things were going, his magazine might be the long-term love of his life. The thought brought an instant wave of sadness.

A woman of faith, Dona was one of the few Christians on his payroll. Not a day passed when she didn't leave him a note of encouragement or a verse of Scripture tacked to his computer monitor. He depended on her more than she'd ever know. For her hard work and sacrifices the past year alone, she deserved something special for Christmas. Finding the perfect gift always proved a challenge—and he liked to pick it out himself—but he'd try his best.

"You're not getting any younger," Dona said, breaking into his thoughts. One hand slid to her hip. *Here it comes. Mama Dona's advice for the day.* It wouldn't be a workday without it, but he adored it—and her. "It's time you settle down in a cozy matrimonial love nest and sire a baby Warnick I can hold in these arms before I'm too old to enjoy it." She touched one finger to her cheek. "I feel an age spot coming on as we speak."

Chuckling under his breath, Landon shook his head. "You haven't aged a day since I've known you, and I think 'sire' refers to the animal kingdom. You'll be glad to know I'm starting to work on my"—he cleared his throat—"love life."

Dona's brows rose and that infectious grin grew broader. "Give me a name, please. That's all I'll ask for now. Promise."

He understood she asked in part so she could pray for him. "Amy. Amelia, actually."

She gave him an approving nod. "That's a very pretty name. I'm sure she's a wonderful girl if she's caught your attention. About time someone did, not that they haven't tried. Tell you what: every morning you can give me a little tidbit about her. In case you feel like sharing. Good for the soul, you know."

"Bye, Dona," Landon said. "Thanks for letting me know about Ted and taking care of all the travel arrangements."

"You're welcome. Back to work now." Giving him a broad grin over her shoulder, she sashayed from his office, once again humming that infernal wedding march.

Knowing Dona, she'd come up with any number of reasons to waltz into his office in the coming days. Fine. He'd find out more about Amy Jacobsen to satisfy his efficient assistant's curiosity. Getting her off his case was one thing, but the way those green eyes lit with excitement when he mentioned Amy's name, he hoped he didn't live to regret it. But it couldn't be a fluke. Flukes had no place in his world.

~

Manhattan Editorial Offices, Habits Magazine – Wednesday, December 4, 2002

"Your thoughts, Amy?" From the expertly-arched brows to the prim, rouged mouth downturned in permanent displeasure, Juliet Hargrove, *Habits* Senior Editor—her boss—awaited her response.

Think quick. "Sounds great. I look forward to writing the piece." Of course, knowing the topic or subject would make her assignment a whole lot easier. Amy smoothed a nervous hand over her skirt, hidden from view where she sat in front of Juliet's desk. Never in her life had she acted so unprofessional. Retrieving her pen, she scribbled a few words to lend the illusion of taking notes.

Juliet steepled her fingers. "As I mentioned in our editorial meeting, the pre-publicity buzz on this one is big. It'll be to our advantage to snag one of the first interviews with this guy. Being a faith-based book, I knew you'd be the one to do it—and the author—justice. I know you won't disappoint me."

Amy nodded. "I'll do my best." She closed her mouth. *Wow.* She was beginning to sound like a puppet and needed to jump back in the game. The faith-based angle was intriguing since Juliet normally stayed far away from anything "spiritual." Even so, she sensed grudging respect from her boss and was never belittled or ridiculed because of her faith. "I appreciate the opportunity." Whatever this assignment was, it was important enough to warrant her boss's attention.

"Very good." Juliet closed her purple notebook with a definitive snap. That bulging planner, crammed full of notes sticking out every which way, was the woman's most valuable accessory. The joke in the editorial offices was Juliet had sprouted an extra appendage. "I'll have Marcheline bring you the preliminary material the research staff has gathered. I'm sure you'll want to add your own notes to determine the angle for your interview." Gucci chic and glamorous with not one dark hair out of place, her boss nodded, her customary signal of dismissal. Juliet's porcelain complexion was unlined and flawless, her smile a rare occurrence. After all, if she dared upturn those lips, she might crack something.

Amy lowered her eyes, ashamed of her unkind thoughts as she prepared to leave. "I'll look forward to doing the piece." *You already said that.* Positivity and confidence were traits Juliet admired and rewarded, but repetition? Not so much.

"Excellent. I'll expect a first draft on my desk no later than Friday morning after you return from your trip. You know how to reach me should you need anything."

"Yes, thank you." Now she knew how she'd spend her time on the return flight. The scent of Juliet's expensive but cloying signature perfume lingered in her nostrils as she departed. Back in her own office, Amy twirled a pencil, lost in thought. If she asked one of the other editors about this assignment, it would only highlight her inattentiveness in the editorial meeting and give someone else ample room to move in on *her* story. As much as she hated it, it was every person for themselves, and she couldn't prove vulnerable and risk losing her job.

Twenty minutes later, Juliet's longtime assistant, Marcheline Boudreau, rounded the corner of her office. Rushing forward, she dumped a bulging file in the middle of the desk. Red—the color reserved for the best "red hot" assignments. "Okay, this is everything I have."

"Thanks." Her interest piqued, Amy reached for the materials sliding precariously close to the edge of the desk. As she stopped them from taking flight, she noted the woman's frazzled expression and gestured for her to take a seat. "Everything okay, March? You look like you're having a rough morning. Sit down and rest for a couple of minutes. Want some water?"

Brushing short dark curls streaked with gray away from her face, Marcheline shook her head. Faint beads of perspiration dotted her brow. "I'll be okay, thanks. Nothing I haven't done before. Only a million and one things on Juliet's to-do list before noon. Sometimes I think life's too short for all this stress and I'd be happier handing out perfume samples at Sak's. Any perfume but the one my boss wears, that is. Had enough of that one to last a lifetime." Marcheline gestured to the folder. "If only we were all so lucky to get your assignment, young lady. Take a gander at the author." Opening the folder, she slid it across the desk. "This man can read me a bedtime story anytime."

Amy gasped and jumped to her feet, sending the chair spinning into the wall behind her desk. "I don't believe it! He actually took Marc's advice." Shaking her head, she held up the professional press photo. "Papa Bear." In jeans and a white button-down shirt—perched on a wooden stool with his sleeves rolled, arms crossed—it captured Sam Lewis to perfection: handsome and serious, but with enough of a grin to reveal the deep smile lines on either side of his mouth. Intelligent, piercing blue eyes bore into hers. Sam's signature black Stetson sat balanced on one knee. It was one of the most natural author photos she'd ever seen, guaranteed to make women swoon, but not threaten other men.

"Papa Bear? So, I take it you know this man pretty well?" Marcheline dropped into the chair and leaned one elbow on Amy's desk, giving her a wide-eyed look. "Give it up, girlfriend. I need all the juicy details."

"I've actually spent a good deal of time with Sam Lewis and his wife, Lexa. He's the Domestic Missions Director for TeamWork, the same organization I work with here in New York. They're based in Houston, and I've also gone on a few longer missions with Sam. That's how I first met him."

"Now I remember. Didn't you go to some ranch in Montana with TeamWork a couple of years ago, right before Thanksgiving? I only remember because Juliet was stomping around . . ." Marcheline shook her head. "Never mind. Suffice it to say you're missed when you're not here."

"Good to know." Amy lowered the photograph to her desk. "Montana was more a personal mission Sam cooked up to help my friend, Natalie, and her husband, Marc. They were newlyweds, she fell down a flight of stairs, lost her memory, was pregnant . . ." She stopped. "Long story, but the mission was a rousing success. Marc's an advertising powerhouse in Boston and knew a great idea when he heard it. Tell you one thing: if any man's qualified to write a book about marriage, it's Sam."

"Well," Marcheline said, "it's encouraging to hear men like that still exist, but they're getting harder to find by the minute."

Amy smiled. "As a matter of fact, I'll be seeing Sam and Lexa next weekend in Baton Rouge since it's a TeamWork wedding."

"Don't remind me you're leaving us." Her lips slid into a pout. "I've got to mentally gear up for it."

"I'll only be gone for a few days. You'll blink and I'll be back." *Wait a minute.* Now the pieces were slowly fitting into place. Juliet's comment about the assignment concerning a man of faith. The upcoming wedding. The background research on Sam would have revealed his position at TeamWork, and her boss probably knew of her involvement. Although she'd never discussed it with Juliet, she often talked about her projects with her coworkers. The office wasn't that big, and they all knew too much about each other's personal lives as it was.

Marcheline rose to her feet. "I'd better get moving onto my next task. Everything from the research department is in the folder. If you ever need to know anything about an assignment, you call on me." Intense, brown eyes stared into hers.

Amy frowned. "Was I that obvious?"

"Don't worry, honey. Juliet's always in her own little world. I don't think she noticed, but I wanted to make sure to get this stuff to you before anyone else got their sticky paws on it."

"Thanks for watching out for me, March. You're the best."

"Welcome. No worries. You'll be fine." Marcheline departed with a small wave.

For the next couple of hours, Amy waded through newspaper clippings and information the research team had collected from various sources. *He finally did it. Stinker.* Her best friend, Winnie, once mentioned Sam was making notes for a possible book, but that was the last she'd heard of it. Sam or Lexa, for that matter, hadn't breathed a word of this exciting news during the whirlwind weekend in Houston three months ago for Winnie's wedding to Josh Grant. Next to her dad, Sam was one of the most humble, godly men she'd ever known. He wouldn't have wanted to detract from his friends' celebration by announcing his own news.

Her eyes focused on the advance press release in her hand. *Seven Rules of Marriage: A Husband's Guide to Loving Your Spouse.* Good title. She smiled, remembering how he'd met Lexa—the petite, spunky spitfire who challenged as much as attracted him—in the San Antonio TeamWork camp more than five years ago. Theirs was a great love story someone should write one day. Amy noted the projected publication date for Sam's book: May 2003. LCJW Publishing, New York, New York. *Hmm . . . never heard of it.* Sam wouldn't have agreed to this venture without a solid partner. When they talked, she'd have to ask him about his publisher. "Kudos, Mr. Lewis. Well done."

Amy clicked on her e-mail folder and started a new message.

Hi Sam and Lexa,

Guess which junior editor at Habits *magazine has the honor of writing an article on Sam's upcoming book? I can't tell you how happy I am for you, Sam, and I can't wait to see you both. Let's carve out some time for an official interview, either before or after Beck and Kevin's wedding. Please give little Joe a big kiss for me. I imagine he's getting so big now and is probably walking or trying to ride a baby armadillo (sorry, Lexa, couldn't resist). I hope Lexa's feeling better with the new addition coming soon to the Lewis family and the growing TeamWork crew. Can't wait to see you in Baton Rouge.*

Lots of love,
Amy

Within the hour, she had a reply:

Hi Amy,

Sam and I would love it if you'd come to Houston after the wedding and stay with us for a few days, if your schedule allows. We'll bring you from Baton Rouge (or I'm sure Winnie and Josh will be happy to do the honors). It'll be hectic before the wedding, but afterwards, you can relax with us at the house and have plenty of time to interview Sam. He's looking forward to it, and I can't wait to catch up with you. Please say you'll come. Kissing Joe for you now.

Love,
Lexa

No sooner had Amy pushed the SEND button on a reply e-mail with her acceptance of the kind offer than the phone rang, making her jump. Queuing a copy of the e-mail to print, she picked up the phone without bothering to check caller ID. "Amy Jacobsen."

"Hi Amy. Landon Warnick. I hope this isn't a bad time."

Amy straightened in the chair. Placing one hand over the receiver, she grunted a few quick times to clear her throat. To her extreme annoyance, her heart palpitated. *What am I, fourteen?* She moved her hand over her heart, as if that would slow it down. *Project warmth without too much enthusiasm.* "Hi there. Your timing is actually very good." Normally a man waited a minimum of three days after meeting her—if not a week—before calling. Not that it mattered since she turned down most of them, anyway. Why waste their time if she wasn't interested? But Landon Warnick struck her as an unconventional man who made up his own rules. In part, that's how he'd forged a name for himself in New York publishing circles in barely more than a decade. Impressive, and another reason to like him.

"After meeting you last night, I started thinking about something when I got home."

"Always a good thing." She put a hand on her knee to stop it from pumping up and down. Closing her eyes, she waited. If he used the word *connection* or—heaven forbid—*vibe*, all bets were off.

"I was remiss in not asking you to dinner when I had the opportunity." *Oh, he's good.* "I knew I'd regret it—"

"Oh, I'm sure you—" *Be quiet and let the man talk.*

"For at least the next fifty years." When she didn't answer—too stunned to speak—he chuckled. "Amy? You still there?"

"Um, yes. I'm checking my schedule for the next fifty years." *Is this guy for real?*

He laughed. "Good. I was afraid I'd already lost you. Listen, I know it's late notice, but I was hoping you could meet me for dinner tonight?"

She shoved aside the nagging part of her brain urging her to play it cool and tell him she had other plans. Playing by the rules was never her preferred way of doing things either. "I have another commitment, but it's not until seven-thirty." If she timed it right, she could manage both.

"Then how about we meet for an early dinner? Would that work with your schedule?"

"Yes. I'd like that." *That's the best you can come up with?*

"Great. Let's say Kyle's on Madison at five-thirty?"

"Lovely. I'll see you then." *What woman your age talks like this?* Maybe an aging, snooty debutante. Her brain must be stuck in neutral. If asked, would she remember her own name? Good thing Landon was decisive instead of playing the annoying "where do *you* want to go?" game. Still, she hadn't acted like such a *girl* in a long time. Disconnecting the call, she stared at the cradled receiver. The upcoming wedding in Louisiana with some of her dearest friends, the opportunity to interview Sam and now a spontaneous dinner date with a fascinating man? Life couldn't get much better.

Turning back to her work, she hoped she'd be able to concentrate instead of watching the minutes tick by on the clock. Up until now, her life had been relatively uncomplicated. *Dull, that's what it was.* Now, it was full of anticipation, ripe with possibility. *Ripe? Girl, you* do *need a date.* Although Amy generally preferred quiet, she had to admit a little excitement never hurt. Try as she might, she couldn't stop her heart from picking up speed. Again.

~

The driver grunted when Amy climbed in the back of the taxi. "Where to, lady?" He was hunched over, his balding head down. From the way the man's right shoulder moved in a rhythmic manner, she assumed he was updating his mileage log. She gave him the address for Kyle's and settled on the ugly, cracked leather seat, trying not to inhale the stale smells of smoke, perfume, alcohol and other things about which she'd best not speculate. As he pulled into the line of traffic, the driver gestured to the row of office buildings to their right. "You work for one of them big publishing companies?"

She'd been in hundreds of New York cabs but this was a first—a talkative driver who asked a question. His dark eyes met hers in the rearview mirror. "Yes. I work for *Habits* magazine."

He whistled under his breath as he switched lanes. "My daughter reads that one. She's seventeen, a high school senior and says she wants to be a writer." He laughed. "Or a model. Or a Broadway star. Hazard of living in New York. Next week it might be something else, but she seems to like writing more than anything else. Gets the highest grades in her English class."

"What does she write?" Interesting a girl that age would be interested in *Habits* considering its median target market was twenty-six-to-forty, single or married urban career professionals with an average of one child. He could be mistaken or trying to ingratiate himself, but—no matter the man's motives—she preferred to give him the benefit of the doubt.

"Stories. Real good ones, too. None of that dark, death and dying stuff a lot of kids write these days."

"What's your daughter's name?"

"Angelina. Angelina Delgado."

Amy smiled, reminded of the shy little girl with the same first name Lexa befriended in the San Antonio TeamWork camp.

"Listen, I know it's a lot to ask, but would you—"

She could see where this was headed. "Sure. I'll give you my card. Tell Angelina to e-mail a couple of her stories to me or whatever she wants. If I see potential, I'll make a call or two." Best not to promise much without seeing Angelina's work first. "There's a number of small and mainstream teen magazines, and they're always looking for new, fresh young voices. It'd be a great place for her to break into the market and see if she'd like to pursue it as a full-time career."

The driver stole a quick glance, looking at her over his shoulder with a proud papa grin as he stopped for a light. "You'd really do that?"

"Sure. I'll be happy to do what I can if her work shows promise." She pulled one of her business cards from her wallet and handed it across the seat when he stopped at the next light.

Taking the card, the driver glanced at it then tucked it in his top pocket. "Thanks. You're a real nice lady, Ms. Jacobsen." A few blocks later, he stopped at the curb in front of Kyle's. Scurrying around the front of the car, he moved quickly for his rotund frame. With a tip of his cap, he opened the back door and took her hand to help her onto the sidewalk. When she paid the fare and told him to keep the change, a generous smile slid across his broad face and the corners of his eyes crinkled. "I'll tell her to send you something. Angelina Delgado. Remember that name."

"I'll watch for her e-mail." Giving him a parting smile, Amy pulled her wool collar closer as a bitter blast of wind hit her full force. Shivering, she burrowed her chin and mouth into the warm scarf wound around her neck. Hurrying toward the entrance of Kyle's, she wondered what awaited her behind the restaurant door.

Chapter 7

ALTHOUGH IT WAS dark outside, the streetlights illuminated the sidewalk enough for Landon to witness Amy manage the impossible: completely charm a Manhattan taxi driver. He chuckled as the burly man opened the door and assisted her from the cab. From his brief conversation with her at Café Eduardo, he was more than intrigued. Surprised but pleased she'd accepted his last-minute dinner invitation, he'd been inordinately distracted most of the afternoon by the prospect of getting to know her.

This was a woman who carried herself with confidence, her shoulders squared with a slight lift of the chin. Amy possessed an inherent grace. Not quite tall enough to be a model—about five-foot-eight by his best estimate—she was lovely in a girl-next-door way that radiated a natural sensuality. He doubted she was aware of the power she must hold over men. She'd transfixed *him* by the simple act of stepping out of a taxi and walking toward the entrance. Women this gorgeous were usually preoccupied with their looks and dressed to please a man with high heels that couldn't be comfortable and body-hugging clothing. While he appreciated those things from an aesthetic standpoint, he'd learned a long time ago it was little more than window dressing. He needed more. The woman walking into Kyle's now might be the perfect woman to challenge him.

Opening the front door, Landon smiled as Amy came inside. The bells decorating the holiday wreath on the front door jingled as she swept past him, bringing with her a rush of cold air. When she turned to him, her warm, generous smile was capable of thawing the deepest freeze. "Thanks." Shivering, she started to remove her gloves. "I think they're frozen to my fingers and I was only outside for a minute or two."

"Here. Let me help you."

She raised both hands. "I don't think I've needed anyone to do this for me since I was five." With her bright eyes and pink-tipped nose and cheeks, she gave him a smile reminiscent of a wide-eyed child, full of the wonder of the Christmas season.

"Glad I could help. I think it's a first for me." He smiled and resisted leaning closer to get a better look at her eyes, an arresting mix of gray and green.

"They're both."

"Excuse me?" She'd picked up on his fascination. *Smooth.*

"Most people have the same reaction. I'm used to it. Mitch's eyes are identical. We got them from our grandfather on Mom's side."

Ah, yes. Eric Carlisle. "I can't comment on Mitch's eyes, but on you, I definitely like it." When Amy lowered her gaze, denying him the pleasure, he hastened to reassure her. "Sorry if that comment made you uncomfortable."

"No worries. It didn't."

He offered his assistance as she shrugged out of her coat. In her heels, she reached the top of his shoulder. His eyes skimmed over her professional navy business suit and crisp white blouse. The pencil skirt and jacket couldn't disguise her curves, but he'd much rather see a woman more relaxed and comfortable in jeans and a sweater. Save for one small button at the top, her blouse was buttoned all the way to her neck. While he appreciated modesty, he had to wonder if Amy was afraid to reveal her femininity. Something about her stirred him in a way he'd be hard-pressed to define. She was beautiful, yes, but perhaps it was a glimpse of a sweet innocence beneath the confident exterior. Unless he was way off the mark, the junior editor was unassuming and guileless. He prayed she had the solid backbone to withstand the demands and pitfalls of their chosen profession.

Change the subject so she doesn't catch you gawking. "You managed something not many women can do. I'm impressed."

The glance she slanted his way was curious. "Thanks, I think, but what would that be?"

"You prompted uncommon chivalry from a Manhattan cabbie. That's an amazing feat."

She unwound the long scarf circling her neck. "Only because he had an ulterior motive. He has a daughter in high school who wants to be a writer."

"Did you tell him she should walk in the opposite direction as fast as she could?"

"No," she said, the corners of her mouth curving. "I told him she should run."

They shared a smile. "How'd he know you're a writer?" The hostess appeared and took Amy's coat and scarf, telling them she'd return shortly with the claim ticket.

"You must have missed it." With one finger, Amy drew an imaginary line across her forehead. "It's usually written up here." She shrugged. "He probably runs that route a lot and knows the building is full of publishing houses. For all I know, he's been asking all his fares the same question and I'm the only one who took the bait. I gave him my business card and told him to have her send me something. I like to help if the opportunity presents itself and I see potential."

"That's very generous of you. You never know when you might stumble on the next writing phenom." He remembered those days—helping young writers achieve their goals, fostering the dream. The luster had tarnished a bit, but he still loved mentoring when he could. *Don't give too much of yourself, Amy.* He'd hate to see this lovely woman burned by the ruthlessness of those fueled by selfish ambition. New York, and the publishing world in particular, overflowed with blood-thirsty sharks who'd devour and then regurgitate writers without a second thought.

The hostess handed him the claim ticket. "Would you like your regular table, Mr. Warnick?"

"Sounds good, if it's available. Thanks, Gretchen." He gestured for Amy to go first, but not before catching her raised brows. As they threaded their way through tables, he nodded at a few acquaintances. It was a decent crowd for a cold weeknight. Piped-in holiday tunes and bright, twinkling lights strung around the perimeter of the restaurant added to the festive atmosphere.

"I imagine you know the staff at most of the popular Manhattan eateries."

He helped her into a chair at the small, out-of-the-way table before taking the one beside her. "It can get noisy and this way we can hear each other without shouting across the table."

She surveyed the restaurant. "Makes sense. This is my first time here, but some of our staff come here after work sometimes."

"The answer is no," he said.

"No?" She shook her head. "Did I ask a question?"

"I only frequent a few restaurants and you've happened to be in two of them in as many days. One by chance—if you want to call it that—and one by choice."

Her smile reappeared. It was quite infectious with a hint of mischief. Best of all, it reached her eyes. "I don't believe in chance or luck as a matter of principle."

He nodded. Good answer, not that it was a test.

"Thank you for inviting me tonight," she said. "A busy man like you, I realize you probably don't leave your office so early most evenings. All things considered, you look remarkably well-rested."

Amy grew more intriguing by the moment, drawing him in with her sense of humor. "A large part of making a success out of the magazine is surrounding myself with the right people and a not-so-little thing called delegation. I highly recommend it." His eyes met hers. "As a matter of principle."

They shared another smile, and it felt good. "Intelligence and common sense will take you far in life," she said. "Speaking as a junior flunkie, I can understand the wisdom of delegation."

He waited as she ordered a half-Coke, half-Diet Coke before ordering an iced tea, but his smile disappeared. She'd called herself a flunkie last night, too. Self-deprecation was one thing, but not understanding her worth was another. Was she being incredibly humble or did it go deeper? "If you don't recognize your value, then Juliet's not doing her job."

"Fine then. I'm brilliant." She held out her hand. "Feel free to slap my wrist for trying to be semi-humble."

Taking the menus from the waiter and handing one across the table to her, he figured he needed to soften that last comment in case she'd taken offense. "I've read a few of your pieces in *Habits*. You're an exceptional writer."

The corner of her right lip quirked slightly higher than the left. "Thank you, but I have to ask if you read them before or after we met last night?"

Implicating Mitch wasn't in his best interest. "If it appeases you, I started out as a"—he cleared his throat—"junior flunkie. You don't know how it pains me to use that terminology, and not because it's a lowly position."

"Of course not, but it sounds like you know my illustrious boss pretty well."

"Juliet and I went to Columbia grad school together; my point being that part of the job is knowing your competition."

"Oh?" she said, raising a brow again. He figured she'd probably give him a skeptical glance quite often. "Part of the whole keeping your friends close and enemies closer theory?" She narrowed her eyes. "Mr. Warnick, if you invited me to dinner to coerce me to divulge hidden secrets, you're sorely misguided." Her tone implied she was teasing. "You'll find I'm loyal to the end."

Landon chuckled. "You have an active imagination. Okay, I'll call off the water torture. Sure, we're competitors, but we can keep each other sharp. We both want to produce the best possible magazine for our readers, and *Habits* and *New York Scene* share a lot of subscribers. Think of it like your church softball team. The players all have varying temperaments, professions, levels of economic status and interests."

Thanking the waiter for the half-and-half, Amy took a sip, appearing to mull over her response. "True enough, but why did you say *your* church softball team?"

"Semantics. Do you play?" *Mitch mentioned it when he told you about Amy. Play it cool.*

"Yes, but how could you know that?"

"It's a hypothetical example to illustrate the whole teamwork aspect."

Her eyes widened at that one. "You're familiar with TeamWork?"

Digging the hole deeper. "Only that it's a great concept, even better when carried out." For now, he needed to keep the conversation moving forward to the next topic.

She stared at him for a long moment. "I may regret asking this, but what else do you know about me?"

If she knew all he *did* know about her, she'd no doubt slap his face, stomp out of the restaurant and out of his life. No way that was going to happen. "For one thing, I suspect your eyes change color, reflecting what you wear." *That's one of the dumbest things you've ever said.*

Looking away, a slight smile creased her lips. "Well, now, that's hardly impressive since you already mentioned it. Besides, I think that statement could apply to most people. And their eyes." A self-conscious awareness passed over her features. While Amy was intelligent and sophisticated, she wasn't worldly—a significant difference and a refreshing change from what he glimpsed in many women who wore jadedness like she must wear a favorite pair of well-worn jeans.

"Then again, you're hardly 'most people,' Amy. Right now your eyes are the color of pale emeralds. Exquisite." He busied himself with his menu again, chastising himself for that perhaps ill-advised observation. It was too much, too soon. She didn't seem the type to bow to intimidation or scare away, but his bluntness had gotten him into trouble more times than he could count. With Amy, he didn't want to push her away. With this woman, he had the feeling nothing came easily, but he thrived on the challenge.

"Tell me something: what else do you know about me? Do I also like walks in the rain, sushi by moonlight and ice skating at Rockefeller?" Her tone lightly teased, the glint in her eye irresistible as the right corner of her lip curled again. "Never mind. That makes me sound like . . ." She lifted her chin, giving him an impish grin that caught him completely unaware.

Digging deep, it took him a few seconds to muster a coherent response. Amy was too good to be true. Nothing thrilled him more than a good bantering session with a sharp, intuitive woman. "Know what I find most intriguing about your little list?"

"Other than it makes me sound like a beauty queen?"

"Does the tiara fit?"

"Bite your tongue." When she scrunched her nose, he was officially captivated.

"You more than meet the qualifications." That comment slipped out unaware. *Watch it.*

"Well, um," she said, darting her gaze away from his, "thank you. Tell me, are you always this—?"

"Honest? Usually." He decided to take the straight approach and prayed it wouldn't lead to a crash-and-burn. "*Do* you enjoy those things solo, Amelia? The walks, the sushi, the ice skating?"

A slow flush of pink colored her cheeks. "I detested sushi the one time I tried it, I adore walks in the rain, but I only ice skate if bribed since I can't afford to hobble around on crutches. So, tell me, do you also know my middle name?" When he shook his head, she twisted her mouth. "Guess you didn't dig deep enough. It's hardly a secret, but tell me, are you also always this—"

"Direct?" His eyes searched hers. "My mother's one of the wisest people I know and she passed on some very important nuggets of wisdom, including to always state my case upfront."

"In that case, Mama Warnick must have also advised you a little more small talk is wise before hitting a woman smack between the eyes with personal information you've learned about her life. If you want honesty, it makes me uncomfortable." As if to underscore her point, she shifted in her seat and lowered her gaze. "On the other hand, score one for healthy respect for your mother. Always a good character trait although I'm afraid it's getting rarer every day."

"I'm sorry, Amy. I didn't mean to make you uncomfortable," he said, feeling a twinge of regret. "In the same vein of being completely honest and direct, I think you're as challenging as you are beautiful. Another rarity."

"I'm not that uncomfortable, and please don't change the subject." The cute twitch resurfaced.

"I thought it was the same subject."

She looked away a moment and sucked in her cheeks. "You're a flirt of the worst kind."

"Which kind is that?"

Those lovely eyes lifted to his. "The extremely dangerous kind that's prompting me to get up from this table, thank you for the lovely dinner invitation, retreat gracefully with my head held high and my dignity—and everything else—intact."

With that comment, he almost choked on a quick sip of his iced tea. Putting his napkin over his mouth, he coughed and resisted the strong urge to loosen his collar. Man, it felt tight. *You deserved that one.*

"Oh, did I say something wrong?" She'd forced a kittenish tone into her voice and batted her lashes with an innocent look. From all appearances, she was trying her best not to burst out with laughter.

"Not at all. Matter of fact," he said, tossing his napkin on the table, "sounds like a plan. I'll go with you."

"I meant *solo*." She traced a finger around the rim of her glass and surveyed him beneath veiled lids. "Seriously, why did you invite me to dinner? A man like you is nothing if not single-minded." Picking up her menu, she moved her eyes across it, but he knew she listened.

"A man like me?" That was one of the more intriguing lines he'd love to investigate. "Please don't make me sound so calculating, Amy." He waited until she lowered her menu. "Forgive me for stating the obvious, but I didn't invite you here tonight to share casual conversation about the weather and the state of the economy."

"Precisely. You must be thinking of making an investment in something."

"True. Your time at NYU was well-spent." He flashed his most brilliant smile.

Her eyes widened. "You're incredibly infuriating."

He needed to tone it down. "In two years, I predict we'll be working the *Times* crossword puzzle together on Sunday mornings." *Brilliant. Way* not *to be subtle.* Landon hoped he hadn't pushed her too far with that comment, but it remained a distinct possibility.

Amy coughed and brought a quick hand up to her chest. "Excuse me?"

"You heard me." *Now you sound arrogant.* He swirled his iced tea and took a long drink.

"For one thing, I go to church most Sunday mornings."

He held her gaze. "Great. I need to get there more often, but I'm an early riser. You?" *Why not add presumptuous to the list?*

"None of your business." She appeared a bit dazed.

It was fascinating how her eyes transitioned from green to gray and back again in the span of only a few seconds. He hoped he wasn't coming across as a total phony and supercilious—a good word he'd come across in the crossword puzzle the week before. "You don't think I can be a man of faith and still do what I do?"

"No, I'm not saying that at all. I suppose it depends on whether you're talking about being a journalist or an in-your-face, world-class flirt."

Landon frowned. "I guess I deserved that one, but that's the second time you've called me a flirt. I prefer to call it innocent bantering."

"Bantering between a man and woman generally implies flirting," she said. "I doubt anything you do is ever innocent or casual."

"That's purely an assumption on your part, and please explain . . ."

When another small smile lifted her lips, he found it difficult not to stare. He hadn't engaged in a conversation this long with a woman in more than a year. Harmless little flirtations here and there, but not full-on bantering like this. It was *great.*

"Meaning you have a purpose for everything. For instance, have you ever engaged in banter with a woman that *couldn't* be construed as flirting?" She waited a few seconds. "Are you trying to remember or are you simply pausing for dramatic effect?"

He made her wait long enough to see her squirm. Amy raised both hands in the air. "Okay, that's long enough. Ding ding ding. Time's up."

"Bantering between a man and woman is nothing more than clever use of language—verbal sparring—and isn't that what we're doing right now? We both love it because it's what we *do.*" He leaned closer. "Admit it. It challenges you, gets your blood pumping and excites you like nothing else." He sat back in his chair, surveying her. "Trust me, it's been a lot longer than you'd think."

"I'm not going to hazard a guess."

"I didn't get where I am by being vague and pointless, Amelia."

Amy released a deep sigh, but whether from resignation or exasperation, he couldn't know. "It's Amy, please. Just . . . Amy."

"Why? Amelia's a beautiful name. It suits you well."

"Humor me."

"Fine. I'll only use Amelia when I'm perturbed with you, want your undivided attention—" he paused, wondering how she'd respond—"or am completely enamored with you. Here's honesty for you: it's difficult to maintain a relationship because I'm so . . . forthright, as you pointed out. Have you found that to be true, too?"

Taking another sip of her drink, she surveyed him over the edge of her glass. "Depends. Are you speaking in terms of personal or professional relationships?"

"Both," he said. "But more in terms of a romantic relationship."

"I . . . I . . ." For once, she seemed at a complete loss for words.

"Like I said, you and I are a lot alike." *Time to back off.* He retrieved his readers from the inside pocket of his suit coat and positioned them. Opening his menu, he was aware she did the same. "Do you see anything on the menu that sounds appealing?"

"I can't seem to concentrate on the menu right now, thank you very much."

"Are you hungry?"

"Not really. You?" When her gaze met his, his pulse accelerated to a dangerous level.

"Same. Want to go somewhere else?"

"As long as you don't consider me a cheap date." She graced him with another glimpse of those mesmerizing, chameleon-like eyes. "What do you have in mind? Provided it's not your apartment or penthouse or wherever you live—or otherwise at odds with your Christianity or mine—sure, I'm fine with it." Putting her napkin beside her plate, she rose to her feet and allowed him to help with her chair. That concession pleased him more than it should.

"Great. Shall we?" Time for Round Two. He hadn't looked forward to anything more in recent memory.

Lead the way, Amelia.

Chapter 8

PULLING A SMALL card from his wallet, Landon slipped it beneath the more-than-generous tip for a soda and iced tea. Amy figured it must be his business card. Apparently, the man never missed an opportunity. Finally a man who could challenge her—and irritate her. And attract her like no other man she'd ever met. Her words to Mitch about finding exactly this type of man smacked her in the face as she threaded her way through the tables on her way back to the front of the restaurant.

Waiting while Landon retrieved their coats, she hid her smile as the hostesses eyed him. What must it be like to be the subject of such adoration? After he helped her into her coat, she wrapped her long scarf around her neck and tucked the ends into the collar. A twinge of self-consciousness nipped at her, knowing he watched. "So many layers at this time of the year," she said, tugging on her gloves.

"Do you need help?"

"Nope," she said, "I can handle it this time. See?" She held up both hands. "All done. Ready to go?"

"Absolutely." He ushered her closer to the front door. "I have an idea. Completely above board, in case you have any qualms."

"I'm not generally a qualm kind of girl, but I'll admit to a healthy curiosity." Her fascination with him grew by the minute.

Landon held the door for her as they headed outside. When he whistled and raised his arm, a cab sped toward them before they could reach the curb.

"Very impressive." She didn't bother hiding her admiration. "That skill comes in handy, especially at this time of the year."

Opening the door of the taxi, he stepped aside. "After you." Ducking his head, he climbed in behind her and closed the door. "Central Park West, please."

The driver turned in his seat and gave her a toothy smile. "Well, now, look who's in my cab twice in one day. How'd I get so lucky? Must be fate. I called Angie earlier and told her about meeting you and what you said, and she got all excited."

"Great," Amy said. "I'll look forward to it, but tell her to take her time and send her best work."

As the taxi pulled into the flow of traffic, Landon leaned close. "Like I said before," he said, voice lowered, "very impressive winning-over-the-taxi-driver skills."

Her breath quickened. "You already said th—" Nearly nose-to-nose with Landon, she stared into those brilliant sapphire blue eyes. They were so clear, sharp and missed nothing. Thankfully, he moved a few inches away, breaking the spell. Turning her head, Amy stared out the window as the driver turned onto Fifth Avenue. A blur of shoppers, laden with bags, scurried into stores and boutiques. "I love seeing the stores decorated for Christmas and everyone's in such a festive mood."

"Are you from New York originally?" Landon's question stirred her back to reality, making her grateful for good, basic getting-to-know-you conversation.

At least he didn't know everything about her personal life. "I was born in California, outside LA, but my family moved to the Philly suburbs when I was six. I grew up there."

"What does your dad do?"

"He was a pastor, but he died four years ago of a stroke. It happened quickly, and he didn't suffer. It's just hardest on those left behind." The last part of her statement was a bit rushed and quiet, but she knew he heard.

"I'm sorry. Is your mother—?"

"She still lives in the home I grew up in. It's one of those old rambling houses with lots of fun places to hide and a big backyard. Great for kids and animals."

"And I know you have one brother, Mitchell, the hotshot Wall Street broker."

Glancing back at him, Amy smiled. "He'd love to hear you call him that. He's thirteen months older."

"You two look so much alike I thought you might be twins."

"It's a common misconception—no pun intended—but no. We have a sister, Celeste, who's four years younger than me. She graduated from Bryn Mawr this past May and works at a marketing consulting firm in Philly." He was asking questions about her life, but she didn't know much about *his* life behind the public persona. "So, tell me. Are you from New York? I don't detect the accent, but I can't pinpoint it otherwise."

"Believe it or not, I was born in Texas. Austin."

"That's surprising. I never would have guessed."

"Oh, believe it, darlin'."

"Is that regret I hear?"

"Texas roots go deep and far, and when I go home for a visit, it doesn't take long for the drawl to come back full force, and the Stetson and boots to come down from the shelf. With more dust on them than I'd like."

"Some of my closest friends live in Houston."

"Then you probably also know something about Texas pride."

"Know about it, yes," she said, "but understand it? That's something else entirely."

"I know we haven't known each other long, Amy, but I'd like to be your friend, too."

"Now, there you go again. I wouldn't be with you in a New York cab going to points unknown if I didn't consider you a friend, or a trustworthy acquaintance at the very least." Twisting her glove-covered hands in her lap, she wondered where this conversation was headed. "Landon," she said, hating the hesitancy in her voice, "here's the thing."

"Tell me." He turned to face her and their knees bumped. "What's the thing?"

You started it, so spit it out, no matter the consequences. It might spare you future heartache. "I get the strong impression you make it a habit to . . ." She hesitated and lowered her gaze. No way would she voice her thoughts aloud and she'd said too much as it was. Although she'd had her share of boyfriends, none of her relationships lasted more than a few months. Even Marco the bartender had made his intentions perfectly clear, but the man seated beside her was in a whole different league.

She didn't expect Landon's hearty laugh. "Surely you, of all people, understand you can't believe everything you read. Or hear. Or see." His gaze held hers. If it was possible, she sensed he could see past her insecurities straight to her soul. "Want to know what I'm thinking right now?"

His words startled her. "Not sure."

After the driver pulled to a smooth stop, Landon opened the door and gave her hand a gentle tug. "We're here. Come with me."

"Do I have a choice?" Although she muttered it under her breath, Landon must have heard because he released her hand.

"You always have a choice. Say the word and I'll take you straight to the church, no questions asked."

The driver lowered his window and looked from her to Landon and back again. "So, are you two gonna stay or am I taking the lady somewhere else?"

A few more awkward moments passed. "Your choice, Amy," Landon said, "but I'd really like you to stay."

"Answer one question."

Landon had the grace to appear repentant. "Anything."

"How'd you know I was going to church tonight?"

The silence between them grew uncomfortably long.

"Hey, buddy? What's it gonna be? I gotta get moving already. Time is money." Rolling his eyes, the driver drummed his fingers on the steering wheel.

"It was a guess, that's all." Landon's eyes bore into hers, bright in the dim light of the street lamp. "You mentioned going to church most Sundays, and based on some other things about you, I figured you might attend a church service mid-week."

For a moment, she wondered if he was mocking her, but his expression was full of admiration, his tone untouched by sarcasm or cynicism.

"If you want to leave, I won't stop you," he said, "but I'd really like it if you'd stay." Pulling out his wallet, Landon handed a bill to the driver before positioning one hand on the back door. She wondered if he had one of his cards in his gloved hand, not that it was important.

Amy hesitated only a few seconds before nodding to the driver. "Please don't let us keep you." She avoided looking at Landon. If he wore a self-satisfied smile, she didn't want to see it.

"Good enough. Thanks again, folks." The man tipped his hat before pointing his finger at Landon as he closed the back door. "Mister, you take good care of Amy Jacobsen. She's special, this lady."

"I couldn't agree more, sir."

As the driver pulled away, Landon took a few steps closer. He was incredibly handsome in his black wool coat, his cheeks flushed with the cold night air and those unbelievable eyes resting on her. A shock of dark hair falling across his forehead made him look a bit rakish, the only aspect of his appearance slightly out-of-place. "Thank you."

"For what?" Her feet were starting to feel numb or she'd be content to stand and stare at the man forever.

"For staying. And giving me an opportunity to redeem myself for my audacity and probably stepping completely over the line."

She gave him a small nod. "Welcome. So," she said, "where to next?"

"Carriage ride?" He waved his hand toward a waiting hansom.

"I'm not sure I have time."

"Sometimes you have to make time."

The man made a good point, so who was she to protest? Holding out his hand, he assisted her as she climbed into the carriage. When he seated himself beside her on the bench seat, she caught a whiff of his fragrance. "I like your cologne. It's the same one I gave Mitch last year for Christmas."

"Great." He chuckled. "Just what a guy wants to hear—that he reminds her of a woman's brother. For the record, my usual scent or whatever is plain old soap, but my long-time assistant sprayed me unaware before I left the office."

She laughed. "A fly-by spritzing? Sounds like fun."

"I suppose so. Okay now," he said, grabbing a thick blanket on the seat beside him. Spreading it over their laps, he scooted closer. "Like it or not, we're expected to snuggle. Meet me halfway?"

"You're a smooth operator, taking a girl someplace freezing cold so you can sit close." His nearness was exhilarating. The horse pulled them at a leisurely pace. An older couple strolled nearby, hand-in-hand. A man helped a little girl into another hansom while a woman waited inside. The night air was sharp and crisp, tempered by the aroma of roasting nuts on the street corners and grilled steaks from nearby restaurants. *Please don't let my stomach rumble and betray me, Lord.* She looked around, giving into a smile as she spied a young man holding mistletoe over a girl's head as he leaned in for a kiss. "It's so clear and beautiful tonight."

"I'd say so."

She slanted a glance his way, suppressing her grin. "You can do better than that. If you flirt this much, how do you ever get any work done?"

"I only flirt like this around women I'm seriously interested in, which isn't often, contrary to your blanket assumptions."

"Enough with the puns," she said, "but again, we don't really know each other. If you want blatant honesty, I'm not sure if I can trust you."

He studied her and appeared more puzzled than offended. "Why not? Christians can't flirt? We can't enjoy one another's company?" When he turned sideways, their knees touched again, sending an electric current shooting through her several layers of clothing. "If you think I've violated any of God's commands, please clue me in. However, if I've offended your sensibilities, I hope you'll accept my sincere apology." He sat back against the seat and blew out a breath. "So much for redeeming myself, huh?"

With his brow furrowed, his earnestness was obvious, and she swallowed her next comment. "I don't offend that easily."

His gaze was warm as he turned to her again. "I *do* like you, Amy. A lot."

"In spite of my better instincts and questionable judgment, I like you, too," she said. "So, why don't you give me your class ring, I'll string it around my neck and we can go steady?"

His hearty laughter broke the stillness of the night. "Maybe that sentiment smacked of adolescent longing, but it's true all the same."

"Point taken and reciprocated." Leaning her head against the back of the carriage, Amy gazed upward. Her breath escaped, curling a lazy path into the dark of the night. "I feel like I can touch the stars, they're so bright tonight." He mirrored her, settling on the seat and gazing upward. They shared a comfortable silence broken only by the steady rhythm of the horse's hooves hitting the cold, hard pavement. She wasn't sure whether to call this a first date or not, yet a sudden, irrational urge to kiss him seized her. *I'm so food-deprived, I'm hallucinating.*

What good Christian girl thinks about kissing a man she barely knows?

Apparently one who hasn't been kissed in way too long.

Chapter 9

"CARE TO SHARE your thoughts?" Landon asked.

"Not on your life." Honesty had its limits, especially with someone she'd only met the day before. This whole experience was so strange yet wonderfully weird, and it made her dizzy. Aware he studied her profile, Amy dared not meet that blue-eyed gaze, afraid of what he'd see . . . or was it the other way around?

Reaching for her hand beneath the blanket, Landon squeezed it before releasing her. As the carriage neared the end of its ride, he jumped down to the pavement with the ease of a seasoned athlete. "Put out your arms and lean toward me. I'll catch you." The unexpected gentleness in his tone surprised her.

Amy frowned when she glimpsed the steep drop to the pavement. "It looks a lot further down than it did on the way up to the carriage." She caught his amusement. "Normally, I wouldn't hesitate, but wearing heels gives it a whole different perspective." Not that a man would understand that. What a ninny. *Close your eyes and pray he catches you.*

"Trust me." Standing on the sidewalk below, he opened his arms.

Hesitating only a moment more, she did as he asked but closed her eyes tight as she stepped out of the carriage.

Catching her—his hands around her waist, holding her close—Landon lowered her to the ground. "You can open your eyes again now." His warm breath caressed her cheek. "Hungry yet?"

She'd just experienced one of the most chivalrous, romantic moments of her life and struggled to find her voice. "Um, sure. I can eat something now. You?"

"I could be convinced. How far is your church from here?"

"Too far to walk."

When she relayed the address, he nodded. "Isn't there a coffee shop near that corner?"

"Yes, as a matter of fact. How'd you know?"

"Another guess. Name a New York City block that doesn't have a coffee shop somewhere nearby."

"True enough. Let's go."

"Great." His smile grew wider. "Why don't we eat a light supper and then I'll drop you off safe and sound by the doors of the church by seven-thirty? After all," he said, taking her by the hand and escorting her across the street, "I promised you dinner." Reaching the street corner, Landon raised his arm and whistled. Sure enough, a cab pulled to the curb within seconds.

"How do you do it?" she asked as they hopped inside.

"You must have missed it," he said. "It's an elective at all New York universities."

Seated at a corner booth a few minutes later, Amy was thrilled when he asked a blessing after their food arrived. Not the garden variety "Thank you for the grub," his prayer was earnest and heartfelt, the kind that could only be faked by a skilled Broadway actor. Having been around a few professional actors in her lifetime, she could usually spot insincerity in a heartbeat.

For the next forty-five minutes, they traded stories and anecdotes. She enjoyed hearing about his work at *New York Scene* as she sampled her clam chowder. In turn, Landon seemed amused by her stories of life at *Habits*. The way he swirled his French fries in ketchup—two at a time—was fun to watch. She nearly drooled as he dug into his cheeseburger with melted Swiss cheese and grilled mushrooms. He asked thoughtful questions and paid attention to her answers. She discovered he was an only child and loved to fish with his dad as a kid. A hint of sadness crept into his voice at the mention of his father but he spoke lovingly of his mother.

They shared a slice of strawberry cheesecake—at his insistence—and sipped coffee. She noted he favored his left hand as he stirred in one creamer and sugar. Her dad had been left-handed, as was Mitch.

Although Landon's questions were of the basic getting-to-know-you type, it didn't feel like an interview—which it would from some in the publishing industry—but more a genuine I-want-to-know-you-better discussion. Still, she wished he'd talk more about himself so it wasn't such a one-sided conversation. Leaning his chin on one hand, elbow propped, Landon prompted her to tell him more about her growing up years and laughed at her stories of childhood pranks Mitch played and the ways in which she and Celeste retaliated. His expressive eyes seemed to drink in the nuances of her face. With some men, such close scrutiny might have bothered her, but in spite of her earlier misgivings, she felt at ease with him.

Standing outside the church a short time later, Amy nodded at her fellow church members as they climbed the steps. The rush of warm air coming from inside the church each time someone opened the heavy front doors was inviting, but she was reluctant to say good night. Several of the women cast curious glances her way as they hurried past them. Hopefully, they wouldn't ask questions she wasn't prepared to answer. Landon held open the heavy wooden door for Velma King, the elderly prayer warrior who'd beseeched the Almighty for well over a year to "bring a mate for dear, sweet, lonely Amy Jacobsen." Thanking him, Velma beckoned to her and leaned close. "Bring that handsome fella inside with you."

"Mr. Warnick." Hugh Farber's resonant voice rang out in the night, making Amy jump. The church's star tenor pumped Landon's hand. "What a nice surprise and always a pleasure. Are you going to the Christmas dinner next Tuesday?"

Amy listened—and studied him a bit beneath surreptitious eyes—as Landon explained he'd be out of town and the men exchanged a few more pleasantries. Then it was Jonathan Kimball's turn. "Thanks for all the toys you and your staff donated to our Christmas drive, Landon. Much appreciated."

When Jonathan disappeared inside the church, Landon gave her a small smile. "It would seem some of the members of your church and I belong to the same civic and charitable organizations."

"I have a question."

"Ask away, but then I need to let you go inside." He glanced at his watch. "I'm sure they've already started."

That was the last thing on her mind. "Tell me, do you ever stay home or are you always a man about town?" Perhaps that wasn't the best way to pose the question, but he didn't seem to mind.

"Hardly, and that's the answer to both questions." When she raised a brow, he elaborated. "I'm not a man about town, defined by its usual meaning. First and foremost, it's where I live."

Amy tilted her head and surveyed him. "I'm not sure I understand."

"I've been blessed with so much, and I try to give back when and where I can. A toy drive here, a homeless project there and events with a number of groups. Working hard to make *New York Scene* the best it can be and helping to meet the needs of different organizations makes me feel like I'm making some kind of difference, as cliché as that sounds." His eyes met hers. "I can't *not* do it."

Questions swirled in her mind, but if she voiced them, they'd be standing on the steps of the church all night long. "I like where you live, Landon. Very much."

His eyes softened. "I don't mean to be tiresome, but it's who I am."

"I didn't say I didn't like it," she said, lowering her gaze from his. "But this is better. All your sophisticated talk can be a little exhausting sometimes, especially at the end of a long workday."

Covering her gloved hand with his, he took a step closer. "I've enjoyed getting to know you better tonight. I hope you'll agree to do this again soon."

She lifted her eyes. "Promise me something."

"Of course. Name it."

"If I agree to see you again, will you please be 'coffee shop Landon'? Not that I'm setting conditions."

He appeared momentarily startled, his expression full of something akin to regret. "'Coffee shop Landon' it is."

"Well, then, yes. Let's." *How silly.* Still, it was all she could think of to say. The man had her uncharacteristically tongue-tied. "I'd like that." With his track record, that probably meant he'd call tomorrow. "One more question. What did you mean when you mentioned other things about me that clued you in that I might attend church on Wednesday nights?"

"You have a joy that radiates from the inside out. It's rare and incredibly special." Leaning close, he planted a soft kiss on her right cheek. His lips were warm and gentle.

What is this man doing to me?

Mischief danced in his eyes. "I'd like to move that kiss slightly to the left, but not wanting to offend you wins out." Releasing her hand, he stepped back. "I wanted you to know the thought's there." He tapped one gloved finger on her nose. "That's not the inner flirt talking, it's plain truth."

Amy let out a small moan.

A hint of male satisfaction curved his full lips. "Was that actually a little moan?"

She laughed and shook her head. "Yes, I do believe it was."

"A good moan or a 'please get away from my lips now' moan?"

"It was more a groan along the lines of I can't believe how irreverent we are to stand on the steps of my church discussing such a thing. But thanks for the thought."

"Time for a compromise." Leaning forward, Landon planted a whisper of a kiss on her other cheek. "I'm scheduled to go out of town tomorrow for an extended trip, but I'm expected to attend a benefit dinner for a children's center on Saturday the twenty-first. I need to make an appearance, shake a few hands and stay long enough to say a few words. We can stay for dinner there or go somewhere else. Whatever you'd like. Please say you'll come."

The question in his eyes, the hope in his voice, was unexpected and sweet. *He really wants me to go.* "It sounds wonderful, but I'm leaving with Mitch on the twenty-first to go home for Christmas."

His barely-concealed disappointment endeared him to her more. "Then I'll call you when I get back in town and we'll arrange something closer to the New Year."

Inhaling a deep breath, she smiled as she turned to go inside.

"Amy, one last question?"

She paused and glanced back over her shoulder. "Yes?"

"Would you mind if I join you here at the church sometime?"

"You're welcome anytime, Landon. Good night."

That smile of his was dangerous. "Good night."

Amy knew he watched as she disappeared behind the heavy wooden door. Inside the church, she heaved a deep sigh as she removed her coat, resisting the urge to flatten herself against the door for support. She'd heard of the phenomenon of being weak in the knees and thought it was complete nonsense—until now. Being in Landon's company brought about a rush of emotions, and she suspected it might take some time to settle down from the natural high of spending time with him.

Concentrating during the study was impossible, and Velma turned the pages as they shared a Bible. Amy covered her mouth when the well-meaning woman lifted yet another petition in their prayer circle. Something about bringing "the man of Amy's dreams into her life." In her mind, she replayed her conversations with Landon. She had no idea he'd be so . . . how best to describe him? One or two adjectives couldn't do the man justice. Enigmatic, charming, intelligent, fascinating, flirtatious? They all made the list. Not to mention unbelievably gorgeous. Then again, he was a bit arrogant—or was it confidence? Presumptuous—or was it optimistic? Pushiness could also be mistaken for forward-thinking. *Calm down. It was one date.* No reason she had to make up her mind about him this minute. Or this week. Or month. *Okay, enough with this.*

From all appearances, Landon acted on his personal convictions. The more she thought about it, his magazine articles *did* contain spiritual threads—subtle but solid. Nothing thrilled her more. Call it the charm of the Christmas season, or the stars in her eyes. As much as anything else, Amy needed to believe—at least a little longer—in the *fantasy* of Landon Warnick.

Chapter 10

Thursday, December 5, 2002 – Mid-morning

"AMY? A WORD in my office." Not punctuated with a "please," it was a command performance, not a mere request.

"I'll be right there, Juliet." Replacing the phone, Amy's pulse jumped. She scrambled to find her notepad on her messy desk as she tried to squelch the rising sense of dread. Didn't work. *What have I done?* Only once before had she been summoned to the massive corner office by the woman herself—in a similar stern tone—and she'd endured a tongue-lashing. She'd listened, apologized, and shoved aside her pride and a sharp retort although she'd done nothing wrong. Then she escaped to her office for a good cry and a few soothing words from Marcheline. Developing a thick skin in the publishing environment was a difficult challenge. From what the other staffers told her, being reamed out by Juliet was a rite of passage inherent with her position. After all, her two predecessors each lasted less than a week at *Habits*, so she must be doing something right. Somehow, that knowledge brought little comfort as Amy started down the hallway.

Five minutes later, Marcheline ushered her into Juliet's office, but not before giving her a reassuring wink. Cradling the phone on one shoulder, Juliet motioned for Amy to take a seat. She swiveled out of view in her massive leather chair while Amy doodled on her notepad. Her fingers were shaking so hard, she almost dropped the pen on the carpet. She clamped her hand on her thumping leg and deep-breathed a few times.

Finished with her phone call a minute later, Juliet got straight to the point. "Amy, can you explain why Landon Warnick is calling you here at the office?"

She certainly hadn't expected *that* question. "It's personal, Juliet, not business." *How does she know?* Amy masked her frown. A nosy editorial assistant or staff member must have overheard her take Landon's call yesterday. After all, anyone worth their salt recognized the rival publisher's name. Funny though. She didn't recall calling him by name at any point in their conversation.

"He's not trying to steal you away, is he?" Rising to her feet, Juliet paced by the side of her desk with one manicured hand poised on her slim hip.

Steal me away? Phrasing aside, she didn't appreciate the insinuation. *Be calm.* "I have no intention of leaving, and I can assure you Landon's not trying to recruit me for his magazine."

"I should hope not." Juliet leaned against her desk, arms crossed. "Knowing him, I can certainly understand why your head might be turned. He has a certain . . . quality. Be forewarned where that man's concerned. You might believe he's wooing you personally, but chances are, he has an ulterior motive. You're a talented writer, Amy, and you're important to me, to *Habits*."

Stunned, Amy swallowed her shock and met Juliet's hard gaze. "Thank you for the vote of confidence."

"I understand you had a date with him last night." Her voice sounded raspier than usual. Although it could be caused by a cold, she didn't sound nasal. Most likely, she'd taken up smoking again. The woman was classic Type A. From what she knew, Juliet barely ate and rarely got a full four hours of sleep each night.

Amy tamped down her rising anger. Was someone spying on her? That made no sense. Sure, they'd been in very public places, and Landon was considered one of New York's most eligible bachelors. Had someone photographed them together? She envisioned the caption beneath a photo of them in the society pages: MYSTERY BRUNETTE SHARES COZY CARRIAGE RIDE IN CENTRAL PARK WITH LANDON WARNICK. *Anything but that.* Mitch would never let her live it down. Why would anyone feel the need to go running to her boss with that information?

She shifted, struggling to appear nonplussed. "Yes, I met him for dinner, but with all due respect, may I ask why my personal life is a concern to either you or the magazine?" She prayed her boss wouldn't either misinterpret the question or find it impertinent. "It was after working hours, on my own time."

Juliet tossed her head and narrowed her eyes. "I suspect he wants to steal you away and put you to work for his magazine. He's done it before and he'll do it again. I'm sure he impressed you with his knowledge of you and perhaps of the articles you've written."

A hundred different thoughts fluttered through Amy's mind. That was the second time Juliet used the word "steal." She closed her mouth, unsure what to say. During their time at the coffee shop, Landon mentioned a few of her articles and the topics—enough to understand he'd read them as opposed to surface skimming. She'd been flattered, and although the things Juliet said were true, it didn't mean Landon's intentions were underhanded or that he harbored an ulterior motive. The man had rushed to the aid of a possibly dying man. She refused to believe he would be . . . disingenuous. "He can't steal me away if I'm not interested in leaving. I'm happy here at *Habits*, and I trust you know I'm a loyal employee."

"Of course. My point being you're one of our best, and Landon knows it. The man is famously tenacious and stops at nothing to get what he wants."

Curiosity got the better of her. "When you say 'he's done it before,' what do you mean?"

Juliet returned to her chair and picked up her gold-plated fountain pen, twisting it between her fingers to the point where Amy wanted to grab it from her hand. "You know how I despise this kind of talk, but I also need you to understand something. About three years ago, we had a young writer working here. Very pretty and a talented writer. Landon took a 'liking' to her, shall we say, and lured her away. She subsequently defected from us with barely a decent good-bye, much less two weeks' notice. Apparently, the man's charms are irresistible."

Amy sat back in her chair, unable to meet Juliet's stare. The whole idea disheartened her. "Surely you're not implying he'd mislead me for the sole purpose of gaining a new employee?"

Juliet's brow arched. "Cozy carriage rides in Central Park aren't normally the way one conducts business, although with him, I suppose anything's possible. I'll admit he's an excellent writer and publisher. I'm not saying he plays dirty, but what I *am* saying is he knows how to play the game to get what he wants." She finally put down the pen and fixed her with a firm gaze. "I knew it was only a matter of time before your talent became a known commodity, Amy. However—" she said, narrowing her eyes—"I'm only going to tell you this once: stay away from Landon Warnick."

Rising to her feet, Amy's heart pounded. She'd fought for breath since Juliet mentioned the cozy carriage ride. Squaring her shoulders, she prepared to make a hasty retreat from the office. This was ten times worse than anything she could have imagined. "As I said, I'll take it under advisement. Thank you." How she got the words out, she wasn't sure. *And why am I thanking her? Polite to the end, you are.* She ignored Marcheline as she hurried past her and down the hall to her office. The walls closed in on her, the narrow corridor endless. Although she felt like slamming her door, she was careful to close it quietly in spite of the tempest raging inside her.

A wave of nausea overwhelmed her as she crossed her arms over her middle and leaned against the window sill. Tears stung her eyes as she digested Juliet's words. One thing she'd learned was not to accept anything or anyone at face value. Good or bad, most everyone had ulterior motives. As a journalist, she needed to be fair and honest and not make hasty judgments. Was her boss's warning a thinly-veiled threat? Could her position at the magazine actually be in jeopardy if she saw Landon again? The thought stunned her. Surely the terms of her employment didn't expressly forbid seeing him socially. Juliet made regular appearances at cocktail parties and dinners where Landon would be in attendance. They moved in the same circles, after all. Such occasions were commonplace and inevitable. Like it or not, certain obligations came with the position.

Stumbling to her desk, Amy dropped into her chair and stared straight ahead, lost in thought. Never would she have expected anything like this to happen. As it was, she rarely dated, by her own choice, and now she'd been told in no uncertain terms—by her boss, no less—to stay away from the first man who'd intrigued her in years. From the top of the mountain one day to the pit the next. Had the whole world gone crazy? Perhaps she *was* every bit as naïve as Mitch suspected.

~

Later that same afternoon, Amy focused on her edits for the next article due. She jumped when the intercom buzzed, interrupting her concentration.

"Amy, you have a delivery at the front desk."

With a frown, she pushed the button on her phone. "I'm in the middle of something, Lana. Is Nathan around? He can either bring it to me or I'll come get it later."

She overheard a muffled male voice—deep and vaguely familiar—in the background. "The delivery's on its way back to you now."

"Okay. Thanks." Sensing a presence in the doorway within the minute, she glanced up to see Landon leaning against the doorjamb. Oh my, this guy was more handsome than a man had a right to be in his dark suit. Tailored to absolute perfection.

"Hi, Amy." The way he said her name with that velvety-smooth, deep voice did untold things to her.

Lord, can You please have a little mercy? When I said I needed help, this wasn't exactly what I had in mind.

"Landon. What a nice surprise." Rising to her feet, she wondered if she'd chewed off all her lipstick. Frustrated with her edits, she'd also tugged on her hair and hoped it appeared halfway presentable. Preliminary notes for the piece on Sam were scattered across her desk along with a couple of articles she was editing. Smoothing one hand over the top of her head, she moved from behind her desk and waved him inside. "Come on in, but excuse my mess."

"It's my fault for dropping by unannounced," he said. "One of the signs of an effective editor is a chaotic desk. At least that's what I tell myself. My assistant, Dona, has fits about my lack of organizational skills, but she learned early on not to rearrange anything. I won't keep you, but I wanted to bring something to you."

"How thought—" Amy's words stuck in her throat as he moved his hand from behind his back and held out a small bouquet of daffodils. For the second time in as many days, he'd stolen her breath in a most unexpected, wonderful way.

"Daffodils?" She focused on the fresh blooms. "They're my favorite. How . . . how . . ." she said, taking them from him. "How did you find them at this time of the year?" Tears stung her eyes. The sentimental gesture touched her more than if he'd brought her the rarest, most expensive roses.

"I was hoping for a smile, not the opposite. Let me run down to the corner and—"

"No, please. I love them." *This man makes all the right gestures. Is he incredibly sensitive or just way too smooth?* "Trust me, they're happy tears. This is . . . very special." She turned back to her desk. "Let's see. I'll need to find a glass or something to put them in. Surely one of the other ladies has a vase around here somewhere, but I'm not sure where." She stopped. Being in this man's presence transformed her into a blathering idiot. Taking a deep breath, she gave him a shaky smile. "Let's try this again. Thank you, Landon. Should I ask how you know I love daffodils?" She eyed the bright yellow flowers with appreciation.

"Confession time." His sheepish grin was as surprising as it was charming and relaxed his features. "I called your brother."

"I doubt he could tell you my favorite color or food, but in this case, he got it right." Her mental tug-of-war continued.

"Actually, I think he was testing me," Landon said. "Probably thought he was throwing me off by naming an out-of-season flower."

"I'll make sure he knows you passed the test. Aced it, as a matter of fact."

"Mitch and I are a lot alike. For one thing, we love a challenge."

"I see. Are you giving me a rare glimpse into the elusive male psyche on a Thursday afternoon?"

"Perhaps, but I should think my intentions are more obvious than elusive." He glanced at his watch, affording her a few precious seconds to regain her equilibrium. "I have an appointment and then need to catch a plane in a few hours or I'd love to ask you to join me for a cup of coffee." Landon's smile broadened. "So you could pick my brain and explore the male psyche to your heart's content."

Still digesting his comment about intentions, Amy felt the telltale flush invade her cheeks. "The thought's there, and that's what counts." She sniffed the flowers. *Silly girl. Daffodils don't have much of a scent.*

"I wanted to thank you again for last night," he said. "Tell me something."

"What's that?" Amy walked with him toward the door, thankful he hadn't burst out laughing because of her silly floral *faux pas.*

"Why daffodils?"

Her lips lifted with the hint of a smile. "Well, it's certainly not because daffodils smell so wonderful." Catching the amusement in his eyes, she continued. "It's more what they represent. Rebirth. Renewal. The earth awakening after the long, cold winter. I love that Easter's usually around the same time, and it's a reminder of the resurrection and the Lord's promise to return." She blew out a breath as she fingered one of the sturdy, lovely blooms. "I love the color—so vibrant and full of life. The promise of new beginnings."

The way his gaze bore into hers made her wonder if she'd said too much. She hadn't intended for it to sound leading. *It really doesn't take much for you, does it?*

"I see promise in what's happening between us, and hope you do, too."

True to form, he'd found the perfect segue in her last statement. "Between us?" This was happening way too fast.

"Surely you feel it, too." Stepping closer, Landon's gaze roamed a languid path over her features.

She felt kissed although he hadn't touched her. "Uh huh." Her tongue seemed to be stuck to the roof of her mouth, and it's all she could think to say. When one of her coworkers passed by, Amy lowered her gaze, her heart pounding. Landon's presence in the *Habits* office could stir trouble. If her senior editor hadn't personally witnessed his visit, she felt sure someone would be more than happy to tell Juliet. Wonderful.

But the man brought her daffodils, so she'd defend him to the end.

"By the way, my best guess is blue," he said.

"What's that?" Either Landon was being obtuse again or her brain had departed on the express train.

"Your favorite color."

How could he know? "Mitch?"

Landon shook his head with a small smile. "Not this time. I'll talk with you again soon. Until then, stay well." He departed before she could form another thought, much less a coherent word.

Amy's eyes widened when she spied Marcheline headed down the hallway in her direction, carrying a cut crystal vase half-filled with water. "Here. You might need this," she said, handing it to her with a wry grin. "I want your life. What a gorgeous man, and trust me, any guy who goes to the trouble to find daffodils at *this* time of year? He's interested in more than friendship, honey."

Don't let your boss hear you say that. After thanking March, Amy turned and glimpsed Juliet a few doors down, talking with another editor. *Too late.* Her arms were crossed and she glared in her direction. With a quick nod of acknowledgment, Amy ducked her head and darted back into her office. As much as she liked Landon, she was thankful he'd be out-of-town for a couple of weeks. Good thing she'd be gone for a few days, too. Give Juliet time to cool off. She'd also pray a little holiday cheer might soften her forbidding superior. Writing a great piece on Sam was the overall best strategy to maintain her boss's favor.

Arranging the daffodils in the vase, Amy prayed Juliet wouldn't visit her office with another somber warning. She'd need to be careful and stay low on the radar until her trip to Louisiana. The prospect of getting away from New York and being with her closest friends in the world grew more appealing with each passing minute.

Chapter 11

Wednesday, December 11, 2002 – Late Evening

HEARING THE TONE signaling an incoming e-mail, Amy scooted over to her desk. *Angel777.* With raised brows, she dropped into the chair and clicked on the new message, quickly skimming it. Angelina Delgado. Although happy to receive the e-mail, the timing was bad. The e-mail had two files attached. Blowing out a breath, Amy debated whether to take a look or save them for later. Her curiosity piqued, she printed them out and left them on her desk. If she needed a break in her pre-wedding trip chores later, she'd take a peek.

After balancing her checkbook, doing three loads of laundry and taking care of a half-dozen last-minute details—she took a breath an hour later and stopped to read the first attachment. It was a funny, bittersweet story of growing up the only daughter in a family of six brothers in a small, cramped house in Queens. When she picked up the second story and took a quick glance, it captured her immediate attention.

Grabbing an afghan and curling into the corner of the living room sofa a couple of hours later, she sipped a cup of coffee while she read through the second story, titled, "Just Maybe." It was a heartrending, first-person account of a young girl finding herself where she never expected to be—pregnant.

I guess I'm not supposed to ask why it happened. It's not like Dante forced me. We'd been getting closer and the warning signs were there. The way he ran his hand over my arm. His gentle, coaxing words. The kisses on my forehead, my cheeks, my chin . . . . I feel unlovable most of the time, but Dante makes me feel like I'm the most important person in the world. Me. A short, sarcastic and not-very-pretty girl from the wrong side of town. Maybe it's only for today, maybe for a few more tomorrows, maybe for a lifetime.

No one ever paid much attention to me before. My mom doesn't like me, my dad hates me, my brother and sister tolerate me. My art teacher says my paintings "show promise" and I might have a chance to "make something of myself" someday if I work hard and take graphic arts classes. I don't know if she really means it or not, but I think she does. I guess some people really are good on the inside. Not because they have *to be but because they* want *to be. I don't know. Maybe it makes them feel better about themselves to help someone like me. Maybe they'll find more favor with God. And now, because of what I did with Dante, I've got a little person inside me. It's weird. I run my hand over my belly, and I can't feel anything, but the lady at the clinic says I will soon enough. Is that what I want?*

"I'll pray for you," the blonde lady with big blue eyes tells me the next day as I walk to the clinic. "I've been where you are. I understand." She looks like an angel, so I'll call her that in my head. She has the most honest eyes I've ever seen. As I stand on the sidewalk, she hands me one of those pamphlets that show babies at different stages of development inside the

womb. It looks interesting. Then this horrible fat man rushes toward me, holding a homemade sign with baby parts and fake blood stains all over it, screaming and spewing spit and venom in my face. He calls me a baby killer. Me, a baby killer? I'd rather kill him *than my baby.*

I back away and turn to go inside. A big bruiser of a woman bars the front door. "Think about what you're doing," she says. She crosses her arms and plants her feet—encased in actual combat boots—and stares me down.

"I am," I assure her. "Please let me inside."

"Not if you plan on taking the life growing inside you. God will never forgive you."

Someone takes me by the arm—not rough, but with a gentle hand. I look into the blue eyes of Angel. "Come with me," she says while telling the mean woman to step aside. Bruiser spits on the ground and says some very unkind things. But she moves.

Ten minutes later, we sit inside the clinic, Angel and me. When she asks me if I want her to leave, I tell her no. I mean it. I want her to stay. She gives me comfort. The only one I told was Dante, but I have the feeling he might never come around again. When I start talking, the tears come. Then more. Angel pulls me in her arms and rocks me, hugs me, holds me.

"Why does everybody have to be so mean?" I ask. "They accuse me of wanting to kill my baby. I love my baby. I don't want to kill her." I've started calling her that because it's not fair to call her "it." If the baby's a boy, that's okay, too, but I'd really like a girl. I can put bows in her hair and frilly socks on her tiny feet. Be the kind of mom mine never was. "Don't they get it?"

"No," Angel says. "They don't."

"But you do. Did you keep your baby?"

She shakes her head. "No." It comes out a sob and now it's my turn to hug her. "I have other kids now, but I'll never forget my first baby." She thumps her chest with a curled fist. "I hold him here in my heart always, and I know I'll see him when I get to Heaven."

"How do you know?"

"Because I'm his mama. A mama knows her child, no matter what."

That makes me think a minute. "I mean, how do you know you're going to Heaven?"

"Because I have a friend in Jesus." She squeezes my hand. "He's with you all the time. He wants *to be there, but you just have to invite Him to take the journey with you. Your mama gave* you *a chance to take your journey, and now it's your turn to give your baby that opportunity. But you don't have to do it alone. Let Jesus help."*

When they call my name, Angel stands beside me and reaches for my hand and says a quick prayer. Something about Jesus knowing every hair on my baby's head, her first word, everything about her. It's probably somewhere in the Bible. Those are some of the most beautiful words I've ever heard. I never thought about it that way before. Never thought much about God at all, but I know I don't hate Him. Angel's right. My mama's not perfect, but she gave me a chance. And now God's given me someone else to care about. My baby isn't a condemnation of who and what I am, and it's not a punishment for what I did with Dante. She's a special gift. *For me, a short, sarcastic, not-so-pretty person. I guess if God thinks I look okay on the inside, then maybe I* am *good enough? Just maybe.*

I look at the clinic lady and say, "This is Angel, and she's coming in with me."

The woman looks annoyed and checks her chart. "It says you're here for a termi—"

"Well," I say, "somebody got it wrong." I'm not saying it because I want to make Angel happy, or to satisfy Venom Spewer or Bruiser. They must not know Jesus if they act like that. No, I'm doing this for me and my baby.

When Angel squeezes my hand again, I know everything's going to be okay. Just maybe.

Putting the pages on the nearby table, Amy shook her head, dazed. *Why do I stand at the door, on the outside looking in?* For the last few years, she'd handed out flyers and counseled women about pro-life and pro-family pregnancy alternatives through her church and inner-city TeamWork projects. *I need to take that hand and walk through the door if that's what a girl needs, Lord.* A verse—also a song—she'd learned as a child in Sunday school came into her mind. *Behold, I stand at the door and knock; if anyone hears my voice and opens the door, I will come in to him . . .*

Climbing into bed, she pondered Angelina's stories. With some tweaking, the first story was good enough to warrant an editor's attention, but it was the second story that captured her heart. It was one of the most honest and insightful pieces she'd read in a long time, and to think it'd been written by a young girl. But that's why it was so good. If Angelina wasn't the girl in her story, it had to be someone she knew well. The sad fact was, because of its subject matter, she wasn't sure where—or *if*—she could place it in the hands of an editor for publishing consideration, but it did deserve to be read by more than a Christian audience. For that matter, it should be read by more than teens, although it might reach that age group on a more relevant level.

As she snuggled under the covers, she closed her eyes. Perhaps "Just Maybe" was intended for her eyes only, the same as she'd been in Angelina's father's cab twice in the same day. The Lord's ways were marvelous and unpredictable and never ceased to amaze her. *Thank you, Lord, for opening my eyes. I pray I can make a difference in someone's life. Just maybe.*

Chapter 12

Thursday, December 12, 2002 — Late Evening - Baton Rouge, Louisiana

"AMY! OVER HERE!"

How she adored that familiar, sweet drawl. Turning toward the greeting, Amy waved as she spied Winnie. Hurrying toward her, Amy dropped her carry-on overnight bag and purse on the floor of the airport terminal and embraced her best friend as though she hadn't seen her in years, not months. "It's so great to see you. Thanks for coming to get me."

"You, too. I wouldn't let anyone else come."

Pulling out of their hug, Winnie gave her pale blue business suit and ivory silk blouse an approving once-over. "You look terrific, sweetie. As pretty as I've ever seen you."

"Right back at you," Amy said. With her cheeks flushed and blue eyes bright, Winnie was lovely in her jeans and a stylish wool jacket. Her blonde hair fell in loose waves around her shoulders instead of being contained in its usual ponytail.

"I take it you went straight from your office to the airport?"

"Guilty." Amy didn't want to admit how close she'd come to missing her flight. She'd put her new shoes and exercise regime to the test at LaGuardia. "You'll be happy to know I've promised myself I won't touch work" —she raised both hands in the air— "or think about it, until I get to Houston to interview Sam. But that's a fun assignment, so it doesn't actually count. Until then, I'm not going to worry about deadlines or anything publishing-related." Maybe if she said it out loud, she'd believe it.

Winnie tilted her head. "Something's different about you. Besides, you can't fool me. That creative imagination of yours never sleeps."

"I can't believe Sam didn't breathe a word about his book before now. That was quite a shock, but a great one. I'm so happy for him." She darted a glance at Winnie. "Surely you knew about it?"

"Only that he mentioned back in June that he was jotting down some notes. You know Sam. Once he sets his mind to something, it's as good as done. I think he's still trying to get used to the idea and there are days he wants to strangle Marc for suggesting it in the first place. This whole thing's already gotten much bigger than he expected. His publisher's doing a great job pre-publicizing it. Knowing Sam, he'll take it all in stride."

"I'm sure he will. Where's your little twin?" Amy retrieved her things as they followed the small crowd of departing passengers toward the baggage claim.

"Chloe begged me to come, but it's too late and we have such a big day tomorrow. I'm sure she's convinced Josh to read her one more bedtime story. He's a master at doing funny voices and she can't get enough."

"Again, like her mother. You look absolutely radiant, Winnie. Marriage looks really great on you."

A sweet flush colored Winnie's cheeks. "You were always so sure about Josh even when I wasn't. Thank you." Her eyes misted and she sniffled. "Sorry. I'm more emotional than ever these days, what with the wedding and everything. Don't mind me." Digging in her purse, she pulled out a tissue. "It's all good."

Amy gave her friend—the "Mother Hen" of the TeamWork crew—another quick hug. "You three belong together, but you and Josh both needed time to work through circumstances in your lives. I trusted the Lord to work out the details. So, tell me, how are the plans coming along for the new house?"

"We break ground the first part of March." Dabbing at her eyes and tossing the tissue back in her purse, Winnie brightened. "Now that Kevin and Beck are settling in Houston, too, Lexa and Sam tease about installing a revolving door in the kitchen for all the comings and goings of the TeamWork crew."

"Not a bad idea. The more the merrier, I suppose." Amy smiled as they reached the baggage carousel. "Lexa feeling any better?"

"Her morning sickness is lasting longer than expected and she's more tired, so she has her moments. Joe's walking now, so—combined with the catering business—she stays busy. Lexa's got more energy than anyone I know, but she's finally learning to slow down and acknowledge when she's overdoing it. Sam helps as much as he can, and he's been cooking dinner a couple of nights a week."

Amy raised a brow. "Sam and cooking in the same sentence? The man has many talents, but that's a stretch unless peaches are an ingredient."

Winnie laughed. "He tries, but it's a good thing Lexa likes spaghetti. Sam's a lot of fun to watch with Joe. Last week, I found the little guy sprawled across his daddy's chest, a storybook on the floor beside them in Sam's office at the house, both fast asleep. Oh, listen to this: Beck got him a little pair of cowboy boots and—"

"Don't even tell me that child has a baby Stetson," Amy said, laughing. "Sam's such a good man. You got yourself a gem, too, Mrs. Grant, but going back to the catering, Cassie tells me Doyle-Clarke Catering is in huge demand these days. You and Lexa have worked hard to build your clientele, and it sounds like the hard work is paying off."

"Thanks. Cassie's helping us full-time now, and she's a hard worker and is great with the advertising. Marta and Gayle work some of the weekend events and we've hired a few part-time helpers, mostly mothers from our church. Christmas is our busiest season, and for the first time ever, we had to turn down a couple of catering jobs this weekend."

"I'm glad you can take a break. You deserve it." Amy watched as luggage from her flight started around the carousel. "Can you believe Beck and Kevin are finally getting married? After watching that shy man skirt around her for years, and then with Adam wanting to marry her and take her to England . . ."—she waved her hand—"there were times I wasn't sure this day would ever come. I was more confident in you and Josh, but please don't tell Beck I said that."

"They've both grown a lot, even in these last few months," Winnie said. "They're solid and downright adorable together. Sam's gone through pre-marital counseling with them, and they're more than ready to be married. Helping to plan this wedding has also been great to keep my mother-in-law busy and focused since it's only been six months since Dad passed away. Rebekah worried it was too soon to plan a big church wedding, but Lorena insisted. Just like she encouraged Josh and me not to delay our wedding."

"I'm sure having Chloe in her life has been a blessing, too. Let me grab my suitcase and then we're on our way." As she toted her suitcase behind her and Winnie carried her overnight bag, they discussed wedding details as they walked to the parking lot. "You didn't bring Ladybug?" Amy asked after storing her luggage in the trunk of the dark blue BMW.

"Ladybug doesn't exactly fit Josh's masculine image, especially this weekend. I love it when Josh drives Chloe around town in that little yellow car, though. He can barely fit inside and it's pretty cramped, but he does it for her." Winnie's voice choked. "It's amazing how well they've adjusted to each other, although the first time Josh raised his voice, Chloe absolutely crumpled. Even as young as she is, it's like she's known all along Josh is her dad. Every time she calls him 'daddy,' I melt." Winnie shifted on the seat to face her, eyes bright. "Do you know what our little girl said yesterday?"

"As smart as Chloe is, anything's possible," Amy said, her heart uplifted by the love and pride in her best friend's voice.

"Thanks. When we were on our way here to Louisiana, she said, 'Daddy, your eyes are green just like mine and they twinkle when they look at Mommy.'" Winnie paused, catching her breath. "My daughter has a romanticized view of life—and yes, maybe she's seen too many animated movies with twinkly-eyed characters—but she shares so many wonderful qualities with Josh, especially a sense of whimsy and fun and seeing the best in people and situations. And you know what? I hope she never loses those qualities."

Reaching across the seat, Amy squeezed her hand. "Me, too." They talked more as Winnie drove them out of the airport and merged onto the highway. Amy's phone buzzed. Tamping down the hope it might be Landon, she saw her mother's number light the display. After assuring her mom she'd arrived safely, she promised to call her later in the weekend to tell her all about the wedding. She caught Winnie's smile as she replaced the phone. "Do mothers ever stop worrying?"

"No, and you'll find out firsthand one of these days. Okay, I've waited long enough," Winnie said with a big grin. "You've met someone. Tell me about him."

I'm too transparent. Then again, Winnie was uncommonly perceptive and could read her better than anyone besides her brother. Amy launched into her story. After talking non-stop for five minutes straight, she ended with Juliet's warning. "Wow," she said, catching her breath, "and to think I wasn't even sure what to say about him."

"It's great to see you so happy. You're usually very cautious about meeting new men."

Amy glanced her way. "You know I have to be."

"Yes, but from what you've told me, you can trust Landon's not after your money."

She hated discussing money and shifted in her seat. "It's not really mine, anyway, but money made from a few successful films and countless Broadway shows."

Winnie exited the interstate before answering. "Your grandfather didn't leave you the Manhattan walk-up and a trust fund to burden you, sweetie, but to make your life easier. He was a great actor and invested his money wisely to help his family."

"Not that I don't appreciate it because I do," Amy said. "Sorry if I sounded like a spoiled and ungrateful heir." Her grandfather's money had afforded her a top-notch education, opportunities and a quality of life she wouldn't have enjoyed otherwise.

"You didn't," Winnie said. "I think having those resources has made you careful and wary out of necessity. Just like your grandfather"—she glanced her way—"and from what I know, you've turned your personal gain into blessings for others. From what you've told me about Landon, he shares that philosophy."

Amy nodded. "Landon has this fierce intensity about him. He embraces life head-on and says whatever's in his head. While I admire that, his blunt honesty is also very unsettling. He challenges me and makes me think, but not in a 'this could get old real quick' kind of way. It's more a 'this could be fun' way. On the other hand, the man's exhausting." Laughing, she shook her head. "Did that make any sense?"

"It did, and he sounds perfect for you. Being in the same business, you understand each other."

"True, but we might also drive each other crazy."

Winnie's trademark giggle slipped out, warming her heart. "*Good* crazy."

"But what about Juliet's warning? I can't afford to lose my job, and I can't believe she'd have legitimate grounds to fire me."

"I guess that's where the trust factor comes into play," Winnie said. "You've never been one to listen to idle gossip and you have great instincts. The best advice I can give you is to pray and know I'll pray for you, too. Take it day-by-day. You've got all the time in the world to explore this relationship and see where it might be headed."

Amy blew out a deep sigh. "Thanks. You're right. I've been praying, but I guess I should ramp it up."

~

After Amy checked in at the inn, Winnie helped her find her room on the third floor.

"I have your dress and I'll bring it to you tomorrow morning after breakfast," Winnie said. "The TeamWork crew is gathering in the restaurant downstairs at nine. Sam's reserved a private room for us."

"It'll be a nice change to sleep in a little. I can't wait to see everyone and catch up on their news. As you know, an awful lot can happen with this group in a very short time." Amy shared a grin with Winnie and stifled her yawn. Now that she'd arrived, she was tired and welcomed a good night's rest. "Thanks for picking me up at the airport and listening to me jabber on and on."

"Anytime. As far as Landon is concerned, any man who puts that sparkle in *your* eye is going to mean something in your life, sweetie."

"Oh, that reminds me. Come inside the room for a minute and I'll show you his picture." Winnie waited as Amy retrieved the latest issue of *New York Scene* from the front pocket of her bag. Flipping through the first few glossy pages, she held it up for her to see.

"My, my. He's very handsome," Winnie said, taking it from her. "Looks like a charmer, and he reminds me of someone else we know."

Amy frowned. "Really? Who's that?"

Winnie handed back the magazine with a smile. "Sam."

Glancing at the photo, Amy shrugged. "I guess I can see the resemblance in the dark hair and blue eyes, but without the smile lines and the tinge of silver at the temples. Landon's personality is a lot different from Sam's, but they're both strong men."

"I think it's more in his posture and facial expression," Winnie said. "I need to go check on Chloe and make sure Josh isn't keeping her up. You get settled in and get some good sleep tonight." Reaching into her purse, she dug out a small slip of paper and handed it to her. "Here's a list of our room numbers and extensions I made for everyone. Most of us are here on this floor. We're in 302 and Sam and Lexa are in 310. Marc and Natalie are in the room two doors down from you. If they get too rambunctious, just call Sam."

Amy laughed in the middle of another yawn. "I don't want to know. Does our crew take up this entire floor?"

"Not quite, but give us a few more years." With another quick hug, Winnie turned to go. "I'm so glad we're all here together. Sweet dreams, and I'll see you in the morning."

~

Friday morning dawned bright and unseasonably warm, and the forecast for Saturday promised to be glorious. After her shower, Amy left her hair to dry naturally. Pulling on her new pair of jeans—two sizes smaller than three months ago—she dressed them up with a pale pink silk blouse and stylish but comfortable brown leather ankle boots. After brushing her teeth and slicking on a touch of lipstick, she fastened a white and pink pearl necklace around her neck and a matching bracelet on her wrist. Although she loved jewelry, she didn't wear much at work since it could be distracting and cumbersome. For special occasions like this, though, she indulged.

Lexa waved to her from the middle of the long table as she entered the private dining room. "Amy! Come over here and give me a big hug." Sitting next to her, Sam talked with Eliot Marchand and Dean Costas, two of the quieter TeamWork volunteers. Catching her eye, Sam smiled and Winnie waved from the opposite side of the table.

"I'm so glad you and Sam are taking the whole be fruitful and multiply command seriously," Amy said, moving around the table to kiss Lexa's cheek before putting one hand on Sam's shoulder. "Hey, Papa Bear."

"Great to see you, Amy." Sam rose to his full height—all six foot five inches—and she leaned into his embrace. He gave the best hugs in the world, and she clung to him for a few seconds.

"Where's your adorable lookalike son?" she asked.

"With my mom and dad for the weekend. They're in grandparent glory, and he's having more fun with them than he would here. You'll see Joe when you come to Houston in a few days."

"Can't wait," Amy said. "When's your due date, Lexa?"

"Valentine's Day." Lexa winked at Sam.

Natalie rushed over to give Amy a hug. "You look gorgeous!" She leaned close and lowered her voice. "Marc and Sam have a competition going to see which one can populate TeamWork the quickest. So far, we're letting them win."

"I heard that," Marc said, coming up behind his wife and giving Amy a peck on the check. "Hello, Daydreamer. For the record, I want everyone here to know I'm doing my part to keep up with the old man. Since Gracie's not with us this weekend, who knows what might happen?"

"Too much information, Marc. Stop it." Natalie gave her husband a love swat. "Okay, I'll bite," she said, directing the comment to Lexa and Sam as

Marc helped her into the chair beside Lexa. "Something's up with you two. It's written all over your faces. Time to share it with the whole group."

"My wife, the teacher, ladies and gentlemen," Marc said, seating himself next to Natalie. He looked over at Sam. "The question's on the table, old man. What's up?"

Sam's deep smile lines surfaced and he glanced at Lexa, who nodded. "Since you've asked and we're among friends . . . we're expecting twins this time. Girls."

"I knew it!" Marc slapped one hand on the table, and Natalie and Lexa exchanged amused glances. "Congratulations, buddy."

Josh entered the restaurant with Chloe beside him. "Aunt Amy!" Releasing her father's hand, the child ran to her, throwing her arms around her middle and hugging her tight. Josh gave her a wink and a broad smile.

"Hey, Buttercup." Amy kissed the top of the little girl's blonde, curly head and felt the familiar tug on her heart. "Let me look at you." She stepped back and smiled. "What a big girl you're getting to be! You're going to look like a princess in the wedding tomorrow. Are you excited?"

Chloe's curls bobbed up and down. "I like your boots."

The whole group turned as a glowing Rebekah entered the room, hand-in-hand with Kevin.

Chloe scrambled into the chair beside her mother as Amy embraced the bride-to-be. "Beck, you're going to be the most beautiful bride ever. I couldn't be more thrilled for you and Kevin."

Kevin moved forward and kissed her cheek. "Great to have you here, Amy. Now the group is complete." His gaze encompassed the entire group, and she listened as Kevin greeted everyone. The deep love reflected in Rebekah's eyes was the kind of love she could only dream of finding one day. She started to tear up again. *Stop welling up like an old maid with no prospects.*

"I say let's get this party started," Josh said, taking the seat on the other side of Winnie.

"Sounds good to me," Marc said, raising his juice glass in a toast.

After a few more minutes of catching up on each other's news, Sam asked the blessing and they departed in small groups to the breakfast buffet. The aroma of fresh coffee, cinnamon rolls, bacon, sausage and eggs made Amy's stomach rumble. Filling her plate, she took a seat on one end of the table with Cassie, Marta and Gayle—the unnamed but obvious "singles" section.

Without giving names, Marc relayed amusing anecdotes about a few famous clients in his Boston sports advertising agency. Lexa and Natalie shared the milestones and antics of their toddlers. When prompted by the others, Sam talked about his book and the plans for a marketing blitz. Winnie told them how Josh thrived in his new position working alongside Sam as TeamWork general counsel, and Kevin told about his wife-to-be's job heading up the various school operations for TeamWork's domestic missions. Beck glowed as she spoke of the success of Kevin's new lumber store outside Houston, and Josh shared about the growing success of Lexa and Winnie's Doyle-Clarke Catering and made mention of Cassie, Marta and Gayle's invaluable help. Dean told them about opening new Texas locations in his chain of leather stores.

Amy sat back, content to listen until Lexa asked her to share about her work at *Habits*. She kept it brief, but shared a couple of humorous anecdotes about recent interviews and stories and told them about her plans for the article on Sam.

True to form, Eliot remained quiet, but those sharp, intelligent eyes missed nothing. He was the mysterious one. Call it a hunch, but Amy suspected one of these days, this guy would surprise them all. Although Sam must know what he did for a living, no one else was privy. Along with his buddy, Dean, Eliot was a loyal volunteer and had served on several missions, including the one in Montana. Moving her gaze to Marta, Amy couldn't miss the glances the pretty blonde with the unusual violet eyes exchanged with Eliot. Another TeamWork pairing? It made sense, but again, she felt the odd-woman out.

Get over yourself. What's with all the Miss Lonely Hearts thoughts lately? She could blame it on the wedding. Weddings always stirred up thoughts and feelings to reinforce her single status.

"You okay?" Cassie gave her a gentle nudge accompanied by an understanding smile.

"Yes, thanks," she said, sipping her coffee. "This love business sure is great, isn't it?"

"As pretty and successful as you are, I'm sure you have men clamoring for your attention."

"Hardly, but I haven't been too interested, either." Amy shrugged. "Keeps life less complicated."

"Forgive me if I'm off the mark or out of line here," Cassie said, swallowing a last spoonful of strawberry yogurt, "but are you hoping to maybe complicate your life sometime soon?"

Words to ponder, but best to divert the question. "How about you? Are you seeing anyone?"

Cassie shook her head. "Not really. As Josh mentioned, I'm getting more involved with the catering business, especially since Lexa's due soon, so"—she gave her a small grin—"I'm not looking for a complication either."

"It's understandable. You're at the stage in your life where you want to focus on your career. You've got plenty of time for everything else later."

"Don't misunderstand," Cassie said. "If the right man comes along tomorrow, I might be interested. My prayer is I'll recognize him."

I've got to find a way to introduce her to Mitch sometime. With her long, naturally-wavy auburn hair and flawless porcelain skin, Cassie was a natural beauty. Her Alabama accent was warm and captivating, and she was intelligent and quick-witted. She didn't fit the image of the cool, sophisticated type Mitch normally dated. Then again, her brother dated a lot of women she'd never met. Mitch and Cassie shared a like compassion and intense desire to help others. Good starting point for a relationship if ever there was one, but she knew Mitch wasn't ready yet.

Gayle nudged her shoulder. "I hear there's a groomsman who can't get here until right before the wedding, and he's a journalist. Imagine that."

Amy's brows rose. "Oh? I haven't heard anything."

"His name's Cooper," Gayle said. "From what Beck said, Kevin met him through an on-campus ministry at A&M, but he was a few years older. He worked on the newspaper staff."

Interesting. "Do you know who Cooper works for now?"

"Not sure. Maybe he's been globe-trotting and covering some breaking news feature or interviewing someone famous. I think he's paired up with you to walk down the aisle tomorrow. Can't imagine why they'd think you two might hit it off." With her classic features and beautiful, deep red hair, Gayle reminded Amy of a young Maureen O'Hara, a gracious Hollywood star she'd once met at a dinner honoring her grandfather.

Amy snapped back to the present. "Imagine that," she said. She loved to talk shop with someone who shared her passion for words, so the prospect was intriguing. "I'll look forward to meeting him." She found it amusing how so many assumed a journalist's life was fascinating and full of ongoing adventure. While it could be exciting, it usually involved lots of the mundane—endless phone calls, constant prodding to get one decent quote and research followed by hours spent at the computer to write and then edit an article. Hardly a glamorous life, but she might as well let others enjoy their illusions.

The rest of the morning was full of wedding events and details, so many Amy thought the better option might be to elope like Sam and Lexa had done in San Antonio. Granted, their circumstances were a bit unique with a year's separation thrown into the mix, but elopement sure saved time and money. *Listen to me, thinking about such a thing.* Cassie's words came to mind about praying she'd recognize the right man of God's choosing if and when he came into her life. That seemed a wise sentiment, and a prayer she could likewise adopt with no hesitation.

She inhaled and then released a slow breath of relief when Winnie helped her into her bridesmaid's gown shortly before lunch. "Oh, thank goodness it fits. Not bad for only one fitting, huh? The deprivation diet and all the jogging on the 'dreadmill' worked. I'm glad we're doing this before lunch, though, and not after. After that huge breakfast, if I keep eating like that, I'll split the seams on the way down the aisle."

"Oh, stop it already," Winnie said, marching her in front of the full-length mirror in her room at the inn. "Whatever you do, don't say anything like that to Beck or she'll panic. Don't want to give the bride nightmares. Besides, if you'd lost any more weight, this gown would hang on you, but right now it fits you like a dream." While modest, the neckline was scooped and draped slightly off-the-shoulder. Their eyes met in the reflected image. "The color matches the green in your eyes perfectly and really makes them stand out. You're absolutely gorgeous, sweetie."

"Thanks," Amy said. "I have to say, you're a big boost for my ego."

"Just telling the truth." Winnie gave her a sly grin. "I only wish Landon could see you in it."

"There you go again." Although she smirked, she wasn't altogether displeased by the comment. After she slipped out of the dress, Winnie hung it on its padded hanger while Amy dressed. "What do you know about this guy who's supposedly paired with me in the wedding?"

"Not much other than he was one of Kevin's good friends at A&M and was the editor of the campus newspaper. They called him"—Winnie hesitated a moment while zipping the garment bag over Amy's dress—"Cooper the Scoop . . . no that's not right. Hang on." She snapped her fingers. "Coop the Scoop Warren. That's it. Kind of catchy, don't you think?"

Amy laughed. "Kind of corny, but yes, it's rather cute. Maybe I can corral the guy into a dance at the wedding reception and we can talk shop. Could be fun." She hoped to dance at least once during the course of the evening, and Coop the Scoop might be the one to share a dance.

During the church rehearsal late that afternoon, Lorena Grant, Beck and Josh's widowed mother and self-appointed wedding coordinator, confirmed she'd paired Amy with Cooper for the recessional. Amy didn't want to think about what would happen if the world-hopping journalist—or whatever the man did now—didn't make it in time for the ceremony. Although perhaps walking solo down the aisle might be fitting. She could practically hear Mitch's voice in her head. *Get over yourself. You're not the only single person in the world. Have fun with your friends and then come home to the real world and get on with your life.* Imagined or not, she'd heed that advice. She shook her head, thinking she should plan some relaxation time on a secluded beach.

An elegant sit-down dinner at a nearby restaurant followed the church rehearsal. Sam, Marc and Josh toasted Rebekah and the girls roasted Kevin, sending them all into fits of laughter. Amy's jaws hurt from all the smiling and laughing, and she was more relaxed than she'd been in months. Everyone should be so blessed to have such friends. She'd worked elbow-to-elbow with these people, her best friends in the world, building houses together—dirty, dusty and bone-tired—the *best* kind of exhaustion. They'd fallen to their knees in prayer for one another. The admiration and love between Sam's TeamWork volunteers was unconditional and one of the greatest blessings in her life. The kind of easygoing camaraderie that came from baring their souls and sharing things they'd never shared with anyone else. She could be herself and not always be expected to be the consummate professional or worry about criticism and backbiting. The same bonds of deep friendship helped her now—at least momentarily—to push aside her constant thoughts of a certain handsome publisher in New York.

No matter how much she loved being with her friends, one thing was an eventuality: it wouldn't be long before Landon Warnick resurfaced in her life. One way or the other.

Chapter 13

Saturday, December 14, 2002 – Baton Rouge, Louisiana –Rebekah and Kevin's Wedding

AMY AND THE other attendants fell silent as Rebekah entered the church vestibule, her mother and Winnie assisting with her short train.

Breathtaking, Amy thought.

Beck's gown was simple yet elegant, befitting the statuesque bride. Made from white silk with an exquisite lace overlay, the column-style gown featured an off-the-shoulder neckline highlighting her beautiful neck and shoulders, three-quarter-length sleeves and an empire waist that draped over Beck's gentle curves to the floor. She wore pearl and diamond teardrop earrings and her long, blonde hair hung in loose waves cascading down her back beneath a crown of flowers matching those in her bouquet. A veil made from the same lace as the overlay of her gown fell to the middle of her back.

Marta led the way as they all crowded around her like beauty pageant contestants to the newly-crowned queen. Beck smiled when Winnie fussed and warned them to keep their distance.

To distract her, Amy asked, "So, Winnie, is that an orchid of some kind in the bouquet?"

Winnie glanced at the flowers she held while the other ladies talked quietly with Rebekah and Lorena. "I think it's cymba-something." She shrugged. "I know more about food than flowers." Combined with the red roses, and ivy and holly representative of the Christmas season, it was festive and lovely.

"It's called a cymbidium orchid," Gayle said. "Natalie told me."

"You look beautiful, Aunt Rebekah," Chloe said. Amy smiled at the childlike wonder in the little girl's face and the sweetness of her voice as she gazed up at the bride. "Like the lady on top of a wedding cake."

Laughing, Beck leaned over and gave her a hug. "Thank you, Chloe. You're the prettiest flower girl in the whole world." The compliment sent the little girl into a fit of giggles as she performed a pirouette. In her white organza dress with a green satin bow the same color as the bridesmaids' gowns, she seemed thrilled with her important role in the ceremony. The small wreath of red rosebuds and baby's breath atop her blonde curls threatened to topple from its perch as she twirled in a full circle. When Marta handed Chloe a basket of red rose petals, the beaming little girl held it up for her mother to see.

Josh, as handsome and debonair as ever in his black tuxedo, rounded the corner where the ladies waited to begin the processional. His eyes lit at the sight of his wife, her blonde hair upswept in an elegant French twist. When he tried to give her a kiss, Winnie turned her head and pointed to her cheek. Obliging her, he gave her a quick peck before crouching to eye level with Chloe, opening his arms. The youngster ran to him and he folded his arms around her, hugging her close. "My girls are so unbelievably gorgeous."

Amy waved one hand at him. "Josh, you've got to stop. You're a dangerous man to have around a bunch of women at a time like this. Fair warning: my heart's so full right now the waterworks might burst any minute. Now scoot. It's almost time to escort your sister to that darling man waiting for her at the front of the church." Amy caught Winnie's smile and the loving glance she exchanged with Josh.

"Yes, boss." Josh saluted her and gave his daughter a wink. "Do you remember what to do, Buttercup?"

Chloe nodded. "Yup, Daddy."

Amy's eyes welled again since it was the first time she'd heard Chloe publicly use the name "Daddy."

"Beck," Josh said as he walked toward his twin sister, "you've never looked more beautiful." Taking one of her hands in his, he reached for his mother's hand with the other. "I wish Dad could be here," he told them, "but it's my honor to take you to your groom. Kevin's a blessed man."

Amy looked away when Lorena leaned close for a private word with her children. She breathed in deeply, chiding herself to stay strong.

"I'm thankful you're here for Dad," Rebekah said. She waved her hand in front of her face and blinked back tears. "Listen to Amy. Don't get us too sentimental." She accepted the tissue Winnie handed her and dabbed the corners of both eyes. "Have you seen Kevin?" A traditional bride, Rebekah insisted her groom not see her until the ceremony—not even a peek—so the wedding photos would all be taken afterward.

"The man's beside himself, in a good way, of course," Josh said. "Trust me, sis, Kevin's the happiest man in the world tonight. He can't wait to whisk you off to your Hawaiian paradise. Does this old heart of mine good to see you so happy."

"If you're old, then you're also calling me old, too, so stop it." Rebekah kissed his cheek. "I love you."

"You too, squirt." He turned to Lorena and held out his arm. "Mom, it's time. Ready?"

Dressed in a long gown with a floral pattern of ivory and green, Mrs. Grant gave them all a warm smile. Placing her hand on her son's arm, she thanked them for sharing this joyous occasion. Lorena was one of the most gracious, genteel southern women Amy had ever known. This evening, she was positively regal, but the sadness in the widow's eyes tore at her heart. She'd witnessed that same look in her own mother's eyes.

Taking a deep breath, Amy's gaze moved to the bride. A new serenity had settled in Rebekah's lovely features since she'd last seen her at Josh and

Winnie's wedding. Knowing she and Kevin were in the center of the Lord's will for their lives must have a lot to do with how calm she appeared. She watched as Winnie lowered and arranged Rebekah's veil. As happy as she was for all her friends, Amy swallowed a sudden surge of jealousy. Lowering her eyes, she turned in the line as everyone stepped into their places.

Natalie entered the vestibule from a side door, her gown swishing with every movement. "Amy, your groomsman finally made it here." Leaning close, she lowered her voice. "Cooper swept into the church like some kind of mysterious, international spy or something, already dressed in his tux. Tall, dark and dangerously handsome. I'm guessing there might be mistletoe at the reception."

Amy's pulse palpitated, but she managed a smile. "How nice for you and Marc." Not that those two needed mistletoe as an excuse. "You look beautiful, Natalie. Marc's going to fall in love with you all over again." Natalie winked before taking her place. Chewing the inside of her cheek, Amy turned her head. Kiss some man because it's a romantic evening with dancing and mistletoe? Handsomeness aside, no way was *that* going to happen even if he was a world-class journalist and they had an entire shopping list of things in common. She'd never kissed a man on the first date, although Landon had seriously tempted her to break that rule.

When the door opened and Josh returned after escorting his mother, Amy heard the string quartet playing to one side of the sanctuary. Josh offered his arm to Rebekah. "Time to take the most important walk of your life, sis. Shall we?" Beck's shoulders rose as she inhaled a deep breath, the first glimpse of nerves she'd allowed. With a nod, she placed her hand on Josh's arm and they positioned themselves at the end of the line of bridesmaids, followed by Winnie and Chloe. The first strains of the processional were heard as two ushers opened the doors. In her excitement, Chloe's bouncing caused rose petals to fall on the carpet. Winnie corralled her, whispering for her to retrieve them.

Amy kept her gaze trained toward the front as two of Rebekah's college friends from LSU headed down the center aisle first. With a quick glance around the sanctuary, she estimated at least two hundred people packed the pews. As the ladies began the processional, low murmurs rippled through the congregation.

"Go, Amy," Winnie coached from behind. "It's your turn, sweetie. Start walking." Her words were accentuated by a none-too-subtle but gentle nudge on her back. Keeping in mind the way they'd practiced at the rehearsal, Amy paced her steps behind Natalie, staring at her friend's gorgeous dark hair, upswept like hers for the occasion. The key to this whole going-down-the-aisle routine was making it appear effortless. She'd done it enough times, she should be a pro. For some reason, she was nervous. Probably because these were her closest friends, it heightened the level of emotion. Concentrating on what she was doing, Amy counted under her breath. *You can do this.* One step, pause, one step, pause.

Settling into the rhythm and making her way down the aisle, she scanned the lineup of groomsmen—all so handsome in their black tuxedos with green satin cummerbunds matching the gowns and white rose boutonnières—standing with Kevin at the front of the church. Kevin's cummerbund was ivory, and his rose was red. Understated elegance.

Where's this Cooper what's-his-name? As she moved forward, one foot in front of the other, she smiled and attempted to look natural for the photographs.

If she gave into her emotions, she'd sink to the floor and weep with joy. *Goodness, get a grip.* Trying to focus her energies elsewhere, Amy scanned the groomsmen again as she continued to move forward as if in slow motion. It was quite possibly the longest walk of her life. Standing next to Kevin were his fun older brother and quiet younger brother, both serving as his best men. Next came Eliot, Dean, Marc, a guy from Kevin's church and another from A&M. Josh would soon join them. What a *big* wedding party—eight attendants each, plus Chloe. Standing at the front beside Pastor Scott from Rebekah's home church, Sam caught her eye and gave her a reassuring nod. *Lord, bless that man.*

After inclining her head toward Sam, Amy caught movement from the side of the church. A door opened and a man—who had to be her groomsman—entered, stepping into place between Kevin's church and college friends. She clamped her lips together not to make a sound and prove herself a fool. What on earth? *This is Rebekah and Kevin's special day. Don't spoil this moment for your friends.* Hopefully her eyes weren't bulging with disbelief, but she couldn't stop staring. Amy almost stumbled as she reached the front. Pivoting in position, she stole another quick glance, trying not to openly gawk. Natalie was right: the man was devastatingly handsome and swoon-worthy. Forcing her eyes away, she tried to ignore Natalie's wink and knowing smile. *Is this the most vivid daydream of my life?*

This man was no Cooper Warren. Oh no, *this* man was Landon Warnick.

Pasting on another smile, she hoped it appeared halfway natural. *Smile at Lexa, wink at Winnie as she comes down the aisle, focus on Chloe—something. Anything.* Her heart pounded so hard she thought she might have a heart attack. Had time ever moved this slow? Amy stared at the carpet as if it was marked with a big red X and fiddled with her small bouquet with those cymba-whatever orchids and red roses. Cassie, Marta and Gayle had all come down the aisle and Winnie was now at the midway point, followed by Chloe. Thankfully, the little girl captured everyone's attention as she dropped the rose petals, pausing every few steps and waving to the congregation, giving Amy a few precious seconds to steal another peek. She couldn't help it. Her jaw slacked before she forcibly closed it. Turning his head, Landon's blue eyes met hers before he nodded with a small smile.

Is this really happening, Lord?

The congregation rose as the organist struck a few chords, cueing Josh to bring his sister down the aisle. A quiet sob caught in Amy's throat as her gaze centered on Kevin at the exact moment he spied his bride. A tear slipped out, and she wiped it away. As if drawn by some invisible force over which she had no control, she lifted her eyes to her groomsman. Her heart skidded to a stop when he winked.

What's Landon doing here in my *world, with* my *friends?*

Chapter 14

FEELING FAINT, AMY swayed but somehow managed to stay upright. Landon made a slight movement but she warned him with a stern glance to stay put. Inhaling a few quick calming breaths, she blinked hard several times as she darted another quick glance in his direction and felt her cheeks grow warm. Forcing her gaze forward and pasting on the best semblance of a smile she could muster, Amy's eyes fell on Lexa.

"Are you okay?" Lexa mouthed. Although Beck wanted Lexa in the wedding party, the very pregnant mother-to-be opted instead to hand out wedding programs and invite guests to sign the keepsake book. Like Sam's reassuring nod—Lexa's smile now gave Amy immeasurable comfort from where she sat a few rows behind Mrs. Grant and other family members. In her pale green dress, her long blonde hair flowing about her shoulders—a change from her usual braid—Lexa would be the perfect focal point. It would seem she desperately needed one.

Across the aisle from Lorena sat Kevin's parents, Elizabeth and Richard, and a number of their relatives. A contingent from Kevin's home church and employees from the family's lumber business filled most of the pews behind them. Since her heart attack in March, Kevin's mother had rebounded well and looked lovely in a slightly lighter shade of green than the attendants' dresses. Richard kept a protective arm around his wife's shoulders and bent low to listen as she whispered in his ear.

Startled from her reverie, Amy's eyes misted as Josh lifted Rebekah's veil and whispered a few words before kissing her cheek. With a quick squeeze on Kevin's shoulder, he took his place in the line of groomsmen. Glancing from Kevin to Landon, Amy's mind worked overtime. *What's the connection between these two men?* Was it a surprising coincidence—something else she didn't believe in on principle—or were there other factors at work?

Sam read several verses of Scripture and asked a blessing on the couple. "Rebekah," he said, his gaze falling on her, "the greatest gift God bestowed on us is the gift of love. He sacrificed His own beloved Son so that through His death and resurrection, we might find our salvation and hope of eternal life. I've watched you and Kevin grow emotionally and spiritually the last few years as you've both looked to the Lord for guidance and sought His will for your lives, both as individuals and as a couple. I rejoice that He's led the two of you to this moment, to pledge your love to one another in His presence and in front of these witnesses."

Sam's focus moved to the groom. "Kevin, the Lord has blessed your obedience and faithfulness to Him and to this woman beside you. Speaking on behalf of Lexa and myself, and our entire TeamWork family, we're overjoyed to share this beautiful day with you and Rebekah as you pledge your lives and love to one another." Placing his Bible on the podium, Sam stepped forward and grasped their hands in his. "Beloved friends, as you begin your marriage and travel this journey together, it's my prayer you'll practice the virtue of patience"—he waited for the quiet laughter to fade—"maintain the deep bond of friendship, enjoy the passion of physical love and the hope of shared tomorrows, accept the riches to be found in a personal relationship with the Lord, pursue new ways to serve Him and embrace the precious blessing of children to carry forward your godly legacy."

Helpless to stop them, Amy wiped away a few more tears and wished she'd had the foresight to tuck a tissue in her bouquet. She smiled her thanks when Cassie pushed one into her hand. Keeping her eyes trained on the ceremony, she listened to the heartfelt vows and observed the ring exchange. As Lorena and Elizabeth clasped hands and walked up the three small stairs to light the unity candle on the altar, Amy stole another glance at Landon. She wasn't sure what she saw in those gorgeous blue eyes when they locked on hers, although it appeared his surprise matched hers.

"Kevin, you may now kiss your bride," Sam said.

Smiling, Kevin slipped his arms around his bride's waist and lowered his head to meet her upturned lips. When they ended the kiss—sweet and appropriate if not a bit longer than necessary—he chuckled and whispered something in Beck's ear. Her cheeks flushed with color, and she leaned against him for a brief moment. Raising her head, she lightly caressed his face before giving him another quick kiss. He captured Rebekah's hand and the radiant couple faced the congregation for the first time as newlyweds.

"Ladies and gentleman," Pastor Scott announced, "may I now present to you Mr. and Mrs. Moore—Kevin Curtis and Rebekah Nicole. May God richly bless your union."

While most in the congregation observed polite wedding decorum, the TeamWork men cheered. Amy, Natalie and Winnie all laughed when they heard a few stomps, no doubt from Sam and Marc. When those two men were together, they were the rowdiest. After Winnie handed Rebekah her bouquet, the couple headed back down the aisle to begin the recessional.

Landon offered his arm to escort her as they met in the center aisle. "Shall we?" Determined to get through it with dignity, Amy placed her hand on his arm but avoided direct eye contact. As the attendants started to file out of the sanctuary, she smiled for the cameras again as they walked behind Natalie and Marc. Goodness, his forearm was strong, and she caught a faint hint of the same cologne he'd worn before. Well-wishers rushed around the wedding couple in the vestibule, forming an impromptu receiving line. Thankfully, no one paid her and Landon any attention.

"I didn't know you'd be here," she whispered as he guided them to places in the long line. With so many attendants, it stretched the entire length of the vestibule.

"That makes two of us because I didn't know *you'd* be here." He leaned close, speaking for her ears only. "Don't know about you, but I'm positively giddy."

She shot him a sidelong glance, trying not to laugh. "Coop the Scoop?"

He chuckled under his breath. "One of my nicknames."

"Well, whatever your name is, you look . . . quite handsome tonight." Although Amy didn't know what to make of the man, she could still be polite. Flirtatious, too, from all indications.

"And you, Amy, are beautiful." Narrowing his eyes, he tilted his head to one side, surveying her. His admiring gaze took in her hair interwoven with baby's breath. Men had no clue what went into making a hairstyle appear this effortless, but the appreciation in those incredible eyes made it worth every painstaking minute. "We can talk privately later. Save me a dance at the reception. A long, slow one." Well if that comment didn't send shivers of the best variety up and down her spine and everywhere in between.

Without answering, Amy skirted the peripheral of the gathering. She mingled with the others, exchanging comments about the wedding, not remembering what she said from one minute to the next. Catching Landon's eyes on her more than once as she laughed and talked with her friends, she pretended not to notice—all the while wondering if she was being way too obvious.

The photographer's assistant ushered them back into the sanctuary not long after and positioned Amy in front of Landon, angled slightly to the right. When the photographer asked each of the groomsmen to rest their right hand on the hip of their bridesmaid, she inhaled a deep breath. *Be a grown-up*. Landon complied while she steeled herself not to act ticklish and giggle like a little girl. His nearness was disconcerting, the warmth of his breath fluttering the curly wisps of hair on the back of her neck as he repositioned his stance.

Separate group shots followed and Amy smiled at the antics of the groomsmen.

"Boys will be boys," Winnie said, coming to stand beside her.

Natalie joined them. "That's why we love them so much," she said, her voice soft with emotion. Cassie was right. Time to at least consider a romantic complication.

"Everyone follow us to The Glades," Josh called out to them all, scooping a sleepy Chloe in his arms as the photo session ended. "Food, dancing and general merriment all around. See you there."

"We're right behind you," Sam said, circling Lexa's waist. Marc did the same with Natalie as they all paraded out of the sanctuary.

"Amy, come join us." Arm-in-arm with Marta and Gayle, Cassie gave her a conspiratorial wink. "The fearsome foursome of TeamWork shall ride together."

She laughed. "I'll be out in a minute. I need to grab my evening bag."

"Good grief, I almost forgot my purse," Gayle said, hurrying behind her into the small dressing room off the side of the vestibule. "Glad you said something."

"We'll save you both a seat," Cassie called over her shoulder.

"Don't think that'll be a problem," Marta said as they headed out the front doors of the church. "Have you seen the size of the limo?"

As they emerged from the church a couple of minutes later, Amy stopped as she reached the outside stairs, surprised to find Landon waiting. Hands in his pockets, he was alone. He waved his hand toward the waiting limo. "I thought you might need an escort."

She shook her head with a small smile. "What gave me away: the trip in the aisle or the near faint by the altar?" Self-conscious as she started down the stone stairs, Amy gathered the long skirt of her gown in one hand, but she was too late. Her heel caught on the hem of her dress and she stumbled. "Oh!" Caught off-balance, she gasped and extended her arms in an attempt to stop from falling.

In one quick movement, Landon steadied her with a warm, firm hand beneath her arm. "I've got you." His calmness soothed her racing pulse.

Placing a hand over her wildly-beating heart, she deep-breathed a few times before giving him a nod. "Thank you for saving me from certain humiliation if not acute embarrassment. Much obliged."

"I like playing your hero, but I trust this isn't a habit with you."

She inhaled a deep breath of the refreshing, clear night air. It was a cold evening, crisp and invigorating. "You know, you'd think Grace is my middle name, but surprisingly it's not. It's your fault I was discombobulated in the first place."

Landon laughed. "That's a fun word. You've got to love weddings." He stayed by her side as they descended the remaining steps to the sidewalk below. For the first time, it struck her how his accent was different. She remembered him telling her the drawl came back quickly when he returned to his native Texas. They were only one state away, after all. He'd been on a trip, so maybe he'd gone home to Texas for a visit. *That must be it.*

Any more attempts at private conversation were nixed as they waited with the other attendants at the curb. Hopefully during the evening she'd get her chance to voice the questions crowding her mind. Amy sighed as she spied the classic silver Bentley that would carry the newly-married couple to The Glades. Kevin carefully assisted Rebekah into the backseat and then shared a few words with Josh, Sam and Marc before climbing in beside his bride.

Josh and his girls, including his mother, settled in the BMW in line behind the Bentley as Marc and Natalie, Sam and Lexa, and several of the other groomsmen and bridesmaids piled into the white stretch limousine. Amy found a spot between Cassie and Marta.

Sam leaned against the seats of the limo, stretching out his long legs. "Ah, finally a car that can accommodate me." Lexa scooted close and snuggled into the curve of his arm. He kissed her forehead. "You okay, baby?"

Lexa nodded. "Fine. Just a little winded." Moving her hand in a circular pattern over her stomach, she closed her eyes.

"Joe doing okay with your parents?" Natalie asked.

"Great," Sam said. "If he *was* here, Joe would be half-toddling, half-crawling after Gracie."

"Oh no, my friend," Marc said, moving his arm around Natalie. "Gracie's the one who'd be doing the chasing." Drawing his wife closer, he whispered in her ear. With his arm around her, he lightly caressed her bare shoulder.

"My mom and dad are keeping Gracie in Connecticut this weekend," Natalie said. "We would have brought her, but"—she stole a glance at Marc—"our daughter can be quite a handful when she gets going." She ruffled her fingers through her husband's blond hair. "Like her handsome daddy."

Amy stared out the window and suppressed her sigh. As much as she loved her friends, she willed the limo driver to go a little faster.

Marc laughed. "Should I be flattered or insulted?"

"I have the feeling I'm in for real trouble in about sixteen years," Sam said, keeping his voice low.

"What do you mean sixteen years?" Marc said. "Guaranteed, your daughters will have you wrapped around their little fingers and toes before you even leave the hospital. You'll be as big a pushover as me, if not more. Plus, you're getting double the fun, Cassidy."

"Remember, I have twin sisters. We'll talk, Sundance," Sam said.

Trying not to be obvious, Amy's gaze gravitated to Landon. He was engaged in an animated conversation with a couple of groomsmen, so she indulged the opportunity to study him unaware. His skin was tan since she'd last seen him, a healthy, natural golden color. His hair was styled the same, only shorter. She eased forward on the seat, trying to get a better view. *Is that a scar on his forehead?* Sure looked like it, but it was difficult to tell. Settling back again, she rearranged the skirt of her dress and made small talk with the other bridesmaids.

After the limo pulled in front of The Glades, they watched as a smiling Kevin stepped from the Bentley and assisted Rebekah. Waving to their friends, they led the way inside. Next Josh escorted his family. Staying behind until the others climbed out, Amy found Landon again waiting for her. Offering her his hand, he assisted her from the car.

The next hour flew by as they enjoyed a sumptuous buffet, followed by Kevin picking up his guitar and introducing a new song he'd written for his bride as a wedding gift.

"Pass the tissues around," Amy whispered to Marta. "We're going to need them."

A talented musician and worship pastor in his new church in Houston, Kevin's songwriting talents had matured since their mission in Montana. His strong tenor voice held a new confidence. Sitting at a long table with the other bridesmaids, Amy became acutely aware of Landon at the next table as she listened to the groom's heartfelt lyrics and beautiful melody. *It's like some kind of magnetizing Warnick radar.*

After dinner and a few rousing toasts, they all moved into a small ballroom where a live jazz band played in one corner.

"Not many places are better for jazz than Louisiana," Josh said, giving Amy a hug as he breezed by at one point. "Have a great time."

Moving one hand over her heart, Amy resisted the urge to cry again as Rebekah and Kevin shared a first dance. *What's wrong with me?* Crying at any given moment was so unlike her. Cassie came and stood beside her, nudging her shoulder, giving her great comfort in their solidarity. Next, Josh danced with his sister while Kevin danced with Lorena. Sam danced with Rebekah, followed by Marc. Soon enough, Kevin cut in and tapped Marc on the shoulder, sweeping his bride back in his arms. From his determined expression, he wouldn't be surrendering her to anyone else the rest of the evening.

One by one, her friends paired off and moved onto the dance floor. Spying a chair on the perimeter of the room, Amy dropped into it. Velma King's prayers sprang into her mind. Clutching her evening bag like a drowning woman clinging to a life preserver, she closed her eyes. *Be strong. You are not alone.*

"I believe this is our dance." Startled out of her daydreaming, she opened her eyes. Sam stood beside her, his hand outstretched. Putting her hand in his and rising to her feet—loving this man more than ever—her smile was shaky as he guided her toward the dance floor. She darted a grateful glance in Lexa's direction, but her friend was engaged in conversation with Lorena.

Sam turned her beneath his arm with flawless execution.

"Looks like you've had a few lessons," she said. "I'm impressed."

He chuckled. "You can thank Marc. After he witnessed me trouncing Lexa's feet in Montana, he arranged for dance lessons, insisting they were mandatory for the preservation of my marriage."

As they danced together, Amy felt Landon's gaze on her. *What's he waiting for? It's not as if my dance card's full tonight.* Marc and Natalie moved closer until they danced beside them. No doubt Marc wanted to start a dance-off and they all laughed as Sam made a big show of not allowing Marc to switch partners. In a quiet corner, Josh danced with Chloe tucked against his chest, his other arm curled around Winnie. Rebekah and Kevin talked with their guests. Marta and

Eliot continued their game of cat-and-mouse, occasionally joining together for a dance. Something was definitely up with those two.

Leaning forward on her tiptoes as the song ended, Amy kissed his cheek. "Thanks, Papa Bear."

"It's my honor," he said, guiding her through the other dancers to the edge of the dance floor. He lowered his hand on her shoulder. "Will you be okay?"

Blinking back tears, she lowered her gaze and looped the dainty gold chain of her evening bag around one finger. "Am I that obvious?"

Sam tipped her chin, his gaze tender. "Ah, Daydreamer. Your time is coming."

Amy nodded as he departed and dropped back into her chair. Cassie, Marta and Gayle were all on the dance floor with guys from the wedding party and having a grand time from the looks of it. Good for them. *Pull yourself out of this chair and go have a great time instead of sitting here moping.* But, somehow, she couldn't do it and stayed where she was.

Lexa slipped into the chair next to hers while she was pondering her options. At least her expression was kind, not pitying. "It'll be your turn soon enough, sweetie."

Amy managed a small smile. "Your husband told me the same thing. Will it really?" Heaven forbid she sounded whiny. Nothing would be worse. "I've put up this brave front for so long about not needing—or wanting—a man in my life."

"And now you're having second thoughts?"

Amy's sigh was heavy. "Tell me the truth. At the risk of winning the Miss Lonely Hearts crown tonight, am I desperate and deprived or destined to spend the rest of my life alone? Pick one or all of the above." Although she disliked the sarcasm in her tone, she couldn't stop it.

"None of the above," Lexa said, her surprisingly deep Texas drawl soothing and calm which did wonders for her nerves. "Take it from my experience. Without really intending to, I did so much to frustrate and anger Sam in that San Antonio TeamWork camp by not following directions and making a mess of things by trying to show him how capable I thought I was. But the Lord knew. He transformed my shortcomings into personal strengths, and took two imperfect lives—coming from different pathways to faith and trust in Him—and now look at us. I didn't have a family, but He blessed me with not one, but two: the Lewis family and my TeamWork family."

Reaching for Lexa's hand, Amy held on tight. "Sam didn't stand a chance, and trust me, he knows as much as anyone how the Lord blessed him with *you*. When he blew back into the camp after finding you'd gone rogue out at the worksite on that Sunday afternoon, we knew." She gave her dear friend a watery smile. "We *all* fell in love with you."

Lexa squeezed her hand and they smiled as Kevin's parents danced nearby. Following Lexa's gaze, Amy watched as Josh danced with his mother. The depth of love passing between them touched her deep insde, reminding her of the closeness Mitch shared with her mom.

"Amy, I don't think you realize how much you've changed since San Antonio."

She turned to face Lexa. "What do you mean?"

"Remember when we were in the marketplace and that horrible screaming match started, leaving Angelina cowering and defenseless in the middle of it all? And then I barged in and gave that woman a piece of my mind?"

"Yes," Amy said with a small smile. "It was pretty unforgettable. You were so fearless and self-confident. In that moment, you were my heroine. You inspired me to become more independent and assertive."

"I'm thankful everything turned out so well, for Angelina's sake. But do you remember your reaction?"

Amy shook her head. "Not really. I didn't run away screaming, but neither did I help you." She could feel the rush of heat and lowered her gaze from Lexa's. "I'm sorry."

"Don't be. That's not what I meant. Most people would have done the same thing. A few months earlier, I'd have reacted the same way, too. I'd never talked to anyone like that in my entire life. This is what I want to tell you: the woman you've become is strong and full of confidence. You face life head-on because you know the Lord's with you every step of the way." Lexa anchored two gentle fingers beneath her chin and captured her eye contact. "You're beautiful, Amelia Jacobsen, and the man of God's choosing is out there. He's waiting for you just as you're waiting for him, and you're both trusting the Lord for His timing. I have no doubt in my mind He has a very special man handpicked for you, sweet girl." She tapped her chin and released her hold.

"Thanks, Lexa, but that's a whole lot of waiting in that next-to-last sentence."

"As a matter of fact," Lexa said, leaning close and lowering her voice, "the answer might be walking toward you right now."

Chapter 15

"CARE TO DANCE, Amy?" Landon nodded to Lexa. "If you'll excuse us, Mrs. Lewis."

As Landon led her toward the dance floor, Amy caught Lexa's wink.

Turning her toward him, he slipped one hand over hers and his other hand rested lightly on her hip. The open admiration in his eyes was unmistakable. As he began to dance with her, she sensed his quiet strength. This was a protective man, a man of uncommon manners and chivalry. While keeping an appropriate distance between them, his slow gaze moved across her features, intoxicating and heating her in unexpected ways. Like nothing she'd ever before experienced, making her heady. Amy lowered her eyes, her heart vulnerable and open. Weddings were notoriously romantic, and she couldn't fall into the trap of unrealistic expectations because of one romantic dance, one incredible night.

Pulling back, she met his blue-eyed gaze. Something about him struck her as different. Perhaps it was the lack of bantering and his more subdued and serious manner. As much as she'd thrilled at their exhilarating exchange in Manhattan, she felt equally drawn to this quieter, more reflective side of him. How easy it would be to fall for this man. She hovered at the precipice as it was, unsure whether to follow her instincts, her mind, her heart. Or were they all one and the same?

"Is something wrong?"

"Not at all. Did you learn to dance this well at A&M?"

He chuckled. "No. Dancing wasn't a skill I acquired in college." The other ladies eyed them and she understood their curiosity. If the situation were reversed with any one of them, she'd wonder about such a rapid-fire familiarity and instant attraction with a man. She'd need to set them straight, especially Winnie. Surely she recognized him from the photo? Having only spent a few hours in his company, Amy knew him better than most men. If she denied their strong attraction, she'd be lying to herself. *You* want *to know this man.* The gentleness in his touch as he held her, and the tenderness in his eyes, captured her overactive imagination and sent it spiraling into romantic daydreams. Never had her daydreams been this vivid.

As if reading her thoughts, Landon increased the pressure of his hand on her back. The gesture was intimate, perhaps unconscious. "What were you thinking about just now?"

Afraid to meet his gaze, Amy turned her head and met her reflection in a wall mirror. "How weddings hold incredible power." Giving her a smile she wouldn't soon forget, he picked up the pace, swaying to the music, dipping and twirling her a half-turn.

"Power?" He turned her under one arm and brought her close again. "How so?"

Intensely aware of him in every way, Amy struggled for coherency. "They lend themselves to feelings of romance and love."

"Granted, weddings might jumpstart feelings of romance, but the power is overwhelmingly in the force of attraction between two people."

A minute later, her smile sobered, as did his as they slowed their pace until both barely moved. "In this case," she said, not believing what she was about to say, "you and me. Tonight. In this place."

The color of his eyes deepened, the lines around his mouth softened. "I believe I saw a private alcove. Care to join me?"

"Why would we want to go somewhere private?" Her eyes searched his. Surely he could hear the rapid beating of her heart, her staggered breathing.

"We need to finish what we started here on the dance floor. Come with me." From the corner of her eye, she saw Winnie shake her head and whisper something to Josh. They both watched as she left the room beside Landon with her hand firmly encased in his. She gave her friends a sheepish smile and a shrug. He led the way to an elegant, brocade-covered settee in one corner, partially hidden by a large potted palm.

"You're a very intriguing woman, Amy." Waiting until she was seated, he dropped down beside her. He leaned against the soft cushions and slid his arm along the back of the settee behind her.

"I suppose we should talk." The tremor in her voice betrayed her. Her lack of experience in these things must be more than obvious, but she hoped he didn't find her ridiculously naïve.

"Sometimes words aren't necessary."

Interesting thing to say for a man whose livelihood is words. She shivered. Slipping out of his jacket, Landon draped it around her although the shoulders swallowed her. Amy busied her hands by smoothing her fingers over the pattern in the brocade of the settee. "I suddenly feel like one of those girls at a middle school dance who sneaks under the bleachers with her boyfriend." She glanced at him with the hint of a smile curving her lips.

Landon's eyes never left her face. "Somehow I get the impression you never did that."

She matched his gaze, keeping it steady. "What gave me away?"

With an achingly soft touch, he brushed the pad of his thumb in a light path across her cheek. His expression was one of wonder. "You shivered."

Leaning into his touch, Amy closed her eyes, lost in the moment. *This man is dangerous. I need to thank him for the dance and depart gracefully.* "I should probably go."

He grabbed her hand, intertwining their fingers. "One last dance?"

"Here?" Her pulse raced.

"Why not?" Standing, he encircled her waist in one effortless movement. "Dance with me, Amy," he whispered, his lips against her temple, causing more shivers.

"There's no music," she said, as if that made any difference.

"Ah, but God didn't give us an imagination to waste."

Where this man is concerned, Lord, that's certainly true enough. Allowing herself to relax in his arms, Amy gave into the wonder of the night.

"Do you hear the music now?"

Feeling dazed, she nodded. "Yes."

As he kept them dancing, Landon moved his hand to the back of her neck. His lips hovered above hers, his eyes lingering on her mouth. "May I?"

"You may." Raising her head, she lowered her lids, inviting him.

Landon's lips molded perfectly to hers. When her lips quivered beneath his, he stroked her cheek again with a feather light touch and then anchored his hand on the side of her jaw. Heat simmered beneath the surface as he kissed her, his mouth searching but with a restraint that surprised and pleased her. Their chemistry was undeniable, threatening to drown her with its dizzying strength and power. How long it lasted, she couldn't know, but she belonged in this man's arms.

With a deep sigh, he finally pulled out of the kiss and rested his forehead lightly against hers. "Thank you." His voice sounded rough and husky, deep with emotion.

Not knowing how to respond, Amy gave him a small smile and tugged his jacket closer about her shoulders, loving how his masculine scent lingered in the fabric. Never in her life had a man asked permission to kiss her, never before had a man thanked her.

"When are you returning to New York?" he asked.

"Wednesday. I have to be back in my office on Thursday morning."

The softness in his eyes stole her breath. "I have a few days off, too. Why don't we spend some time together?"

His question sent her pulse shooting to the stratosphere. Lowering her eyes, she returned to the settee. "I'm driving to Houston tomorrow with Sam and Lexa. Believe it or not, I have an assignment while I'm here in Texas."

"Interviewing Sam about his marriage tome?"

She nodded, wondering how he knew, too dazed to ask.

"I'm heading back to Austin tomorrow. Would you mind if I talk Sam into borrowing you for a day or two? I could show you around my hometown, and then we could drive to Houston together."

"You want to 'borrow' me?" Her senses slowly returned, balancing her equilibrium. "I'm not really sure what that means, but when you borrow a book from the library, you promise to return it, safe and sound." *I hope that didn't sound as dumb to him as it did to me.*

"It means you can trust me and I'd never do anything to harm you. I'll keep you *safe and sound.* Promise." Sitting beside her again, he took her hand. "There's something about you, Amy. I'd love the opportunity to get to know you better while we both have some free time. Is that something you'd like, too?"

"That sounds like something the girl hiding under the bleachers with a boy would do." They shared a smile. "Not that you need Sam's permission to take me to Austin, but where would I stay?"

"I'll take care of all the arrangements. You could stay at my parents' house, but I'm not sure it's the wisest idea to subject you to that. Don't misunderstand. They're great, but I don't think you want to listen to my stepdad's boasts of his fishing conquests or listen to my mom talking about her latest recipe. I'll figure out something." His eyes met hers. "Please say you'll come."

Chapter 16

AMY SWALLOWED HARD, knowing the die was cast. If Kevin—one of the most honest, faithful, upstanding Christian men she knew—trusted Landon, he had to be one of the good guys. The best, actually. That's all her heart needed to know. "Yes, I'll come." Her heart started beating wildly again.

"Great." His smile stretched across his face. "I'll talk to Sam before the evening's over. I suppose we'd better go back in now or there'll be speculation."

"I'm sure it's already too late for that." Putting her hand in Landon's as he pulled her to her feet, Amy hooked her arm through his. *Let the inquisition begin.*

"Okay, bridesmaids, gather round," Winnie said, waving as she spied her. She made sure she positioned Amy directly behind Rebekah. "Beck's getting ready to throw her bouquet, so we need all of you over here." When she tried to dart away, Winnie anchored her to the spot.

Wriggling free of Winnie's hold, Amy called to Cassie, Marta, Gayle and the other two unmarried bridesmaids. "If I'm doing this, you are, too."

Beck waited until all the ladies, including Chloe, gathered in a semicircle behind her. Knowing Winnie, she was conveying silent signals of some sort to her sister-in-law, hoping the bride had extraordinary throwing skills, not to mention precise backward aim. Sure enough, Beck turned around and tossed the bouquet straight into her hands. She didn't have to move an inch, and she certainly didn't try to catch it.

"Well, if ever I've seen a direct sign." Winnie leaned close. "You're next, sweetie."

"And *you're* wicked," Amy said.

Landon talked with some of the men nearby. At least the sight of her holding the bride's bouquet didn't send him running from the room.

Soon after, Rebekah and Kevin prepared to leave, still dressed in their wedding finery. She knew they were staying somewhere local and then flying to Hawaii tomorrow, but not too early . . . at Kevin's insistence. That thought made her smile. Hugging all her attendants in turn, Rebekah gathered Amy close. Flushed with excitement and anticipation, she'd never looked more beautiful, her luminous eyes a sparkling, deep emerald green. "Everyone adores Cooper, Amy. Kevin says he's a great guy and he thinks you two are a perfect match. I hope we'll be dancing next at *your* wedding."

She smiled and squeezed the bride's hand. "Be safe, Beck. The ceremony was beautiful, and I'm thrilled for you and Kevin. Have a great honeymoon."

"Thanks," Rebekah said. "We'll talk soon."

Amy nodded, tears of joy filling her eyes. "Love you both."

"You, too." With a quick kiss on her cheek, Rebekah moved on.

Amy's brow furrowed. *Wait a minute.* Questions danced in her mind. Beck must not be thinking straight. Considering the woman had just married her dream man, it was understandable. First, Gayle referred to him as Cooper, the globe-trotting journalist, then Winnie called him Cooper when she helped her try on her bridesmaid dress. Good grief, even Natalie referred to him as Cooper the super spy or whatever before the wedding ceremony. Could Cooper be Landon's real first name? Maybe he used one name for his personal life and another for his professional life? Although an uncommon practice for men, it was still a possibility. Her grandfather's real name wasn't Eric Carlisle, but actors adopted stage names all the time.

"Whatever your name is, I like you. A lot," she said under her breath. Covering her mouth, Amy stifled a yawn. It had been a full, exhilarating day, but it was getting late and she was growing more weary by the second.

Hearing laughter coming from outside the reception hall, Amy lifted the skirt of her gown and started down the front steps, being slow and careful. JUST MARRIED was scrawled on the back window of the Bentley and bells and streamers dangled from the back bumper. No doubt Josh, Marc and some of the other groomsmen had been busy while she and Landon shared their private tête-à-tête in the alcove.

Standing on the stairs and watching as the newlyweds climbed into the Bentley, she smiled and waved as the elegant, silver car pulled out of the parking lot. The group was more subdued as the limousine transported the remaining members of the wedding party back to the church a short time later. Standing in groups in the parking lot, they said their quiet good nights and good-byes.

Try as she might, Amy couldn't get a decent tidbit out of Marta as to what was going on between her and Eliot. Although she didn't deny the attraction, Marta only gave her a cagey smile and then changed the subject.

Landon strolled over where she talked with Cassie and Marta. After greeting the other ladies, he grinned. "May I drive you back to the inn?"

Ignoring the stares of the other ladies, Amy smiled. "That would be lovely. Give me a few minutes to gather my things inside."

"Take as long as you need."

Motioning to get Winnie's attention, she signaled her friend to meet her on the church steps.

"Amy Jacobsen, I never would have believed it if I hadn't seen it with my own eyes," Winnie said, shaking her head as they walked into the dark church together. Pulling a key from the pocket of her lightweight coat, she unlocked a side door and flipped a switch, illuminating the vestibule. "Macking with that man in the alcove."

Here it comes. "I wondered how long it would take you. Down, *Mother Hen.* I'm a grown woman, perfectly capable of taking care of myself. And really, Winnie, who under the age of eighty says 'macking' anymore?"

"Well, you know what it means." Winnie's giggle escaped as they entered the small room where the ladies had stored their personal belongings. "Then again, you're all about the words, aren't you? Except for when you're macking with a handsome man, of course."

Hearing the other attendants coming into the church, Amy lowered her voice. "So, I suppose everyone knows I was kissing my handsome groomsman tonight? Kissing him *good*," she added for Winnie's benefit.

"If we didn't before, we sure did when the two of you walked back into the reception hall. You've got the man's attention, that much is obvious, but I need to ask you about Landon."

"What about him?" Amy concentrated on folding the top and jeans she'd worn to the church earlier, and placed them in her overnight bag with her boots.

"Meet me back outside in a few minutes," Winnie said.

Amy knew it was a lost cause to try and put off the questions, so she might as well address them now. Retrieving her cosmetic items from the vanity area, she tucked them in the top compartment of her case before zipping it closed. Gathering the rest of her things, she draped her garment bag over one arm. Slipping out of the church with Winnie close behind, she carefully started down the steps.

"When you arrived on Thursday night, you were positively glowing after meeting Landon in New York," Winnie said, putting one hand on her arm, stopping her. "Then you meet a handsome man at the wedding—one who lives here in Texas—and suddenly you're infatuated with *him*? It's unusual for you to find one man you're interested in, and now all of a sudden, you have two?" She shook her head. "Forgive me, but it seems so . . . well, out-of-character for you."

Amy paused on the steps, scanning the parking lot. Landon waited beside what she assumed was his rental car, talking with Chase the A&M guy, and Travis the church guy, for lack of knowing what else to call them. "It's getting colder out here by the minute, Winnie. Are you sure you want to get into this now? I'm coming to Houston soon enough. We can talk then."

"Talk to me now. We all noticed your preoccupation with Cooper tonight," Winnie said. "And vice versa. I can see you really like him, but I don't want to see you get hurt."

"I appreciate that more than you know, but maybe for once in my life I don't want to do what's safe or right, proper or whatever." Noting Winnie's wary look, Amy plowed on. "What everyone doesn't seem to get is that Cooper *is* Landon. He's the same guy I shared a date with in New York, the carriage ride, the odd but wonderful conversation . . ." She blew out a breath. "Sure, Cooper might have been his nickname in college, but trust me, the man is Landon Warnick."

Confusion clouded Winnie's eyes and she frowned. "But . . . wait a minute. For one thing, Cooper's last name is Warren and he lives in Austin. Josh told me, and he got it from Beck, who obviously knows from Kevin's association with him. This makes no sense. I mean," she said, rubbing her fingers over her forehead, "sure, he looks a lot like the guy in the photo you showed me, but he's also different somehow." She put one hand on her hip. "For one thing, does Landon have a drawl? Because Cooper sure does."

"No, but *you* have a drawl—as do Lexa, Sam, Josh, Beck and Kevin—and I don't hold it against any of you." Amy started back down the stairs.

Winnie sighed and hurried to keep up. "Hear me out on this, Amy. Please."

Stopping again, she flashed Winnie a bright smile. "No, Landon doesn't have a drawl, but his voice sounds pretty much the same—deep and sexy as all get out, if you want the absolute, God-honest truth. It makes me positively shiver. Look, Landon told me he's originally from Austin and the drawl comes back when he's home in Texas." Darting a glance at him, she was grateful he was engaged in conversation. "He mentioned his parents still live in Austin, and maybe he has a place there, too." She shrugged. "Makes sense. As far as the last name, I have no clue except that Warren is awfully close to Warnick. My best guess is Warren's his real last name but he uses Warnick professionally since it's not as common."

"And that doesn't bother you?"

"Why should it? My grandfather used another name professionally."

"But Landon's not—"

"Need I remind you that *your* business is called Doyle-Clarke Catering? It's not Grant-Lewis Catering, and you're not changing it because you're married now, are you?"

Winnie snorted. "Not the same thing and you know it."

Amy curled one arm around Winnie's slender shoulders. "I like Landon. He's a very nice man in spite of his boldness." *Some would call it cockiness.* "And in spite of the fact that it seems like he's a fast worker." *Some would say he has hidden motives.* "I appreciate your protectiveness and your love and concern, but it's okay. Promise."

"Didn't he know about your involvement with TeamWork and know you might be here?" Winnie asked.

That question stopped her. "We had one date—less than three hours together. I mentioned I had friends in Texas, but other than a brief mention of TeamWork, we didn't discuss it, shocking as that might be to you. Look," she said, as they walked together down a few more steps, "it's not like we've had time to share each other's darkest secrets, spill our guts or otherwise compare notes about every organization we're both involved with . . ." Her voice trailed as she glimpsed Winnie's expression. "Short answer? He's probably as surprised as I am to find out we have mutual friends in common. As a matter of fact, I'm thrilled about it."

"I'm not accusing him of anything, but I can see the wheels turning in your brain, trying to rationalize this guy."

Amy felt like a child being chastised and almost stomped her foot. If she did, it would only reinforce Winnie's point and further encourage the interrogation. She stilled her foot and along with it, the inclination to act out her feelings of aggravation. Taking a deep breath, she kept her voice steady. "Why are you so suspicious of this guy all of a sudden? You're the one who said I have great instincts and am level-headed. Trust me on this one. You can get to know Landon better when we come to Houston."

Winnie's eyes widened, bright in the reflected moonlight. "You're still coming to Houston with Sam and Lexa, right?"

Amy shifted from one foot to the other and stared at the pavement. "Um, not exactly. Landon offered to drive me there by way of . . . well, Austin."

"He what? Now you're taking a road trip with him?"

Amy wanted to sink into the steps, and she dared not look Landon's way. Surely he and everyone else in the church parking lot heard her friend's outburst.

"I have half a mind to call your mother or Mitch, young lady." Winnie massaged her forehead again. "Remember the Alamo," she muttered.

Amy stifled her gasp. Now she really wanted to go with him, to prove a point if nothing else. "What on earth does *that* mean?" When Winnie stopped and gave her a penetrating look, Amy narrowed her eyes. "We're talking about a completely different set of circumstances from you and Josh in San Antonio. Besides, I trust Cooper . . . Landon, whatever."

"Don't you see?" Winnie asked. "You don't even know what to call him. Use a little discernment here. If you're not completely clear on the man's identity, do you think it's wise to go on a trip with him?"

Amy forced her hands to her sides, resisting the urge to cross her arms. "So, what you're really saying is you don't trust *me*."

"Of course, I do, but I also noticed the way you two looked at each other in there tonight, the dancing and the macking in that cozy alcove . . ."

"Enough with the macking!" Gathering the skirt of her dress, Amy turned to leave. Irritated as she was, she couldn't risk another stumbling incident. "I'll see you in Houston."

"Sweetheart," Josh said, walking over to them and slipping his hand around his wife's waist. "Time to get going. Chloe's sleeping in the car."

"Josh, you've got to talk some sense into my best friend. Seems she's temporarily lost her mind."

"If this is about her groomsman, no need to worry. He's a solid guy and we all think he and Amy make a great match." When Josh gave her a wink, she could have kissed him. "You have the TeamWork man stamp of approval, Daydreamer."

"Well, thanks for that," she said, turning her head, trying not to laugh. She avoided Winnie's glare.

"I can see when I'm outnumbered, but I still have my concerns." Gathering Amy in her arms, hugging her close, Winnie released her a few seconds later and cradled her cheeks between her palms. "I love you and I care. I'm just tired, confused and . . . ." She darted a glance at her husband.

Amy's eyes widened. "You're pregnant!" She clamped a hand over her mouth and prayed no one else heard.

"We sure are," Josh said. She'd seen plenty of smiles from him, but none more infectious than the one creasing his face now. "You're the first to know, so we'd appreciate it if you'd keep it on the down-low."

"Of course," Amy said, finding it difficult to believe Lexa didn't know. "How far along?"

"Only about a month," Winnie said, snuggling into the curve of her husband's arm. "We weren't planning on another baby this soon, but you and I both know God sometimes has other plans."

"Well, I'm thrilled for you. Chloe—and everyone else—will be ecstatic. Good thing you've hired extra helpers for the catering business. You're going to need them." Amy grinned at Josh. "I'm sure you're relishing hopping onto the whole 'let's populate the TeamWork crew' bandwagon." Her eyes widened. "Hey, you might have twins, too."

"Oh, let's hope not," Winnie said with a tired smile. "One at a time is all I can handle."

"Have fun, Amy. We'll see you in a few days." Josh tweaked her cheek and led Winnie toward their car.

Winnie blew her a kiss over her shoulder. "Love you, sweetie. Be careful."

"Thanks. Love you, too. See you soon."

~

Checking her phone for messages as she packed her suitcase the next morning, Amy noticed a call from an unfamiliar number, a Manhattan exchange. She hadn't taken her phone to the wedding or the reception, not wanting to be bothered. In case of an emergency, she'd given Sam and Lexa's contact information—as well as Winnie and Josh's—to her mom and Mitch. Sinking onto the bed with a leftover yawn, she retrieved the message.

"Hi, Amy. I had a great time with you the other night. I'm sorry we can't get together until after Christmas, but I'll look forward to seeing you again. Until then, I hope you're well and having fun wherever you are and whatever you're doing this weekend. I'll be thinking of you and I'll give you a call when I get back to New York."

An odd feeling washed over her, bathing her in indecision and uncertainty. Her fingers shook as she fumbled with the phone, double-checking the date and time of the voice mail. The message registered during the time she was at The Glades for the wedding reception. Listening to the voice mail a second time, Amy mentally checked her facts, her heart racing. The night before, she'd walked the recessional on Landon's arm, danced in the man's arms and kissed him until she was glowing and near-giddy. He'd arranged with Sam to drive her to Houston and then given her a light, sweet kiss in the lobby of the inn before saying good night.

Was this some kind of sick, twisted prank? If so, why would Landon play with her mind? Her mind raced out-of-control, and her head pounded with unanswered questions. So many questions. This was surreal. If Landon was in New York City, then who was the man here in Baton Rouge? A man who looked enough like him to be his twin, or at least a blood brother? Could he really be Cooper Warren and no relation to the publisher of *New York Scene*? The thought made her cheeks redden as a tumult of emotions rushed through her, filling her with dread to the point where she groaned out loud. Embarrassed and confused didn't begin to cover it. No wonder Winnie was concerned, as well she should be. As always, her best friend's instincts were spot-on. Maybe it was true that pregnancy *did* heighten a woman's senses while infatuation must have diminished hers.

For the next few minutes, Amy replayed every conversation she'd shared with him since spotting him at the front of the church. *The wedding program.* Rummaging through her evening bag, she remembered she hadn't wanted to fold it in order to squeeze it into the bag. Winnie had grabbed a few for her and said she'd give them to her in Houston, but she'd glanced at it at one point. *Think.* From what she could recall, the wedding party was so large all the names weren't individually listed.

"Who doesn't list the attendants?" she asked in the quiet of the hotel room. They'd all been introduced to the wedding guests at the reception, but she'd been helping Cassie fix something on her dress after the ladies were introduced, so she'd missed hearing his name. Still, everyone and their mother had called him Cooper, both before and after the ceremony.

Oh, no. This can't be happening. Amy dropped the phone as though it burned her fingers and sat up on the edge of the bed. Closing her eyes tight, she slapped one hand on her forehead. *What kind of fool am I?*

"Lord, what did I do? Who did I kiss? Who *is* that man?"

Chapter 17

NO SOONER DID Landon step inside the lobby the next morning than he knew something was wrong. *Very* wrong. Dark storm clouds loomed overhead and an ear-splitting clap of thunder boomed outside as he strolled across the lobby in her direction. Waiting in the lobby, legs crossed, hands clasped over her knees, Amy startled at the ominous sound. My, but she looked fetching dressed in jeans and a pale blue sweater. Much prettier than he'd imagined, and that was a whole lot of gorgeous. Either she wore very little makeup or was quite skillful at applying it. As beautiful as she'd looked for the wedding, he preferred this more natural Amy. Her dark hair was pulled back in a ponytail and a few wispy strands escaped on the sides of her face. Sure enough, she tucked them behind her ear, first one and then the other.

Although he gave her his best smile, she barely acknowledged his presence. As he approached where she sat in a wing chair, she glanced at her watch, licked her lips and fidgeted. Her gaze darted around the small lobby, taking in everyone and everything except him.

"Good morning, Amy." Removing his Stetson, he sat in an adjacent chair and ran a hand over his hair. "Missed you in the church service this morning."

A fleeting expression of regret surfaced in her features. "Yes, well, you'd think a pastor's kid could remember to show up for church."

"You're allowed. It's been a busy weekend for all of us." Did she actually feel miserable or guilty because she'd slept in? "Don't beat yourself up about it."

"Oh, don't you worry about that. I'm not." She shifted her position and uncrossed her legs while her arms found their way across her chest like some kind of invisible shield. The sarcasm in her tone was difficult to miss as she narrowed her eyes. "You certainly look like the urban cowboy this morning." Her all-encompassing glance swept over his well-worn boots, heavy suede jacket with white fleece collar, stonewashed jeans and black Henley. From the glint in her eye, she didn't seem displeased with what she saw.

Determined not to let her sour mood dampen his high spirits, Landon resolved to charm her out of her funk or whatever this was. After watching her squirm for a couple of seconds, he'd had enough. "Look," he said, scooting to the end of the chair, "is something wrong?" Leaning forward, not wanting other guests to hear, he rested his crossed arms on his knees. "You look like you could take the sting out of a rattler bare handed and not blink twice." He brushed a section of dark hair away from his forehead and raised his brows.

Her eyes widened. "Where'd you get that? Some kind of cowboy euphemism handbook?"

Stiffening, he pursed his lips. *Whoa.* "Believe me, I could have been much more blunt. Maybe I should go outside and come back in again once you've recovered the lovely lady from the wedding. She's the one I was hoping to drive to Houston . . . by way of Austin. Now she had spunk, but at least she was civil and polite."

"Fine with me because I'm not sure I want to go with you."

He ran a hand over his jaw. "What's that supposed to mean?"

She met his gaze head-on and he was shocked at the anger glimmering beneath the surface. "I'm sorry. I'm not normally this defensive and spiteful, but I'm . . . well, I'm very confused. To say the least."

"I can tell. About what? Talk to me. Tell me what's on your mind. Let me help."

"Okay, here's a question for you. Exactly who *are* you?"

"Very funny. Surely you know who I am, especially after last night." When she didn't crack a smile, his grin sobered fast. "Really, Amy," he said. "What's up? I'm the same guy."

"Why is everyone calling you Cooper?"

Interesting question. He needed to hear her out and get the reasoning behind her questions. Did she doubt him? Not trust him for some unknown reason? "It's part of my name. I was on the newspaper staff at A&M and my nickname was 'Coop the Scoop.' Why? Who exactly do you think I am?"

"For the record, I don't go around kissing strange men."

"Well, neither do I, so we're even on that point. Women, either. You think I'm strange?"

"Maybe. I don't know." She slapped her hands on her jeans-clad thighs and rose to her feet. She started to pace in front of the chair. "I'm not quite sure of much of anything right now."

Her words startled him back to the present. *What's going on here?* "Care to enlighten me? Give me a name?"

She narrowed her eyes. "Do you have a twin who happens to live in New York?"

"No, I'm an only child."

Plopping back down in the chair, she sat forward and rocked back and forth, fiddling with the sleeve of her sweater. "You see, here's the thing."

"Tell me. What's the thing?" Surely that would bring her around.

Amy snapped her head up and stared at him for a few seconds. "I . . . I, um . . . ." She took in a deep shuddering breath and cleared her throat. "When I danced with you last night, and . . . kissed you, I . . . well, believe it or not, I thought you were . . . someone else."

"Who on earth—?" He stopped. *No way. She doesn't know who I am?* Perhaps the more important question was: *Who does she* think *I am?*

"Not long before coming here to Louisiana, I had a date in New York with a publisher named Landon Warnick. It was only one date," she added, as if he might be upset at that revelation. "So it's not like I'm being disloyal or anything."

This conversation grew more interesting every time she opened her pretty mouth. Shifting in the chair, he assumed what he hoped was a neutral expression. His heart pounded against his chest, and his mind scattered in a hundred different directions. "Go on." Stupid thing to say, but he needed to hear her out. Like everything else about this woman, it promised to be fascinating. Then he'd tell her the truth, they'd share a good laugh and get on their way to Austin. If nothing else, her assumptions made for a great story. At the moment, he wasn't sure whether to act indignant, curious or just plain mystified.

"I have to say, in all honesty, I'm glad you're *not* him."

That got his attention real quick, but not in a good way. Pushing up farther in the chair, he grunted. "Why do you say that?"

"Because Landon—as wonderful as he is in many ways—can also be a bit arrogant, completely presumptuous, borderline rude and, if my boss is correct, sneaky and underhanded and will stop at nothing to get what he wants."

"Is that right?" A rising cloud of anger stirred in his gut. It wasn't so amusing anymore and he prayed he didn't say something misguided. "What exactly did you tell this . . . Landon, is it?" Now he'd done it. He'd stepped over the line and there was no turning back. "Did you tell him to stay out of your life?" *Oh, what a misguided fool you are.*

"No, but I told him flat out I didn't know whether I could trust him."

He didn't like the triumph surfacing in those gorgeous eyes. "What'd he do? Run away like a coward?" He forced a grin. One thing was clear: Amy was more than a challenge. She was a woman with which to contend.

"Not at all. He laughed it off and didn't give it a second thought. The resemblance between the two of you is quite extraordinary, though. Both in looks and . . . well, pretty much everything." She leaned closer, peering at him, tilting her head. So close, he caught a whiff of her perfume—it was nice, not overpowering and stirred his senses.

"Do you want to touch my face or something?"

She sat back again. "Of course not. Sorry."

"I assure you, I'm real. Pinch me and you'll find I'm all flesh and blood, but you know what they say. Everyone has a twin somewhere in the world." *Stop talking now.* "But does this other guy have my charm and savoir-faire?" He could have slapped himself. Of all the harebrained, idiotic, misguided, stupid things he'd done in his life, *this* was—hands down—his lowest moment. Absolute worst. "Why don't you think you can trust him, if you don't mind my asking?"

She stared at the floor for a long moment. "He's too smooth, and my boss thinks . . . well, it doesn't matter." She waved her hand. "I'm not sure I believe her, anyway."

"Did you say he's a magazine publisher?"

"Right. A great one called *New York Scene.* It sounds like it's about Manhattan nightlife or something, but it's not. If you ask me, it's not the best name for the magazine."

That one hit a bit below the belt. "You don't say."

"But Landon's one of the sharpest, best, most intuitive writers around. He's amazing in so many ways."

"You're not sure you can trust him. Let me guess. Your boss doesn't like him because she thinks Landon's out to steal you away and put you on his payroll?" He grunted again and shifted in the chair. *Good luck sleeping tonight, you liar.* With every word, he dug himself in deeper. Judging by the way she looked at him, maybe he'd said too much already. He needed to confess. Then she'd know what a huge jerk he really was. *Then you won't have a chance with her*—ever. That last thought stopped him cold. Now that he'd found her, call him selfish, but he didn't want to risk losing her. Not at least without an opportunity to prove himself. Might take a lot of doing, but he had to try.

"Exactly. How could you know that?"

Her question brought him back to reality. "I've been in publishing, remember, and I also know a little something about business practices." His eyes met hers. "I'm sure Landon knows how talented you are and only wants whatever's best for you in the long run, but who am I to talk about it in the first place?" He'd gone off the deep end of the pool with that one, but it was starting to get a little fun. *You're not only a fool, you're a perverse one.*

She twisted her hands in her lap. Oh, she was intriguing. Even more so when she was nervous or fired up about something. Her nerves seemed to have calmed a little, but he wanted to still those antsy hands or else he'd kiss her senseless.

"You see, Cooper, when I agreed to go to Houston with you—by way of Austin, of course—I thought you were Landon."

He allowed the hint of a grin. "I doubt Sam Lewis would have agreed to this arrangement if he didn't trust me. Keeping his TeamWork crew safe is one of his top priorities."

She nodded and appeared to breathe easier, the taut lines around her mouth relaxing. "You're right," she said, "and I trust you, too, or I wouldn't even consider going anywhere alone with you."

"Although you thought I was someone else, you like me as Cooper, right?" His conscience stabbed him hard on that one. Thankfully, she didn't seem to notice the little slip tucked into that sentence.

"I wouldn't have kissed you if I didn't like you. Two *times* I liked you."

Landon rose to his feet. "The offer of a ride's still good, but if you'd rather find another way to Houston, I'll understand, considering the circumstances. Bottom line, Amy? I'm the same guy you danced with last night. Still the same guy . . . in every way." He fixed his gaze on her and she didn't disappoint. Raising her chin, the firm line of her mouth softened before she relented and graced him with her lovely smile. Ah, that smile. If she hated him the rest of her life—which was possible after the next few days—he'd forever remember it. Another loud clap of thunder made him jump, and she visibly startled. "It's okay," he said, attempting to sound as calm as possible. "A display of God's power." *Or His wrath.*

She was quiet for a few moments, her tumultuous thoughts evident behind her blank gaze. Finally, she said, "Perhaps against my better judgment, I'll go with you. I need to go upstairs and get my things and then check out. I'll be right down." Rising from the chair, she headed toward the elevator.

"Let me help you."

She paused and turned back to face him. "It's not necessary. I'm perfectly capable."

"Capability isn't the issue. You have bags and I have muscles." Seeing the look on her face, he raised his hands and fought the urge to grin. "Okay, that didn't come out the way I meant it, but we'll leave the door open so the dorm mother won't be alarmed. How's that?"

She rolled her eyes. "Stop reading that stupid cowboy rule book, will you?"

He laughed and followed her into the elevator, wondering how many prayers for forgiveness he'd be saying the next few days, not to mention the rest of his life. If he wasn't mistaken, relief tinged with amusement danced in her eyes. "I promised to take you to breakfast. Why don't we start there and then play it by ear?"

"Since I already agreed to ride to Houston with you, and all my friends must have left by now, I think we're more or less stuck with each other."

"I can't think of anyone I'd rather be stuck with," he said. "If you're honest with yourself and me, you'll admit you're looking forward to this little road trip."

"My, my, someone's being mighty optimistic." The reemerging humor in her voice was encouraging. "I just hope I'm not making one of the biggest mistakes of my life."

"No need to be so dramatic," Landon grumbled. Man, he'd dug the hole deep and wide and he needed to find a way to somehow climb out of it or die trying. *Now who's being overdramatic?* Problem was, if he somehow managed to dig out of that pit, Amy would be waiting for him at the top—with a heavy shovel and more than ready to throw him right back down in that big, stupid hole.

Chapter 18

"SO, TO BE perfectly clear, you were kissing Landon what's-his-name last night, not me." He leaned against the doorframe as Amy opened the door to her room and led him inside. Knowing he watched, she left the door ajar. When she shot him a look, Cooper raked one hand through his short, dark hair. "I guess that explains why you kissed me like *that.* Wow. Ego bruiser, that one. I just thought I was one really blessed guy."

"Well, no. Apparently, I was *that* easy," she said. "Weddings bring on all these ridiculous romantic feelings, and you're . . ." She waved her hand in his direction. As uncomfortable as it made her, she suspected he was pretty good at reading her mind. "Do I really need to finish that sentence?"

The hint of a smile crossed his face. "My ego says yes, but my overriding sense of logic says you'd better not. Appreciate the thought, though. I have to ask, what happened to make you think I'm *not* Landon?" How she wished she could read his mind right about now.

"I got a voice mail message from him saying how much he enjoyed our date. He said he hoped I was having a good time wherever I was and said he'd look forward to seeing me again. That's when this horrible feeling came over me and I realized this was a case of mistaken identity."

"Not so sure about the horrible part."

She smirked. "You know what I mean. I'm usually fairly intelligent, but in that moment, I felt like the world's biggest fool. I have a photo of Landon in my bag. I can show you later, if you want. That way, you can see who I'm talking about and understand why I thought you were him."

He slanted an incredulous glance her way. "Not necessary, but let me get this straight. You carry this guy's photo around with you?"

"Yes, but not really." She blew out a breath. "It's in his magazine. He's the publisher and editor in chief, after all."

"You seem pretty impressed by that, in spite of the fact you think the name of his magazine is all wrong."

"And you sound a little jealous." *Why would he care or feel threatened?*

He scoffed. "Yeah, right. I can hold my own against some publisher guy any day of the week. What else you got?"

"For the record, I didn't kiss Landon." Glancing his way, she glimpsed something resembling wounded pride flitting across his features. Strange.

"I didn't ask. Still, good to know, although it's not exactly the most rousing recommendation for a guy. But," Cooper said, tossing his hat on the closest chair, "since you brought it up, why not?"

Amy chewed the inside of her cheek, trying to conjure up a plausible answer. Why she said it in the first place, she had no idea. *Oh, Lord, You have a warped sense of humor sometimes. How small* is *Your world, anyway? Really, what are the odds?*

"Wart on the chin? Bad teeth? Acne as a teenager?" He snapped his fingers. "I know. Foul breath or bad—"

She held up one hand, laughing. "Stop it. He's a very—extremely—handsome man, and believe me, the thought was there, if you must know." She darted a quick glance at him and started gathering her belongings.

"You *do* realize you just paid me a big compliment."

"Get over yourself." She walked into the bathroom. Tossing a few last items into the overnight case, she grabbed it but stopped short when she spied him sprawled in the side chair. "Don't get too comfortable over there."

"I figured it out. He scared you by coming on too strong."

She lifted her chin. "You're in serious danger of the same thing. It's . . . disconcerting."

Cooper shrugged. "Fine. Don't tell me. I was only curious." He unfolded his tall frame from the chair and rose to his feet.

"Is that all you can think about? Why do you care one way or the other, considering you pretty much won that round anyway?"

"Hey, you're the one who keeps bringing up the man, so I'm thinking there's some hidden guilt rolling around in there somewhere. And, for the record—as you put it—you're not easy, Amy." His eyes softened, his voice gentled. "As a matter of fact, you strike me as the type of woman where nothing comes easy."

"What's that supposed to mean?" She started tapping her foot and crossed her arms over her chest.

"Nothing," he said. "Just that you're definitely worth getting to know."

Opening the closet door, she felt his eyes on her as she retrieved the hanging bag and draped it over her suitcase. "Let me get my jacket and then we're on our way."

"You still haven't answered my question."

"Which one? You asked a number of them." *This is what I get for skipping church.* But no, the Lord didn't work that way. *Churlish. That's the word for how you're acting.* Though she recognized it, it was still hard to stop. An apology would be advisable, but she couldn't bring herself to do it. Sparring with Cooper was fun, as it'd been with Landon. That thought gave her pause. *You're such a wanton woman, flirting with these men.* She'd need to spend extra time on devotions tonight.

Cooper's blue-eyed gaze pierced holes straight through her as he removed his suede jacket. The way his black Henley stretched over those broad shoulders, a couple of buttons undone at the top, should be outlawed. Not to mention the slightest hint of stubble peppering his jaw. She'd always been more attracted to the Landon type—professional, dressed impeccably in a business suit, oozing self-confidence—but Cooper flipped all those preferences upside down although the man was no stranger to confidence.

Talking would be good. "What do you think you're doing? If you don't want me to rethink this whole thing, please put your jacket back on. Although"—she hesitated for a long moment—"perhaps we should, um . . ."

He tilted his head to one side, surveying her through narrowed eyes. "Should . . . what?"

"Set some ground rules for this little road trip."

"Sure. Go ahead. You first." Cooper nodded toward the bed. "May I?"

"May you what?"

He chuckled. "Relax, Amy. All I want to do is sit. You're not afraid of me for some reason, are you? Rest assured, I'm not out to steal your virtue or take advantage of the fact I'll have a beautiful woman in my car for the next eight hours or so." When she raised a brow, he sobered. "I'm teasing. Come on, lighten up. It'll make this experience a whole lot more enjoyable for both of us." Crossing the room, he sat on the unmade bed. For some reason, she *always* made the bed in hotel rooms, but not today. "Hmm. Comfy." He bounced a few times on the mattress as if testing it.

"And that's supposed to make me feel better about this whole thing?"

He laughed. "What, me bouncing on the bed or the virtuous comment?"

"Pretty much all of it."

"Since you seem to want to spell it out, I have some ground rules, too. Want to hear them?" He patted the bed beside him. "Care to sit down so I can at least talk to you at eye-level?"

After parting the curtains to allow light into the room, Amy sat in the chair he'd vacated beside the small table. Crossing one leg over the other, she swung her foot back and forth, stopping when she caught his amused glance.

"Sounds like you don't trust yourself," he said. "The way you're acting smacks of it, too."

"Maybe I don't."

"So, it's not *me* you're worried about? It's you? Has a man done something to hurt you in the past?" His eyes widened. "You're not afraid of men for some reason, are you?"

Amy shook her head, fighting the urge to laugh. "That would be a definitive no." What a conversation, and in her hotel room, no less. Her shoulders slumped and she blew out a breath. "It's more my being immature and stupid. Cut me some slack. I've never been in a situation like this before. I honestly wouldn't blame you if you said to forget the whole thing and leave me sitting here in this inn, left to my own defenses."

Cooper shook his head. "Don't insult yourself. Want to know what I'm thinking?"

When she didn't answer, he strolled over to where she sat. The man could walk across a room like no one else—not really a swagger but with incredible confidence bordering on bravado. Propping both hands on the arms of her chair, he pinned her with that piercing gaze he'd mastered so well. Although his appearance was so similar to Landon, Cooper definitely had his own distinctive personality. When he leaned close, his breath warmed her cheek, unnerving her even more. *This man makes me dizzy and more than a little crazy.* "I think you're every bit as nutty as you are beautiful. At the moment, it's a toss-up which one would win out. Tell you one thing, though." That sexy, slow grin emerged. "I sure wanna stick around and find out."

Amy gasped and turned her head. With the movement, her hair escaped the confines of the loose ponytail and fell about her shoulders. Glimpsing Cooper's dumbstruck expression, she understood exactly why she was skittish about this whole arrangement. His eyes skimmed over her face and trailed upward to her hair. The man's audacity was appalling, the look in his eyes nothing short of presumptuous. Then why did she feel so drawn to him?

Maybe he's more like Landon than I presumed.

Finally, he stepped back. Crossing the room, he sat back down on the bed again and clasped his hands together. "So, tell me about these ground rules."

"Okay. I'm a Christian and don't believe in . . . hanky panky before marriage." Try as she might, she found it difficult to breathe. "I think it's important to get that information out there right from the start."

"Good. I agree, but did you actually say hanky panky?"

"What? You want a definition? You know very well what it is, and having me say it out loud serves no purpose."

"I didn't ask you to define it. I know what it is."

"Do you agree because you're a Christian or because you simply don't believe in"—she sucked in a deep breath—"pre-marital . . . sex . . . for moral, ethical or other reasons?"

Cooper fixed her with those gorgeous eyes. "God won't strike you down because you said the word, Amy. I gave my heart to Jesus when I was ten. Then I got stupid for a while, if you want to talk stupid. I'll tell you when we can have a conversation that's not in your hotel room or a moving car. Suffice it to say I'm older, I've wised up and I know right from wrong in God's eyes and that's how I now choose to live my life."

She nodded. "Here's the thing, Cooper."

For a second, an odd expression flitted over his handsome face. Leaning back on his elbows, he cocked his head to one side. "Tell me. What's the thing?"

Why did he have to act so comfortable on the bed in her hotel room? Easy going was one thing, over-familiarity another. Not to mention his question was the same one Landon asked during their carriage ride in Central Park. As a matter of fact, he'd said it earlier, too, during their discussion in the lobby. Amy moved her hand to her forehead, frowning. *This is too strange.*

"Are you okay?" Genuine concern tempered his question.

"Trying to take it all in. I guess we'd better get on the road soon or we'll never get to Austin."

"Sounds like a plan, but what were you going to say?"

Lowering her hand, she met his gaze. "This must be a habit with you. Okay, I'm going to lay it on the line here. I feel really weird, knowing how we kissed last night. The glances, the looks, the dancing, feelings . . . all of it, and now we'll be spending time together in very close quarters for the next two days."

"I know. I feel the same way, but I'm glad you're telling me 'right from the start,' as you put it."

She gulped. "You do?"

He looked momentarily confused. "Do what?"

"Know how I feel?"

"You're not exactly a shy wallflower. One of the things I appreciate most about you is your honesty. Trust me, that's a very good thing. The way I see it, after this adventure together, we'll either be madly in love or desperate to be rid of each other." He pushed himself off the bed and onto his feet. "I have an idea." He stepped closer to where she sat and held out one hand. "Stand up."

"I'm not quite sure I like your tone."

"Humor me. Stand up." He leaned close to where she still sat in the chair. "Please?"

Uncrossing her legs, Amy slowly rose to her feet but—not wanting to appear overeager—took her sweet time.

"Here's the plan: we kiss"—he held up his hand when she started to protest—"once before we head out on the road, then we make a pact not to do it again unless either of us wants another round when we say good-bye in Houston." Standing in front of her, with barely an inch separating them, his eyes searched hers.

Her lips settled in a firm line. "You're crazy. Why would you think I'd want to kiss you? I don't even know you."

"I hate to state the obvious, but that didn't stop you last night."

She tried to ignore his smug grin but found it difficult to get past the broad shoulders and all-too-inviting smile. "Is this some kind of test?"

"Not really. It's more to prove a point."

"I might regret this, but what point would that be?" Amy lowered her gaze and avoided his direct eye contact since past experience had proven it to be hazardous for her emotions, not to mention her best judgment.

"That we're adults capable of self-control even though we'll be fighting it the entire time."

"It?"

"This." Tugging her shoulders toward him, Cooper lowered his head, his lips a heartbeat from hers. The male pride curving his mouth annoyed her to no end, but not enough to stop her from tilting her chin upward. *What a pushover I am.* She hadn't known how much until now. Moving one hand to the back of her neck, he sifted through her hair with slow, gentle fingers. *Oh, that's good.* She dropped her hands to her sides as he pulled her close and she detected the wonderful combination of Irish Spring and minty mouthwash. As he lowered his head, his mouth hovering above hers, she closed her eyes, anticipating this more than she wanted. The kiss was soft, his lips brushing over hers before becoming more firm in a fabulous déjà vu of the night before. Oh, the things this man could do. All too soon, Cooper released his hold on her and stepped back a few paces. "Yep, that should do it."

Her emotions as tangled as her hair, Amy turned aside. *No fair.* Touching her lips with shaky fingers, she cleared her throat and willed herself to speak and not come across like a complete imbecile. "Let me put my hair up again and then we need to get moving."

"I like it down."

She stared at him for a long moment before clearing her throat. "It doesn't really matter what you think, now does it? Give me a minute and I'll be ready." Retrieving her hair elastic from the carpet, she walked over to stand in front of the mirror. She knew he watched, and she focused on smoothing her hair, avoiding eye contact. Her fingers still shook, and she bit her lower lip in frustration.

"Don't pull too tight."

"You're an incredibly infuriating man." She paused, remembering she'd said that very thing to Landon. *It's official. I've gone mental.* With renewed vigor, she twisted the band around her hair in a quick ponytail, making certain it was secure. "How long did you say this pact should last?" She cringed with the realization her question made it sound as though she was anticipating another kiss.

"Until I drop you off in Houston, but it's your call. Feel free to break it anytime, Miss Irresistible."

"Please don't call me that."

Grabbing her suitcase and overnight case with one hand and looking back over his shoulder, Cooper's wink was playful. "It's better than a few other nicknames I can think of."

Staring at his back as he headed into the hallway, Amy grunted. "Insufferable." Grabbing her purse and the hanging bag with her bridesmaid gown, she stalked out of the room behind him, not bothering to close the door. *Oh yes, this is going to be an interesting couple of days.*

As she followed him to the elevator, she remembered Cooper hadn't told her any of his ground rules. Maybe it didn't matter since the primary one had already been laid out and sealed with a kiss, which in retrospect might not have been the best way to seal their agreement. But it would do. Amy swallowed her smile as Cooper held the elevator doors and ushered her inside.

"Austin or bust." He stood so close she felt his warmth.

Lord, grant me strength.

Chapter 19

"SO, TELL ME what wonderful things Texas mamas tell their boys." Swirling her French toast in syrup with no shame whatsoever, Amy brought it to her lips, smiling as she savored the delicious bite. They were only two of a handful of patrons in the restaurant next door to the inn. Quiet was good, and it suited her mood fine and dandy. Thankfully, the storm had already passed through the area, and now the sun winked at her through still-dark clouds. The man seated across from her both mystified and confounded her. One thing she knew for sure: she'd never smell Irish Spring again without thinking of Cooper Warren.

He smiled. "Nah. I'd much rather sit here and watch you eat. It's an art unto itself."

"Right," she said, stabbing another bite. Why was she eating like she hadn't consumed anything the past week? Making up for lost calories was one thing, but this was ridiculous. "It's hardly a phenomenon. I more or less starved myself and worked out like a crazy person to fit into that bridesmaid dress." Seeing the look on his face, she raised a hand. "No comments, please, especially flattery. I already know your opinion on the subject."

"I think watching you say or do anything is a treat."

She put down her fork. "Didn't your mother ever tell you not to be so flirtatious?"

He laughed. "Mom taught me to always hold doors for a lady. She told me to always listen very carefully to what a woman says, and that sometimes there's a difference between what she says and what she means. That one can get tricky. I learned how to prepare and cook at least five meals, how to clean the dishes and sort and wash laundry so all my whites don't turn girly pink."

"This is good stuff. Go on." Amy finished her French toast all the while eyeing her honey dew melon.

"She taught me to respect a woman's right to say no." He paused as if to gauge her reaction, but she wasn't about to give him the satisfaction. "She taught me to appreciate fine art, great classical music and gourmet food. I learned the value of a dollar and how earning money isn't as important as the joy derived from doing something you love. That I should dole out at least five compliments a day and try to find at least five wonderful things in God's creation each day and thank Him."

Amy's eyes met his. "Your mother sounds very wise."

Cooper nodded. "That she is."

"Well, in that case, I hope you haven't disappointed her too much." She let out a giggle at his apparent surprise. "Sorry. I couldn't help it. From what I can tell, you turned out okay, although I'm sure you were a mischievous kid."

"Right back at ya." When he winked, she felt warmth invade her cheeks.

"Hopefully, you learned some wise lessons from your father, as well." His eyes fell and he turned his head, but not before she glimpsed the pain. "I'm sorry." Immediate regret filled her. Wanting to grasp his hand in hers, she refrained. "Forgive me. Apparently, I've touched a raw nerve."

Finished with his eggs and sausage, he lowered his fork to his empty plate and pushed it aside. "It's okay. My dad wasn't around much, and when he was, it would have been better if he'd never been there at all."

"But you mentioned your dad and his fishing stories."

"Right. My dad used to take me fishing when I was little—younger than ten—but I'm mainly talking about my stepfather. He married my mom when I was fourteen. Cooper shifted in his chair. "Can we please agree not to talk about my dad?"

"If that's what you want, but I'm a good listener."

"I know."

"I have one brother. Goes by the name of Mitch," she said, wanting to break the awkward silence. "He's thirteen months older and we give each other grief on a daily basis. Mitch is a stockbroker and finds it fascinating I'm a writer since he can't string together two coherent sentences to save his life."

"You sound very close."

She nodded. "We are. For a kid who teased me mercilessly, kidnapped my kitten and held it for the ransom of a candy bar when I was six, and set me up on one too many blind dates, I guess he wasn't so bad. Mitch is one of the most kind, generous, loving people I know."

His features relaxed when he smiled, a welcome sight. "He's blessed to have you as his biggest fan. Hang on to that relationship, Amy. Don't ever take it for granted."

~

"So, how long is this road trip?" Amy followed as Cooper led the way to the little white rental car in the hotel parking lot. She thanked him as he pulled the passenger door open and waited while she climbed inside. Putting her purse on the floorboard, she fidgeted, fussed and fiddled. Never in her life had she puzzled over how to position her legs in a vehicle. To think she was going to spend the next two days with this man had her mind reeling.

"Seven hours, give or take, depending on stops." Closing her door, he came around the front and slid behind the wheel. "Honey, please tell me you went before we left the hotel?"

"If you can please refrain from calling me 'honey' and making bathroom jokes, I think you'll find I'm a very agreeable passenger." Reaching into her purse, she pulled out a magazine and smoothed its curled pages on her lap. Anything to keep her fingers and mind occupied.

After pulling the car out of the parking lot and onto the main road, Cooper slanted a glance her way with a quirked brow. "Anything interesting you can share?"

"Not unless you'd like to know the best way to shave around your knees without getting nicked or how to . . . oh, never mind." *Better not to read about the best way to please your man.* He probably had his own ideas about that subject.

"Well, the shaving advice might actually come in handy. Angling around the slight cleft in the chin can be tricky. Being all curved like the knee and all."

"You don't have a cleft in your chin."

"Glad you noticed."

"I was pretty close to you a few times in the last twenty-four hours, so yes, I noticed. Why don't you tell me what degree you earned from A&M, Coop the Scoop. Journalism?"

"Shaving, of course."

She laughed. "Mine's in toasting bagels."

"Better." He darted a quick glance her way.

"What's better?"

"*This* Amy. The more relaxed version who's fun-loving and charms me senseless. As far as my degree, it's a whole lot more fun if you guess."

"Why can't you come right out and tell me? Must everything be a game with you? And it wasn't journalism even though you were the campus newspaper editor?"

He grinned. "You checked me out, huh? Asked a few questions at the wedding, did you?"

"No. That information was volunteered. No inquiries involved."

"Not journalism. You already know I went to A&M with Kevin, and he sells lumber."

"Kevin does much more than sell lumber and you know it. But, okay, let's see." Pretending to ponder the options, Amy tapped her index finger over her lips. "I know. You sell lightbulbs at Home Depot."

With the force of his laughter, Cooper almost lost his hat. He clamped one hand on the Stetson, removing it. "Sorry, I forgot my manners. I should have taken this off in the first place." Handing it to her, he ran a quick hand through the thick, dark waves.

She spun the Stetson on her hand, giving it an approving glance. "It's very nice, but why are you giving this to me?" Made from deep brown felt, the hat was sturdy and well-constructed. When she angled it on her head, it drooped over her right ear. "What do you think? Is it me?"

"You'd better take that off." His lips twisted as he darted a quick glance her way.

"Why? Because it looks better on me than you?"

"Exactly."

She grunted. "Like I said, you make everything a game."

"Not true. You ask leading questions and definitely bring out my latent flirting genes."

Latent nothing. Twisting in her seat—as best she could from the confines of the seat belt—Amy gave the hat a light toss, thankful it landed upright on the backseat. "Wasn't proper training in Stetson removal one of those rules your mama taught you all those many years ago?"

He chuckled. "You are so not subtle. I'm thirty-three and a half. Exactly. You?" He slanted a glance her way before refocusing on the road and negotiating a turn. She was grateful he was a safe driver—not overly cautious, but defensive.

"I'm twenty-seven. And your birthday is June fifteenth, but you still haven't answered my question."

"Your lightbulb comment wasn't far off. Electrical engineering. And for a word person, you're not too bad at this math thing. Kudos."

"Thanks. Electrical engineering, eh? That's interesting," Amy said. "I imagine you'd be pretty handy around the house."

"You must not have heard the joke about how many engineers it takes to screw in a lightbulb. All brains and no common sense."

"You certainly don't act like any electrical engineer I've ever met."

"How many are we talking, exactly?"

"A few. You sure don't kiss like one either." *What am I saying?*

His brows rose. "Oh? Kissed a few engineers, have you?"

"Not a one. Well, not until you. I'd imagine an engineer would be an entirely technical, by-the-book kisser." *Now I'm talking about* kissing *styles?* "Which you most definitely are *not.*"

"Well, having never kissed a journalist before, I'd have thought it'd be noisy, wordy or clinical."

Noisy? Clinical? Amy chewed the inside of her cheek to stop her laughter and tried to keep a straight face. "In spite of my better judgment, I have to ask which category do I fall into?"

"None of the above. You're definitely in the creative category."

Her phone rang and she busied herself rummaging through her purse, grateful for the interruption. Digging it out of her purse, she shot Cooper a warning glance. "Not one word."

He made a show of zipping his lips as she answered the call.

"So, how was the wedding?" Mitch asked.

"Great. Beck was gorgeous, Kevin was handsome, everything went off without a hitch."

"As long as they're actually hitched, I'm glad to hear it."

Men. Didn't they know the teasing got old? *I miss you, Dad.* "I'm in the middle of something. Can I call you back later?"

"You've got a man with you, don't you?"

Switching on the radio, Amy startled when it blared through the speaker. "Don't be ridiculous. It's only the radio." She directed a semi-threatening glance at Cooper, but he shrugged and feigned an innocent "Who me?" expression.

"Put him on the phone, Amy."

"Can't do that, but thanks so much for calling. Catch you later."

"And you're misguided. Didn't I warn you about getting in the car with a stranger?"

"How do you know it's not Josh or Sam?"

"Because you've got that little nervous thing going on with your voice."

"I don't know what you're talking about."

Laughing, Mitch mimicked what she'd said, purposely infusing his voice with small tremors. "I learned a long time ago how to interpret those nuances and inflections in your voice. Remember, I know you better than anyone."

"Yeah, well, I'm working on that one."

He chuckled. "Be good."

"Talk to you soon." She disconnected before he could respond.

"Boyfriend?" Cooper said.

"Worse. Mitch." She put away her phone. "Being overprotective, as usual."

"Don't be too hard on the guy," he said. "Ten to one, he'll call you again within the hour to grill you for more details, hoping to catch you alone. I'll be happy to talk with him, if you want."

Turning her attention to the magazine, Amy flipped the pages. "Not necessary. How about I read one of these advice columns? That could be fun."

"Sure, but only if we both give our opinion."

"That certainly sounds fair." For a half-second, Amy entertained the idea of fabricating some story about a woman torn between two men who happened to look very similar, but no, she read the article as printed. The problem posed was about a married woman who'd been having a secret love affair with a fellow office worker. Now the affair had ended, and she sought advice on whether to confess the affair to her husband, especially since she professed to still love him.

After reading the article out loud—with Cooper nodding every now and then to indicate he listened—she lowered the magazine to her lap. "So, what do you think she should do?"

"First of all, an affair with a fellow office worker is wrong on so many levels. She should definitely confess the affair to her husband. If he loves her, he'll accept the truth, appreciate her honesty, and then work on righting whatever was wrong with their relationship in the first place. After all, no woman who's happy in her marriage is going to look elsewhere." Tapping his hand on the steering wheel, he appeared more than satisfied with his answer. "Your turn."

Amy shifted on the seat toward him. "Bear with me a second and hear me out. Suppose there wasn't anything really wrong in her marriage. Theoretically, let's say they had a good, emotionally satisfying relationship but he left something to be desired physically for whatever reason. The lure of someone more exciting proved too great and she finally succumbed to the temptation."

The muscles in Cooper's cheeks flexed. "That's a bit shallow, wouldn't you say? Come on, Amy. Just because the poor guy might have a hump back or something? A physical imperfection or frailty doesn't excuse a woman for being unfaithful to her husband."

"I'm not saying that," she said. "I'm just . . . thinking out loud."

"Well, while you're doing all that thinking, maybe you could realize you didn't answer the question. You only proposed one idea as to *why* she might have strayed in the first place."

She relented. "You're right. She should confess the affair to her husband, even if it hurts him terribly. You already know me well enough to understand my staunch policy on honesty always being the best policy. Was psychology your minor in college?"

He shook his head. "No." After that, he remained silent.

Leaning her head against the seat, she was content to watch the passing scenery although there wasn't much to see except dilapidated billboards, open fields, abandoned tractors and cowboy outlet stores. Finding a contemporary Christian radio station, Cooper cranked up the volume, occasionally singing along. He was probably shocked she could sit still for an extended period and not flap her jaws.

"You have a nice voice," she said.

"Thanks. Feel free to join me. Jump right on in whenever you want."

"Trust me. That's not something you want to hear."

"Try me."

"No, thanks. I'd much rather listen to you." She graced him with a smile sweet enough to turn horseradish into honey.

That was all the encouragement he needed, it seemed. Giving her a wide grin, he burst into another boisterous song, although this time he made up half the words and resorted to *la dee da* more often than not. Snuggling down into the seat, Amy hid her smile. This little adventure might prove to be quite agreeable after all.

Chapter 20

"NEED TO STOP?" Cooper asked an hour and a half into their trip.

"No, I'm fine. Let's keep going." A few minutes later, the radio signal began to fade, spitting out more static than music. She turned it off. "So, you never told me *your* personal ground rules."

He shot her a skeptical glance. "Sure you want to hear them?"

"I wouldn't have asked if I didn't. Is there some reason you think I wouldn't want to hear them?"

"You're mighty defensive, little lady. What's got you strung so tight?"

"I beg your pardon?" she asked. "If anyone's defensive, it's you, and that line sounds like it came straight from a John Wayne movie. I gave you more credit for originality than that."

"I'm sorry. You're too good to be true."

"Glad I could fulfill your teasing quotient for the day. Is that a backhanded compliment?"

"If you want it to be."

She shook her head, uncertain how to read this man in any sense of the word.

"Okay, the ground rules," he said. "Of course, the no hanky panky rule applies. No smoking, no drinking, no bad language and no using the Lord's name in vain. Of course, those last few are general rules for everyone, but I don't need to worry about any of them with you, am I right?"

"Right."

"Then there's the rule about talking about beloved but deceased pets. You don't do it. Neither do I want to hear about designer shoes, handbags or the latest craziness with any Hollywood superstar couple. I could care less. Neither do I want to talk about personal care items, television shows, diets, decorating or food preparation tips or the latest antics of some overpaid professional athlete. And whatever you do, please don't tell me about the latest scandal in Washington or which disgraced politician or spurned mistress has written a bestselling book about his or her affair. Shall I go on?"

Amy laughed. "No, I think that covers everything I might possibly want to talk about on this trip. You could have saved yourself a lot of trouble by asking me politely to shut up, you know."

"I'd never tell you such a thing because I give you more credit than to talk about those things in the first place," he said. "Besides, I can think of much better ways to make you quiet. Unless the pact's still in place, and then I'd have to get a little more creative."

"Are you always this weird with women you hardly know?" A vision of Landon popped into her head again, and she pushed it aside.

"Honestly? Only the ones to whom I'm strongly attracted."

Don't ask. "And have you been strongly attracted to many women in your lifetime?"

"Attracted, yes. Lots of times. Strongly attracted? Maybe five times. Acted on it? Three times, but nothing lasting or long-term ever developed. Hoped it would last? Only once."

Don't ask. "What happened?"

"I'm looking at her."

Amy gasped. *You deserved that one.* "What? That's impossible."

"Why?" She detected the humor in his voice, but Cooper was straight-faced and kept his eyes trained straight ahead.

"For starters, you don't know me."

"What do I need to know? I could very easily fall in love with you, Amy. What's not to like? It's obvious you're no serial killer, gold digger or after anything other than my good looks and charm."

She slumped back against the seat, massaging her fingers on both temples and shaking her head.

"Careful. You might dislodge something up there."

"Oh, you!" she hissed. "One minute you're telling me you'd like to marry me and the next you make me feel like a complete idiot."

"I didn't say anything about marriage. I said I hoped it might last. And you're no idiot."

"Well," she said slowly, as though talking to a small child, "saying you hope a relationship might last pretty much means marriage in my book. Surely a man who has no casual hanky panky as a ground rule doesn't believe you can have a lasting relationship without the benefit of marriage."

"I thought we'd already settled that back at the inn. Sorry, couldn't resist. Now that I've got you all flustered, do you agree we should take this one step at a time?"

She narrowed her eyes. Why was it she couldn't stay angry with this man any longer than she could hold her breath? "Was that little stunt intended to get me all . . . all . . ."

"Flustered? Or hot and bothered," he said. "Take your pick."

"Stop this car, Cooper. Stop it right now." Amy grabbed the door handle, her fingers clenched tight. If her words didn't sound commanding enough, surely the glare she gave him would convince him to pull over since she didn't relish the idea of jumping from a moving vehicle.

"Calm down," he said. "I never meant to offend you. Really. Forgive me." He quickly pulled the car to the side of the road. "Please stay in the car. I'd never forgive myself if you hitchhiked and got kidnapped—or worse. We're heading toward the Texas border, and it's not exactly known as the safest state around."

"At least you have capital punishment in Texas, right?"

"I know one way to get you to smile again. Look at me, please." His voice was quiet.

"I will not."

"Don't be childish."

"I am not." This whole scenario was wonderfully absurd, but she dared not give him the satisfaction of giving into a grin.

"Then look at me."

Turning her head slowly, she met those blue eyes. As she suspected, one look and she melted. What a hopeless romantic. Like it or not, she was quickly falling for this man. Worse yet, she sensed he knew it.

"That's much better," he said. "It's almost time for lunch. What do you say we pull off at the next exit that looks promising and find someplace to eat?"

"If you promise to behave yourself."

His smile thawed her even more. "Promise."

Chapter 21

"I STILL WANT to know what that last conversation was all about. But not now," Amy told him, trying her best not to shake her head again and have him joke about dislodging brain cells. *Like they're just flying around in there willy-nilly.*

Deciding on a family, sit-down restaurant called Kleinman's a short time later, Amy excused herself to go to the ladies room after they'd been ushered to a booth.

"Don't be long," Cooper said, stretching his arm along the back of the booth. Great. Next time she'd request a table. She rolled her eyes and stalked off in a bit of a huff although they both knew it was for show. The man was entertaining, she'd give him that much.

No sooner had she dried off her hands than her cell phone rang. She hesitated, half-wishing it was Landon, half-hoping it wasn't. Picking up the phone, she glanced at the display. Mitch.

"Hey, Mitch." Slowly exhaling, she leaned against the counter, cradling the phone against her ear.

"You gonna tell me now?"

"I'm a grown woman, you know. Believe it or not, I can handle life on my own when I'm outside the scope of your protection."

"Look, being serious here for a minute. It's not like you to take off with some guy. You're usually a lot more cautious. See, I was right—and maybe a little prophetic—when I said I should be worried about you taking off with some stranger in a car."

"He's not just any guy. And he's not a stranger."

"Oh? Who is he then?"

"I appreciate the big brother act, but you've got to trust me for *some* common sense."

"I do, but humor me for my peace of mind."

"His name is Cooper Warren, and he was a groomsman in the wedding. The quick rundown is that he went to A&M with Kevin and was the campus newspaper editor. Now he lives in Austin. Electrical engineer . . . or something."

"And where are you going with him?"

"To Houston via Austin by car."

"Why?"

She glanced at the ceiling, staring at a sprinkler head, trying to figure out how to shorten this conversation. The sound of her tapping foot reverberated in the small space. "Short answer? He offered." No way she'd tell him she accepted Cooper's offer under the assumption he was Landon Warnick. It sounded crazy enough in her head. No way could she say it out loud.

Silence for a few seconds. "How do you think Landon will feel when he hears you traipsed around the dusty Texas countryside with this Cooper guy?"

"It's December, so it's not dusty, and I owe Landon nothing. We've had one date, Mitch, so it's not like we're in a relationship."

"Really? From what you told me, he's your dream man. Then you go off to Louisiana for a wedding and now you're on a road trip with some other guy? Where's your sense of loyalty? Not to mention propriety."

She frowned. "First of all, the jury's still out on the dream man part. Landon's charming, but he's also pushy and overconfident at times. Like someone else I know. And let's not get into the morals clause here."

"Did Landon scare you off?"

"No, of course not. I'm not saying that." *Why does he sound defensive?* "I just get the feeling he'd be pushy and want too much too soon. I don't know," she said, frowning. "Can't a girl enjoy a few casual dates without going through an inquisition? I know you have my best interests at heart, but I need to figure this one out for myself."

"Nothing with you is ever casual, especially going on a road trip."

Her hand slid down to her hip, pushing aside Winnie's similar concerns when they resurfaced in her mind. "Tell me this: is it something about my personality that attracts such strong men? Do I have some kind of 'Pick me! I'm gullible!' sticker stuck on my back?"

"In my case, blame it on genetics so you're stuck with me. In Warnick's case, I haven't a clue. Promise you'll keep your cell phone turned on during your little holiday adventure."

"Will do. I have to get going now, and thanks for checking in. I'll talk with you again soon."

She heard him say "You'd better" before disconnecting.

Lost in thought, Amy walked back into the dining area. She tried not to think about the fact that a man who looked so much like Landon waited for her. Cooper watched as she dropped into the booth beside him. "Oh, sorry, I wasn't thinking." She startled when he reached out one hand to stop her from moving and pulled her back down beside him.

"Your first instinct was better. Are you okay? You seem . . . distracted."

"I'm fine." She forced a smile even as she questioned her brother's uncanny ability to make her feel disloyal to Landon. While the man sitting next to her in the booth looked a whole lot like the publisher, he was much freer with his comments and emotions. Both men were attentive, sensitive to her needs, possessed a quick wit and a good sense of humor. Not to mention drop-dead handsome. Since she *was* on a little holiday, why not go with it and enjoy the male attention for once in her life?

Cooper nudged her shoulder. "If you don't perk up soon, I may be forced to break that pact just to put a silly grin on your face."

"When do I ever have a silly grin?" She hesitated. "Do I really?"

"No sillier than mine. And when people say 'I'm fine,' it usually means the opposite. If you need to talk, I'm a good listener and not such a bad guy once you get to know me."

"I don't think you're a bad guy, Cooper." *Anything but.*

"Did Mitch call?"

Astonished, she opened her mouth to speak but closed it instead.

"That's what I thought. He's only doing his job. Don't be too hard on the guy."

This was seriously weird. Mitch sounded defensive about Landon and now Cooper was supportive of Mitch? *The world's gone crazy. Or else I am.*

The waitress came to take their orders, but they hadn't taken the time to look over the menu. "I'll have a grilled cheese on wheat and whatever soup you have," Amy said pushing the menu to the edge of the table.

"Chicken noodle okay?"

"Great, thanks. With a glass of milk, please. Skim, if you have it."

"And you, sugar?" The young waitress gave Cooper a flirtatious smile, but he didn't seem to notice as he studied the menu. She couldn't be much older than sixteen or seventeen, but it was difficult to tell beneath the layer of heavy makeup and iridescent blue eye shadow.

"Can I still order breakfast?" he asked.

The girl's pink-glossed lips curved in a seductive smile. If she batted her eyes any faster, she'd take flight. "You can order anything you want, honey."

Amy's eyes widened. Cooper's Adam's apple moved up and down in his throat but he kept his eyes trained on the menu.

"The breakfast special will be fine, thank you."

"Scrambled eggs or over easy?"

Because of the provocative way the girl asked the question, Amy gave her a withering look as Cooper finished ordering his breakfast of scrambled eggs, sausage links and an English muffin with strawberry jam.

Closing his menu, he picked up Amy's and handed both to the waitress. "Coffee with cream, too, please."

"Be right back with your coffee. And your milk," she added, tossing Amy a retaliatory glare.

"That was interesting," Amy said, trying to keep the disgust from her tone as the waitress swayed her hips and winked at a thirty-something man several tables away.

"Nothing more than a small town girl trying to liven up her day, I imagine." Cooper sat back in the booth and crossed his arms. "You're all I need to keep the day lively, and I mean that as a compliment." He caught her grin before she could hide it. "At least it brought your enchanting smile back. I've missed it." Surprising her, he planted a light kiss on the tip of her nose.

"Careful. Doesn't that violate one of your all-important road rules?"

"Nope. I never said anything about a kiss on the nose. And please stop staring at my lips. That should be one of my road rules, too, come to think of it. It's driving me kinda nuts. Your eyes are entirely too full of longing and need."

"It's nothing more than hunger," she said, feigning offense. "For food."

"You're the best ego boost I've enjoyed in a long time." His lips curled in that charming yet maddening way.

"Tell me something," she said.

"Yes, I like breakfast. I think every meal should have at least one breakfast item, preferably eggs or sausage. Or sausage and eggs."

She laughed. "Fun fact to know and tell. Question two: do you have women hitting on you like that all the time? Although in the case of our waitress, she's jail bait."

Cooper shrugged. "I don't know. Maybe. I notice it sometimes, but find it more amusing that anything else." He wiggled his brows. "Don't tell me you're jealous?"

"Don't flatter yourself."

"You need me in your life, Amy, and I'm going to prove it to you by the time you get to Houston."

Her jaw dropped. "You've set a timeframe for yourself?" Crossing her arms, she snorted. "Please tell me you're kidding."

"I never joke about important things like that. Remember, a trained engineer deals with units of measure and electrical components. We're precise, logical and some would say obsessively technical."

"Okay," she said, mulling over his words. "But from all indications, you're also a spontaneous and atypical engineer. I may regret asking this question, but what unit of measure and electrical component are you talking about? And what do either one have to do with anything?"

Waiting as the waitress set Cooper's mug of coffee on the table, Amy watched as he stirred in one creamer and one sugar. After putting the spoon on a napkin, he took a sip. "Ah, good and strong, the way I like it." Lowering his mug, he captured her gaze, holding it steady. "In terms of you and me, the unit of measure would be the amount of emotional attraction and the electrical component would be the amount of physical attraction."

Amy gulped. "I see." Gathering her thoughts, she focused on a toddler banging on a stainless steel highchair tray for a few seconds. *I know how you feel, kiddo.* Returning her gaze to his, she met those piercing blue eyes. "How about I save you some time?"

Cooper almost spit out a mouthful of coffee. Slamming down his mug, coffee sloshed over the edge as he raised his fist to his mouth, coughing. "Thrilled as I am, you'd better explain."

"I don't need whatever timeframe you've set to recognize the idea of having you in my life is more than tempting. Being completely honest here, no man has ever made me question my stand on . . . certain things . . . before marriage."

Catching his look, she frowned. "Don't overinflate that statement. I'm talking about coming on this road trip in the first place with a man I don't even know very well." Turning her head, she blew out a breath. "I must be crazy."

He took another sip of his coffee. "I was only referring to kissing, but it's good to know where you stand on the issue. You're beautifully transparent." His eyes sparkled with mischief, and he looked like he fully expected her to slap him silly. "Question for you: why *did* you come on this road trip with me?" His question sounded more curious than defensive, but it made her squirm.

Good question. Come up with something plausible to answer the man.

"Amy, let me—"

She held up one hand. "You asked a question, so give me a minute."

Drumming his fingers on the top of the table, he waited. When she frowned, he stopped. "If I may hazard a guess, I think you wanted a little adventure in your life."

"Are you implying my life is boring?"

"Not at all. I'm saying you play by the rules, and that's a good thing."

Her words to Winnie on the church steps the night before about not always wanting to do the safe thing, the right thing, flooded her mind. "I look at it more as following the Lord's leading in my life."

"So, you're saying you think the Lord's hand is in this"—he waved his hand between them—"relationship between us."

Amy slumped farther down in the booth. "I'm not sure what to think. Like you said, let's take it one step at a time." She shot him a look. "Just be thankful I spared you the whole self-righteous, abstinence speech, which I've perfected over the years, by the way." Taking a small sip of her milk, she avoided his gaze.

"Thanks for that." He chuckled. "You're refreshingly candid, Amy. I'm not quite sure what to make of you either except to say I find you enchanting. I could come up with a whole bunch of adjectives to describe you, and that's after knowing you less than twenty-four hours."

"Oh, I'm sure you'll have a whole list of adjectives before our little adventure is over."

"Don't wish it over too soon," he said. Why did he suddenly sound disgruntled?

Once their food was delivered to the table by their thankfully subdued waitress, Amy bowed her head as Cooper asked a blessing.

"Amen," she said as he ended the prayer.

"That looks like good comfort food." His tone held amusement as he slathered strawberry jam over his toast.

"It is," she said, picking up her soup spoon and dipping it in the steaming broth. She inhaled deeply and smiled. "Why do you think I ordered it?"

He stopped chewing and gave her a cockeyed grin. "Needing comfort today, are you?"

She paused with her spoon halfway to her bowl. "Do you think it's possible for us to have a conversation for one minute without irony, innuendo, teasing or—heaven forbid—flirting?" She formed an "O" with her lips accompanied by raised brows.

He laughed. "What do you say we give it our best try?"

And so, for the next thirty minutes they tried. The conversation flowed easily and she discovered they had much in common. They traded stories about their lives, steering clear of any career talk—much to Amy's delight—and discussed their fitness routines, favorite foods and pet peeves. Whenever he laughed, a number of ladies in the coffee shop looked his way. An irrational sense of satisfaction rushed through her when he paid them no mind.

His accent was intriguing, a drawl tempered with something else she couldn't define. He radiated an effortless, natural charm. Beneath the teasing persona, her road companion was a decent guy. Great guy, actually. With each passing minute, she warmed to him even more. The fortress she'd erected around her emotions was crumbling fast. If it existed in the first place.

The conversation turned more serious when he told her he invited Jesus into his heart when he was ten, in the tree house in his backyard, of all places. "I was stinking mad because I was the only kid who didn't have his father with him at the Little League end-of-the-season banquet." Cooper scratched his head and gave her a sheepish grin as he fiddled with the handle on his empty coffee mug, refilled for the third time. "He promised he'd be there, but as usual, some work thing came up at the last minute. When I got home, I threw down my glove and stomped outside and used some choice words I'd only heard but never used. Mom heard me, but she let me stew around for a while until I calmed down. Then she climbed up into the tree house and sat down beside me, Bible in hand. I think she was afraid the tree house wouldn't hold her, but it was sturdy. That's one thing Dad did right, anyway."

In his expression, Amy glimpsed the long-ago hurt in the little boy he'd once been. She put her hand in the middle of the table. Their eyes met, and he covered her hand with his, giving it a light squeeze.

"What did your Mom say?" she asked, slowly withdrawing her hand.

"She told me how God doesn't want us to harbor resentment for wrongs. It helped when she said she knew exactly how I felt." His sigh was heavy. "I know she did, in ways I probably don't want to know. As I listened to her read some favorite verses of Scripture, it really impacted me—in a way it never had before—and I wanted what she had: the kind of peace and confidence she radiated from the inside out. When I asked her about it, she said it came from Jesus." Pausing, the tautness around his eyes relaxed. "So, I started confessing all the anger about my dad and recounted every bad thing I'd thought about or done in my whole life. Mom finally stopped me and she knelt beside me as I prayed to ask Jesus into my heart."

He rubbed his hand over his jaw and gave her a cockeyed grin that tugged somewhere deep inside.

"Your mother sounds like a wonderful woman," she said. "Mitch was the one who led me to Jesus when we were barely older than toddlers." Her smile sobered and a tear escaped. "And now I'm praying my brother finds his way back." Sweeping her fingers beneath her eyes, she heaved a deep sigh. "He lost his best friend on 9/11, and for a while he blamed God. It changed him, and he became more cynical and suspicious, but he's slowly coming back around."

It was Cooper's turn to take her hand. "Glad to hear it. I'll pray for him, too."

She gave him a half-smile through watery eyes. "Thanks."

They enjoyed the rest of their meal as he told her more about his days as a college newspaper editor. From the way his eyes lit with enthusiasm, his passion was obvious.

"Why didn't you pursue a journalism career after you graduated?" she asked, finishing her sandwich and stacking the bowl on top of her empty plate.

He cocked a brow. "Who says I didn't?"

That question threw her off for a moment. "One of the TeamWork girls thought you were a globe-hopping journalist." Her eyes widened. "I know. Maybe you're an undercover reporter and go on secret missions? Was that why you were late to the wedding?"

A fleeting expression of surprise skittered in his eyes. "I've been known to write a story or two, but I was late because my flight was delayed."

Now she was being the silly one. Wiping her mouth with her napkin, she shook her head. "I'm sure you have plenty of stories to tell, but we should probably get moving now." She grabbed the check from the table and reached for her purse.

"I'll take that, thanks," Cooper said, tugging it from her grasp.

"You're doing all the driving. Surely your male pride will allow a woman to treat you."

He pulled his wallet from his back pocket and rose to his feet. "It has nothing to do with male pride, but you're not paying. Case closed." He put a generous tip on the table for their waitress and waited for her to scoot out of the booth.

Waiting at the front counter as he paid their tab, Amy observed as the bus boy cleared their table. Picking up a small card from the table, he glanced at it before tucking it in the pocket of the smock he wore over his clothes. *Hmm . . .* Lost in thought as they walked back to the car, she overheard voices nearby, angry but muffled in what sounded like a heated discussion. Picking up speed, she headed in the direction of the commotion, stopping short as she rounded the corner of the building. *What on earth?*

Chapter 22

THEIR WAITRESS WAS backed up against the red brick wall, hands behind her back, facing a couple of mangy, long-haired guys. Only a few inches from her, they appeared to be in their early-to-mid-twenties.

Cooper plowed into her from behind. "Whoa! Sorry." His hands fell to her waist, steadying her.

"My fault," Amy said under her breath. With a low growl, she ground her jaw and stomped toward them. "What do you think you're doing? Leave her alone!"

The two guys backed away a few feet. Visibly shaken, the girl cowered, her brown eyes wide and luminous. In her thin cotton uniform, she clutched her arms across her chest and shivered as she ran her hands up and down her bare arms. Without a second thought, Amy untied the fabric belt on her jacket and shrugged out of it. Moving behind the waitress, she draped it around her slender shoulders. The hurt and sadness in the girl's eyes, too world-weary for one so young, pierced her heart.

"What's your name?" she asked, not seeing a name tag as the teenager buttoned the jacket with shaking fingers.

"Tamara," one of the guys said.

Amy turned and stared them down. "You're still here?" How she'd love to smack the smug expressions off their faces. Tempting as it was, smacking wasn't a Christ-like response. *Love them and show them by example.* Unclenching her fists, she raised her chin and glared at the two guys. "Want to tell us what's going on here?"

Cooper stepped in front of the guys—boys really, now that she got a good look at them up close and personal. "I suggest you leave the lady alone." Confident. Commanding. John Wayne-like. *Impressive.*

"Ah, man, she ain't nothin' but trailer trash, anyway." The taller, mangier one waved his hand in dismissal and started to walk away.

What a horrible thing to say. Her instincts made her step closer to Tamara.

"This guy thinks he's gonna teach us a lesson," the other one taunted, standing his ground, challenge in his eyes. Amy's stomach tightened as he smacked one balled fist against his palm. Cooper could take this kid in a heartbeat, but hopefully no one would resort to violence. The first guy turned but stayed his distance.

"You're right about that," Cooper said, pushing one finger against the taunter's chest. "Back off, boys. You both need to learn some respect and manners. You never treat a woman like this and you sure don't talk about a lady in a disparaging way."

"Dis—what?" The first one scratched his head.

When she caught a glimpse of his teeth, Amy cringed, wishing she could drag him to the nearest dentist's office. Before or after she made sure he shaved and washed his hair was the question. Her eyes moved to Tamara, but the girl slumped further against the wall and avoided her gaze.

"Didn't we cross the state line?" Cooper said to her.

Amy snapped back to attention. "Yes, we did."

"You kids from Texas?" He'd taken them off-guard, and the startled looks on their faces would have been comical if the situation wasn't so serious.

"Yeah," the one said. "You stupid or something? What of it? And we ain't no kids."

"I beg to differ. If you were Texas men, you'd know how to treat a woman right. Maybe your mamas didn't teach you that lesson, but you'd best learn it now unless you want to spend a majority of your sorry lives staring at four concrete walls without the benefit of female companionship. Personally, I wouldn't recommend it."

The second kid glared at him in wide-eyed disbelief. "So, you don't wanna fight?"

Cooper's mouth twisted. "No. I guarantee you," he said, forcing him against the wall, "if we fight, you wouldn't come out on the good end. Trust me on that one."

"We're leavin' already," the kid said, raising his hands and stepping away. "You got lucky this time, Tam," he called over his shoulder as both guys sauntered in the opposite direction.

As soon as the boys took off, Tamara closed her eyes and slid down the wall. Amy rushed forward and the girl collapsed against her. Sobs rolled from her in waves. Holding her close, Amy suspected this child hadn't been held like this in a long time, if ever.

Leaning her head on Amy's shoulder, Tamara buried her face against her sweater, soaking it with mascara, glittery eye shadow and tears. Amy smoothed her hair and murmured comforting words to try and keep her calm since she seemed to hover on the edge of hysteria. Closing her eyes, she said a quiet prayer, but loud enough for Tam to hear.

"What . . . what are you . . . you doing?" Tamara sniffled, pulling back and wiping the back of her hand over one cheek and then the other. Black mascara was smudged under both puffy eyes and her cheeks were flushed.

"Saying a prayer."

"For me?"

It was difficult to tell whether her question bespoke defiance or simple curiosity.

"Yes. You seem to need it right now."

"Oh." Tamara slumped against her again, and Amy glanced at Cooper as she tightened her hold. He stood a few feet away, hands pushed deep in his pockets, appearing a bit awkward.

"Cooper, here. Take my purse." She shrugged it from her arm and dropped it to the concrete. With one foot, she kicked it across the pavement in his direction. "I have a package of tissues in there."

He shot her a skeptical look as he picked up the purse. "That's breaking a cardinal rule. My mama told me never to open a woman's purse. Under any circumstances. Never. Very bad thing."

Amy rolled her eyes. Tamara stopped sniffling and stared at him.

"Normally, that's true," she said, "but I have nothing to hide. I give you permission, so do it. Please." She gave him a smile to sweeten the request.

"Do you need a ride somewhere?" Cooper asked Tamara after she blew her nose and dabbed at her eyes. Her smeared eye shadow made her look more bedraggled and haggard. She shook her head, not answering. Shuddering again in the chilly air, she wrapped her arms across her middle.

"Here. Let me help clean you up a little." Taking one of the tissues Cooper handed her, Amy used a gentle touch, dabbing at Tamara's eyelids and then on the delicate area beneath both her eyes. It was impossible to remove all traces of the eye makeup, but as she worked, Amy revealed her clear skin. *Beneath it all, she's only a vulnerable, hurting kid.*

"Why are you being so nice to me?" Tamara sniffled and stared into the distance. "Why do you care? Because it's almost Christmas? Is this your good deed for the day?"

Amy's heart sank at the heavy sarcasm in the girl's voice. "You looked like you needed a little help, and a friend."

"I don't have any friends, and you don't want to be one neither." Her frown grew deeper.

"That's not true, but in order to have friends, you need to be one, too. It works both ways." Balling the tissue, Amy tossed it toward her purse. Out of the corner of her eye, she saw Cooper throw it in the nearby dumpster and then lean against the brick wall, watching them.

"Surely you have girlfriends you can talk to at school," Amy said.

"I dropped out."

Amy tried not to show her surprise. "How old are you, Tamara?"

"Almost seventeen. And call me Tam."

Tam's brown eyes were less defiant and filled with something more like defeated resignation. "Care to tell us what that little scene was all about? Why were those guys hassling you?"

"I don't owe you any explanations."

"True enough, but if you want to talk, I'll listen."

"You don't know nothing about my life. Look at you," Tam said, waving her hand up and down in front of her. "Dressed in your fancy clothes. You probably have a nice car that's not patched together and you pray it gets you to the end of the street much less to work. A high-paying job with meetings and power lunches. Friends with lots of money and country club memberships. A family who cares . . ." Her voice faded and Amy saw the tears behind the wounded words before Tam's wet eyes focused on her. "You've seen me in action." She looked over at Cooper. He shifted his position and shoved his hands in the pockets of his jeans again but remained expressionless. "I got a little too friendly, that's all," she said with a shrug. "Those guys . . . they kind of expected something. It's nothing. I'm used to it."

Amy sucked in a quick breath. *Lord, give me the right words.* "I buy my clothes at sample shops, I don't own a car and my job pays lousy but I love it. Some of my friends have money and others don't have much at all, and my family is great. The way I look at it, everything I have is a blessing. The family I was born into wasn't my choice, but what I do with my life *is* my choice. You can have what you want, too, but God expects you to work for it. He never said it was easy. The things I had to work hard for—and the sacrifices I've had to make—make achieving and earning certain things more precious."

"I'm not easy," Tam said, the defiance back full-force.

"I didn't say you are. I meant *life's* not easy." Putting both hands on her slender shoulders, Amy forced the girl's eye contact. "Here's the thing, Tam. You can't flirt with every good looking guy. You don't know the kinds of people that are out there, the kinds of things that can happen. Yes, there's a lot of very good people—good men—but you have to be able to see the difference. You can't go around putting yourself out there and tempting them or it'll eventually get you into serious trouble. You need to learn how to tell the difference. It's something called discernment, and I'm going to pray you find it. Sooner rather than later. If you ask God, He'll help you."

"You sound smart and all, but I don't really believe in God."

"Well, God believes in *you*." Amy could tell she'd caught her attention. The "really" in her statement gave her a little wiggle room. "Are your parents around?"

Tam shrugged. "Mom works all the time and my stepdad's usually drunk or else hitting on her."

Amy's heart ached and she swallowed the hard lump in her throat. "Does he hit *you*?"

The girl shook her head. "Nah. I think he knows if he did, I'd hit him right back."

"Do you have anyone you can talk to? A friend?" She motioned to the restaurant. "A lady who works here, maybe? In case things get too tough at home, you need someone you can confide in or at least someplace you can go where you know you'll be safe."

"Not really. I mean, yeah, there's one nice lady named Kaye, but she's got enough kids and grandkids of her own to take care of. She doesn't need me hanging around."

Retrieving her purse from the ground, Amy reached inside and pulled out the small case with her business cards. "Here. Take this." She handed one to her. Taking it, the girl scanned it before meeting her eyes again. "I want you to call me if you need anything. Anytime. Anywhere. If there's a way I can help you, I will, but you have to let me know, okay?"

From the corner of her eye, she caught the skepticism written in Cooper's expression from where he still leaned against the brick wall, arms crossed, watching them.

Tam frowned and half-nodded. "Thanks." She glanced down at the card she held in her hand. "Amy."

"God's given you unique and wonderful gifts, Tam."

The girl's eyes grew rounder. "Really? What gifts do you think I have?"

"You're smart and resourceful. Anyone can tell that much. You've got so much to look forward to, so much to see and do." She smiled and made sure she had Tam's eye contact. "Beneath all that makeup is a very pretty girl, but you need to use discernment and make the most of the opportunities God hands you. Then, you'll be able to really shine."

"Thanks," the girl mumbled, her lower lip trembling. She looked on the verge of crying again and caught her breath as she looked up at her with tearful eyes. Straightening up, she squared her shoulders and ran a hand over her rumpled uniform, smoothing it.

"Do you need a ride somewhere?" Amy asked.

Tam shook her head. "No. I was on my break and they're probably looking for me. I hope I'm not in trouble. Can't afford to lose this job. I was only supposed to have twenty minutes, but I don't know how long I've been out here. Longer than twenty minutes, I reckon." Starting to walk away, she paused and began to unbutton her jacket. "Sorry. Here's your jacket."

"Keep it. Besides, it looks better on you than me."

Tugging the jacket closer about her, Tam nodded. "Thanks." She started toward the corner and paused. "Amy?"

"Yes?"

"Merry Christmas." Her glance included Cooper. Coming back over to her, she leaned close. "He's really fine."

Amy smiled but hoped he couldn't hear Tam's words or read her lips. "Tone down the flirting. You don't want to invite trouble. Save it for the right man. He'll come along at the perfect time in your life, but you want to be there waiting for him when he walks through the door."

She could tell Tam listened but she turned the corner and disappeared from view without another word.

Moving behind her in a flash, Cooper lowered his suede jacket onto her shoulders. With gentle hands, he turned her around to face him, bringing the jacket together in the front, his eyes never leaving hers. "I'm breaking the pact." His lips met hers in a kiss more sweet than passionate, perfect for the moment and her jumbled emotions.

"In case you haven't noticed, I don't always play by the rules either. We lasted all of what? Five hours?" She laughed a little and brushed away a tear.

"You don't know how glad I am about that." He released his hold on her. "More like four hours and thirty-four minutes. Shall we get back on the road to Austin now?"

"I'd say so. We've had enough excitement."

He grinned. "Be careful what you wish for."

Chapter 23

"THAT WAS A beautiful thing you did back there." As he opened the car door and Amy climbed inside, Landon noticed she shivered. After starting the engine, he cranked up the heat. "Austin or bust." He drove a couple of blocks toward the interstate and glanced her way. Her shoulders shook, her head turned toward the window.

"Amy?" She didn't answer but fumbled with her purse on her lap.

"Are you crying?"

"No," she said, her voice small. When a sob escaped, she clamped a hand over her mouth.

He pulled into a deserted parking lot and stopped the car. Not knowing how to help her, he watched, feeling as helpless as he had back at the restaurant. The woman beside him wore her heart on her sleeve, and he loved her desire to help others in tangible ways. She possessed a depth of compassion he rarely glimpsed. Stuck in the confines of the car, and with freezing temperatures outside, he struggled with two immediate options: pull her close and comfort her or huddle in his seat like a stoic coward.

He glanced at her purse. "Do I have your permission?" When she nodded, he reached for it, thankful the package of tissues sat near the top of her bag. Plucking one out, he handed it to her. Accepting it with a grateful smile, she dabbed at her eyes as a few tears streamed down her cheeks.

"I'm sorry," she said in between sniffles. "I don't cry often, but I feel so bad for Tam and girls like her. Did you see the emptiness in her eyes when she said she didn't have any friends? She's only a lonely child without anyone to care for her, so she turns to men for affection and mistakes it for true love." She sniffled again. "That's one of the saddest things I can imagine."

When she turned those beautiful eyes on him, something inside shifted. A pale yet brilliant green, they'd never looked more intense, sparked by deep emotion. They also held a question, as if she hoped he'd have the answers for the world's problems.

"You demonstrated love to Tam and fulfilled a physical need," he said. "She's a lost kid, but hopefully she'll wake up and realize not everyone's out to take something from her."

Her shoulders still shook and she lowered her head to her hands. "I'm sorry. You can start driving, if you want."

"No way I'm going to leave now." Not sure what she wanted him to do, he sat back and waited, feeling helpless yet resisting the urge to pull her into his arms and hold on tight.

"Please?" she asked, her voice muffled.

When a few more seconds passed, she tilted her head, indicating she needed him to come closer. Reaching for her, he brought her to him, as close as possible within the confines of the car's bucket seats. Smoothing her hair away from her eyes, he kissed her forehead and leaned his head against hers. "Let it out. Whatever you need." At his words, she sobbed even harder. His heart swelled as she cried in his arms, and a strong, foreign urge to shelter and protect this woman flooded through him. He was glad she was comfortable enough to cling to him and share her hurt, but with every passing moment, he felt like the worst kind of scum for not revealing his true identity. With her so upset, it sure wasn't the right moment now. Problem was, would that moment ever come? As compassionate as Amy was, she was also feisty and wouldn't tolerate dishonesty.

"I get pretty emotional with stuff like this. You might as well know that now."

"I knew you were beautiful, but now I can add words like stubborn." He tipped her chin and waited until she met his gaze. "Feisty, fearless, loyal, kind and unbelievably compassionate."

"You're saying some really nice things to me—about me—all of a sudden.

He eased into a grin. "Stick around, sweetheart."

"Don't call me sweetheart. Please." Turning her head, she pulled out of his arms and glanced back at the restaurant, closing her eyes.

As soon as she left his arms, he experienced a loneliness that shocked him. *Lord, help me. I'm already falling hard for her. Forgive me for deceiving her.* Knowing she prayed, it drew him to her more. And pierced his heart to its core.

~

Another hour down the road—spent in relative quiet—Amy yawned and struggled to sit up straighter. A flash of yellow-gold caught her attention in a field. From what she could tell, it was a golden retriever. Why was the dog running abandoned on this deserted stretch of highway? "Cooper, pull over. *Now.*" Placing one hand on his arm, she twisted in her seat, craning her neck as she stared out the back window.

Easing his foot off the accelerator, he pumped the brake and edged off the highway onto the slightly-sloped shoulder. Gravel crunched beneath the tires as he stopped the car. "Are you sick or something?"

"Or something." After flinging the passenger door wide, Amy scooted out and sprinted into the open field, releasing puffs of air as she ran. At least the terrain was flat and the weeds weren't high, allowing a wide range of visibility. *Please don't let there be any strange creatures anywhere around here.* Thinking about the possibility of a personal encounter with snakes or armadillos—anything other than a dog or cat—made her cringe.

"Amy!" Cooper called from behind. "What are you doing? Promise I'll gargle at the next stop!"

The crispness in the early afternoon air was refreshing, and she'd never been so thankful she'd stepped up her recent workouts. Catching another glimpse of her target, she headed east, easing into her stride, praying she wouldn't stumble. At least the dog had veered away from the highway. "There she is!" Pointing as she ran, not stopping or looking over her shoulder, she heard the pounding of his boots on the ground behind her.

As she closed the distance between her and the dog, Amy slowed to a fast walk. "Here, girl!" She slapped one hand on her thigh. A hard shiver ran through her, but it wasn't as much the cold as fear for this beautiful creature running wild. "Come here, Lassie," she said, employing her most soothing tone. "What a gorgeous girl you are." Stopping, she caught her breath and projected her voice to carry across the field. "Come see me, pretty girl, and I'll give you a special treat."

Cooper stopped beside her, hands on his hips, breathing heavily. "Thanks for the workout, but Lassie? Really?"

"Please don't mock me."

"Have you ever *had* a dog, Amy? That's probably an insult."

"Rin Tin Tin, then. Toto. Cujo. Whatever."

"Did you know Lassie was supposed to be a girl, but only male dogs played the role—if you can call it that—because their coats were thicker and looked better on camera? Not to mention males are bigger and it took longer for child actors to outgrow—"

She rolled her eyes and moved her hands to her hips. "You're just a walking encyclopedia, aren't you? Keep your facts to yourself. I have a dog to round up here."

"I'm here to help."

Cooper followed as she moved forward, being careful to be as nonthreatening as possible. Above all, she didn't want to spook the dog.

"Sure. Hand me one of those granola bars you've got stashed in your jacket," she said.

"How'd you know . . ."

"Hand it over." Amy held out her hand while keeping one eye on the dog. "It's been sticking out of the top of your pocket most of the day." The dog sat on the hard ground, panting, brown eyes wide.

Digging into the ground with the toe of his boot, Cooper handed over one of the bars. "I'm sure you have a plan. So, where do you suggest we take her . . . or him?"

"This dog's definitely a female."

"I thought females aren't as predisposed to running away as males."

Amy shot him a quick glance. "Depends on the company she keeps, I'm sure."

"Tell you what. Let me handle this one." Walking in the dog's direction, Cooper pulled out another granola bar. "Ten to one I'll have her in my arms in ten seconds or less."

She grunted and stalked after him. "I never wager, but I imagine that's pretty much a personal challenge for you around any female, isn't it?"

Halting his progress, he turned back toward her with a slow, easy smile. "Jealous?"

"Keep walking."

"I don't believe it. You're jealous."

"Of a dog? That's absurd, and you're overly competitive." She watched as he approached the dog, stooping at even level as he outstretched his hand, offering the granola bar. Although she couldn't hear his words, Cooper murmured sweet enticements. Within three seconds, the dog was eating out of the man's hand. *Traitor.*

"Can you come over here and get a good grip on her collar?" he asked.

Amy's boots crunched on the hard, cold ground. "She sure is a beauty, isn't she?"

His eyes shifted to hers as she stooped low and curled her fingers around the well-made leather collar. "Yeah, she is, but I doubt she knows it."

She led herself right into that one. "Not very original, mister." Amy leaned closer and inspected the collar. "What do you know?"

"Something interesting?"

"This collar was sold through a chain of leather stores here in Texas owned by Dean Costas, one of the TeamWork guys. He was at the wedding. Lives outside of San Antonio."

"Eliot's buddy? Nice guy. Quiet. It's interesting how so many different people from all different walks of life and from all parts of the country are involved with TeamWork." He paused until she looked up at him. "Isn't it?"

She averted her gaze, but her pulse picked up speed.

"Amy?"

"Hmm?" She bent close, studying the dog's tags. "Cooper, meet Anson." She smoothed one hand over the shiny, clean coat. "She's obviously not a stray. Poor baby must have wandered away."

"With a name like Anson, she probably belongs to some yuppie couple in the suburbs."

She laughed. "Suburbs? Right, of Nowhereville?" Leaning forward, she kissed the side of the dog's nose and ruffled behind her ears. Leaning into her touch, Anson's long, pink tongue emerged again. "Don't be scared, sweet baby. We'll take good care of you."

Rising to her feet, Amy surveyed their surroundings. "I'd say it's time to move her to the car. There's a phone number for a veterinarian on her tag, but unless you have your phone, mine's in the car. Hopefully, we can reach someone who can tell us where to take her." Cooper didn't budge. "Fine." She shifted Anson and slid both arms beneath her. Gritting her teeth, she bent her knees and started to lift the dog.

"You're too impatient. Give a guy a half-second, will you? Allow me." Coming around to the other side of Anson, Cooper scooped her in his arms in one swift movement and headed toward the car. "Do you attract this much trouble everywhere you go?"

She huffed. "Usually. It's one of my primary goals in life. It would be unconscionable to leave this beautiful dog roaming alone out here. Someone's bound to be looking for her."

"No doubt. I need you to open the door for me. The car key's in my right front pocket." Anson squirmed as Cooper halted beside the car; he hugged the cumbersome canine closer to his chest. "The sooner the better. This girl's pretty heavy."

"Okay, but not a word out of you." Feeling awkward, Amy reached into the front pocket of his jeans and quickly pulled out the key. She unlocked the door and watched as he lowered Anson to the backseat.

"Hop in," he said, angling his head. "Let's keep Anson between us while we figure out what to do so she'll be less inclined to lead us on another chase."

"I don't think she's going anywhere. She's pretty tuckered out, aren't you girl?" Doing as he asked, she climbed in the car. Amy stroked the top of the dog's head. "I'll call the vet. Can I borrow your phone? Mine's in my purse up front."

"It's in my overnight bag." His tone sounded a bit wary. What did he have to be nervous about? Climbing out of the car, he was back in less than thirty seconds. "Give me the number, and I'll call."

As she read the number from the tag, Cooper dialed. A few seconds later, listening, he frowned. "It's an answering machine." His frown deepened. "I'll leave a message and pray Dr. Patsy checks and answers her messages on Sundays." After leaving his name and the basic facts, he disconnected. "I say we give her ten minutes to call back and then we find the local police station or state trooper's office."

"Okay, sounds like a plan," Amy said. "Thanks for being a good sport about this."

"Wouldn't miss it. Ever had a dog?" He stroked the retriever's thick fur.

"We had a couple growing up, both labs, one yellow and one chocolate. And we had one cat. You?"

"A few dogs, all mutts. They're more affectionate, I think. I'm not home much now, so it wouldn't be fair to a poor dog. My parents have one. Goes by the name of Buster." He chuckled and scratched behind Anson's ear. "Buster sure knows how to make a guy feel loved and appreciated."

If he was expecting a comeback, Cooper wasn't getting one from her. She was content to sit and watch him with Anson. The dog brought out the softer, more gentle side of him, one she liked very much.

"Want me to turn on the car for warmth?" he said.

His question startled her from her thoughts. "I'm warm enough for the moment. Besides, I can always cuddle with Anson."

Surprising her, he started to sing. Warble was more like it. "I'm sittin' in the backseat with a beautiful girl and a big old dog between us on a cold December day. Startin' a romance made in Texas Heaven. What a thrill it is for this heart of mine." He paused, laughing, and started in again, exaggerating his crooning. Closing his eyes, he moved one hand over his heart. "Her love and this old dog'll keep me warm all the rest of my days."

Amy listened to his nonsensical lyrics and meandering country tune—complete with an affected twang—and burst into laughter. "Shhh," she said when Anson startled. "It's okay, girl. Cooper's being silly, but beneath that flippant exterior, he's a pretty good guy and means well."

"It was the first thing I could think of to keep us entertained."

"Mission accomplished. Of course, if it was a legitimate country song, you'd make mention of heartbreak, beer, a horse or a pickup truck and somebody done wrong."

He laughed. "As opposed to what, an illegitimate country song? To my knowledge, that's what half of them are about, anyway. Not that they don't have their place."

When the corners of Cooper's eyes crinkled, Amy's breath caught in her throat. *He looks so much like Landon right now.* It was enough to drive a girl batty. She couldn't help but wonder how the other man would react to the situation with Tam and now with a runaway dog. Lost in her thoughts, she jumped when his phone rang.

"Hi, Dr. Patsy. Thanks for calling back." He listened and nodded a few times. "Right. We found her on the side of the highway. Tags with your phone number and the name Anson. Where are we, Amy? Can you see that next mile marker?" He pointed toward the front window.

She squinted against the sun's glare and gave him the number. After he repeated it, his eyes grew wide. "Yes, ma'am. We'll find it. Thanks a lot. Lord willing, we'll see you in a few minutes." Shoving the cell phone in his pocket, Cooper slid out of the backseat and slammed the door. In lightning speed, he hopped behind the wheel and started the engine. "Strap yourself in and keep one hand on Anson."

"What's the emergency?" Amy half-laughed but did as he asked. Feeling playful, she couldn't resist teasing him. "Don't trust yourself in the backseat of a car with me?"

"Yeah right," he said, buckling in and pulling back onto the road. "I had my chance but restrained myself, if you noticed. Maybe another time."

Her eyes grew wide and she held onto Anson as they both slid across the seat, leaning to the left as Cooper made an illegal U-turn in the middle of the highway. She gulped as he floored the accelerator, headed in the opposite direction. "I pray a state trooper didn't witness that," she mumbled under her breath, burying her face in the soft, sweet-smelling fur of Anson's neck. At least the dog seemed calm. Amy raised her head as the car accelerated. "If you're auditioning for the Indy 500, don't bother. No one's out here to clock your speed."

"As I suspected—but didn't want to alarm you—this dog's about to give birth, Miss Dog Rescuer. Since I don't want to pay a whopping fee for cleanup of this rental car, I'm getting Anson to Dr. Patsy as fast as humanly possible."

No comeback came to Amy's mind. "Carry on, then. To Dr. Patsy's!"

Cooper glanced at her in the rearview mirror, his eyes meeting hers for a split second. "Like I said, you invite trouble."

"Admit it. You love it."

"Didn't say I didn't."

Although he drove fast, he was a skillful driver. *Thank you, Lord.* Amy continued to soothe Anson and they both stayed quiet. A few minutes later, he pulled into the driveway of a small, one-story white clapboard house. The sign out front read Patsy's Vet & Pet Care. Stopping the car, Cooper opened the back door and swept the dog in his arms. He shoved the door closed with one knee and headed up the walkway.

Grabbing her purse, Amy scrambled out of the car and followed him. Before they reached the front door, it opened and a kindly, middle-aged blonde woman wearing oversized glasses and a white coat with DR. PATSY embroidered inside a red heart, welcomed them.

"I can't tell you how thankful I am you called. Please bring her right back here." She led them down a hallway and into an adjacent room then gestured for Cooper to put Anson on a table. "I need to examine her and then we'll let nature take its course. Interested in a puppy, folks?" She pulled on protective gloves and gave them a bright smile and a wink. "A nice young couple like you could give one of them a good home. Good experience before having a little one of your own."

Amy grunted and looked the other way. "We're not . . ." She closed her mouth.

"They're purebred and show quality. Worth a fair price, and I'd give you one in exchange for your kind efforts."

"Thanks, Doc, but we're not in the market for a puppy yet, are we sweetums?" Cooper glanced at his watch. "As a matter of fact, we need to get back on the road now since we're supposed to be in Austin sometime today."

"I know her owners will be extremely grateful for your kindness," Dr. Patsy said. "If you want to leave your names and contact information, there might be a reward in it for you."

"Knowing Anson's safe and where she belongs is all the reward we need. Thanks."

"Merry Christmas to you both." Patsy turned her attention back to Anson. "I'll let you find your way out, if you don't mind."

"Of course. Take care, Anson. Come on, honey." Draping one arm around Amy's shoulder, Cooper steered her down the hallway and out the front door.

"Honey?" Amy couldn't stop her grin as he closed the front door behind them. Her giggle escaped.

Cooper chuckled as they walked to the car. "I like 'sweetums' better. People seem to think we're a couple, anyway, so I figured why not go with it? The thought keeps me all warm and toasty inside." He ushered her into the car.

"I'm exhausted or I'd offer to drive," she said, leaning against the headrest as he started the car. "Are you okay?"

"Just great." He gave her one of his infectious grins. How easily she could get used to them—all shiny with straight white teeth. Plus an honest-to-goodness twinkle in those blue eyes and what she suspected was more than a hint of mischief.

Chapter 24

"SO, TELL ME what a lovely young journalist from New York City wants for Christmas."

"I haven't had time to think about it, but I really don't need anything. Certainly not from a man I don't know very well."

He snorted. "To be clear, I asked what you wanted, not what you needed. And while it's true we haven't known each other long, we've already shared some unique experiences. I'd venture to say you know me better than a lot of dates you've had. Am I right?"

She pushed herself farther up on the seat. "Now you're suggesting I date men I barely know?"

"No, are you?"

Closing her eyes, she counted to three. Opening them, she found his eyes on her. "Are you trying to get us killed here? Eyes back on the road, please."

"You caught me in a moment of weakness. I'm sure you give gifts all the time to people you don't know, have never met and will never meet."

"What kinds of gifts are we talking here?"

"The gift of time, for one. You help build houses with TeamWork, and I imagine you help out at your church in some volunteer capacity—Sunday school, kids' ministries, nursery, Bible study."

"I try to help where there's a need," she said.

"That's the best kind of gift. I can think of one thing you'll need."

She shot him a curious glance. "What's that?"

"If you're not too tired tonight, I'd like to take you to the mall."

"It's Sunday, remember. They'll be closed."

"Oh, right. What time do stores normally open on Monday?"

"Depends on whether you're talking about a drugstore, a twenty-four hour supermarket or a department store."

"Somewhere nice. One thing I'm not is cheap," he said. He sounded a tad defensive. "Discount stores are fine and dandy when I need antifreeze or fishing equipment. Although," he said, darting a glance her way, "thawing and reeling is a pretty good idea right about now."

She smirked. "Don't get your feelings all twisted in a snit. I wasn't implying you're cheap, but I'm not touching the rest of that statement with a proverbial ten-foot pole."

He angled his head in her direction. "Touché. You're a quick study, but you still didn't answer the question."

"I think the department stores open by ten, but you really don't—"

"Then we'll go tomorrow morning. Humor me. This is something I'd really like to do for you."

"I have absolutely no idea what you're talking about, but since I'm more or less at your whims or mercy, I suppose I don't have a choice."

"You always have a choice, Amy. Remember, my mama told me a woman has the right to say no to anything." He gave her chin a quick tap before returning his focus to the highway. "You can't get respect if you don't first give it. Most importantly, when a woman says no, you respect her wishes."

"Your mother is a very wise woman. In all honesty, I imagine it'd be hard for most women to say no to you regarding most anything." Maybe she shouldn't have said it, but it was true. *Can you ever learn to hold your tongue?*

"Sounds like a backhanded compliment. Are you including yourself in the 'most women' category."

"Of course not."

He laughed. "Didn't think so, but a guy can hope. Like I said, nothing comes easy with you. There is one exception to the rule."

Something stirred inside her. "Do I want to know?" Amy stared straight ahead, her mind racing. Trying to guess what he'd say at any given moment kept her on some weird kind of adrenaline rush but it was also exhausting.

His brow furrowed. "Sorry. It's not the right time for this discussion."

"You brought it up." Now she really wanted to know.

"I'll tell you when the time is right."

She nodded. "I'll trust you to know when that is since I have no clue what you're talking about."

"You've got a deal."

He exaggerated his drawl, and she couldn't resist her smile. Nestling further into the seat, Amy closed her eyes. He'd stolen her breath . . . again. She liked this man she barely knew. Liked him a whole lot more than she should. Worse, perhaps, she trusted him and was in serious danger of the very thing she feared for her brother—surrendering her heart too easily and too quickly. Her greatest fear? The barriers she'd tried to build to keep him out of her heart were tumbling by the wayside, faster than a stack of children's blocks.

~

Sipping hot chocolate during a short break, Amy savored the flavor, watered-down though it was. Dispensed from a vending machine in the otherwise abandoned rest stop, it was scalding hot. Curling her fingers around the cup, she inhaled the steam, thankful for the warmth. With the sun dipping lower on the horizon every minute, the temperatures had dropped fast. Adjusting Cooper's jacket on her shoulders, she absently glanced over the display of colorful tourist brochures. Stifling a yawn, she was glad they'd soon be in Austin—a little over an hour away. A hot shower and a warm bed never sounded so inviting.

"Ready?"

Amy startled from her daydreaming to see Cooper already by the door, one hand poised on it. "Coming." They walked in silence to the car.

"Everything okay?" he asked after helping her inside and sliding behind the wheel.

"Appreciating your good manners. If I ever meet your mama, I'll have to thank her."

"Thank you."

"That's all you have to say?" Surely the man had another comeback.

"Shh. I'm relishing the compliment." He turned the key in the ignition several times. Nothing. After trying a few more times with no response, he hit one fist on the steering wheel in what seemed like a rare display of anger. "I don't believe this." Closing his eyes, he leaned his head back on the seat and exhaled.

Stay calm. Another adventure. Amy stole a glance, but his eyes were still closed. "Um, Cooper, are you praying, cursing under your breath, power napping or thinking?"

He opened his eyes. "Figuring out the next move with a good dose of prayer on the side."

"At least you can't blame this one on me."

"Of course not. I guess it's time to call the rental car company. The contract's in my overnight bag. Be right back." A minute later, he leaned against the side of the car, and she heard him speaking.

Frowning, Amy hopped out of the car and shrugged out of the jacket. His eyes held a question as she draped it around his broad shoulders, but she glimpsed the gratitude in his expression.

He covered the phone with his hand. "Go back inside and stay warm. I'll be there in a minute."

Five minutes later, Cooper strode into the small building. If the tautness in his expression didn't warn her of his disgruntled mood, the set of his jaw and hunched shoulders did.

"Should I ask?"

"Not if you want the answer," Cooper said. "Sorry." His eyes were lined and heavy; he rubbed a quick hand over his brow.

Amy brushed dark hair off his forehead and glimpsed the scar. With one finger, she traced its outline. "How did this happen?"

"Teenage foolishness. I flipped on a motorbike and hit the ground running." His gaze softened as she removed her hand. "Okay, here's the situation. There's nothing the rental car company can do since we're in the middle of Nowhereville, Texas on a Sunday. They advised me not to tinker with the car since it's a rental and trying to repair it would violate the terms of use agreement."

"You're saying we're stuck?" Amy bit her tongue not to whine. She'd never been one to do it before—although she'd had plenty of circumstances to warrant it—and she wasn't about to start now. "Isn't it their contractual obligation to either remedy the situation or make amends in some way?"

"They're sending a driver, and he'll take us wherever we want within a twenty-mile radius. Plus they're refunding the full rental fee." Cooper shrugged. "At least it's something."

"They can't send another rental car?"

"They don't have one available anywhere near here until sometime tomorrow."

Might as well accept it and move forward. Complaining wouldn't get them any closer to Austin. "So, what do you suggest?"

"Since it's pretty clear we're not going to make it to Austin until sometime tomorrow morning at the earliest, the most pressing need is finding a place to lay our heads for the night. Let's pray there's a motel within twenty miles."

Crossing to a nearby bench, Amy plopped on it and hugged her arms over her chest. "What if there's not?"

Cooper dropped down on the bench. "Where's that positive, optimistic spirit I love?" Leaning close, he nudged her shoulder.

"I'm afraid it's gone missing. I'm trying my best not to venture into whine territory here—that's w-h-i-n-e."

He chuckled. "Oh, I don't know. A glass of w-i-n-e doesn't sound so bad right now."

"I'm sure we don't need to go far to find you a watering hole." Amy laughed when he elbowed her.

"Don't worry. There'll be no imbibing tonight. I need all my faculties and wits about me."

"This day keeps getting better, doesn't it?" she said.

A grin curled his lips. "That's one way to look at it. It's also what God's given us, so we might as well accept it."

"Maybe you could call your parents or a friend in Austin to come out here—wherever we are—and get us? We're not that far away, are we?"

"You want total honesty? I'm beginning to really like the idea of being stranded with you, especially since the original purpose of this trip was to get to know each other better. I was going to get you a room in one of Austin's best hotels, but given our current circumstances, what's the difference whether you're in an Austin hotel room . . . or somewhere else?"

"Are you absolutely positive that car won't start?"

Reaching into the pocket of his jeans, he pulled out the rental car key and dangled it in front of her. "Be my guest if you don't believe me."

Amy shook her head, frowning. "That won't be necessary."

Stretching out his legs, he leaned against the wall beside her, shoulders touching. "If you'd be kind enough to watch for a white van, I'm going to try and grab a little shut-eye."

"Sure. Here," she said, guiding his head to her shoulder. Then she thought better of it. "That's probably not comfortable."

"I'm not going to bypass one of God's opportunities." Adjusting his position, Cooper smiled.

The silkiness of his hair was irresistible and Amy ruffled her fingers through it before running them over his scalp in a light, circular pattern. Her mother used to do the same thing for her when she was tired.

"Mmm . . . that's nice."

Her shoulder started to ache not long after, but no way was she going to move or shift him. Something about such a strong man giving up control for even a minute proved he trusted her. Soon, she felt the rise and fall of his breathing and the steady rhythm of his heartbeat.

Amy felt the blood drain from her face. *Lord, I don't know much about this man, but I trust him. Problem is, should I?* "But I trust You," she said under her breath. Stealing a kiss on the small scar on Cooper's forehead, she leaned her head against his.

Chapter 25

WITHIN A HALF hour, a white van pulled in front of the rest area. It had to be their ride since no one else was around. Tapping him on the arm, Amy kept her voice low. "Cooper. Wake up. The van's here."

He ran a hand over his eyes. "Thanks. Let me talk with the driver first. Wait here, and I'll be right back." A couple of minutes later, he returned and retrieved their bags. Chivalry was alive and well in Nowhereville, Texas.

Gathering her purse, Amy hurried outside as Cooper loaded their cases onto the van. Offering his hand, he assisted her on the steps. A rush of hot air blasted her as she took a seat in the middle. "Whew, from one extreme to the other." After thanking the driver, she scooted over to make room for him. When he climbed in beside her, she was more aware of him than she wanted.

He leaned close, keeping his voice low. "By the way, there's only one motel in a twenty-mile radius."

I will not complain. I will accept my circumstances with a good attitude. "Fine. As long as it's got a bed and a hot shower, I don't care." When she spied his quirked brow, she stifled a groan. "It's one of those seedy, by-the-hour places, isn't it?" *So much for positivity.*

"Not for us, it's not."

Not sure how to respond, she focused on the nothingness passing by outside the van. She yawned a few times and felt her lids growing heavier every second.

"Come here." Moving one arm around her, he nestled her close. "My turn. You were there for me, and it's time to repay the favor. Lean on me."

She gave him a grateful smile. "Don't mind if I do. Thanks." Snuggling against his shoulder, she gave into the temptation to catch a few minutes of rest. He smelled so good, all masculine, and he was warm. "I can hear your heartbeat."

"Then you know how fast it's beating with you in this position." His hold on her shoulder tightened. "Don't think of moving."

A half hour later, after talking with the desk clerk at the motel, Cooper took her by the elbow and led her back outside. The van driver had already departed and their bags stood in the small lobby. "Why are we outside? I realize it was hotter than a sauna in that van and this actually feels good after that inferno, but—"

"I wanted you outside when you scream. At least it'll muffle the sound."

"You'd better explain." She tapped her foot in an impatient rhythm on the concrete walkway. She'd done that a lot when in this man's presence. "Let me guess. There's no room at the inn?"

He shook his head back and forth, but the corners of his mouth twisted.

"Just spit it out, whatever it is." She stopped her foot and stared. "Don't tell me this fleabag motel doesn't have a vacancy." Aware her voice rose, she didn't bother mincing words or trying to be quiet.

"Oh, they have a vacancy all right, but there's only one room available."

"What?"

"You heard me. Come on, let me escort you." Going inside the small lobby, he picked up their bags and headed back out and down the sidewalk. "We're looking for Room 116." He stopped. "Are you coming?"

"Of all the stupid clichés," she sputtered, glancing around the parking lot as she followed him. "I don't see a hubbub of activity around here, so it makes no sense."

"According to the manager, they're currently doing renovations and not many rooms are available right now."

"Well, *that* makes more sense." Her words came out more a mutter and she coached herself to be more upbeat, calling on the inner cheerleader she'd been in school. "I guess there's nothing else we can do but make the best of it, right? And thanks for carrying my bag."

"That's my girl. I mean, that's the spirit," Cooper said, his voice wry. "I hope you know I had no idea any of this would happen. It's not like I planned it."

"Of course not." Amy's stomach rumbled, reminding her it'd been hours since their last meal. Cooper must be starving, too, for more breakfast food or whatever. "I hope there's a place to eat around here that's open. Vending machine food doesn't sound very appealing. Unless you've got more granola bars stashed in your bag."

"I'll ask the clerk. There's bound to be a local pizza or hamburger joint, but I have a few granola bars left if we get desperate. Or we can save them for a quick breakfast."

When they reached the room, they discovered it only had one bed—a double. Her brows rose. "I suppose you didn't know about this either?"

"That there's only one bed? Call me silly, but I assumed there were two doubles. I can always get some extra linens and sleep in the bathtub."

"I'll call and see if they have any cots." Dropping onto the bed, she ran one hand through her hair, fighting the strong urge to cry a steady stream of tears if not a full-on, sobbing gush. "I'm trying to make the best of this situation. Give me a minute." She surveyed the room through narrowed eyes.

"Let me make sure the heat works before we settle in." Fiddling with the dials on the thermostat control, Cooper switched it on. Within a few seconds, she heard the sputtering and rattling of the heating unit. She almost laughed when he said, "I guess that means it's working?"

Amy eyed the cheesy art prints nailed to the walls, the plastic cups and ice bucket and small coffee maker on the desk. At least the television looked new, unlike everything else. "Why is it even the cheap motels have a really big, nice TV?"

"I don't know. Been in a lot of cheap motels, have you?"

"Be quiet. It's a generalization." She gave him a warning glance. Stretching out on her back, she covered her eyes with her arm. "I'm absorbing. Be right with you."

~

Amy's eyes fluttered open and she propped herself on her elbows, dazed. She blinked hard. Cooper sat by the table in the far corner of the room, reading by the light of a floor lamp. As she struggled to awaken more fully, she thought she glimpsed eyeglasses. When he shifted and turned toward her, no glasses were in evidence.

Lowering the magazine, he smiled. "Hello, sleepyhead."

"What time is it?" She yawned and sat up on the bed.

"Almost seven-thirty."

"That late?" She ran a hand through her disheveled hair and frowned. "Wow. Sorry. Hope I didn't snore."

"You didn't. You were very lovely in your sleep," Cooper said. "You actually smiled and whispered my name a few times. Sounded pretty hot."

Amy drew in a quick breath. "Surely not."

"I'm teasing. Relax. But you did make a rather odd sound."

Oh, no. She groaned. "It's probably the one I make when I'm exhausted. It started when I was a little girl. Did it sound sort of like a little clucking noise?"

"That's the one." He laughed. "I think I'll call you 'My Little Hen.'"

"Not if you want to make it through the night."

"Oh, but we're in Texas now. Don't forget the capital punishment thing. Do anything to me and you'll pay the ultimate price."

"What are you reading?"

He held up the latest issue of *Habits*. "Never miss an issue."

Her mouth gaped. "If I didn't know better, I'd say you bought it since we met, but considering I've been with you most of—" She waved her hand. "Never mind. Doesn't matter. Glad to see you read something other than engineering journals or whatever."

"I can appreciate a high-quality magazine. Reading about the newest method of screwing in a lightbulb isn't nearly so interesting as some of the articles I've read in *Habits*." He gave her a pointed look and flipped a few pages.

"But it's mainly a New York magazine. Where did you, how did you . . . ?" She stared at him, at a loss for words.

"Wanna see the subscription label?" He pointed to the small white rectangle on the front cover.

"You're a *subscriber*? So, you know . . ." Why was she faltering? *Spit it out, woman.*

"I know you're one of their best editors and a terrific writer in your own right. You should do more of it. For instance, I just read a fascinating piece on a woman's shelter in New York and how they're helping the women find jobs and get back on their feet again. Eye-opening stuff. The story of the girl named Rita was riveting." He put the magazine on the table. "It's obvious the junior editor who wrote the piece holds a close personal interest. And, if I may say, your articles are why I buy it. It gives this particular magazine a very nice balance. Some of the other pieces are more, well . . . let's say the magazine could be called *Highbrow*."

"Are you saying it's fluff?" Tucking her hands beneath her, she shifted on the bed.

"Sometimes it is. Hope that doesn't offend you."

Amy shook her head. "No. It's your honest opinion and I can certainly appreciate that. Besides," she said, lowering her gaze, "I agree."

"Ever think of leaving and going to another magazine?"

Mitch's comments at Café Eduardo came to mind, and she frowned. "You and my brother should join forces. He asked the same question."

"Great minds think alike. Something to consider, anyway."

"Perhaps." She rose to her feet. "Ever read *New York Scene*?"

His eyes widened and he looked like she'd shot him with a stun gun. "I've read it, yes."

"What do you think of it?"

He hesitated before answering. "I like it enough." Rising to his feet, he stretched his arms above his head. "If we're going to eat, I suggest we get going."

Accepting his hand, Amy slid off the edge of the bed. "First, I want to show you something." He watched as she opened her suitcase and pulled out the copy of Landon's magazine. Finding the page with his photo, she opened it and held it up for him to see. "This man," she said, pointing to it, "is the publisher of *New York Scene.* Landon Warnick." When he turned away, unresponsive, she put it back in the suitcase. "Surely you see the resemblance? It's uncanny, really."

He nodded, but remained uncharacteristically quiet. Putting away the magazine, she stole a peek at the photo and wondered where Landon was and what he might be doing.

Shoving aside that line of thinking, she took in their surroundings. "Are we really staying here tonight, Cooper?"

"Yep. If you were hoping to wake up and find different circumstances, I'm sorry to disappoint you."

"That wasn't disappointment speaking," she said.

Silence greeted her for a long moment. "Why don't we see what Mr. Lewis has to say about a situation like this." Grabbing the book from his suitcase, Cooper made a big show of opening it to the table of contents.

Amy stared. "Where . . . where did you get that? Sam's book hasn't been released yet."

"It's an ARC copy, and a perk of being one of Kevin's groomsmen. I'd say it's perfect for the single man as well as a married one. Lots of great tips," —he grinned—"for how to win a woman and keep her happy. Judging by Sam and his TeamWork crew, I'd say he's an authority on the subject and eminently qualified to write this book." Running his finger down the page, Cooper shook his head. "As I suspected, there's not one chapter about what to do when you're stranded in a fleabag motel in Texas, no car, it's freezing outside, we're hungry and the very real potential for an axe murderer in the next room."

Amy smirked. "Don't remind me. So, based on what you know of Sam, what do you suggest his advice would be for a situation like ours?"

He quirked a brow. "Define 'situation like ours.'"

She lifted her chin. "One man, one woman, unmarried, both Christians with no choice but to spend the night together in the same room."

He closed the book with a definitive snap and sent it back to its place with a well-aimed toss. "I was going to suggest calling Sam. Knowing what I do of the man, he probably has friends in every corner of Texas—if not the globe—ready and waiting to come to the rescue of one of his TeamWork maidens."

Her hands found her hips. "TeamWork maidens? And why would I need rescuing?"

"You're a proud, card-carrying member of TeamWork, are you not?"

She swallowed hard and resisted the temptation to step backward. She raised her eyes to meet his and steeled herself not to melt. "Sure am. But I don't need rescuing."

"You're most definitely a maiden, though. I know it's an old-fashioned term, but you're an old-fashioned girl, aren't you, Amy?"

"What's that supposed to mean? You make it sound like a bad thing."

"I'm sorry." Stepping back, Cooper ran a hand through his hair. "Trust me, it's a very good thing. I'm not handling this very well. I'm the one who needs rescuing—from my own thoughts, I'm afraid." He lowered his hand and gave her a sheepish look. "Being completely honest here? At this particular moment, I'm wishing you weren't so old-fashioned." When she opened her mouth to protest, he raised his hands. "But I'm also thanking God you are."

For a moment, she couldn't speak before recovering her voice. "Okay, let's agree we won't suggest this to Sam for his next book. And don't think about holding this little situation over my head. I cannot be blackmailed." Her smile escaped as she wagged her finger in his face, an action she could tell annoyed him. "It's one of the unwritten TeamWork credos. Come on. Let's get on with it. Um," she stammered, knowing her cheeks must be flaming, "I mean time to . . . do something. I realize how that sounded, but you know what I mean. Something about you makes me lose my senses sometimes and I become completely inarticulate." Admitting it was worse.

His eyes never leaving hers, Cooper took one slow step in her direction, then another, and then one more until he was standing in front of her.

Amy stood her ground though barely a hand's length separated them. His nearness did things to her. Unsettling things. Warmed her all over, up and down the length of her and then some. "I'll call for a cot when we get back here after dinner," she said.

"Humor me. Supposing it *was* a chapter in Sam's book, what would the next chapter be titled, Miss Irresistible?" When she gave him a blank look, still flustered, he chuckled.

"How about 'Don't Call Me Miss Irresistible'? That one's a guaranteed mood killer."

"Then be prepared to hear it all night, sweetheart."

She ignored that comment. "Did you find out where we can get something to eat around here? Please tell me there's a restaurant, diner, pizza joint, donut hut?"

"Yeah, there's a place. Grab my jacket and let's go. We only have to walk about a half mile."

That stopped her cold. "Are you serious?"

"A half mile's not that far. Why? Is walking a problem for you?"

"I didn't wear my walking shoes, that's all."

"You didn't bring tennis shoes with you?"

She frowned. "It's not like I expected to go to the gym on this whirlwind trip. I have work pumps—heels," she added, noting his skeptical glance, "the strappy sandals I wore in the wedding and the boots I'm wearing."

His gaze traveled to her feet. "I see what you mean. Okay, tell you what. You stay put, and I'll go get us some food and bring it back. We can have a late supper here and watch something on our big TV. A real slumber party," he said with a chuckle. "Sounds like fun. Are you game?"

"No, no. I'll go with you. It would weigh on my conscience for you to be out there walking all by yourself."

"Why, Amy, are you feeling protective of me?" Reaching for his cowboy hat, Cooper smoothed his hair and anchored the Stetson, running his fingers along the front rim.

"Not really. It's more the need to ward off amorous armadillos and jail-bait waitresses. Besides, I'm not sure I want to be left here alone in this so-called motel." She caught his look. "Don't take it personally."

"I didn't." Grabbing his jacket, Cooper draped it around her.

"This is getting to be a habit with you," she said.

"You love it."

"Didn't say I didn't." She glanced down at her sweater and frowned. "Let me change real quick. This sweater is a mess and I'm wearing more of Tam's makeup than she is."

Five minutes later, she emerged after changing into a pink blouse, combing her hair and brushing her teeth. She smiled at the look on Cooper's face as she reemerged. "Ready to go?"

"You look very pretty. Can't decide which color I like best on you, although I think blue and green are your best colors."

"Thanks, I think," she said as he helped her into his jacket again. "Blue's my favorite color."

"I know that."

Interesting. "What's yours?"

"I like most of them, but red's a favorite."

"Ah, the color of passion." She stopped. *Did I say that out loud?*

He grunted. "Yes, exactly."

After pushing her arms into the sleeves, she started to work the buttons. The shoulders drooped and it was hopelessly big. "I think it's big enough for both of us. Want to share?" She gave him a grin she knew was more than a little flirtatious. *Watch yourself.*

"Hold on." Going to his suitcase, he dug around inside. She watched in silence, wondering what he had in mind. With a triumphant expression, he pulled out a black leather belt. "Here. This should do the trick." He wrapped it around her waist, pulling a little too tight. "Perfect. Entirely fetching."

"Thanks," she said, readjusting it, "but I don't need a corset."

"Yeah, that waist of yours is tiny. I wanna make sure you're all snug and tucked in."

"You're pretty creative when you want to be, aren't you? Wait," she said, glimpsing the mischief in his eyes, "don't answer that. It was a rhetorical statement. My stomach is rumbling, so it's time to go find some food. The fair maiden needs the big he-man hunter to fetch her some vittles." Her laugh escaped. "That's one sentence I never thought I'd say."

"My pleasure." Linking his arm with hers, Cooper escorted her out the door. As they walked, he put one arm about her, drawing her close. Not long after, he started to remove his arm. "Sorry. I shouldn't take liberties."

Amy grabbed his hand, keeping it anchored on her shoulder. "You're not. I was the one who offered to share your jacket. This is the next best thing. Besides, I'd never forgive myself if you caught a bad cold or worse." She tried to match his long stride but couldn't keep up, so he slowed to keep pace with her. "Tell me where we're going."

"It's called Scully's. The night desk clerk recommends the grill special."

"What's that? Considering where we are, maybe I don't want to know?"

"We're safe. Big old Texas cheeseburgers with French fries. All the adventure today has worked up my appetite and a burger sounds great. You?" His smile reached his eyes, and she felt another little piece of her heart floating toward him.

Chapter 26

DIGGING INTO BURGERS at Scully's, Cooper gave a thumbs-up. "You have to admit, this is a lot more adventurous than sitting in a hotel restaurant in Austin. Although that's probably exactly what we'll be doing tomorrow night provided we ever make it there."

"If you're there, it won't be boring. You're anything but stuffy."

Before they started eating, he'd asked grace. His prayer sounded as heartfelt as Landon's in the coffee shop on that night that suddenly seemed so long ago. *Stop it!* The comparisons between the two men were invading her thoughts with more regularity now, and it was enough to drive her crazy. *Lord, why two of them?*

Cooper raised a brow. "If I didn't know better, I'd think you're softening up a bit toward me. That comment sounded suspiciously like a compliment. Next thing I know, you're going to want to break the pact."

She gave him a look. "I hardly think anyone who's kissed you three times needs any more softening up." Covering her embarrassment, she took a big bite of her burger. He must think her a glutton, but the food was so delicious she didn't care. "I can't believe how good this tastes. I think it's the best cheeseburger I've ever had." Using her pinky, she wiped away a dab of mayonnaise from the corner of her mouth.

"I noticed you told them to hold the red onion." He laughed when she tossed her balled-up napkin at him. Should she point out he'd also removed the onion and put it on the side of *his* plate? They ate in companionable silence for a few minutes. "You're right. This tastes great. I was more hungry than I realized."

"It doesn't seem like the wedding was last night," Amy said. "Seems more like a lifetime ago, doesn't it?" Glancing around the small establishment, she grinned at the sight of the cactus in a corner strung with oversized, multi-colored Christmas bulbs shaped like jalapeños and armadillos. A jazzy version of "Jingle Bell Rock" played on the jukebox, and she tapped her foot under the table, noticing Cooper did the same. He'd done the dip and twirl thing with his fries and guzzled Dr. Pepper like it was endangered.

"Is that your way of saying you feel like we've known each other a lot longer?" For once, his tone didn't tease, but he moved his boot over hers and tapped it lightly, maintaining the rhythm of the music without missing a beat.

She snapped back to attention. "I suppose so."

"I agree. Not to change the subject, but care to share how you discovered you wanted to be a writer? I'm sure that's a good story."

Wiping her mouth with her napkin, she took a long swig of her half-Coke, half-Diet Coke. "Third grade. Mrs. Poppycock's class, and yes, that was her real name. At the beginning of the school year, she asked us to write an essay about our favorite summer memory."

Cooper pushed his empty plate to the middle of the table. Leaning his chin on one hand, he paused to thank the waitress for refilling his glass and then gave her his undivided attention.

"My essay was about making friends at summer camp with a girl named Hillary." She hesitated, and an unexpected wave of emotion swept through her.

"You don't have to tell me if it's upsetting." Cooper's voice was low and soothing.

"It's fine. I haven't thought about it for a long time. Hillary grew up in London and Paris and had already traveled more of the world than any other kid I'd ever known."

"Were her parents diplomats?"

"No, but that's what I thought at first, too. Hillary was different than the other kids. She was quiet, and because of it, not many of the others tried to get to know her. But I found her to be exotic and hilarious. She had a great sense of humor, a maturity and a wisdom about her. Hillary enjoyed reading and writing as much as I did, and we bonded over our mutual love of Louisa May Alcott's books. We both loved *Little Women*, especially, because Jo was a writer. One day at the camp, I wandered off the pathway on a nature hike and ventured into the woods alone. To this day, I don't know how she did it, but Hillary found me—shivering, cold, hungry and more than a little humiliated—two hours later. In the cabin later that same night, she was in the bunk bed across from me, and she said, 'You know when you were in the woods today? You weren't alone. God was with you the whole time. I was only telling you what He whispered in my heart. He's always there.'"

Cooper started to say something, then stopped. "Sounds like a very special friendship," he finally said.

Tears stung the back of Amy's eyes as he captured her hand in his. She stared at their joined hands a moment, comforted by his warmth and obvious compassion. "It was." A tear slid down her cheek. Slipping her hand from his, she dabbed the moisture from beneath her eyes with her napkin. "About a month after the camp ended, I found out the reason she was so well-traveled. She had a rare form of cancer and needed to go to those countries to try out new experimental procedures and drugs." Her shuddering breath escaped. "My lovely friend died six months later. Her parents mailed a sweet note to me along with a first edition of *Little Women* they'd bought for Hillary's ninth birthday, her last one as it turned out. They said she wanted me to have it. I'll treasure it always."

Taking her hand again, he brushed his thumb over it in a gentle, sweeping motion. "What a great memory, although I know it's bittersweet. I'm thankful you had a chance to know Hillary, and I'm sure she felt the same way about you."

She appreciated his sensitivity and the kindness she glimpsed in his eyes. "When we said good-bye that last day at camp, she encouraged me to follow my dreams of being a writer. I remember she said, 'God gives us only so many days to touch somebody's life in a special way, so we need to make them count.'" Her eyes welled again. "Of course, I had no idea she'd be gone within a few months. Maybe I should have known something was up since she talked about Heaven a lot. Some of the other kids thought she was morbid about it, but being a pastor's daughter, I didn't think it was strange. She sat out a lot of the games and activities, but I thought it was because of a sensitive stomach."

Taking another deep breath, Amy melted into Cooper's compassion. "Do you know how rare it is to form an instant bond with someone that impacts the rest of your life?" Understanding how much the sentiment also applied to the man sitting across from her, she lowered her gaze. "Hillary was one of those people. Like Mitch, I got mad at God for a while and railed at Him for stealing away such a great person, but then I started thinking about what Hillary told me. In part, that's one reason I try to help runaway dogs and misguided teenage girls and anyone else God puts in my path."

The jukebox started, and a slow country ballad began. "Dance with me, Amy." Standing, Cooper held out his hand.

After only a moment's hesitation, she slid off the chair. Putting her hand in his, she followed as he led the way to a small area cleared as a dance floor. An older couple danced nearby, not speaking, barely moving. The way the man held her in his arms, the way the woman laid her hand on the side of his face, spoke more than words ever could. Cooper's sentiment from the night before was right. Sometimes words weren't necessary. Sometimes being there for someone else was all that was needed. A kiss, a touch, a whisper. Her eyes misted. *Why am I so emotional?*

Cooper wiped away another tear she hadn't realized escaped. Pressing his lips to her cheek, he rested his head against hers. "I hope I don't make you cry."

"You don't." She gave him a wan smile. "You're wonderful."

"Come here." Slipping one hand around her waist, he clasped her free hand with the other.

Without hesitation, Amy leaned into his embrace, her head resting on his firm chest. She heard—and felt—the strong rhythm of his heartbeat through his cotton shirt and moved her hand over his heart. When she felt him stiffen, she was filled with immediate regret. It was too personal, too intimate a gesture and she shouldn't have done it. Embarrassed, she started to withdraw her hand.

Clutching her fingers, Cooper stilled them, holding them against his chest. "You're touching my heart, Amy."

"Sorry about that."

"I'm not. Keep doing it and don't ever stop."

Cooper's hand tightened around her waist as they danced. Closing her eyes, Amy relinquished everything to the moment and pushed aside all the thoughts cluttering her mind. For once in her life, she wanted to enjoy the moment without overthinking it. This night was perfect—the romantic music, the mood, and especially the man holding her in his arms.

When the music stopped, he led her back to their table. "Would you like some dessert?"

"Not really. You?"

"If I gave you my honest answer, I'd send you running all the way back to New York. How about I order us a piece of pie and we can take it back and share it later as a midnight snack?"

The way he looked at her, she couldn't refuse. While he went to the bar and settled the tab, Amy glanced around the small place, noting a few other scattered patrons. It was almost scary how he preoccupied her to the point where she only had eyes for him, oblivious to all else.

"Ready to go?" Putting a carryout bag on his chair, he helped her into the jacket.

After fastening his belt around her waist—ignoring his amusement as she tightened it—she accepted his hand without speaking as they headed into the dark, quiet and very brisk night. Their boots crunched on the gravel of the parking lot, the only sound the strains of the jukebox playing another slow ballad.

Surprising her, Cooper tugged on her hand and pulled her over to the side of the building. Lowering the bag to the ground, he stepped close. "Dance with me one more time." His voice was low, without the customary playfulness.

"Here? I guess this is another situation where I need to use my imagination." Catching his grin, she eased into a smile. "Okay, but if some random creature comes along and absconds with our dessert, don't blame me."

"I'm willing to take my chances if you are." When she nodded, he tugged her close. They danced for a couple of minutes until the song ended. Slowing them down, he kissed the tip of her nose. "Do you feel it, too?"

Her breath caught.

"Did I say something wrong?" Cooper's eyes, bright in the moonlight, searched hers.

She forced a smile but her heart wouldn't stop its relentless pounding. "No, and yes, I feel it, too."

His lips met hers, still curved with his wonderful smile. Moving his hand to cup her cheek, he caressed the line of her jaw with gentle fingers and anchored one firm hand behind her neck. She'd never wanted a man's kiss more.

He sifted gentle fingers through her hair. "In case you missed it, I kind of like you. A lot."

Did Landon and Cooper both subscribe to some "How to talk to gullible, vulnerable, needy career women and win them over" guide?

"What are you thinking?" His hold on her tightened, and when he ran his thumb over her bottom lip and then brushed his lips over hers, she was lost.

"I kind of like you too, Cooper. A lot," she said, surrendering to his kiss. Her breath quickened with the unmistakable stirring of desire when he deepened the kiss. He kept them dancing as his mouth covered hers, and they twirled slowly, making her heady and dizzy with his nearness and the power of the kiss.

Lord, why did you plant this incredible man in my direct path? Are we crazy?

With his arms still around her, Cooper raised his face to the night sky. "Deep in the heart of Texas, huh?"

"Yep," she said, scooping up his Stetson, forgotten on the ground. "Great aim. It fell right on top of the dessert."

"Don't know about you, but I'm not sure I need dessert anymore."

"You are such a flirt. I think you worked up my appetite again. Um, I mean—" Feeling the besotted fool, she hoped the darkness hid her flaming cheeks.

"We'd better put that pact in place again," he said, his voice quiet.

"What kind of pie did you get, anyway?" she asked, falling into place beside him.

"I didn't. I got chocolate cake. I've always heard how women crave chocolate."

"We do. Let's pick up the pace, shall we?" She heard his chuckle as they walked back to the motel in silence. Although they didn't hold hands, he stayed close enough to feel his warmth. She wondered what he was thinking but knew better than to ask.

Chapter 27

"I NEED TO take a shower," Amy said as they reached the motel a short time later. *Probably not the best thing to say.* She was nervous and wasn't sure what to do, how to act. After that dance, and especially that kiss, she was more than a little worried.

"You take the bathroom first. I'm going to turn on the TV and catch up on some NBA scores and listen to the news. Take your time," Cooper said with an encouraging smile.

Hoping he wasn't watching, Amy tried to be as nonchalant as possible about pulling her things from her suitcase. Realizing she'd only brought a nightgown with her and a matching lightweight robe, she hesitated. *Do I put these on or sleep in my clothes?* She pondered her options. On the one hand, while modest, the nightgown wasn't exactly made from a sturdy fabric. If she kept the robe on, the rather sheer fabric of the gown would be camouflaged and not reveal anything. She really didn't want to sleep in her jeans. Now *they* were certainly made from a sturdy fabric, but . . .

"Something wrong?" he asked.

"Nope, everything's just peachy." With another silent prayer, Amy retrieved her nightgown and robe set and carried them in the direction of the bathroom.

"Dropped something."

Turning around slowly, Amy spied what she prayed she wouldn't see lying there in all their pink, lacy glory. Cheeks flaming, she snatched them from the floor, mortified, ignoring his soft laughter. Retreating to the safety of the bathroom, she leaned against the door, breathing deeply, in and out. *You're an adult, so act like one.* Never mind that one of the two most handsome men in her life was in the next room. Putting her hands on her cheeks, she shook her head. Without a doubt, she'd lost some brain cells during the last twenty-four hours.

A half hour later, she emerged from the bathroom, all freshly-scrubbed and clean. The shower had been invigorating with no creepy-crawly creatures to fend off, courtesy of the cold weather. "All yours." She pretended to ignore him as he gathered his toiletries and headed into the bathroom. "I hope I left you some hot water."

"That's okay," he mumbled. "I'm heated enough."

Staring at him, open-mouthed, Amy picked up the bath towel and continued drying her hair. Remembering she hadn't checked into getting him a cot for the night, she sat on the bed and dialed the number for the night desk clerk. She started to speak but stumbled over her words in the middle of the request. After being told a cot would be delivered to their room in a few minutes, she replaced the receiver with a sigh.

Grabbing the towel, she caught sight of Cooper standing in front of the bed. Still fully dressed, hands on his hips, his grin was wide. Maddening.

"Forget something, did you? Maybe drop your boxers on the floor?" She leaned over the edge of the bed, hoping that might be the case.

"No boxers." The man didn't miss a beat. *Oh, this is getting too personal. Help me, Lord. I'm begging You.* "If it makes you feel better," he said, walking into the bathroom and coming back out again, "here." He tossed light blue briefs on the floor with an irritating grin.

"Thank you," she said. "That does make me feel better, in a very strange way."

Walking over to retrieve whatever it was he must have left in his suitcase, Cooper stalked back across the room, stooping to retrieve his briefs with a backward wink before heading back into the bathroom. Soon after, she heard the sound of the shower. As she listened to the local evening newscast and continued drying her hair, she heard him singing. Tiptoeing over to the bathroom door, she pressed her ear against it. He was in the shower singing "How Great Thou Art." Considering it was a fairly difficult hymn to sing, he did a decent job with it. She smiled as the higher notes sounded slightly off-key.

He emerged a short time later wearing navy sweatpants and a well-worn Texas A&M T-shirt stretched a bit tight across his chest and revealing highly impressive upper arm muscles. *Wow.* As he walked across the room, the scent of soap mixed with mouthwash lingered in the air.

Brushing her hair, Amy averted her gaze. "So, you sing in the shower. Hymns, even."

"Only when I'm trying to maintain my Christian testimony and have an unbelievable woman right outside the door, sitting on a bed in the motel room we're sharing." He darted a glance her way. "Just so we're clear, this kind of behavior isn't commonplace with me."

"Thank you for volunteering that information."

Depositing his things in his suitcase, Cooper then draped his jeans over the chair. Amy tried to keep her focus on anything but his masculinity and how attractive he was. *Maybe Christian girls aren't supposed to have such thoughts. Forgive me, Lord, but You're the one who made him.*

A firm knock sounded on the door. "That's probably the cot," he said, reaching into the pocket of his jeans. Pulling out his wallet, he strode over to the door, hidden from her view on the bed. After a few seconds of conversation, he returned with the portable bed. "The guy offered to assemble it, but I told him I'd handle it." Lowering it to the floor, he started to work.

"Thanks. Were you thinking of my reputation?"

He shot her an amused grin. "That, too. You're not really worried about a sullied reputation, are you?"

"Only because no one will know about this except you and me, right? Ever."

"Cross my heart and hope to die in your arms," he said, tugging on the last stubborn leg of the cot. "The way I see it, anybody who'd whisper or accuse us of doing something immoral are the ones with a guilty conscience." He stopped his task and pinned her with one of his deep, piercing looks. "Just because they might succumb to temptation doesn't mean we will. Hopefully this'll be more comfortable than the bathtub." Within less than a minute, he had it assembled. After testing it with one hand, he sat on it to test its sturdiness. "Uncomfortable as all get out, so it must be right."

"Do you want me to put the sheets on for you?" she asked.

"Nah, thanks. I'll take care of it before I hit the hay. Want to watch a movie and share that piece of chocolate cake now? I hate to see it go to waste . . . or we could have it for breakfast?"

She made a face. "Are you serious? Let's eat it now."

"You find us a movie and I'll get it." Grabbing the bag and sitting back down beside her, he gave her a sheepish shrug as he held up one plastic fork. "Do you mind sharing? Or else you can eat what you want and then give me any you don't want. Or eat it all. Whatever you want."

For a change, *he* was rambling, and she found it endearing. Could it be he was nervous? "Not a problem." Sharing this man's germs was the least of her worries. Finding a movie that didn't have any language, violence or suggestive themes might prove more difficult. They finally found a station showing reruns of old TV sitcoms. Laughing together, they each took turns sharing the cake. He sat cross-legged on top of the sheet and she was beneath it. At one point, he offered a bite to her, and she took it. When he raised a brow, she did the same for him, wondering if it was wise, but not really caring.

"I'm done. You take the rest," she said. Pushing the takeout container toward him, she shoved off the bed to go into the bathroom and brush her teeth again.

As soon as she came back into the room, he went into the bathroom and she heard running water and some serious teeth brushing. A man who paid serious attention to his dental hygiene was definitely a keeper. *What in the world are you thinking? Either go to sleep or at least pretend you're asleep.* Her eyes traveled to the cot. The white sheet and blanket were neatly folded on top. She'd won contests in college for making her bed in record time. Sliding out of the bed, she slipped the robe off her shoulders and draped it over the end of the bed but still within easy reach. Setting to work, she unfolded and shook out the sheets. Working her way from top to bottom of the cot, she quickly tucked under the corners. "Very nice," she said, smoothing her hand over the sheet before turning back to the bed.

Of course, God having the sense of humor He does, Cooper came out of the bathroom at that moment. He stopped short. After his gaze traveled the length of her, he averted his eyes and lowered his head, making an indescribable noise deep in his throat. Tossing his clothes on top of his open suitcase, he crawled under the covers of the cot while she did the same in the bed and made a big show of pulling the sheet and blanket up to her neck.

"Thanks for making up the cot," he said.

"Welcome. Did you see the crisp corners? Earned a Girl Scout badge for that one."

"I'll take your word for it. One more thing."

"No cookie jokes, please." She caught his smirk. "Were you a Boy Scout?"

"Made it to Eagle Scout, as a matter of fact." He winked. "Where'd you think I learned my survival skills?" Tossing the sheets aside, he walked over to his suitcase and pulled out his Bible. When he sat back down on the cot, it creaked and sagged a bit in the middle. "Easy does it. Hope you don't hear a crash in the middle of the night."

"My offer to fix up the bathtub's still valid." Pushing up in the bed and leaning against the headboard, she tucked the sheets around her.

"The view's much better from here. Wanna know what I feel like doing right now?"

"Not sure."

"Pray. Wanna join me? You can stay right there. Probably best if you do."

"Um, sure." That suggestion was the last thing she expected to hear, and yet the best idea considering her wandering thoughts.

And so, he read a few verses of Scripture and they prayed together. Amy prayed for everyone and anything she could think of to pass the time. When he grunted and nudged her foot with his, she finally stopped. "Your turn," she mumbled. This man was no stranger to prayer. Nothing rote or routine about it, and she appreciated how he prayed for Beck and Kevin, the TeamWork crew, his mother and stepdad . . . seemingly everyone in his life except for his dad. Something was there, but she didn't want to push him. It wasn't the time. As Cooper finished his prayer, she half-listened as she silently prayed for him and his relationship with his father.

"Feel free to turn off the light now," he said. "Unless you're one of those people who likes falling asleep with the light on."

"No, it's fine." Reaching for the switch, she turned it off, bathing the room in moonlight through the small opening in the heavy drapes. As her eyes adjusted, she saw him cross his arms behind his head, heard his deep sigh.

"Ah, you and me. In a motel room. In the middle of nowhere. In Texas. And no one else knows we're here. Who'd have guessed?"

A grin curved her lips. "*God* knows."

Cooper groaned. "That's right. He does. Thanks for the reminder." He turned on his side, facing her, and propped a fist under his head.

"You're not going to start singing bad country songs, are you?"

He shook his head, grinning. "It's kinda hard for a guy, you know, especially with how fetching you look in that nightgown."

"We shared prayer. Please don't spoil the moment, but thanks for noticing. I didn't time it that way, so please don't entertain such thoughts."

"I love how you think you know what I'm thinking. I have to say, though, God's timing is perfect, isn't it?"

"Thank you, I think," she said, yawning. Better to switch course. "In spite of everything, I had a wonderful day. Thanks for taking such good care of me."

"It was my honor. I'm sorry about having to come to this motel, though."

"That's not your fault, and I'm not sorry. Not at all." It was her turn to sigh. "I mean . . ." she paused, searching for the right words.

"I know what you mean, and I feel the same way."

A loud popping sound made them both jump. Bolting upright, Amy switched on the light. "What was *that*? Please tell me it's fireworks."

He shot her a look. "We've probably got a brawl going on."

Chapter 28

"YOU MEAN WITH *guns*?" Amy said. "What should we do now? Get dressed?"

"No, you stay put. I'll go check it out." By this time, Cooper was already off the cot and shrugging into his jacket.

"Chivalry aside, you don't need to play the hero card. Why don't we call the front desk?"

"They probably heard it, too, and I pray it's a guy on duty. I'd better check that out, too."

"Look, Cooper, I know we're in Texas and all, and I can appreciate your vigilante attitude, but maybe we should stay put and call 9-1-1? They do have that here, right?"

"Yeah, they have it, but in this rural area, you never know where you might find law enforcement at this time of night on a Sunday. Especially since I'm pretty sure that was the deputy sheriff lovin' up a girl in the back corner at Scully's."

"Lovin' up?"

"Yeah. Surely you've heard of it." The grin he gave her could melt an igloo. "Want a demonstration?"

"Remember the pact's in place."

"Ah, yes. You love to remind me. Smacks of 'remember the Alamo,' doesn't it?"

Shaking her head, Amy laughed. "You Texans. So funny."

Sitting in the chair by the table, he pulled on his boots. "You love it."

"Didn't say I didn't." What a sight he made when he stood up with one leg of his sweatpants stuffed inside the boot, one hanging outside.

She stifled her grin. "Cooper, I like you, but I don't want you playing target practice out there with who-knows-what-or-whom. This is serious and you could get hurt. Not to mention you're full of chocolate cake and it might slow you down."

He shot her a look. "Calories won't slow me down, and not everyone in Texas engaged in a brawl carries a sawed-off shotgun. I'm not one to sit on the sidelines, and I'll be fine. Promise."

"Yeah, but a lot of hooligans *do* carry them, and apparently this isn't a case of happy people shooting off firecrackers in the parking lot. I can't let some ridiculous sense of bravado get you killed, so please don't do anything on my account." She shook her head and ran a hand through her still-damp waves. "Tell me this isn't happening."

"Would if I could, sweetheart. I'm more shocked to hear you use the word 'hooligans.' And it's not bravado or me trying to impress you, although I appreciate the concern. It's more a desire to help out when and where I can. Kind of like someone else I know." Another pop sounded and they stared at one another. "Yeah, well, I'd better go check it out."

"Please be careful," Amy said, feeling the strong urge to run to him, throw her arms around his neck and kiss him hard on the mouth. Instead, she sat and twisted her fingers together. "Please don't do anything foolish. Come back to me, safe and sound."

"I'll do the best I can, little lady." Stuffing his Stetson on his head, Cooper gave her a shaky grin and headed to the door. "Lock it behind me," he said before departing.

After doing as he asked, she sank back onto the bed and lowered her head to her hands. *Lord, this day has been . . . well, one of the most crazy, fun, adventurous, terrific days of my life. Please keep Cooper safe. Be with Tam tonight, wherever she is. Help her to realize her self-worth and not get involved with men in a way she shouldn't. Help her to see how special and valued she is in Your eyes.* Raising her head, she frowned. She knew her self-worth and yet she'd been tempted by a man. A pretty girl like Tam with no spiritual training with no one to really care about her? Her heart ached. *Lord, I pray my words today will somehow reach her and she'll seek You in her life. Help her, watch over her and my greatest prayer is that she might someday come to know You in a very special way and hold You close in her heart.*

Thirty minutes later, Cooper blew back in the room. "Man, it's wicked cold out there!"

She looked up from her position on the bed, startled. "Wicked?"

A puzzled expression crossed his face as he removed the Stetson and brushed snow from the shoulder of his jacket. "I thought you'd be more concerned about what happened instead of my choice of a word."

Removing his jacket, he strolled across the floor and hung his Stetson over the knob on the side chair.

"Of course, I want to hear what happened. I've been praying since you left, but I didn't expect to hear that particular word. It sounds . . . odd coming from a Texan."

"I do business with a lot of northeasterners. Now do you want to know what happened?"

"Sure. I'm all ears. Sit. Talk." She watched as he tugged off his boots and peeled off his socks. Mitch had a habit of smelling his socks, and she prayed Cooper didn't share that disgusting practice. She blew out a sigh of relief when he dropped the socks over his boots. Climbing on the cot, he sat cross-legged and propped his elbows on his knees.

"Okay, so a guy and his brother were in a fight. Both pretty much drunk out of their minds. No guns involved. The night manager was the one with the gun. He shot it in the air a couple of times to get their attention and hollered for them to open the door. Then he burst in the room a few doors down from here. I waited outside until he yelled for me to come in and help. Thankfully the manager's a bruiser in terms of size, but it still took both of us to haul the younger guy off his brother."

"Do you know what they were fighting about?"

"Always thinking like a journalist, huh? Give you one guess."

"Hmm . . . Let's see. Which one has a bigger truck? Which one can hold the most beer? Has the most loyal dog? The best—"

"Come on. After three and a half guesses, you can do better than that." When she didn't speak for a few seconds, he quirked a brow and grinned. "Guess which one has the better looking girlfriend, and you've got it."

"How old were these guys, anyway?"

He shrugged. "Twenty-something, I'd guess—the younger one, anyway."

"And were the girlfriends in attendance at this little brawl?" Why that mattered, she didn't know.

Pulling back the sheet and blanket, Cooper crawled beneath them. He stretched out and crossed his arms behind his head, emphasizing those distracting upper arm muscles. "Not supposed to ask that one." His yawn was exaggerated.

She found it difficult to concentrate. "Why not?"

"Trust me when I say I would have won that little competition, hands-down."

"But I'm not—"

He turned his head, and his eyes met hers. "Good night, Amy."

"Cooper?"

He shifted and faced her again. Those sleepy eyes and disheveled hair mesmerized her. *I'm a goner.* "Yes?"

"That was a really brave thing you did tonight, helping keep the peace. You're . . . well, you're my hero."

Cooper's lips slid into an irresistible, sexy smile. "Why, shucks. Thank you kindly, ma'am." He tipped an imaginary hat. "Tomorrow I'll dig out my class ring and we can go steady."

Amy's mouth fell open. She turned her head, swallowing her memory of the hansom ride in Central Park with Landon when she'd said practically the same thing. Her heart rate escalated to a dangerous pace.

"Remember when I said I could very easily fall in love with you?"

"Ye—es," she said, trying to keep her voice steady, but failing. "Kind of hard to forget."

"Well," he said, "it's a whole lot easier than I thought." With that, he turned his back to her and tucked the bed covers around him like a cocoon.

Those words silenced her. Knowing Cooper, he probably said it for that very purpose, stemming the possibility of anything else happening between them. After turning off the light, she snuggled under the sheets and closed her eyes tight. As if that would help. Of course, all she could think about were his sweet words, those fabulous, taut muscles, his sensitivity, generosity and protective instincts . . . those muscles. Fat chance of concentrating on anything else. *You'd think I'd never seen an attractive man before.* Punching her lumpy pillow to make it more agreeable by pounding it into submission, she finally rested her head.

Was that subdued laughter coming from the man on the cot? "Everything okay over there?"

"Everything's fine," she snipped. "See you in the morning."

"Sweet dreams."

Amy was aware he tossed and turned a bit during the long night because she did the same thing. She must have dozed some because she awakened with a start in the middle of the night. As her eyes adjusted to the moonlight filtering through the slightly-parted drapes, her gaze fell on him.

"Hey, sleepyhead." His voice was thick and husky, hazy with sleep.

"Hey there," she said. "Can't sleep?" Both on their sides, they faced one another.

"Not really, which is surprising since I was bone tired when I crawled into bed last night."

"Wanna trade? I don't mind taking a turn with the cot." Although it served its purpose, it couldn't be comfortable. She hoped he wouldn't wake up with a sore back later in the morning.

"A very sweet and generous offer, but no. In case you haven't noticed, I'm generous to a fault."

She laughed a little. "Humble, too. Maybe you should try the bathtub. I could make it real nice and cozy for you."

"You look very pretty bathed with moonlight, Amy."

"Good night. Try to get some rest. You need your beauty sleep."

"Just talking a little Texan with an incredible woman."

"Texan?" she repeated. "Should I ask?"

"Use your imagination and I'm sure you'll figure it out."

Her heart skipped a beat. On the cot, he turned over, and she heard his soft chuckle. Closing her eyes, she knew she wouldn't get much sleep. *And this is why God gave us daydreams.*

Chapter 29

EARLY IN THE morning, Landon finally gave up trying to sleep and slid out of the bed. Throwing on a hooded sweatshirt, he pocketed the key and headed out, determined to run off his frustrations and talk to the Lord. It wouldn't absolve his guilt, but it would help expend excess energy and clear his head. After running five miles, he slowed to a jog and focused on praying about when to tell Amy the truth. He knew he had to do it today, but trusted the Lord to give him a clue when the time was right.

An hour later, freshly-showered, he pushed aside the heavy drapes to allow the first rays of sun into the room. Crossing the room, he sank onto the cot. Still asleep, Amy's lips were parted and her hair partially covered her face. *Beautiful.* She was even more gorgeous in the glow of dawn. Walking over to the side of the bed, he brushed silky dark strands away from her cheeks. With his fingertips, he softly traced them down the length of her jaw to the curve of her neck with a light touch but enough to awaken her. Amy stirred and whispered, "Hmm. That feels good."

He withdrew his hand. That hadn't been his intention, but a thrill of satisfaction rushed through him.

"Do it again, please."

Against his better judgment, he did as she asked. Her eyes opened and she gave him a look of relaxed contentment. He'd almost expected her to shoot upright and demand he get away from the bed, but the expression she wore now was much more of a threat in an entirely different way. Amy was the most tempting woman he'd ever met; her physical beauty was undeniable but she possessed a sweet innocence and purity of spirit that naturally drew him to her.

She yawned and stretched her arms high above her head, blinking hard a few times. "Did you really mean what you said last night, or was it a way to shut me up?"

"It was an effective way to prevent something from happening."

"Thank you for protecting my virtue. You're a very special person."

"Oh, you wouldn't think I was so special if you knew the thoughts in my head last night. I was awake half the night confessing to the Lord." *In more ways than one.*

"My, but someone's awfully honest in the light of morning."

"Here's honesty for you, Amy. You're entirely too enticing in every single way." *Time to change the subject.* "I'm going to be a good cowboy now and rustle up two strong cups of coffee and give you some privacy to get ready. Do you take anything in your coffee?"

It seemed to take her a moment to catch up after his little speech. Shaking her head, she stared at him with those wide eyes that looked greener than ever in the morning light. "How do you know I even like coffee?"

Hoping his expression didn't resemble anything close to guilt, he cleared his throat even while his pulse escalated. "An assumption. Don't all New York girls like coffee?"

"You're right." She giggled, and it went a long way toward making him feel more relaxed. "I crave it most mornings, actually, but I doctor it so much it's not really coffee. Two creams and four sugars. Don't forget your jacket." She slid out of the bed, obviously not thinking about the fact she wasn't wearing her robe. Crossing the room, she retrieved his jacket and held it out to him.

The light coming through the half-opened curtains revealed more than she could know. For his sanity and peace of mind, he needed to get out of there. *Now.* "I'll be back in thirty minutes. Be sure and lock the door behind me." Taking his jacket, he made sure his hand didn't touch hers or it might spontaneously ignite. Mumbling his thanks, he shrugged into it, knowing he couldn't get out of the room fast enough. Opening the door, he welcomed the cold rush of air and blew out a deep breath. He waited outside the door until he had the satisfaction of hearing the lock click in place.

~

"Here you go. Hope you don't mind, but I went ahead and added the cream and sugar," Cooper said.

Amy accepted the cup with a grateful smile and took a tentative sip. The hot liquid warmed her, and she wrinkled her nose as it slid down her throat. "Are you sure you didn't put in four creamers and two sugars instead of the other way around? Not to sound ungrateful."

"Um, yeah, maybe. Sorry. Call me a coffee dyslexic." Cooper sat in the uncomfortable-looking chair by the small table, watching her through narrowed eyes as he sipped his coffee.

"That's probably politically incorrect, but thanks for the morning humor. And the coffee."

"Happy to oblige. Here," he said, digging into the pocket of his bag. "Have a granola bar until we can stop somewhere for a meal later on."

"Thanks." She caught it when he tossed it to her. "I'm not that hungry, anyway. The chocolate cake last night was enough to tide me over." Unwrapping the end, she nibbled it. "You know, this tastes a lot better than it should."

He held up one hand. "Wait a second. You're not allergic to anything, are you?"

"No allergies that I know of. Why?"

"We've had enough adventure lately, and I'm not sure where we can find the closest ER or a doctor. Just trying to keep us safe." He waved his hand. "Carry on. Enjoy."

She met his eyes with another grin. "You're doing a great job of keeping me safe."

"Yeah, well, I try." He grunted and chewed off a big bite of his granola bar and they enjoyed a few minutes of companionable silence. "Ready to go after our little coffee break?" he asked, tossing the empty wrapper in the trash can under the table. When she crumpled her wrapper, he held up the can and she made a perfect basket. "Good aim."

"Yeah, well, I try." They shared a grin. "And yes, I'm all packed. Oh, you forgot your shampoo in the shower. Here." Retrieving it from the top of her suitcase, she handed it to him.

"Thanks." When he took it from her, their fingers touched. Never in her life had she felt what she'd consider anything more than static electricity from the touch of a man's hand, but she felt his touch everywhere.

"Do you feel it?" She put her half-empty cup on the table.

Cooper cleared his throat. "I'd have to be deaf, dumb, blind, dyslexic and numb *not* to feel it."

A grin curved her lips. "Stand up, please."

Accepting her hand, he rose to his feet, but he wore an expression of skepticism. "I'm having a second déjà vu moment here in less than a minute. Something about this scene feels very familiar."

"Need a reminder?" Amy pushed aside her conscience. She'd never acted this flirtatious, but she was enjoying every single second.

He chuckled under his breath. "Wow, you sure are a morning person, aren't you?"

She shrugged. "I guess I am, but I never had the opportunity to find out before."

"Glad to hear it, but I can't. Sorry."

"You can't because you don't want to?"

"Oh, I want to, trust me."

She backed away. "Oh," she groaned, dropping his hand. "I'm completely without shame. Might as well call me the TeamWork Tramp and get it over with. Please forgive me. I hope you know that I've never acted like this with any man before."

Bringing her into the circle of his strong arms, Cooper's nearness and warmth were overwhelming. Amy's breath caught in her throat as she looked up at him, her sleepy gaze drinking in every detail of his freshly-scrubbed, smooth-shaven face. "You want to know why I can't?" His eyes caressed her face, and unless she was mistaken, they were hungry with unspoken need. No man had ever looked at her this way, especially from such close proximity. His arms tightened around her, a good thing since she was melting again inside.

"Uh, huh. Please."

"Because," he said, "number one, my coffee breath is probably pretty disgusting. Second of all and most important? The way I feel right now, if I kiss you the way I want—and the way I think you're asking—I won't want to stop. I *won't* stop. I know better than to start something we can't finish. I respect you too much and I'm trying my best to be a strong man of honor here. But I have to say, sweetheart"—his slow smile easy and warm—"you make it difficult for a guy without trying. For the record, I meant what I said last night. I'm already dreading taking you to Houston and I won't want to let you go, but as much as I'm enjoying this," he said, pulling out of the embrace, "I have someone lined up to drive us into Austin. We need to get moving."

"Well, why didn't you say so?" Zipping her suitcase, Amy sat on the bed and started to tug on her boots. "That was quick work. How'd you find us a ride so soon?"

"When I stopped by the office to drop off the key, a woman named Jacinda was talking to the desk clerk and happened to mention she was headed into Austin. The clerk must have heard our story and all about the ruckus last night, and she told Jacinda we might need a ride. She freely offered and considering she had a tattered New Testament sticking out of her top pocket, I figured we could trust her." His smile was blinding. "The Lord is good on a cold December morning in Nowhereville, Texas."

Amy shook her head. "It must be nice, everything coming to you so easy. And yes, the Lord is good."

He grunted. "No illusions here. Not everything comes so easy. Besides, I figured I needed to come up with an idea to get us to Austin before you suggested hitchhiking with that pretty thumb of yours. Texas may be great for a number of things, but hitchhiking definitely isn't one of them." She laughed and he raised a brow. "You think I'm kidding?"

"I'd never suggest such a thing, especially here in Texas, but you're misguided if you think my thumb's pretty. That's a new line. Last time I checked, hitchhiking was *never* a good idea."

Cooper snorted and unzipped his case to toss his shampoo inside. "Ready to go?" Hoisting her bags and his overnight case, he headed to the door. Pulling it open, he stood aside, waiting.

"Yes, sir," she said. Retrieving her purse and hanging bag, she followed.

~

An hour later, Amy sat sandwiched between Cooper in the front seat of a blue pickup truck driven by Jacinda, the sister-in-law of the best friend's brother's wife of the clerk in the small motel. She listened as they carried on a lively debate about freshwater versus saltwater fishing, but chose to remain silent since she couldn't contribute anything. Cooper attempted to include her in the conversation, but then Jacinda raised another topic of which she knew nothing.

With a start, Amy blinked and looked out the window when Cooper gave her a gentle nudge. She must have dozed for a few minutes. Yawning, she sat up straighter.

Jacinda pulled the truck to a stop at the valet entrance of a stately hotel in downtown Austin. A bellman headed toward them with his cart and an eager smile. Grabbing his Stetson and stuffing it down on his head, Cooper opened the door and slid out of the truck. Not long after, the bellman wheeled the cart into the hotel with her bags, but Cooper held onto his suitcase.

"Thank you so much, Jacinda." Wanting to give the woman something for her trouble—at least enough for gas money—Amy opened her purse.

The woman leaned close. "Never you mind, honey. Your man's already taken plenty good care of me. Why, he paid me enough for five trips. You two have yourselves a great time. The Driskill's one of the best hotels in Texas, if not the entire country. Lots of people fall in love here."

When Amy scooted across the seat, she avoided Cooper's knowing grin. "I didn't hear a word," he said under his breath.

"Sure you didn't, and I'm the world's foremost expert on softwater fishing."

His grin was so inviting. "Saltwater." After helping her from the truck, he closed the door.

She waited while he said good-bye and thanked Jacinda, her gaze scanning the façade of the historic structure. A plaque mounted on the exterior wall explained the building was made from brick dressed with limestone and the original hotel featured three grand entrances, one with the largest arched doorway in Texas. Glancing up, she noted the festive decorations—green garlands with red bows—draped beneath the windows and stretched along the railing of a balcony directly above where she stood.

"Welcome to The Driskill," the doorman said, holding the door open as they passed through the columned entrance and entered the spacious lobby.

Amy paused for her eyes to adjust to the much dimmer lighting inside. A towering, magnificent Christmas tree drew her immediate attention, and the pleasing, soft strains of a harp came from a nearby corner. Their footsteps echoed, and she glanced at the floor, marveling at the inlaid marble and tile. The tree was located in the center of the long portion of the lobby, and a shorter lobby area jutted perpendicular and featured small groupings of sofas, chairs and tables suitable for an intimate meeting or gathering. The lobby was quiet, and the few guests milling about spoke in hushed tones. A lovely, dark-haired woman sat behind the concierge desk and nodded her head with a smile of greeting.

"If you're trying to make up for last night's accommodations, you've more than succeeded," Amy said in low tones, waving her hand around the lobby. "This is way more than I expected."

Cooper removed his hat and ran a hand over his hair, smoothing it down, an increasingly familiar action. "I couldn't bring you to Austin and not show you The Driskill. It's a favorite of mine and a great example of turn-of-the-century elegance." Pride infused his voice. "It was built in the late 1880s by a cattle baron named Colonel Jesse Driskill. Presidents, movie stars have stayed here, and a lot of Texas governors held their inaugural balls here. Take a look around while I go get you checked in."

"Cooper," she said, touching his sleeve as he started to walk away, "I can't allow you to pay for my room. I insist on taking care of it."

"You can insist all you want," he said with a small grin, "but Texas chivalry won't allow such a thing." He lowered his voice. "You deserve the best and this is something I can do for you, Amy." His eyes met hers. "Indulge me."

The man managed to shut her up yet again. Rooted to the floor, she observed as he strode toward the front desk. At this time of the year, a place like this was probably booked anyway and they wouldn't have a vacancy. As it was, the term "vacancy" seemed much too common for such a grand hotel as this.

A few minutes later, Cooper approached where she stood admiring the details of the grand staircase—draped with holiday garlands and twinkling lights—which led to the mezzanine above it. "All set. Your room's on the fifth floor. Normally, it's too early to check-in, but they've made an exception."

She tilted her head and gave him a wary smile. "You don't own stock in The Driskill, do you? In order to have such influence."

"Hardly. But I've attended a number of events here through the years and conducted a few meetings." He shrugged. "Call it a perk."

"Thank you," she said, lowering her gaze and feeling her cheeks grow warm.

"I'm going to catch a cab over to my house for a couple of hours." He nodded to the bellman waiting nearby. "Charlie's going to take you up to your room. Why don't you get settled and I'll be back at one o'clock," he said, checking his watch. "The hotel has a great restaurant called the 1886 Café & Bakery that reopened this past July. We can have lunch there, if you'd like. Then we'll head out for that promised trip to the mall."

"Sounds wonderful," Amy said, "but you don't need to—"

"Yes," he said. "I do." His tone left no room for discussion.

"But this is way too extravagant and—"

Placing his finger over her lips, he silenced her. "Please enjoy and let me pamper you."

Swallowing further protests, she gave him a small smile. "I'll freshen up and meet you here in the lobby again at one o'clock."

"Until then." He graced her with his incredible cockeyed grin before heading out the front doors of the lobby. From the upright posture, squared, broad shoulders and confident steps, this was a man who commanded attention. It was difficult to ignore the interested glances from several women as he passed by them.

She heard a woman's sharp intake of breath from a few feet away where two blonde, middle-aged women watched Cooper exit the hotel. "Hold your horses, Lila. Unless my eyes deceive me, that gorgeous man was Landon Warnick." The drawl was distinctively Texan, and dripping with the affectation of wealth. "It sure is wonderful to see him back in Austin. Pity about his father, but his mama's a real good woman. One thing's for certain: God doesn't make men like that anymore."

Thinking of correcting the woman, Amy opened her mouth to speak, but closed it instead. *It's not your place.* The observations both intrigued and irritated her, but her brain was fuzzy. Landon and her life in New York seemed light years away, but for now, she'd relax and enjoy each moment.

"Ready, Miss Jacobsen?" The bellman's question startled her out of her trance.

"Yes, of course," she said. "I'm sorry to keep you waiting."

"Not at all." He ushered her to the lobby elevators and pushed the button.

As they waited, Amy pointed to the huge, colorful stained glass light fixture in the ceiling near the Christmas tree. "Is that made from Tiffany glass?"

"It is indeed," Charlie said. "You'll see Tiffany lamps in your suite, too." He waited as she stepped inside the elevator. Coming in with the small cart holding her suitcase and overnight bag, he pushed the button for the fifth floor.

"Did you say my suite?"

"Yes. You're staying in the Yellow Rose."

"Oh." Even without being there, Cooper could render her speechless. The doors opened and she stepped into the quiet hallway, following Charlie's lead. When he opened the door to Suite 543 and stepped aside, she gasped. "What did you do, Cooper?" She skimmed the marble entryway, crown moldings, hardwood floors, oversized, floor-to-ceiling windows with custom made tapestry drapes, the small writing desk and an antique dining table with four chairs. The inviting décor featured plush, earth tones primarily in shades of gold, beige, soft browns and yellows, all warm and welcoming. Strolling into the middle of the suite, Amy gave Charlie a sheepish smile. "I feel as though I've been asleep and awakened in some kind of unbelievable, marvelous dream."

He nodded. "I'm happy you like it here, Miss. The Driskill prides itself on treating its special guests to true Texas luxury and charm. This is one of our bridal suites." That stopped her thoughts cold for a minute before she snapped back to attention. "You have a view overlooking Brazos Street, and this is the living, dining and sitting area." Her gaze followed his to an elegant chair and sofa, an area rug and a beautiful tapestry in complementary colors. A lighted ceiling fan softly whirled above her.

"Wait until you see the bedroom," Charlie said with a warm smile. "You ain't seen nothin' yet."

Amy's eyes widened at the familiar phrase since Sam used it on occasion. The magnificent tapestry poster bed stole her breath, as did the antique armoire and Tiffany bedside lamps. Moving over to the side of the bed, she touched a gold, braided tapestry tieback securing delicate white lacy fabric at one of the corners. Picking up the yellow rose nestled on one of the overstuffed throw pillows, she inhaled its fresh, glorious scent.

"You have a personal dressing room with lighted ceiling fan and floor length mirrors," Charlie said, opening a door and showing her the closet before leading her further into the bathroom. "As well as the usual amenities, this room features black Brazilian marble floors, a makeup mirror and vanity lighting."

"Charlie, I can honestly say The Driskill is the most elegant hotel I've ever had the privilege to stay the night."

"Be careful on the floor, Miss. It can get slippery when wet. Use the mat."

"I'll remember that," she said. She'd learned that particular lesson about slippery marble the hard way when she visited her grandfather's Hollywood mansion when she was six. Thankfully, she'd only suffered a mild bump on the back of her head rather than a full-blown concussion or worse. Heading back into the main area of the suite, Amy reached for her purse where she'd left it on the desk and pulled out her wallet. "Thank you so much."

Charlie waved his hand when she offered him a tip. "It's my pleasure to serve you. I trust you'll enjoy your stay at The Driskill, Miss Jacobsen, and please let the concierge or staff know if you need anything at all." Although the words were practiced, the kindly man's smile was sincere.

As soon as Charlie departed, Amy released her until-now-contained squeal of delight. Running back into the bedroom, she sat on the side chair long enough to tug her boots from her feet before taking a running dive and plopping in the middle of the high bed. Her heart beating fast and hard, she stretched out on her back and heaved a deep sigh. Smoothing one hand over the gorgeous comforter, she studied the detail of the wrought iron headboard.

This suite was an extravagance she never would have expected. "You shouldn't have done this, Cooper." A secret thrill of pleasure coiled in her belly, and she rolled over on her stomach, propping one fist under her chin. Surely an electrical engineer was too practical to splurge on something like this, especially for a woman he didn't know well. If he was trying to impress her, the plan was working spectacularly well.

I don't know what Your plan is, Lord, but I like it.

Chapter 30

RIDING THE ELEVATOR down to the lobby a half hour before Cooper's expected return to the hotel, Amy heard a chorus of young voices singing Christmas carols. Turning toward the grand staircase, she saw a group of about twenty boys and girls—third and fourth graders by her estimation—attired in red and green. Moving down the stairs from the mezzanine and singing "Silver Bells," each child stopped on a step until they all lined up on the staircase, facing the lobby. Their angelic voices rang throughout the large lobby area, the acoustics perfect, and Amy clapped with enthusiasm when they finished.

Right on time, Cooper strode into the main lobby. An older, distinguished gentleman standing near the front desk called out a greeting and walked toward him with his hand extended. Amy did a double take when she thought she heard the name Warnick and the two men shook hands. Her pulse took a flying leap. Two mentions of Landon in such a short time? *Could it be possible . . . ?* She shook her head, refusing to entertain any illusions.

Cooper glanced around the lobby as he talked with the man, probably looking for her. Not certain whether she should make her presence known until his discussion was concluded, Amy moved to a nearby wingback chair and seated herself in it, partially hidden behind the fronds of a potted plant.

He'd changed into a crisp, white and blue striped dress shirt but still wore his jeans and held his jacket draped over one shoulder. Inclining his head toward the other man, Cooper listened and nodded as he talked. When they laughed together easily, the resonance of her traveling companion's deep timbre warmed her heart.

What a hopeless romantic you are.

A couple of minutes later, the man departed after giving Cooper a hearty slap on the shoulder. Rising to her feet, Amy relished the broad grin creasing his face as he spotted her and headed in her direction.

"Hello, gorgeous," he said.

"Hello, generous." The grin she gave him was purposely coy. "After last night, are you planning a shotgun wedding to make an honest woman of me?"

Her words stopped him, and he tilted his head, surveying her. "Would you?"

"Would I what?"

"Marry me if I asked you? Right here, right now? I'm sure I could rustle up a minister to do the honors for us."

Amy laughed off the question with a wave of her hand. "I was only referring to the fact that my room is none other than a bridal suite. And, trust me, I have more respect for the God-ordained institution of marriage than to take an impulsive leap into holy matrimony with someone I barely know."

"While I share your respect for marriage," Cooper said, "I beg to differ on the barely knowing you part of the equation. You see, I don't think it takes a long time to know someone well enough to know you want to marry them."

How did the man do it? She couldn't begin to manage a coherent comeback.

Hooking her arm through his, Cooper directed her to the front of the hotel and the 1886 Café and Bakery. After the hostess seated them and the server took their orders, they exchanged small talk and she gave him details of her fabulous suite. Although he listened, Amy knew he was more focused on studying her features than hearing about the accommodations. Something was bothering him. While he wasn't moody, he wasn't as overtly flirtatious, but he listened, asked questions and was quiet. She liked this side of him, and appreciated it while another part of her missed their lively bantering. *The balance is nice.* Maybe he'd discovered something that disturbed him when he went to his house. Whatever it was, Amy hoped it wouldn't taint their remaining time together. She knew the man well enough to know he'd share it with her if and when he felt the need.

When their food was delivered, Cooper reached across the table, covering her hand with his as he said grace. Afterwards, she watched, wide-eyed, as he took a first bite of his self-proclaimed favorite, the well-known "Hangover Burger"—a mile-high burger made from Angus beef, brown sugar and chili-rubbed bacon, a sunny-side-up egg and hash browns on a whole wheat bun. While the man enjoyed his breakfast food, he couldn't eat like this often or he'd weigh five hundred pounds. Noting his amusement as he chewed, she sampled Helen Corbitt's Cheese Soup—another specialty—in a bread bowl. No doubt the delicious soup had a gazillion calories, but for the moment, she couldn't care less.

"The beginnings of The Driskill is sad, really," Cooper said after chewing another hearty bite of his monstrous burger. "Colonel Jesse's story is one of American free enterprise, but it's not without its share of tragedy."

"Tell me," she said, intrigued. "I saw the life-sized portrait of him hanging in the lobby."

Cooper proved a natural storyteller as he held her captive by relaying some of the history and legend of the hotel, adding to its mystique and fascination. "By the time he was forty-five, Jesse had a wife, four daughters and two sons and moved to the frontier town of Austin. He'd already made and lost a fortune during the Civil War by selling cattle to the Confederacy. But the guy was resilient and obviously a shrewd businessman considering he went on to become a rich cattle baron and civic leader. He opened the original hotel in 1886 at cost of around four hundred thousand dollars as a showplace to rival hotels in New York, Chicago, St. Louis and San Francisco. Two weeks later, The Driskill hosted its first inaugural governor's ball." Cooper paused his story and took another bite, chewing his food. "Jesse lost his fortune again a couple of years later when a drought and hard winter killed thousands of his prized cattle. Then he went bankrupt, lost the hotel in a high-stakes poker game and died three years later of a stroke. Legend has it poor old Jesse haunts The Driskill to this day because he wasn't ever able to fully enjoy his namesake creation."

"Is that right?" Amy tore off a small section of the bread bowl and popped it into her mouth, giving him an impish grin. "What does he do? Moo at guests in the elevators?"

Cooper shook his head. "Very funny. No, supposedly Jesse smokes cigars in guest rooms and has a little fun switching bathroom lights on and off."

The corners of Amy's mouth quirked. "Maybe he was a wannabe electrical engineer." She laughed when he wadded up his napkin and tossed it at her.

"Do you want any dessert before we head out?" he asked a few minutes later. "They have some great specialty desserts here, and one of them's acclaimed."

She gave him a look. "If I gave you my real answer to that question . . ."

His smile made her all kinds of silly, the kind of smile that could launch a thousand daydreams. In a matter of days, this man had settled in the trenches of her heart and made himself at home. "Don't you wanna know what it is?"

Amy shook her head, forgetting the current thread of discussion. "What . . . what is?"

When he leaned across the table, lowering his voice, a smoldering sensuality flickered in his gaze. "The acclaimed dessert is the 1886 Chocolate Cake. Sinful and decadent."

Swallowing hard, Amy cleared her throat and pushed her soup aside. She avoided his continued, intense scrutiny. "Oh my goodness, I can't eat another bite. Maybe the cake could be a midnight snack. On the balcony or the mezzanine," she added lest he perceive it as an invitation.

Fifteen minutes later, Cooper handed a valet his claim ticket. The young man lit up with a wide grin. "Ah man, that truck's a sweet ride." Thanking him, he ignored her raised brows as the valet took off at a sprint.

"Here she is," he said a couple of minutes later. A beautifully restored, red and white vintage Chevy truck—with the grinning valet behind the wheel—halted beside them. "Amy, come meet Matilda."

"What an awesome truck. It suits you," she said after he climbed in beside her. "Do you refurbish vintage trucks in your spare time?"

"If I *had* any spare time, it'd be high up on the list of hobbies."

"You seem to have plenty of time right now." She wondered how he'd perceive that comment and dared to steal a glance his way.

"Touché, but spending time with you is paramount right now."

"Why?" she asked. Two could play this game.

"Why not?" He grinned when she rolled her eyes.

"Why Matilda?" she asked as he maneuvered the truck into the early afternoon downtown traffic.

"That one I have an answer for. Matilda was my grandmother's—on my dad's side—middle name. I thought it was fun for a truck like this."

"It is, and no offense to your grandmother, but I hope you don't plan on naming any daughters after her." It was the first time Cooper had mentioned his father without a hint of sadness.

"Oh, I don't know. I think Tilly War—" He stopped, his brow furrowed as he turned left at the next light. "The name Tilly's sort of cute, don't you think?"

"In a pig-tailed, pixie kind of way, I suppose it is." She leaned her head closer to the window, peering up at the skyline of Austin passing by them. "Where are you taking me now?"

"You'll find out soon enough."

"That's what I'm afraid of." That wasn't all she feared.

~

"Now, for your Christmas gift," Cooper said a short time later. They stood side-by-side in front of a Macy's store directory.

"Maybe it would help if you'd tell me what we're looking for," she said.

"Give me a minute. I'll find it."

"May I help you find something, sir?" Amy tried not to smirk. She normally had to wait at the Saks counter in Manhattan an average of twenty minutes to buy her favorite makeup, but in less than a minute, Cooper garnered the more-than-willing attention of a helpful salesclerk. He spoke in low tones to the young woman who leaned closer than her hearing should warrant.

Stop being so snarky. Not wanting to appear in the least bit jealous, Amy turned her head, feeling awkward.

"Second floor, right corner," the saleswoman said, pointing them in the direction of the escalator.

Soft holiday music played in the background and festive decorations adorned the walls and ceiling of the department store. "Let it snow, let it snow, let it snow," she sang along with Johnny Mathis's song, a longtime favorite of her mom and dad's.

"And I thought you didn't sing."

Amy laughed as they stepped off the escalator. "Oh, it's a rare event. Hope I haven't scared you off."

"Sounded good to me. I give you permission for a private performance anytime you'd like."

"Which department are you taking me to? Surely not the lingerie department." Seemed he wasn't the only flirty one. What was *with* her? The temptation to tease him proved overwhelming. At least he'd perked up since their lunch and didn't seem quite as contemplative.

"I like your lingerie fine from what I've seen of it." He shot her a sly grin. "This is about fulfilling a need for you, not a want for me. Sorry to disappoint you, but I have something much more practical in mind. Humor me, please."

Indulge me. Humor me. What's next? When they stepped off the escalator, she pulled him over to one side. "Cooper, you could win a trinket for me at the county fair and I'd be thrilled. You've done so much already. Please don't spend any more money on me."

For a fleeting moment, she glimpsed wounded pride flitting across his expressive face. Her upbringing wouldn't allow her to accept an extravagant gift from a man she barely knew, even if he claimed not to expect anything in return. *Face the facts.* Sooner or later, things would change and Cooper *would* expect something from her. What that was for *this* man, she had no clue.

"It's only money," he said, bringing her thoughts back to the present. "Like I said, this is fulfilling a need for you. Trust me." He grabbed her hand and marched her toward the back corner. "Come with me, please."

She stopped in her tracks, stunned.

"Something wrong?" He stepped close. "Are you okay?"

"It's nothing," she said. "Serious déjà vu moment, that's all." Visions of Landon leading her across the street after their carriage ride invaded her mind. *Lord, what's happening?* Shaking her head to clear her thoughts, Amy forced a smile. "Lead the way."

Her TeamWork friends, especially Winnie, wouldn't believe it. Here she was, allowing herself to be led around by a man. Halting in the middle of the misses coat department, he opened his arms. "Now can you guess what I have in mind?"

"I'd say you want to replace my jacket." She couldn't resist his triumphant grin. He looked like a little boy on Christmas morning, full of enthusiasm, his eyes bright.

"Exactly. Since you were so gracious in giving Tam your jacket, you definitely need another coat. Full-length, short. Whatever you want." He leaned against a column with a wall mirror, twirling his Stetson between his hands. "Have at it."

"You're going to watch while I try on coats?"

One brow quirked. "Is that a problem? Why wouldn't you—"

She raised one hand. "Fine. No need for a fitting room, anyway." Spying a salesclerk nearby, she resisted the urge to sigh. Of course, the woman walked over to Cooper and asked if she could help. Perusing the closest rack of coats, Amy tried not to eavesdrop but heard him say they'd let her know if they needed assistance.

Obliging his request, Amy tried on different jackets and coats of varying styles, fabrics, colors and lengths. Never before had she modeled something for a man other than her dad or Mitch, and those times were rare enough. Although she felt silly as she pranced, posed and twirled, she enjoyed his reactions which alternated between giving her a thumbs-up or a noncommittal shrug. Not one thumbs down in the bunch. Surprisingly, he didn't appear the least bit bored or embarrassed. Some she tried on for the sheer enjoyment of getting his reaction, and he didn't disappoint.

Starting to tire of the process, she finally found a stylish black and white herringbone, fitted at the waist with a matching belt and made to rest on the curve of her hips. On some women, it might be a disaster waiting to happen, but it flattered her figure. As soon as she slipped it on, she knew. *This is the one.* Walking over to the mirror by where Cooper waited, she buttoned the jacket and looped the belt. Designer. Well-made. Great fit. A glance at the tag confirmed her suspicion of the price. *Wow.* If she decided on this jacket, no way could she allow him to buy it.

He let out a low whistle, and warmth flushed her cheeks as she pivoted to face him. Seeing the admiration in his expression, she was overwhelmed with a sudden self-consciousness and an unexpected shyness.

"That jacket is made for you, but it's missing something." Leaning close, sending her pulse skyrocketing, he lowered his Stetson on her head. Shivers ran through her at his nearness, so close she felt the brush of his lips and the warmth of his breath on her temple. "Perfect. Be nice to me and I might let you wear it sometime." With a grin, he removed it.

"Ooooh," she said with a return grin, "would some of your brain cells transfer to me, too?" Removing the jacket, Amy arranged it on the hanger. "This is expensive, and I can't let you buy it." She darted a glance his way.

He snorted. "Nothing doing. That's a moot point we already settled." Taking the jacket, he strolled toward the counter.

The salesclerk offered a convenient shopping pass discount, and although it appeased her somewhat, guilt nicked her conscience as the clerk handed him the sales slip. Feeling awkward, she stepped to the side and turned her head as Cooper hastily scrawled his signature. *He's a lefty.*

"Hold on a minute," Cooper said. As the woman started to drape a plastic bag over the jacket, he pushed the signed receipt across the counter. "Amy, do you want to go ahead and wear it?"

"Sure. Great idea." Although she was plenty warm at the moment, it was pretty chilly outside.

After the clerk located scissors in a drawer and snipped off the tags, she handed the jacket to Cooper and the package of extra buttons to Amy. "Who gets the receipt?"

"I won't be returning it," Amy said. "You should keep it for a tax deduction." He held the jacket as she slipped into it.

Thanking the clerk, he held out the receipt to her. An expression of something indefinable lit his eyes as he waited for her to take it. When she shook her head, he sighed. "Let's not make this an issue."

"All right, but only because you insisted." After opening her purse, she tucked it inside.

Cooper threaded his fingers through hers as they headed back to the escalator. "Thanks for the jacket, Coop." For a brief moment, she rested her head on his shoulder. "I'll think of you every time I wear it."

"You're welcome and I'm honored, but please don't call me Coop."

She raised her head. "I'm sorry if I touched a nerve. Since it was your nickname at A&M—"

"I'd rather be called something else by you, Amy."

"Like what?"

He started to say something, then stopped and cleared his throat. "Cooper will do fine."

As she hopped on the escalator in front of him, she thought she heard him mutter, "For now." Something was definitely up with him. She hadn't put up a fuss about the jacket, his credit card wasn't declined and had cleared immediately, and they'd had a wonderful time. Stealing a glimpse at his profile in the mirrored wall beside them as they rode the escalator back to the ground level, Amy drew in a quick breath. Cooper's head was bowed and it appeared as though he was—praying?

Chapter 31

COOPER DROVE MATILDA to the front gate of a small airport. "Excuse me," he said, motioning to the glove compartment.

"What do you need? I'll get it," Amy said, moving her knees to the right.

"I've got it, thanks." Opening the compartment, he pulled out a badge. Stopping beside the small security booth, he lowered his window and held the badge for the security guard. "I don't have to show ID since I'm a regular here, but after 9/11, it makes me feel better to show it, anyway, as a matter of protocol."

Stepping outside the booth, the guard broke into a wide grin. "Howdy folks. How've you been—"

"Fine, Carl." Cooper stuffed the badge in his coat pocket. "Hope your family's well."

"Yes, sir. Getting ready for Christmas. Thanks for that book you sent for Wendy. Says it'll be a big help and she wanted me to thank you."

"Sure thing. Tell her the best way to thank me is to put it to good use. Carl, I'd like you to meet Amy Jacobsen. She's visiting from New York." Cooper pressed back against the seat and Amy leaned forward to give the man a smile.

Carl tipped his cap and gave her a nod. "Nice to meet you. Good, clear day for flying and you've got a great pilot here."

"Nice to meet you, too, Carl."

The man flies a plane, too?

"Can I please see your driver's license or a photo ID, Miss Jacobsen?"

"Oh, sure," she said, pulling her purse onto her lap and reaching inside for her wallet. "I don't drive much, but the license is still valid." Cooper took the license from her, taking a peek as he handed it to Carl.

After Carl thanked her and waved them inside the gate, Amy turned to Cooper. "You're really a pilot?"

He chuckled. "I really am. You're not squeamish, are you?"

"It depends on what you're talking about."

He grinned. "The roller coaster of your life."

"Flying is one of my favorite things, but once I get up in the air, I don't want to be doing any dipping or flipping around, thank you very much." She looped a circle with one finger. "Please don't tell me you fly one of those Snoopy planes."

"Snoopy planes?" Cooper's laugh was hearty as he pulled Matilda to a stop near the hangar. A number of private aircraft were parked at different angles on the tarmac.

"You know, the old-fashioned kind where you're not fully enclosed and you need to wear goggles and one of those leather caps that covers the ears, and a long scarf around the neck. Gotta have one of those. Like Amelia Ear . . ." She clamped a hand over her mouth.

"I think I can manage to keep it level. You'll be happy to know it's a Cessna 182, not a Snoopy plane. No dipping and flipping today. Were you named for the aviation pioneer?"

Amy shook her head, her hand still over her mouth.

Removing the keys from the ignition, he turned toward her. "Say something now or I'll kiss you to give your lips something constructive to do."

Lowering her hand, she sighed. "I hope I don't meet the same fate as that other Amelia."

"Well, thanks for the vote of confidence. Not exactly what I was hoping for." Cooper shook his head and climbed out of the truck. Coming around to open her door, he reached for her hand and assisted her. "For starters, no one really knows what happened to Miss Earhart. Second, there's the fact I'm an experienced pilot, like Carl said. The third thing you should know is I always pray before I take off."

"That does makes me feel better. So happy to hear it."

Tossing his keys in the air, he led her to a small, white private jet parked nearby. "Amy, meet Madelyn."

"Madelyn?" Eyes wide, she stared at him.

"What's wrong now?"

If she wasn't so stunned, she'd laugh. In both expression and tone, he was a cross between exasperation and amusement. "Nothing." She shifted from one foot to the other. "It's just that Madelyn is my middle name."

He shrugged. "Isn't that something?"

"That's all you're going to say?"

"About the name? Purely a coincidence."

"Come on, Cooper. You don't believe in coincidence any more than I do, but I know men don't randomly nickname their cars, boats, planes, mopeds or whatever." Belatedly, she closed her mouth. "Forget it. It's your private business."

"No need to get jealous. Madelyn's my mom's name." He opened the door. "Climb aboard and make yourself comfortable and I'll be back in a minute. Be good and don't touch anything on my plane."

"As if," she huffed. "Better take your keys in case I get curious." He laughed when she raised her brows and gave him a mischievous grin.

"Scamp."

"You love it," she said, trying not to laugh.

"Didn't say I didn't." Closing the door, Cooper gave her a wink and then hurried toward the hangar.

Amy's stomach flip-flopped with anticipation. She loved the thrill of taking off in a plane, the thrust of the engine, the sheer power of lifting in the air. Pulling out her phone, she checked for messages. She half expected Mitch had called. Or Landon. No messages. With a shrug, she returned the phone to her purse. The pang of disappointment wasn't because Landon hadn't called. In some ways, it was better he hadn't. How could she return to New York and go on a date with him now? Until she resolved her feelings for Cooper, it wouldn't be honest to give Landon the impression she was interested in anything more than friendship. She leaned her head against the seat and blew out a deep sigh.

Cooper climbed into the small cockpit beside her a few minutes later. "This is the pre-flight inspection portion of our program," he said as he adjusted and turned a handful of buttons and knobs on the panel.

Amy remained silent, not wanting to interrupt or distract him. All the controls and blinking lights seemed complicated. She smiled when he started the engine and the propeller rotated as he prepared for their takeoff. "I imagine being an electrical engineer helps you learn these controls. I don't know how you do it. There's so many." Her voice was tinged with an awe she didn't bother to hide.

"It's not difficult, and it's certainly easier than trying to figure out the thoughts in that beautiful head of yours. Here," he said, handing her a headset before pulling one out for himself, "this is how we communicate once we get up in the air."

Listening and watching as he demonstrated how to work the headset, she figured it was simple enough for her mush of a brain to manage. Reaching across her lap, he helped her buckle in, tugging on the strap to make certain it was secure. "Twist around a little to see if you can turn in the seat. You need enough free movement to look out the windows without being overly constricted."

Amy did as he asked, feeling a little silly, knowing he watched every move. "It's fine. Ready for that prayer now." She bowed her head as he prayed for a safe trip and added a few words when he finished.

"Ready?" She loved that mischievous grin.

"You are such a kid."

"You'll know why in a minute. There's nothing quite like flying in the wide open blue sky. It gives you a sense of unbelievable freedom."

"Do we have any time before we're supposed to take off?"

Cooper darted a glance at the clock on the control panel. "We don't really have a time—"

"Oh, whatever. Be quiet." Pulling him by the lapels of his jacket, Amy planted a quick kiss on his lips.

"We can do better than that," he said, tugging her close again and lowering his lips to hers in a very satisfying kiss. "Much better," he said a minute later, releasing her with obvious reluctance. "That's a great send-off, just in case something unexpected happens." He released her, planting another kiss on her nose before leaning his forehead against hers.

"Well, um," she said, "my kiss was for taking such good care of me, but apparently yours was farewell in the event we crash. That's real encouraging coming from the pilot, I have to say."

He laughed. "Maybe we should have waited until we're safely back on the ground, but thanks for breaking the pact."

"What pact?" She gave him a coy grin. "I don't know what you're talking about."

Opening a compartment, he retrieved a pair of aviator sunglasses. "My version of goggles," he said. *Oh my, he looks way too good.* "I've got an extra pair. Want to borrow them?"

She shook her head. "I'm fine, thanks. Now, then, it's time to get this baby up in the air."

After radioing the tower, Cooper taxied down the small runway and the plane effortlessly lifted into the air. Feeling like a kid, Amy pushed as high in the seat as possible and pressed her face against the window, suppressing the urge to say "Whee!" For the better part of the next hour, they soared above the city with Cooper pointing out highlights of interest. Amy peered out the window as she listened, giddy as a small child. His love and appreciation of his hometown was obvious.

"The park directly below you is where Mom taught me to ride a bike," he said before pointing out his childhood neighborhood.

"Wow," Amy said, eyeing the impressive houses—mansions, really—with each sprawling home in the middle of several acres and a swimming pool in the backyard. "This must have been a great place to grow up."

"It could be, yes."

She had the feeling his response had everything to do with his father. Although it was on the tip of her tongue to inquire further, she refrained. Inappropriate timing. Soon after, he turned the plane and headed back toward downtown Austin, elevating the plane to a higher altitude. "The Driskill is directly below us now on your side," he said.

"Yes, I see it! This is so great to see everything from the air."

"Glad you're enjoying the tour." He sounded pleased by her enthusiasm.

"I'll never forget it," she said. When he turned his head, their eyes locked and something inside her shifted. A second later, he returned his attention to the controls.

"Next up is the main campus of the University of Texas. I imagine it's pretty empty right now since the students are on their Christmas break. Even though I went to A&M, I spent a lot of time on this campus with my friends through the years."

Amy spied the bell tower and marveled at the massive football stadium with its giant Longhorn symbol. "Sam Lewis graduated from Texas. I guess it's true what they say," she mused, "it's so spread out and big here. At NYU, everything's . . . well, much more contained, but that was a good thing during the winter months, especially." She darted a quick glance at his handsome, dashing profile. "Why did you go to A&M instead of UT?"

"Engineering scholarship," he said, adjusting a few controls. "And I played football. Both schools have great teams, but I spent some field time as an Aggie whereas I probably would have remained a benchwarmer my entire career as a Longhorn."

"I learn something new about you all the time," she said, smiling. "What position did you play?"

"Tight end. No comments, please."

She giggled. "I wouldn't think of it."

"We're coming up on the state capitol and government office buildings now." He flew low enough for her to see the Texas and U.S. flags atop the capitol. "They have a woman dressed like Lady Liberty on the steps outside to greet visitors and they have dance demonstrations inside the rotunda. It's a fascinating tour and very impressive. Maybe I can take you sometime."

She turned away from the window. "Are you saying—"

"I'm saying I hope you'll want to come back sometime." He darted a glance her way.

Her heart picked up speed again. "I'd like that." She turned to look out the window again. "It's so charming here," she breathed. "I can see why you love it so much."

Concentrated on his task, he didn't say anything for a full minute or more. "We're starting our descent now," he said. "You might feel a little pressure and your ears might pop."

Within five minutes, they were back on the ground. "Thank you, Cooper." Amy removed her headset and handed it to him. "Hands down, that was the best plane trip I've ever taken. It was incredible and very special." When he helped her down from the plane, she felt wobbly, her legs like wet, limp noodles. Giving him a tremulous smile, she grabbed hold of his arm. "Whoa. Feeling a little shaky here."

"I've got you." Cooper slid an arm around her waist, keeping her steady.

"I was fine until I got out." She put a hand up to her head. "Sorry." Closing her eyes, she willed her equilibrium to behave.

"Let me help you into the hangar and get you some water."

"No, I'm fine. This is embarrassing enough, but I can't have you thinking I'm a wimp."

"Nothing about you can be classified that way. The Cessna's pretty smooth, but some people have that reaction if they're not used to a smaller plane. Do you want me to take you back to the hotel so you can rest before dinner?"

"You keep thinking I need to rest. I'm no wilting flower."

He laughed. "I know that."

"As a matter of fact, in New York, I'm capable of working an entire eight-hour day—sometimes more—without the benefit of a nap."

"I was actually thinking maybe you'd like to nap a little . . . with me. In the truck," he added. "No hanky panky involved."

"Oh, you!" Feeling better, she pushed away from his hold and hurried across the tarmac toward Matilda, thankfully feeling much steadier on her feet. Quiet laughter followed her. Smiling, she spun around and ran straight into him. Putting one hand on that rock-solid chest, she lifted her head when he didn't move. Didn't try to kiss her. Didn't say anything. The problem was, she couldn't see his eyes since he still wore the dark sunglasses. That bugged her to no end, as if he hid secrets. Smoothing the wayward shock of hair from his forehead, she ran her finger in a gentle pattern over that endearing, crescent-shaped scar. Beneath her other hand, she felt the rise and fall of his chest, his ragged breathing.

"Cooper," she said, swallowing hard, "I think it's best if we put the pact back in place now."

He looked away and blew out a breath. "Exactly."

As he drove them out of the airport, she sensed the change in their behavior. The constant barbs and back-and-forth exchanges had slowly transitioned into mutual admiration and fascination. Since she was leaving for Houston tomorrow and then heading back to New York late on Wednesday, how could a relationship with this man work by any stretch of the imagination? She closed her eyes and leaned her head against the seat, knowing he watched.

You've brought this man into my life for a reason, Lord, and I'm going to trust You know what You're doing.

She'd never doubted His guidance in her life before, and she wasn't about to start now.

Chapter 32

SHE'D KNOW THAT lush, dark head of hair anywhere. As Amy spied Cooper coming up the grand staircase from the lobby to the mezzanine, all she wanted to do was run to him, run her fingers through those lush waves and give him a kiss he'd never forget. *This is getting ridiculous.*

When he rounded the corner and approached the lounge area outside The Driskill Grill, she couldn't take her eyes off him. In his dark, double-breasted suit with white shirt and deep red tie, he was the most handsome man she'd ever seen. Stopping a few feet away, he moved one hand over his heart. As he made his way to where she sat on one of the loveseats outside the restaurant, she rose to greet him.

"You look ravishing, Amelia." The whispered words thrilled her heart, the kiss on her temple sent shivers everywhere. His glance was admiring as he took in the length of her, making the past few months of diligent workouts and watching calories worth every sacrifice. Not to mention the manicure and pedicure at an obscenely overpriced New York salon. Tossing her classic, black jersey dress into the suitcase at the last minute had also been a very good instinct. The neckline dipped—low enough to make her feel like a woman yet not revealing anything it shouldn't—and the cut emphasized her waist before skimming over her hips and falling to her knees. Paired with the strappy, high-heeled silver sandals she'd worn to the rehearsal dinner and wedding, she'd aimed for classic elegance. A dainty silver bracelet and matching earrings—Celeste's gift for her last birthday—were the perfect complements. As they walked together toward the entrance of the restaurant, she caught him stealing another glance.

Cooper crooked his arm, offering it to her. "Shall we go in to dinner now?" Tearing her gaze from his, she was afraid to ponder what those blue eyes might be telling her.

This is crazy. They hardly knew each other. *And yet we know each other so well.*

Escorting her into the restaurant, he pressed a gentle hand on the small of her back in an intimate yet appropriate manner. Pulling out her chair, he waited until she was settled. For the next two hours, they talked quietly, laughed together and sampled one another's entrées. The cuisine was top-notch, the company even better. Attentive and responsive, he managed to turn the attention back to her whenever she ventured into personal territory. Oh, yes the man was smooth and purposeful. Most people wanted to talk about themselves, and she wondered why he seemed reluctant to share details about his life.

"Cooper," she said as they finished their dinners, "could you tell me a little more about what you meant in Baton Rouge when you talked about giving your heart to the Lord and then—"

"Ah yes, the stupid comment." He took a quick sip of his water. "I fell away from the Lord when I was in my mid-teens and it lasted a few years. For one thing, I was something of an anomaly at A&M because I was both the newspaper editor and an athlete." He gave her a small smile. "Others weren't sure whether I was a geek or cool unless they got to know me. It's almost like I had a dual iden—" He stopped abruptly and cleared his throat. "I got caught up in the whole fraternity and sports thing and wanted to experience the world before I was ready."

"A lot of young people do," she said, wanting him to know she understood.

He nodded. "When I started my career, things took off quicker than I expected and I faced a lot of choices early on." His gaze moved to hers, and she glimpsed a sadness. "Choices I wasn't prepared for, both professionally and personally. I willingly fell into some common traps because of bad decisions. But, I've never been arrested, never been addicted to alcohol, tobacco, drugs or anything else. I've never physically hurt anyone with my bare hands or behind the wheel of a car. For a time, I partied too hard and liked the fast lane too much, but that's all behind me. My mom taught me right from wrong and instilled solid Christian values in me early on, but I was determined to put God to the test. And so . . . I did." After wiping his napkin over his mouth, Cooper laid it on the side of his plate. "The Lord's brought me to my knees a few times and humbled me. He's taught me some invaluable lessons, and some were pretty hard to accept at the time."

Amy's eyes welled and a tear dropped from her lashes. She tried to wipe it away before he noticed, but he missed nothing.

"I've disappointed you."

"Don't be silly," she said, brushing away another tear and dabbing at the corners of both eyes with her napkin. "We all make mistakes. I make a ton of them on a daily basis. If you harbor any illusions that I'm some kind of perfect Christian, you can forget it. I think the main thing is that we learn from our missteps." She lifted her eyes to his. "Witnessing how the Lord can sometimes turn our mistakes into life's sweetest blessings is one of His miracles."

"I don't think you're perfect."

She'd opened her mouth to continue, but closed it instead.

"What I think," he said, leaning close with a smile that reached the deep recesses of her heart, "is you're open to God's leading, and you're willing to follow His call. That's a beautiful quality and a whole lot more than I can say for most people, Christian or not. Besides, if you were perfect, you sure wouldn't be sitting here with me." She adored the way his eyes crinkled at the corners. "All I've learned up to this point helps me appreciate the woman sitting across from me all the more. I've needed a woman like you, but I didn't know it . . . until you came along and tore apart every preconceived perception I had of what a relationship could be."

Shaking her head, Amy stared at him. "I take it that's in a good way?"

"The best way."

Sitting back in her chair, she gave him a helpless look. "We've only known each other for two days. Barely forty-eight hours. This is completely crazy."

"By whose standards of measure?"

"What do you mean?"

"Tell me something." Taking her hand, he laced their fingers together, holding on tight. "How long did your parents know each other before they fell in love?"

She shook her head, wondering what prompted his question. *Love?* "My parents weren't your typical love story."

"No love story should be typical. How long?"

Giving up this line of questioning wasn't on the horizon, it seemed. "Two weeks."

"And when did they marry?"

Turning her head, she blew out a breath. "They were engaged within a month and married the next month." She stopped short of asking him if he'd been talking with Mitch. *Mitch knows Landon, not the man sitting here at the table.* Wanting to ask Cooper about *his* parents, she refrained, given his reluctance to discuss his dad.

"You should know I spoke with Kevin at the reception. I shared with him my thoughts about how special you are."

"You did?"

Cooper took a sip of water and nodded. "Kevin may be quiet, but he's one of the sharpest guys I know. He noticed my preoccupation with you, and he wasn't the only one." The way he trailed his fingers over her wrist in a light caress was tantalizing. Knowing she should withdraw from his touch, she couldn't. "Amy, I can't believe our good-bye tomorrow will be final in any sense of the word." He paused. "Do you?"

"No." The word was quiet. Wiping away another traitorous tear, she dared to meet his gaze.

"I want to see you again. Soon. Please tell me that's what you want, too."

Her resolve softened at the depth of emotion in those incredible eyes. "You know I do. But," she said, waving her hand, "your life is here in Texas, and mine is in New York. We're worlds apart."

"I say we let God handle the details and not fight it. Have you ever been in love before?"

That question took her by surprise. "Not supposed to ask that one." Lowering her gaze, she twisted her hands together in her lap. "I'd hoped to project this image of a sophisticated, professional woman who's had at least one serious relationship in her life." She turned her head and looked away. "I must sound pretty pathetic to you."

"Not at all. If anything, I think the Lord saved you for me."

"*What?*" Fumbling for the right words, she gave him a helpless look. "I do believe . . ."

"You believe . . . what?" The man was uncanny in reading her, as though he could see past any veneer straight into her mind, her heart. "Is that so impossible for you to believe?"

She inhaled a deep breath. "How do you expect me to react when you say things like that?" Glancing at her lap again, she smoothed her napkin, needing something to do with her hands. In the boldness of his statement, if she didn't know better, she'd think Landon sat at the table with her.

"Time is immaterial. We understand one another better—and have more in common—than a lot of people who've been married for years. It's the special kind of relationship that only happens once in a lifetime."

Taking a deep breath, she held up one hand. "One of us has to be rational, and this is happening so fast," she said. "I'm scared, but it's not *you* that's scaring me. You make me feel things I've never felt before and I have no idea what to do with all this . . . overwhelming emotion."

"Well," he said, "we can trade e-mails, burn up the phone lines and talk a little Texan."

"What's Texan? Considering it's the second time you've mentioned it, this must be something important to you." Sipping her water, she relaxed. "Tell me, is it something Christians do? Clarification: something Christians *should* do?"

Cooper's laugh was deep and wonderful. "Flirty talk, sweet talk, but within the bounds of propriety. At least until marriage when it becomes a matter of personal preference and—if you ask me—priority." His grin was borderline provocative, stirring all kinds of emotion. "You know how powerful words can be, Amy."

She snapped up her head. "What did you say?"

"I said words can be very powerful. Don't you agree?" If Cooper sensed she was bothered, he didn't show it as he signaled their waiter for the check.

Pondering his words, she remained silent. As much as she wanted to believe him, doubts niggled at her mind. The biggest problem—one she couldn't admit to this man—was that she'd fallen hard for him. For a split second, she wondered if Cooper really *was* Landon. No, couldn't be. Crazy idea. Why would he mislead her? Still, how could there be so many similarities? It made no sense unless he was some kind of actor. *Or a writer wanting a good story.* She needed to stop this train of thought now . . . it was dangerous.

Chapter 33

YOU HAVE TO tell her. The thought nicked at Landon's conscience and guilt wound its way into his heart, squeezing him so tight at times he almost couldn't breathe. Loosening his shirt collar hadn't helped. He'd dropped all the hints and clues he could think of to point Amy to the truth, so she'd figure out his true identity. *Coward.* An almost unbearable burden rested on his shoulders and he'd been either too chicken, too selfish—or both—to come straight out and tell her. What a sham—he was a man who prided himself on being honest to his core. No Christian man should lead on a woman and act this way. He had no excuses except his own selfishness in not wanting to let go of her. When the truth was revealed, would she hate his guts or find it amusing and laugh it off? Somehow, the latter didn't seem likely.

Slipping his hand around Amy's waist as they walked out of The Driskill Grill, he could tell she liked it but wasn't used to it. A middle-aged man in a tuxedo played a grand piano outside the restaurant and musicians tuned their instruments on the small stage behind him. As they passed by the piano, he pointed out the yellow rose etched in glass on the top. Offering a long-stemmed yellow rose to Amy, the pianist launched into a rousing rendition of "The Yellow Rose of Texas." Landon dropped a bill in the man's tip jar with one of his cards.

"The concierge told me Austin is the 'Live Music Capital of the World,'" Amy said as he walked her to the coat check.

"Sure is. We have the most musicians and music venues per capita than any other city in the world. Okay, you have a choice," he said. "We can stay here and enjoy some great, top-quality jazz or we can go to a winter wonderland outside the city limits. But whatever we do, we'll end the evening with a slow dance here in the lobby before I send you upstairs for the night."

"A winter wonderland sounds whimsical, and whimsy wins every time." She was so open with her heart and emotions, and the affection in her voice—combined with the look in her eyes—simultaneously captivated and haunted him. Helping her into her jacket, Landon called himself a few choice names, hating himself for squandering her affections. *Lord, forgive me.*

The ride in the truck was quiet. He was quickly falling over the edge with Amy and had allowed her access to his heart. It was as unexpected as it was unprecedented. Was love driving his need to know her better? Having nothing to compare it to, he wasn't sure. No other woman had ever jumpstarted his feelings of protectiveness and unmitigated desire like Amy did. They'd passed the ultimate test alone in that motel room. It must be love because he only wanted what was best for her. He could see himself raising children with her. She'd be a great mother someday.

Whoa. Slow down, buddy. Based on your dad's track record, you'd probably be lousy at it. Above all, he didn't want to push her by moving too fast, but how could he help it? In New York, he'd been brash and come on too strong. Now, he was doing the same thing and yet she was right beside him for the ride. *The ride of a lifetime.* In essence, this woman was the girl of his dreams. No other woman possessed such purity, trust and incomparable beauty. He wanted to know more about her—everything about her—but his own stupidity might have sidelined that idea. An overwhelming sadness overtook him.

He guided Matilda into the annual festival of lights on the outskirts of the city, full of multicolored, twinkling lights.

"What *is* this place?" She peered out the car windows like she'd done in his airplane, full of childlike enthusiasm. Joy lit her eyes as she turned back to him. "It's fantastic."

"It's a garden the city transforms into a holiday paradise at Christmas. Come on. Let's take a walk." He assisted her as she slid down from the truck.

Closing the door, he reached for her hand again, pleased by how easily she accepted it—skin against skin without gloves like in New York. The stars in the clear night sky winked from their lofty perch, rivaling the glowing lights surrounding them. Hand-in-hand, they traversed the narrow pathways, a dizzying maze of shades of red, green, blue and white. When she leaned her head against his shoulder, he moved his arm around her.

"Will you sit with me for a few minutes?" he asked. She nodded but didn't speak, following as he led her to a bench and they sat close together. Seeing her shiver even though she wore her new coat, he slipped out of his suit jacket and draped it around her. His gaze slid a luxurious path from her lovely high cheekbones to the lines of her jaw, sloping to her long, elegant neck before settling on the sweet, enticing hollow at the base of her throat. *She's so beautiful, Lord.*

"You're staring."

"I can't help it." He knew she didn't mind. "I've been here almost every Christmas of my life and it's never looked as incredible as it does tonight."

"There you go again, getting all mushy." Her dark hair reflected the lights and he longed to touch it, tangle his fingers in it, draw her near and kiss her until tomorrow.

"There's so much to say." He tipped her chin.

"I know, but I think we already said it all at dinner." She turned her head, avoiding his probing gaze, as though afraid to allow him entrance to her private thoughts. He didn't deserve this woman. But selfishly, he wanted her. *Lord, I need her.* She'd be the solid anchor he'd needed but hadn't known until now. His eyes widened. How had he not seen what he'd been missing for all these years? *Because you hadn't met Amy.*

"Why are you fighting this?" His eyes never left her face.

"You're a romantic fool."

"Guilty. Who'd have thought it? Here's a thought: let's run away together and find adventure across the globe."

"Where would we go?" She nestled into the curve of his arm and they laughed and talked until a comfortable silence settled between them. With the back of one hand, he stroked his fingers across her cheek.

"Cooper, we shouldn't . . ." Even as she said the words, Amy lowered her lids. Those irresistible, soft lips parted, inviting him. When he touched his mouth to hers, she trembled, prompting him to increase his efforts. Loving a woman wasn't easy under any circumstances, but as he covered her mouth with his—tasting, nibbling, savoring—he knew he couldn't risk *not* loving her.

Time lost all meaning and he finally released her. "I have something for you, but it's in my jacket."

"Cooper, no. You've already given me too much."

"Okay, then, if you won't do it, I'll get it."

With a deep sigh, she shook her head and retrieved the small black box from an inside pocket. "What did you do now?" Darting him a wary glance, her fingers shook as she opened the top and spied the gorgeous sapphire locket nestled inside. Judging by the way she ran a reverent finger over it, Amy recognized this was no trinket.

"Turn it over." He sat back, watching with bated breath.

"*Amy, Hebrews 11:1. With love . . .*" Her voice faded to a whisper. Holding it up to the moonlight by its silver chain, she squinted. "I can't make it out if there's a name."

Inside, his stomach churned. This was supposed to be the moment she realized who he was. He quietly quoted, "Now faith is the assurance of things hoped for, the conviction of things not seen." The verse struck him as highly ironic given their present circumstances.

"It's absolutely gorgeous. You've given me so much, and I have nothing to give you."

"You've given me more than you'll ever know. This is my mom's, and her mom gave it to her."

Amy moved her hand over her heart. "That makes it even more valuable."

"She wants you to have it. I told her about you and she gave it to me with her blessing."

Her glance was incredulous. "Why would she give such a gorgeous heirloom to a total stranger? You even had it engraved. I appreciate the thought, but how can I accept this?" Putting the necklace back in the box, Amy tucked it back inside his jacket. "This is such a valuable part of your family heritage, your heart."

Using the pads of his thumbs, he wiped away her tears. He loved that he evoked such strong emotion in her, but hated that he'd made her cry. "My sentiments exactly. I was hoping you'd want to wear it as a reminder of our time together. It would mean a lot to me if you'd accept it, Amy. May I?" She hesitated so long he was afraid she'd refuse more than the necklace. Finally, she nodded without speaking, but still appeared conflicted. Retrieving the box and opening it, he pulled out the necklace and fastened it around her neck.

She touched the necklace and glanced back up at him through watery eyes. "I'm sorry," she said as more tears slipped onto her cheeks. "I don't mean to cry. It's so unlike me."

"You say that every time you cry." This woman had no idea of the emotions roiling inside him. He wasn't proud of his behavior, and every moment that passed and he wasn't honest enough to tell her the truth, made his self-revulsion grow stronger. "Don't be afraid to reveal what's in your heart."

"This must be embarrassing for you, sitting here with me crying on your shoulder."

"You should know I don't embarrass easily, and I could care less what anybody else thinks. God's the only One who knows my heart." He pulled back and took her hands in his. "Amy, I need to tell you something."

Putting her fingers over his lips, she stilled them. "Shh," she whispered, "no serious talk tonight."

"This is important."

"And so," she said, scooting closer, "is this." Leaning close, she planted a warm, sweet kiss on his cheek.

"You'll want to know this. Trust me on that," he said, his resolve melting when she moved those luscious lips to his jaw and headed for the corner of his mouth. Did she have any idea how seductive she was?

Taking her hands, he pulled back. "Please listen."

Withdrawing her hands, she rose to her feet. "This night is too precious, and I'm getting tired. No serious discussions tonight." Her eyes, bright in the moonlight, met his. "I think it's time to return to the hotel now."

"As you wish." Standing beside her, he waited until she reached for his hand. "Promise we'll talk before I take you to Houston tomorrow."

She squeezed his hand. "Thank you, and I promise."

Lord, you know I tried. He couldn't bring himself to spoil the evening, break the connection, especially when she specifically asked him not to bring up anything serious. He'd be up all night, praying for the Lord to give him the right words when he told her and revealed his true identity. Then he'd pray she wouldn't kill him, a distinct possibility.

Dropping her off at the hotel an hour later, he brushed her forehead with a good night kiss. "I understand your TeamWork nickname is Daydreamer."

Amy offered him a dazed smile through sleepy eyes. "Which one of my friends told you that?"

"I'll never reveal my source," he said. "but it suits you."

"Thank you for the most romantic evening of my life." Taking his hand, she pulled him further into the lobby. "You promised me one last dance."

Without a word, he helped her out of her jacket and laid it on the closest chair. As if it was the most natural thing in the world—he the only man, she the only woman—she curled into his chest without hesitation. The contours of her body aligned perfectly with his. "We were made to dance like this." *Made for each other.* With his lips on her temple, he felt her sigh. Closing his eyes, leaning his head against hers, he blocked out everything else. Nothing else mattered. *Lord, please keep me strong. Help me to be worthy of her. I'll tell her tomorrow morning before we leave Austin. If she hates me, I'll fight for her. But I need Your help.*

In the dimly lit, deserted lobby, Landon serenaded his beautiful Daydreamer as he danced with her around the Christmas tree, accompanied by the strains of live jazz wafting down from the mezzanine musicians above. She slid her hand up the front of his jacket. He wrapped her hand in his and drew her close, cherishing this woman and the night, committing it to memory. Come tomorrow morning, it might only be a sweet memory. Twirling her, Landon lowered his lips to hers, losing himself in the pure joy . . . of Amelia.

Chapter 34

FRESHLY-SHOWERED AND BACK in her suite, Amy sat on the bed for a few minutes and recounted her life with Cooper since they'd left Baton Rouge. That exactly what it was: *life.* She'd never met anyone like him, but even the things he did that most annoyed her—the overly-flirtatious comments, the presumptuous confidence—also attracted her. The man was certainly a challenge. The attraction between them was strong and he was physical perfection, except for that crescent-shaped scar, but it only added to his appeal.

She bowed her head. *Father, I've only known him a short time, but it's been a very eventful few days. What is this feeling I have for him? Is it love or infatuation? I'm asking for Your help to discern the difference.*

After the most perfect evening of her life capped by the romantic dance in the lobby, he'd asked if they could push back their trip to Houston until late morning to give them time to talk. Whatever he wanted to tell her, or discuss with her, must be very important. As he walked her to the elevator, he'd been quiet as if his mind was weighted with a heavy burden. Their future perhaps? Was it crazy to contemplate a long-distance relationship with Cooper? How could that possibly work? She glanced at the clock. At almost ten, it was too late to call Lexa. She'd call her in the morning to tell her of the change in plans.

A knock sounded on the outer door of the suite, sending her pulse into overdrive. *Surely not.* Retrieving her robe from the end of the bed, she pushed her arms in the sleeves and looped the belt at her waist. "Who's there?" she asked, approaching the door.

"Room service, Miss Jacobsen." The voice was young, female, Hispanic.

Removing the security chain, Amy greeted the hotel staffer holding a large slice of chocolate cake on a china plate, covered with plastic wrap. "For you, compliments of . . . um, Your Devoted Cowboy. I think that's what I'm supposed to say."

"Thank you," Amy said, resisting the urge to laugh as she took the plate. "Hold on a second and let me get my purse."

"No tip." She shook her head. "Very handsome man, your cowboy. Nice."

"Yes, he is." Amy smiled. "Thank you again."

Closing the door and reattaching the chain, she eyed the cake as she carried it into the bedroom. Eating something this sweet wouldn't be advisable if she wanted to sleep. *Cooper, you shouldn't have.* The man forgot nothing. She left the plate on the small writing desk in the outer part of the suite and returned to the bedroom.

Turning back to the bed, she frowned when she spied her purse sitting by her pillow. Time to do a little housecleaning and toss old receipts. Switching on the news, she half-listened as she scanned the receipts, crumpling the ones she didn't need to save. A story about a homeless shelter in New York caught her attention and she grabbed the remote to increase the volume. "The project is funded by a group of Manhattan and Texas businessmen, part of a Christian organization called . . ."

Amy's breathing grew shallow and she mouthed the word at the same time as the newswoman. "TeamWork." Leaning forward on the bed, she watched a few seconds of video footage of the group in action at a soup kitchen in New York, riveted. She scanned the group of men and women, some she recognized from her inner-city projects. *Landon.* There he was, big as life, smiling and talking with a group of men. In another clip, she spied him helping to stock supplies for a food pantry and then in a final clip, she saw him in a lineup of men, serving food at a shelter.

Landon's part of TeamWork? Since when? Why hadn't he said anything? TeamWork was a huge organization, but with her projects in New York, wouldn't they have crossed paths? Did he know she was a TeamWork volunteer, too? Her cell phone rang, startling her out of her trancelike state. She reached for it, not checking the display.

"Hey, Amy."

"Hi, Mitch. No offense, but it's late, and I'm really tired." She yawned for emphasis. "What's up? Make it quick."

"Hear me out on this."

The somber tone of his voice sent off alarms. "I'm not sure I like the sound of that, but go ahead. Speak."

"Have you ever researched the two men in your life?"

She frowned. "No, I haven't. Unlike you, it's not my first instinct when I meet a handsome man. *Men*," she added, "which sounds weird enough. I take it you have a report. You're making me nervous."

"Excuse me for stating the obvious, but for an intelligent writer trained in research and investigative work, you haven't done your homework."

"Spill it, Mitch the Itch." That childhood nickname was well-deserved tonight. Staring at a chipped nail, she made a mental note to touch it up before leaving the hotel in the morning.

"Okay, there's all sorts of information out there about a Landon C. Warnick, but I can't find a single thing on any Cooper Warren of Austin, Texas or anywhere else for that matter. Can't find any record of him in the alumni records of Texas A&M either, although again, there's tons of stuff on Landon Warnick."

"Is that really so unusual? After all, Landon keeps a much higher profile than Cooper. Some people like to keep their life private. Is that so hard to believe?"

"No, but even so, you can usually find something to indicate the person actually exists. But, like I said, there's absolutely nothing. All I'm saying is, I find it very curious."

Her agitation transitioned into bewilderment. "Surely you're not suggesting I either made up the man or that he doesn't exist. If that's the case, I can assure you he's a living, breathing, fine specimen of manhood."

"Well, thanks for that. Neither am I suggesting the man could have taken great pains to remove all traces of his name from the Internet. You can do that, but it takes a whole lot of time and trouble. You need a good motivation." Her brother's voice dripped with irony.

"I don't like what you're suggesting," Amy said. "I trust Cooper, and I won't listen to any of this since it serves no worthwhile purpose. So, please take your insinuations and doubts and keep them to yourself."

"You can't blame me for looking out for my little sister's heart. I want to make sure the man who's stolen your heart hasn't also stolen something else, or done something he doesn't want anyone to know about. Or simply—"

"What makes you think he's stolen my heart?"

Mitch's sigh was audible. "This is *me*, Maddy."

Her eyes opened wider at the nickname. "Good night, Mitch."

"I'll talk to you again soon," he said. "Please think about what I've said and be careful. That's all I ask."

While she appreciated his protective instincts, Amy wished he hadn't planted the seed of doubt in her mind. A big old seed. Stunned, on autopilot, she put her cell phone on the bedside table and turned down the volume on the TV as she resumed sorting through the things in her purse. Although it kept her fingers occupied, her mind worked overtime, pondering her brother's words.

Rising from the bed, she started to pace, trying to remember all the seemingly "little" things she'd pushed to the back of her mind. She began the mental list, wondering if she should write them down. Landon wore readers in Café Eduardo. She thought she'd seen Cooper wearing glasses in the hotel room, although he didn't use them last night at dinner. Then again, he didn't look at the menu and told her he always ordered the same entrée at The Driskill Grill.

Both Landon and Cooper were at least six foot two or three, both left handed. Cooper said a number of things almost identical to what Landon had said. He'd cut off Carl at the airport and made sure she didn't see his ID badge. Amy's eyes widened as she recalled he'd referred to Sam's book as an ARC copy. How would an electrical engineer know the term for Advance Reader Copy?

What was it he'd said before dinner tonight? She tapped her knuckles against her temple. Something he'd said had triggered a response, but she'd chosen to ignore it. Squeezing her eyes tight, she concentrated. It came to her in less than a minute, and she blinked hard. *He called me Amelia.* Sure, he'd asked her if she was named after Amelia Earhart when they were in his plane, but had she ever told him her real name? *Think, Amy.* Of course, he could have found that information at the wedding or on the Internet. That one thing wasn't incriminating, but—combined with all the other signs—it was enough to give her pause. Serious pause.

The locket. Cooper said his mother gave it to him and wanted her to have it. Running over to the dresser, she retrieved it with shaking fingers. Turning it over, she could now see the name . . . only it was initials. "LCJW," she said in the quiet of the suite. She brought her hand up to her forehead. Landon was also Sam's publisher?

Feeling dizzy, she returned to the bed. Her mind was spinning. Returning to her task, Amy sifted through the remaining receipts. When she spied the Macy's receipt for her jacket, a sense of foreboding overtook her, tightening her throat, making it difficult to breathe. Her fingers shook almost uncontrollably as she moved her gaze to the bottom of the sales ticket. Surprisingly, it was legible. Staring at it, her heart skidded to a stop. The small piece of paper slipped between her fingers and fluttered a slow path to the floor as she fell back on the luxurious comforter and released an anguished groan.

As she'd suspected, the scrawled signature didn't read Cooper Warren.

She'd seen that same scrawl in *New York Scene.* It belonged to its publisher and editor-in-chief, Landon Warnick.

Chapter 35

THE PRISON GUARD ushered him inside and closed the door. Landon approached the small table in the middle of the room and slumped into the steel and black vinyl chair. He focused on the clock in the otherwise utilitarian room—stark white walls devoid of photos, color or anything to stimulate the mind. Providing ample time to dwell on what he'd done. Funny thing how that was the intended effect on the person sitting on the *other* side of the table.

A long time ago, he'd made a vow to the Lord that when and if *he* ever married, he'd never disappoint and betray his wife and family in the countless ways his father had done. No one deserved that, and he had the lingering emotional battle scars to prove it. He'd seen what his dad's betrayal had done to his mom and been on the receiving end of empty promises and personal failure from a man who'd built an empire only to bring it down because of insatiable greed and selfishness. Call it subconscious, but his lousy excuse of a father might be the reason he'd avoided serious relationships. After meeting Amy, his world had spun into freefall and had him rethinking his perspective on life, work and love. He'd done so many things wrong and now was the time to start trying to make them right. Doing it *God's* way instead of his own.

To the point of forgiving this man.

The door opened, and his dad entered, dressed in khakis and a short-sleeved black shirt. Taking small steps, he shuffled as though shackled. Landon tried to hide his shock. In the eight months since he'd last visited, the lines on Jared Warnick's face were more deeply-etched, his eyes rimmed with dark circles. His hair was cut military style but still dark and peppered with silver. Life and bad choices had beaten him down. Most likely, it was his conscience that was chained, devouring him from the inside. Guilt could do that to a man.

Landon pulled himself from the chair and rose to his feet as his dad approached. "Hey, Jared." When the older man took his hand, it felt brittle and not at all like the firm, warm handshake he remembered. He looked shorter, more slight and pale. Nearly four years in a minimum security facility had altered the appearance of this once robust, healthy man. The weathered face reminded him of a homeless man he'd met back in New York. A pang of emotion pricked his conscience. Holding onto his hand longer than necessary, he was at a loss for words.

Jared ran a palm over his grizzled face. "Been a long time."

"Things have been hectic."

"I know you've got a lot of responsibilities. Good to see you back in Texas." His father motioned for him to sit and sank into the chair opposite him. "How's life treating you in New York? Everything okay with the magazine?"

Landon shifted. For a father who'd never shown much interest through the years, this was a switch—conversing like they actually liked each other or shared some kind of relationship. "Things are okay, but that's not what I want to talk about. First, do you need anything?"

With a snort, Jared drew random circles on the table with one finger. "Nothing you can give me, but thanks for the offer. Your being here will do. So, what's brought you around to see me?"

"I need to ask you something."

Blue eyes almost identical to his own bore into him with firm resolve. "Speak. I'm all ears."

Landon grunted and leaned forward, crossing his arms on the table. "Why'd you do it?"

The older man blew out a deep sigh and focused on one of the bare walls. "I wondered how long it'd take you to ask. What makes you finally ask now?"

"Answer the question and then I'll tell you."

A frown creased his dad's forehead. "Fair enough. The short answer is greed. I wanted something I couldn't have, not that I'd expect you to understand."

Landon snorted. "I might understand better than you think."

"Oh?" One brow raised. "From what I know, you've got everything. You worked hard to get where you are, and I'm proud of you." Something suspiciously akin to pride shot through Jared's features.

How he'd longed to hear those words when he was younger. "A few months ago—even a few weeks—I might have agreed. Not now."

"Tell me, then. What is it that you want?" His dad leaned closer. "I guess I should put it another way. What is it you want that you can't get? That's usually the way it works, isn't it?"

"Self-respect is rather hard to come by at the moment."

"What do you mean, son?"

Calling him "son" hit him hard as Landon stared into the eyes of the man who gave him life. The man who'd taught him to always be honest and then let him down by cheating on his mom in every way possible and stealing from the company he'd founded with a few hundred dollars and then spearheaded into a small empire. A living, breathing example of how *not* to treat a woman and let down his friends, his family, his son.

"I'm afraid I've done what you did, in a manner of speaking."

"Ah," his dad said. Deep sadness crossed those once-handsome features. "The sins of the father revisited. A tortured soul can spot another a mile away. I figured as much. So, tell me, what'd you do?"

He tried to ignore the implication of *this time* tacked onto that statement. "I hurt the woman I love, and she doesn't know it. Yet."

"You'd better explain it to me so it makes some kind of sense." Jared settled back in his chair and crossed his arms over his chest.

Landon met his gaze, holding it steady. "I pretended to be someone I'm not. Sort of. It's very convoluted."

His dad chuckled. "It usually is. I've got all the time in the world." He paused. "Tell me. You've come here for a reason and if there's any way I can help you, I'll try."

The words shot straight to his heart. "I'm a fraud." Much to his chagrin, a tear escaped at the same time self-loathing stirred in his gut.

"Meaning you want me to help you out of the self-imposed prison you've put yourself in? Give you the voice of reason from what I've learned?"

Landon nodded. "I never thought I'd be asking, but I want your advice."

"Okay, then. Here's my advice: don't be greedy, selfish and stupid." A smile hovered around the corners of his mouth. "Seems to me there's a simple answer."

"Care to share it with me?"

"Confess. Tell her everything. Humble yourself. If you love her, you owe her that much and a whole lot more."

"I know." Landon poured out his story as his dad listened, asking a question every now and then. He purposely omitted a few details. Things like staying in the same motel room. That was his business to square away with God. Telling anyone else would feel like a further betrayal of Amy, and he couldn't risk harming her any more than he'd already done.

"Sounds like she's worth getting back, son," Jared said when he finished. "One of the biggest mistakes of my life was being too proud to admit I was wrong. That and being too arrogant. If I wanted something, I took it and didn't think twice about hurting anyone else. Funny thing, though. If I'd asked, they'd probably have freely given it to me." Shaking his head, he ran a hand through his short hair. "I hurt the people I loved the most. I should have humbled myself and begged your mama's forgiveness. Should have spent more time trying to make amends. By the time I came to my senses and tried, it was too late. There's only so much a woman can take." He hesitated and waited until Landon met his eyes. "Only so much a son should have to put up with."

Landon held his father's gaze. "Maybe you should have tried harder."

"Agreed, but you and I both know you wouldn't have listened. One of the things you got from me is that hard-headed stubbornness and win-at-all-costs attitude. By the time you were sixteen, you'd already made up your mind about me. Like it or not, son, you're a whole lot like your old man."

That statement brought reality home and with it a revelation. "I doubt I'd have the magazine if I wasn't like you in some respects."

A hint of a smile emerged. "Is that your way of saying I'm not such a bad guy?"

Landon smirked. "It's more of a begrudging thank you. Look, gratitude wasn't in my mind when I came here today, but one thing Mom taught me was respect. In spite of all you did, she wanted me to try and understand who you are. Why you did what you did." He drummed his fingers on the table, lost in thought.

"Your mama's the best woman I've ever known. The way I look at it, I did two things right in my life. Marrying Madelyn was the first."

"And the second?"

"I'm looking at him."

Lowering his gaze, Landon choked down the wad of bitterness lodged in his throat. Never in his life had his dad been this honest with him.

When he lifted his head, Jared's eyes were bright. "Sounds like Amy's your Madelyn."

"You know, Madelyn is Amy's middle name."

"Is that a fact? Don't know about you, but that's no coincidence."

Landon snapped up his head. "My thoughts exactly."

"Tell me your plan."

"Don't have one yet, but I will." He blew out a breath, frustration interwoven with resignation. "My biggest fear is that when I tell her, I'll lose her. I can't let that happen."

"Do what I said, son, and then give her some time. From what you've told me, you did a boneheaded thing, but it sounds like you two had yourselves quite the adventure and got to know each other in the process. You've got a lot in common, work in the same business and live in the same city. I know patience isn't your strong suit, but you're smart and resourceful. I'm sure you'll figure out a way to get back in her good graces. Just plead your case and give her some time."

Rising to his feet, Landon skirted around the table and drew his father into his arms before he could think better of it. He couldn't recall the last time he'd hugged him. Jared returned the hug, his grip surprisingly firm and patted him on the back. That pretty much did him in. Squeezing his eyes tight, Landon willed himself to be strong and not shed any more tears.

As he rang the bell to summon the guard, Jared gave him a wry grin. "By the way, I've still got that Bible you gave me."

"Good. Read it much?" Maybe that was pushing it, but those words were soothing for his heart.

His dad's low chuckle reverberated around the walls of the small room. "Yeah, a little. If it means that much to you and your mama, maybe I should read it. It's not like I'm pressed for time." Jared's eyes settled on him. "From what I can tell, you turned out okay."

Landon nodded, his eyes wet. "I'll be back."

"I'll look forward to it, son. Remember what I said. Go get your girl. Bring her around to meet me one of these days, and don't stay away so long next time."

"I won't." His eyes met his father's. "Thanks . . . Dad."

Jared saluted him as the stone-faced guard appeared and escorted him from the room. The last four years, he'd called his dad every name in the book, and some he'd never mutter out loud, but he'd thought them in his heart. Now he was guilty of the very same sin.

Closing his eyes, Landon sank into the chair again and bowed his head. *Father, forgive me. I've done the same thing as my dad. Not that I blame him. I'm my own man, but fully capable of the same faults. I've hurt the woman I love and pray she'll find it in her heart to forgive me. Help me find the right way to tell her, and help me accept whatever happens.*

Chapter 36

AMY TUCKED THE black dress into her suitcase the next morning, trying not to notice the scent of his cologne still lingering in its fabric. How things could change in the course of a few hours. Last night, she'd spun precious memories slow dancing in the man's arms, falling in love and dreading saying good-bye to him. Sleep had eluded her much of the night. Pounding her pillow, she finally wised up around three in the morning and prayed. Her unrest ebbed enough so she could finally catch some fitful sleep for a few hours but then it started up again as soon as she opened her eyes and climbed out of bed. While she packed, she stewed, chastising herself and grumbling like a crazy person. Wadding up her nightgown, she tossed it on top of the other clothes. Seeing that nightgown triggered memories of their night in that fleabag motel in Nowhereville, Texas. A small smile slipped out before she could stop it.

"You are pathetic!" Shaking her head, she stomped into the bathroom. "What kind of girl goes on a road trip through Texas, of all places, with a man she doesn't know? And allows him to pay for everything and then falls hard for the guy? You're not only naïve, Amy Jacobsen, you're unbelievably stupid."

Her dad always cautioned her and Mitch against calling anyone stupid. "People do stupid things, but don't ever call *them* stupid," he'd said. "It's demeaning and condescending."

She agreed although she'd been known to engage in private name-calling on occasion.

"We were made to dance like this," she said, rolling her eyes and mimicking Cooper—*Landon* from the night before. Funny how situations—and people—could look so different in the light of day. "This is one girl who doesn't have stars in her eyes anymore. I'm done," she said, tossing cosmetics in her overnight bag. Whoa. She'd tossed a bottle with so much force, it could have broken. "Keep calm. Take a deep breath." Although it helped, the effect was fleeting.

Landon had duped, deceived and fooled her. *Lied* to her. That last one was his most heinous offense. Was he a con man? A lunatic? Maybe a deranged twin like in some soap opera? On the other hand, he'd charmed her, protected her and taken great care of her. She and her wayward cowboy made a fine pair. Apparently, she needed mental health services, and quick. Maybe they could go to some kind of weird couples therapy together.

"You sure know how to pick a guy," she said to her reflection in the vanity mirror, twisting the cap back on her nail polish. She chose to ignore the dark shadows beneath her eyes. Let the man see he'd caused her to lose sleep. *No, don't give him the satisfaction.* Searching through the cosmetic bag, she found the foundation she'd brought for the wedding. She squeezed some out and dabbed it beneath both eyes, blending carefully even though her fingers were still shaking to match the quaking in her stomach. "Talk about confusing."

Embarrassment swept through her a short time later when the elevator doors opened while she still mumbled to herself. Inside the elevator, a couple and their young son waited with polite smiles. "Sorry about all this stuff," she said, hauling her bags inside, ruing the bulkiness of it all. Traveling light had never been one of her strong points. She gave the boy a grateful smile when he held the door. She cleared her throat and stared at the elevator buttons, willing it to move faster. When the doors opened to the lobby, the boy tugged out her suitcase and parked it by a chair.

"Thank you." Amy offered the child a small smile which encompassed his parents. "I appreciate your help. Merry Christmas." One of these years, she hoped to have a well-mannered boy like this one. *Good grief, Miss Lonely Hearts is now thinking past the whole "not having a man" whine to "will I ever have a child?"*

"You are pathetic," she said under her breath.

Checking out at the front desk, she was surprised to learn Landon hadn't yet settled the bill. Without a second thought, she plopped down her credit card. No doubt this fiasco would cost her a pretty penny, but it was worth it not to feel any more indebted to him than she already did. Thanking the woman behind the desk, she folded the receipt and stuffed it inside her purse. If she looked at it now, she might faint, and she couldn't risk that happening. She left her bags with the concierge and promised to retrieve them within the hour.

Glancing at her watch, Amy noted she still had a few minutes until he arrived. The night before, she'd noted all the paintings in the lounge area of the mezzanine outside The Driskill Grill. Might as well go take a look at them—something to kill time while waiting for what's-his-name. Anything was better than dwelling on her muddled love life. *From no love life to a big old mess the size of Texas.* Heading toward the grand staircase, she paused a few steps above the lobby floor and lifted her eyes to the likeness of Colonel Driskill.

"Hey, Jesse," she whispered with a wink. "Be good."

She climbed the remaining steps, lost in thought. Wandering from one painting to another, she admired the western landscapes and cowboy scenes. A striking piece in an alcove caught her eye, different from all the others. Slinging her purse over one shoulder, she moved into the alcove to study it at close range.

The vibrant hues and textures were outstanding. A young woman walked in a field under a bright blue sky dotted with a few puffy white clouds. She wore no wedding ring, no shoes. Splashes of vivid blue on the apron tied over her plain brown work dress were shocking by contrast. Wildflowers in purplish blue—most likely Texas bluebonnets—as well as yellow, orange and red, bowed and danced at her feet. With her face raised to the sun, a hint of a smile curved her lips and her dark hair cascaded in waves to her waist. A brown bonnet, its ribbons fluttering, dangled from her fingertips.

Captivated by the lovely painting, she read the gold engraved plaque mounted on the wall beneath it. *FINDING AMELIA*. JACKSON HAWLEY, 1991. *Amelia?* "I think I'm in the *Twilight Zone*," she muttered. Hearing a familiar grunt behind her, Amy drew in a deep breath and turned. Try as she might, her pulse sputtered at how ridiculously gorgeous Landon looked in his jeans, red shirt and that jacket she'd come to appreciate more than she should. Likewise the brown Stetson he held in his hands. *Not fair*.

If she bombarded him with all the questions fighting for precedence in her scattered mind, she'd take a running leap and pummel the cowboy. That wouldn't be the best publicity for the hotel. She could see the headline now: CRAZED WOMAN ATTACKS LOCAL MAN AT THE HISTORIC DRISKILL HOTEL. Calling Sam or Josh for bail money wouldn't wash; she'd never live that one down. So, for now, she'd hear what the man had to say for himself. And then pummel him.

"Good morning, Amy." His gaze—warm with appreciation—slid over her before settling on the sapphire pendant visible between the opening of her blouse. She'd fastened—then taken off—the necklace several times, but didn't dwell on her motivation for leaving it on. What a situation.

With a slight nod, she turned back to the painting, unsure whether to call him Cooper or Landon. If the former, it'd heap more guilt on him. If the latter, it'd put him on the immediate defensive. Why should she care? *Like it or not, you do*. Discussing a work of art seemed a safe enough way to draw him into a conversation.

"*Finding Amelia*. Interesting," he said, raising a brow. "I don't suppose you'd consider it another coincidence?"

"Not at all." She shrugged, feigning nonchalance. "It's not like 'Amelia's' *un*common."

"Neither is it common, especially for the woman I'm looking at now." Blue eyes sought hers and softened.

"It's by Jackson Hawley." Turning back to the painting, she avoided his gaze. "Maybe you've heard of him?"

"Enough to know he died this past year and the value of his paintings skyrocketed. I'm sure this one is worth a pretty penny now. You're right. It's terrific."

When he stepped beside her, bringing the familiar scent of Irish Spring and all that rugged masculinity, Amy tried not to breathe in. *You're hopeless. Keep talking*. "I admire an artist who's true to his vision and paints with honesty and confidence," she said. "In this piece, for instance. Notice the faint lines on her forehead and around her eyes and mouth. The drabness of her gown reflects her life, but look at her face, raised to the sky and the warmth of the sun. There's hope in her expression. The way she's holding her bonnet is significant, too. The ribbons flying in the breeze symbolize freedom, a break from the past perhaps."

"I'm impressed. You got all that from this painting?"

She circled a finger around a small cluster of multicolored wildflowers with one finger. "Sure. Take this area, for example. What do you see?"

"Try as I might, other than the bluebonnets, I see nothing but scraggly little flowers. Love the colors, though. Did you know the bluebonnet—our state flower, by the way—is as important to Texas as the shamrock is to Ireland?"

"I don't doubt it. They're beautiful, but in this piece, they hold particular significance—wild, free, uninhibited."

Landon tilted his head and stepped back a few paces. "Unlike the woman?"

"Exactly," she said, stealing a glance at him.

"Another thing." He pointed to the woman. "The way she's postured, her arms out, the relatively long stride, it seems to me she's gaining confidence as she walks. Like she's embracing her future." His voice was low, contemplative. "I'm sure Jackson had his reasons for making her barefoot, too." When he caught her wary glance, he added, "In terms of being free without anything constraining her feet."

"I think you have a greater appreciation for art than you realized." Why she was talking with him in a civilized manner was another matter altogether.

"It's the company I keep. She inspires me." He captured her gaze. "Tell me, are *you* like the woman in this painting . . . Amelia?"

"In some ways, yes. In other ways, no." Leave it up to him to make the differentiation.

"We need to talk, Amy. It's important."

"I know."

He shifted and averted his gaze, but not before she caught his look of surprise. "I'm sorry it's later than we planned on leaving. There was someone I needed to see this morning. My . . . dad. He's in a prison about thirty miles from here. Minimum security, not that it matters." Based on the tightness in his facial muscles, it was a difficult admission.

No wonder he seemed pained whenever the subject of his father arose. "I had no idea," she said. "I'm . . . sorry." She stopped herself as she was about to call him by his *real* name.

"Well, don't be. He has no one to blame but himself." Landon ran a hand over his brow as unspoken questions lingered in the air between them. The sadness in his face tugged at her heart. Resisting the strong urge to wrap her arms around him, Amy crossed them over her middle instead.

"He committed fraud and embezzled millions from his own company, but he was an even bigger fraud to his family." Landon glanced at her before his gaze flickered to the carpet with the hotel's "D" insignia beneath his boot-covered feet. "You've got to love the irony."

"What do you mean?"

He lifted his eyes to hers. "He's not the only fraud in the family. Amy, I'm not the man you think I am."

Chapter 37

"THERE'S A BALCONY over here." Landon angled his head toward the Brazos Street side of the hotel. "If it's not too cold, we can go out there and talk."

Amy nodded, thankful she wore her new jacket. *The one he wanted you to have.*

Leading her around the mezzanine, he opened the balcony door and waited. Thankfully, no one sat in the rattan rockers or on the bench. Crossing to the balcony railing, she peered over the ledge to the quiet street below, gathering her thoughts. Behind her, she heard his boots on the red tile floor followed by the door closing. Taking a deep breath, she turned.

He dropped his Stetson on the bench. "Care to sit?"

"No, I'll stand, thanks." Chilled—pretty much numb from the heart outward—she ran her hands up and down her arms. Never in recent memory could she remember being this nervous. Being summoned to Juliet's office couldn't compare.

Landon shoved his hands deep into the pockets of his jacket and walked forward a few steps, planting himself a foot away from her. "It's difficult to know where to begin." What sounded like remorse and guilt laced his words, and he ran a hand through his hair.

"The beginning usually works just fine. Why don't we start there?" Inspiration seized her. Turning the tables on him might speed up the exposure of his little charade. Although she hadn't taken a turn on the stage since high school, she'd inherited a few of her grandfather's acting genes. Time to draw on what she'd learned from him, however limited or rusty her skills might be. "Okay, I'll start. Is Landon your twin?"

He snapped up his head and narrowed his eyes. "No."

She feigned a look of surprised innocence. "You're so much alike. Brother then? Surely you're somehow related." She stopped tapping her foot in its incessant rhythm.

"No. Not a brother either."

"Then tell me what I'm missing here." Taking a step backward, she bumped into the balcony railing. She moved her hands behind her and leaned against them. *Slow down, wayward heart.*

"If there's one thing I've learned about you, it's that you have very good instincts."

Guarding herself against the intensity in those eyes, Amy turned her head.

He took a slow step toward her. "About people. About a young waitress, a runaway dog, a little girl at summer camp. Shall I go on?"

"Please do." She fought to calm her breathing, but it proved an exercise in futility.

"You like sharing a blanket in a hansom in Central Park and chocolate cake at midnight. Daffodils in winter, coffee with two creams and four sugars, slow dancing at Scully's—"

"Stop right there." Amy raised her hand and planted it firmly on his chest, preventing him from coming any closer. "How did you—? How could you—?" Her eyes widened as she glared at him. "Who *are* you?" She brushed her fingers over the crescent moon scar, so perfect in its imperfection.

Wrapping his fingers over hers, Landon drew her hand away. "You know *me*, Amy."

"This is maddening," she said, shaking off his hand. "I don't know what to think. Who do *you* think I think you are?" What an absurd question.

"I'm Landon. Landon *Cooper* Jared Warnick, to be specific." When she didn't speak, he reached into his back pocket and pulled out his wallet. Opening it, he held it in front of her and pointed to his New York driver's license. "Exhibit A."

She leaned closer. "I can't see it. Your thumb's in the way."

Giving her a look, he yanked it out and held it up in front of her. "Now can you see it?" He looked about ready to spit.

She darted a glance at the photo. "Ye—es," she said. "Very flattering photo for a mug shot."

"Not the picture, you beautiful nutcase. The *name*." He shoved it at her again.

"You'd be well-advised to lower your voice and not resort to name-calling." The indignation in her voice wasn't lost on him based on the lines furrowing his forehead as he tucked the license back in his wallet and returned it to his back pocket.

"You know," she said slowly, drawing out her words for maximum effect, "for a man who's all about being upfront and honest from the start, I find it interesting how you couldn't be straight with me." She crossed her arms. "It's about time you finally got around to your little confession. I wasn't sure how much longer you could keep up this ridiculous farce."

He grunted something unintelligible and the muscles in both jaws worked furiously. "You knew?" The pacing started again, back and forth a few times before he stopped. "You *knew*? Have you known all along, and you've been waiting for me to dig the hole deeper?"

"Get over yourself, but yes, you had me fooled and I must be the world's most colossal fool not to have seen it coming. Sure, there were hints here and there pointing me to the truth, but I didn't dwell on them because why on earth would I believe you'd ever do such a thing in the first place? Winnie and another of the TeamWork girls thought your last name was Warren and everyone was calling you Cooper. As soon as I saw you at the front of the church, I knew you were Landon even though you looked different enough with the tan, the haircut, the scar on your forehead. Then when the phone message from *Landon* was delivered a few days late, I was—"

"Discombobulated?"

"Yes, to say the least." Their eyes met. "Then there's the accent. I think that's what really tipped the scales. Care to explain?" Powerless to stop it, she tapped her foot in a rapid staccato. Staring at the ground, Amy shuffled her boots and shot him a look of disgust. "I studied my junior year in London, but I didn't come back home and call everyone 'love'"—those last few words were spoken in a feigned British accent—"say it's half past five instead of five-thirty, hold my fork upside down and shovel food onto my fork with my knife!"

Landon shook his head and ran a hand through his hair. "The way your mind works is fascinating. In answer to your question, when I come back home, the accent comes right back and I don't even think about it. If you'll remember, I told you that during our date in Manhattan."

"Yeah, well," she said, blowing out a breath, "you said a lot of things that night. You made me dizzy with all the things you said."

"Dizzy good or—"

She stared. "You really are incredibly infuriating, you know that?"

"Come on, Amy. No jury in the world would convict me of premeditated deception."

She snapped up her head. "Fraud. That's what it's called."

The way his lips thinned and his eyes hardened, she knew she'd pushed him too far. Admittedly, it was a low blow, but the man deserved it. He'd brought up the irony of it all in the first place.

"Fair enough." Pushing the Stetson aside, Landon dropped onto the bench and leaned forward, elbows on his knees. "When I saw you coming down the aisle at the wedding, you were so beautiful. I've never known a woman who makes me crazy like you do." Catching her look, he added, "I mean that in all the best ways. After our date in Manhattan, I couldn't wait to get back to the city so I could spend more time with you. Get to know you better. Dancing with you at the wedding and then that kiss . . . . Every single thing in my life paled in comparison to that moment." He shook his head. "Can we please put this behind us, have a good laugh, chalk it up to a great story and ride into the sunset together?"

She shook her head in disbelief. "Is it really that easy for you to sweep deception under the rug? Sweep, sweep," she said, moving her hands back and forth as though holding a broom. "You lied to me!"

"Haven't you ever—at least once in your life—wanted to be someone you're not?"

"I can't say I haven't ever thought about it, no, but you took it too far. Way past acceptable boundaries, Landon. A minute's too long for deception. You kissed me knowing full well I thought you were Landon the night of the wedding. Then you made me doubt my sanity the very next morning when I thought I'd kissed a perfect stranger!"

He shook his head. "How *does* your mind work? I hate to point out the obvious, but I *am* Landon. And, for the record, you didn't really know Landon that well when you went to the wedding and kissed him."

She stared. "You really are nuts, aren't you? Talk about sanity. Make that insanity. You're walking a very thin line here talking about yourself in third person. I suppose now I should start spouting things about how Amy feels?"

"I started to tell you I was Landon in the lobby of the inn in Baton Rouge, but you wouldn't let me get a word in edgewise—"

"I did—" She stopped and clamped her lips together, motioning for him to continue.

"I tried to tell you last night, but you stopped me. I should have blurted out my name right then and there, but like you said, the night was too perfect and I didn't want to spoil it. Tell me, how did you figure it out?"

"Mitch. Good thing he's looking out for my best interests since I'm apparently incapable of it myself. What a fool I've been."

His shoulders slumped. "You're not a fool. This whole thing started out because of what you'd call my male pride."

When he paused, she nodded. "Go on."

"You insulted me personally, and that was bad enough, but when you started in on my magazine, you crossed a line." Those blue eyes were gorgeous even as they sliced through her with the force of his anger. The man was really fired up now and it infuriated her.

She could contain herself no longer. "Ooohh! Then why didn't you just leave? Climb into that rental car and drive off into the sunset in Nowhereville, Texas all by your lonesome? Were you so mad because I insulted you—and your magazine—that you wanted to get back at me by dragging me along in your crazy charade? Because you had something to prove?"

"For starters, yes, I needed to find out if you really meant those things you said or if you were only . . ."

She waited, but he hesitated for a long moment. "Only . . . ?"

Rising to his feet, he walked toward her. Catching the look in her eye, he stopped a good two paces away. "Let's look at the facts here. I had a situation where a woman I wanted to get to know better completely enchanted me with her wit, humor, beauty and everything else about her. But then she told me straight to my face she couldn't trust me. You have a brother, so you should have a modicum of understanding of how men love a challenge. Can't resist them, as a matter of fact. You bruise a man's ego big time by saying you can't trust him, sweetheart. Call it misguided, but I think I did a pretty fair job of convincing you." Landon leaned close. "These last few days? That—*this* was me. More than the guy in the fancy suit in Manhattan is or ever will be."

Her snort escaped. "Well, then, why don't you shuck the fancy suits and wear your jeans and Stetson and drawl away? I'm sure that'd thrill your legion of female followers."

"Amy, I know I've been the worst kind of Christian. I never should have done it, and I don't know that I can ever adequately explain myself, but even in my deception, I showed you who I am. In here." He tapped his curled fist on his chest. "Everything I said to you this whole trip was true. About my background, my family and especially about my feelings for you."

Her eyes grew large. "The things you said as Cooper that were the same things Landon said to me, you did that on purpose, didn't you? You were somehow hoping I'd get wise and call you on it because you were too chicken to just come right out and tell me? And please don't call me sweetheart."

"A part of me wanted you to catch me. You're a very intelligent woman, and I knew you'd eventually figure it out. But I needed to be the one to tell you—for my own peace of mind, not that it's helping much at the moment. Here's something for you to chew on: maybe you didn't want to know the truth. Ever consider that possibility?"

Her mouth gaped. "Why would you think something so completely ludicrous?"

"Because maybe—just maybe—it's crazy enough to be true."

Huffing out a breath, she tapped his arm. "Let me see your wrists."

"Why?" Nonetheless, he raised them for her inspection.

She pretended to examine one wrist and then the other. "Well," she said, "I figured there's an ID bracelet to identify you as an escaped mental patient from the state hospital. Are you wearing a straitjacket beneath your clothes?"

"Okay, that's enough," Landon said, shaking free of her grip. "I'll admit I'm guilty of a big—okay, huge—lapse in my mental faculties, but it's not like I'm delusional. Can we at least talk about this like rational adults without hurling insults at each other?"

She snorted. "How many sane, rational people do you know who go around impersonating someone?"

"Don't you mean impersonating themselves?"

"That's even crazier! Now you decide to be rational? You know exactly what I mean and none of your explanations are going to change the facts. And to think I thought I'd fallen for you." *Why did I have to say that? I'm such a fool.* "Turns out, the whole time, it was a lie, a carefully calculated mirage." She snapped her fingers. "I know. In your spare time, you're also an off-off-off Broadway actor."

"Yeah, right. My singing's halfway decent, but I can't act my way out of a paper bag. I'll leave that to your esteemed thespian grandfather."

Amy inhaled a quick breath. "You know about . . ."

"For the record, darlin', you didn't just think you fell for me, you fell in head first, eyes wide open."

"Don't darlin' me, Cooper—Landon!" She raised her hands in exasperation, and took over the pacing routine he'd abandoned. "I don't know what to call you right now. Guaranteed, it's nothing flattering. You're not really a Texan anymore, either, as much as that must pain you." When he opened his mouth, she held up one palm. "Don't start spouting some hackneyed cliché like 'born a Texan, always a Texan.'" Unable to control the flood of emotions, she bit her lip and turned aside. Her composure had gone on holiday along with her common sense. Amy felt his presence directly behind her. Closing her eyes, she drew in a deep breath, releasing it slowly.

"Amy." Lowering his hands to her shoulders, he turned her around. "Look at me. Please." His voice was low, his tone unbearably tender as he lifted her chin with one finger. Opening her eyes, her lashes fluttered over misty eyes. "If you'd asked me point-blank if I was Landon at any point during our trip, I would have told you the truth. You didn't ask my last name, didn't question. You accepted me for who and what I am even when I tried to point you to the truth."

"Sugarcoat it all you want, but one thing I can't tolerate is deceit. What you did was low. And cruel." Her roller coaster emotional stability was in question now. If she stayed angry, she wouldn't dissolve in tears.

Dropping his hand, he stepped back. "I take full responsibility for deceiving you, but I never meant to be cruel. If you honestly believe that, then I can only pray you'll accept my heartfelt apology."

"Don't you see? The sin of omission is every bit as dangerous and wrong."

"I agree." Raising his arms to his sides, Landon stepped back. "As long as we're getting everything out, I might as well tell you the journalist in me considered pretending to be a twin brother or something. It could have been a good exposé on what it's like to look exactly like someone else and walk a day in their shoes. You know, the publisher versus the cowboy . . ." Seeing the look on her face, he stopped. "Okay, this thread of discussion is getting me nowhere fast. This is what you need to know: I crossed the line at the point where I decided to go along with your misperception and pretended to be Cooper. It was the point of no return. After that, I knew if I confessed, you'd reject me and push me away forever. I realize I'm running the serious risk of that very thing right now, but—"

She looked up at him through watery eyes. "Landon, how can I ever trust you, knowing what you did?"

"Because I've never done anything like it before in my life and you have my word I never will again. If you give me a chance, I'll share so many honest feelings you'll be sick of me. *Sick*. If you want, I'll tell you every single thing—no matter how big or small—that's going through my head."

"Now you sound chauvinistic. You're already on shaky ground, so don't push it."

"We're going in circles here," he said. "Look, I know it in no way excuses what I did."

"That's the most intelligent thing you've said yet!"

He captured both her hands in his and held them tight, his face hovering right above hers, his lips a heartbeat away. "I didn't want to, but God help me, I've fallen in love with you, Amy. Believe *that.* I was impressed and infatuated with you when Mitch first told me about you. Then when I met you . . ."

Withdrawing her hands, Amy stepped backward. Her heart pounding, she brought a hand to her chest. "Wh—" she gasped, her breath ragged, "wh—what do you mean when Mitch told you—" Digging deep, she couldn't find the words.

Beneath his golden tan, Landon's face paled. "After meeting your brother at the Knicks game and then seeing him again at that charity event, I almost called Mitch to see if he could arrange for us to meet, but—and this is the part I want you to understand—I decided against it. I wasn't supposed to be at Café Eduardo that night. My advertising director was home with a sick child and I had to pinch hit. So whatever you're thinking in that beautiful head of yours, it wasn't a deliberate set-up."

He lowered his face into his hands for a long moment while she waited. Finally, he raised his head. "Every woman I've ever dated wanted something from me other than my love. They either wanted the prestige or the money that comes with success. The couple of times I had an ongoing relationship with a woman, I kept my dad being in prison a well-guarded secret. When they found out, they dumped me." When he raised his eyes to hers, they were wet with emotion. "The worst part of all is that I've prayed for a woman like you, a woman of strong faith, to come into my life. Someone who might love me for who and what I am on the inside—not the outside—and now that I've finally found you, I blew it." He rose to his feet. "Never mind. I can't expect you to understand, but you're imprinted on my heart and that won't ever change."

The sadness in his soulful eyes and the exhaustion in his face tore at her heart, ripping it straight down the middle, and an ache stirred deep inside her. "I'll find my own way to Houston," she said.

"Nothing doing," he said. "I might be a royal jerk, but I'm no heel. I've arranged for another pilot to take you. A driver will pick you up at the airport and take you to Sam and Lexa's."

"Landon, I can't accept—"

"It's called keeping you safe." His eyes met hers. "Call it my parting gift. I promised to take you and I intend to keep my word. I just won't be delivering you in person." When she raised her brow, he blew out an exasperated sigh. "Figure of speech."

Amy fought the strong impulse to tear up again. This crazy cowboy had her all kinds of emotional, and her senses threatened to spin like an out of control merry-go-round. The man could silence her with a well-chosen word and stir passion with the soft brush of his lips over hers. A well-known and respected New York publisher who also happened to be the most ridiculously handsome, infuriating, confusing, irritating man she'd ever met.

"We'd better get moving." He hiked his sleeve and checked his watch. "It'll take thirty minutes to get to the airport if the traffic cooperates. I'm driving you there, so—like it or not—you'll have to put up with me a little longer. I hope you're not planning on giving me the silent treatment the entire way."

"Do I have a choice?"

He stopped and stared. "You know the answer to that one."

Without another word, Amy started for the door. "I don't know what to say to you right now, but I suppose I can come up with something to talk about if it'll keep you from singing." Flinging open the balcony door, she stalked toward the grand staircase.

Chapter 38

EMOTIONALLY SPENT AND bone-weary, Amy reached for the pilot's hand as he helped her step aboard the plane. "Nice to meet you, Miss Jacobsen. I'm Tony Koenig."

She forced a small smile. "Thanks, Tony. You, too." As she moved to one of the four seats behind the cockpit, Landon climbed inside with her bags.

"Do you want me to hang the bridesmaid dress?"

"It doesn't matter. You can put it anywhere."

What an inane conversation, but it was safe since it was clear neither one of them knew what to say next or how to act. From the corner of her eye, she noticed he hung it in the back of the plane.

Landon paused in the doorway. Finally, he raised his eyes to hers. "Jack's doing much better, by the way."

She stared. "Jack from Café Eduardo?"

"The same. He's home now and recuperating."

Swallowing hard, she fought more tears. "I'm glad to hear it. I've been praying for Ellie, too."

Landon's Adam's apple slid up and down and the muscles in his jaws clenched. "I'll talk to Mitch when I get back to New York and try to explain myself."

"You don't know Mitch very well," she said. "Better let me do it. I might be furious with you, but I don't wish you bodily harm."

Landon lowered his eyes and rotated the Stetson in his hands. "Be well, Amy. I'll pray for a safe trip and have fun with your friends in Houston." Without giving her a chance to respond, he shoved the hat down on his head and exited the aircraft. Twisting in her seat, she watched as he strode across the tarmac to where Tony talked with another man in a mechanic's jumpsuit. A minute later, Landon addressed both men and appeared to do most of the talking. Fingering the sapphire locket, Amy unclasped the chain and held it in her palm, staring at it as tears slipped onto her cheeks.

When Tony returned to the plane, she inhaled a deep breath as he slammed the door, securing it. Something about it seemed so . . . final. She didn't know what she expected for the end of the road trip, but she'd never felt such a heaviness in her heart.

"Tony," she said, unbuckling her seat belt and sliding out of her seat, "I need five minutes. It's important."

Giving her a hesitant look, the pilot reopened the door and stood aside. "There's a storm brewing and we need to circumvent it. We leave in ten minutes."

"Thanks. I'll be right back. Promise." Within seconds, she jumped down to the pavement and headed toward Landon. With his head lowered and slumped shoulders, he walked toward Matilda. Thank goodness he moved slowly or he might have already been halfway out of the airport. Amy's pulse throbbed in her ears as she raised her voice. "Landon! Wait!" A departing plane drowned out her words and they floated away with the wind. *I can't let him go like this.* Opening the door, he climbed inside the truck. "Landon!" Breaking into a run, she sprinted toward Matilda.

Raising his head, he tipped back his Stetson and squinted. A faint smile creased his lips, but as she drew nearer, the sadness in those gorgeous blue eyes shredded her heart. How could she be so infuriated by a man and yet feel her heart slipping into his? This love business could be a beautiful thing, but why did it have to hurt so much?

Slightly out of breath, Amy halted beside the truck. "I wanted to tell you . . . thank you . . ." *Why am I stumbling over my words?* "Thanks for bringing me safely to Texas." *Say it.* "In spite of the way things turned out, I had a great time."

His eyes narrowed but not before she caught the flicker of surprise. "You're welcome. It was my honor." He started to tug the door closed, but she grabbed it, holding it firm. "You have a plane waiting, Amy. Time to go."

"In a second." She stepped to the side of the door so it wasn't a barrier between them. "Tell me the truth. You could have told me who you were anywhere along the way between Baton Rouge and Austin. Why didn't you?"

Running one hand over his jaw, he stared into the distance before focusing on her. "Like I said, I was already in too deep. Call me selfish, but if I'd told you the truth, you wouldn't have come with me. I couldn't risk that happening. I wanted—I *needed*—to hang onto the dream a little while longer."

"Which dream is that?"

His eyes softened. "You, Amy. *You're* the dream."

Swallowing her tears, she stared at a sign posted on the hangar. "Where are you going now?"

"Not sure. Out of your life, if that's what you want. Your call." His words stunned her and she grabbed onto the door again, gripping it as if it was holding her upright. "My prayer is that—in time—you'll be able to forgive me." His eyes held the regret of a hundred tomorrows.

"Miss Jacobsen!" Tony called from the door of the jet. "We need to leave now."

She turned and nodded, her vision blurred. "I'm coming." The words choked in her throat.

Quickly stepping out of the truck and moving around the door, Landon caught her sleeve. Leaning close, he brushed his lips over her cheek. Achingly sweet. Beautifully tender. "Bye, Amelia. I hope all your dreams come true."

"Yours, too." It was barely more than a murmur, lifted by the slight breeze and her daydreams. "Bye." Reaching for his hand, she placed the locket inside and closed his warm fingers around it. The stricken look on his face wrenched at her heart and shattered it even further.

She hurried back to the plane and scrambled aboard. With tears streaming down her face, she closed her eyes as she heard Tony on the radio and felt the rumble of the engine. Amy didn't dare glance out the window until the plane had taxied and started its ascent.

Her sobs escaped as she spied her cowboy leaning against that red and white vintage Chevy truck, clutching his Stetson over his heart.

Chapter 39

YAWNING, AMY STRETCHED, feeling as tired as though she'd put in a full day at work when the driver pulled the car into Sam and Lexa's driveway outside their two-story, red brick home. That's what mental stress and exhaustion could do to a body. As she climbed out of the car and thanked the driver, Amy smiled as she noted the holiday decorations adorning the windows and the front entrance. The door opened and Josh hurried onto the walkway, pulling on his jacket. "How's my favorite journalist?"

"Hey, Josh," she said, shivering with the cold, loving his quick hug. "I didn't expect to find you here, but it's always great to see my favorite attorney. I'd say it's beginning to look a lot like Christmas."

He gathered her bags from the trunk of the car and dug out his wallet, but the driver stopped him. "Already taken care of, sir."

Walking beside Josh, she wondered about Landon's reaction when he'd discovered she'd paid for her stay in the Yellow Rose suite at The Driskill. Contrary to what she knew of him, he hadn't said a word about it. Of course, that could have been another reason he was so quiet during the ride to the airport. That and the fact she made it clear by her body language—arms crossed, body turned toward the window—she didn't much feel like making small talk.

"Sam and Lexa had a meeting downtown this afternoon." Josh stepped aside for her to go into the house first. "After you called Lexa to say you'd be arriving later, she asked us to come and be your welcoming committee. I'm currently between meetings and figured you'd want some time alone with Winnie, so I'll keep the kids occupied while you talk." Coming in behind her, he closed the door.

"You're a good man, and your consideration is duly noted." Amy caught Josh's grin as she glanced around the spacious living room. "This is such a great house." The scent of pine filled her senses and she admired the tall, fresh Christmas tree in one corner by the fireplace. Her survey took in the high ceilings and large windows, lending an airy, light feeling. Books lined one wall and photographs another. Throw pillows and personal touches—fresh poinsettias and a vase of fresh seasonal flowers—added to the home's charm. Spying her favorite photo of Lexa and Sam on one wall, she smiled. In her arms, Lexa held yellow roses and the love and joy radiating on both their faces was infectious. It'd been taken on the night in San Antonio when they'd surprised everyone by getting married immediately after his return to the States from his year-long overseas mission. As she always did, Amy saluted the photo of Sam's lookalike younger brother, Will, currently training as a future NASA shuttle commander.

Pushing open the swinging door from the kitchen, Winnie emerged, looking pretty as ever in jeans and a dark pink, long-sleeved tee. With her blonde hair swinging behind her in its customary ponytail, she could be mistaken for a teenager. "About time you got here!"

Dropping her purse on the floor, Amy ran to the welcoming comfort of her friend's arms. "Am I ever glad to see you. You don't know how much." Biting back a sob, she tightened her hold around her friend's slender shoulders. Winnie patted her on the back, and Amy noticed Josh's concerned expression where he watched from a few feet away. A slight tug on the bottom of her jacket caused her to pull away.

"Aunt Amy, why are you crying?"

"Oh, Buttercup, these are happy tears." Brushing moisture from her cheeks, Amy scooped Chloe into her arms. "I'm just so"—she swallowed more tears and forced a brightness into her voice—"happy to see you and your mommy and daddy. I have to store up a whole bunch of hugs to keep me warm through the rest of the winter in New York. It can get pretty cold." Planting a kiss on the child's rosy cheek, she smoothed back an unruly curl. Chloe was a miniature embodiment of both her parents: the mass of glorious blonde hair, cute button nose and mouth were Winnie's, but the green eyes were all Josh, as was her ready smile and charm.

"Come on, monkey," Josh said, holding out one hand. "Let's go pick out a book for you to read to Joe when he wakes up from his nap."

Amy gave him a grateful smile as she lowered Chloe to the floor. Josh nodded as he led his chattering daughter toward the stairs.

"And *you*, come with me," Winnie said, leading the way through the swinging door and into the kitchen. She motioned to the counter stools by the butcher block table in the middle of the kitchen. "Have a seat and tell me what's going on since I can tell you're about to implode. Want a cup of coffee?"

"Sure, thanks, for both offers. I rarely turn down coffee, and a listening ear sounds even better." She lowered her voice. "Am I still keeping your secret about impending motherhood?"

"Yes, you are," Winnie said with a small giggle, "but I'm sure it won't be long before everyone knows. We don't want to say anything yet until I'm a little further along, although I'm sure Lexa already suspects."

"Understood. You look great, though. Feeling okay?"

"Yes, but just tired from all the catering stuff and keeping up with Chloe. And Josh," she said with that sweet, telltale newlywed blush invading her cheeks. "How about something to eat or nibble on? There's leftover salad, quiche and muffins from a lunch we catered yesterday."

"Matter of fact, I could eat a little something. Didn't cross my mind, to be honest. Maybe a muffin to go with my coffee might be nice. Thanks."

"Banana nut okay? I'll heat it up for you."

"Perfect. My mouth's already watering." She watched as her friend moved around the kitchen, as comfortable as though in her own house. "I'll admit, I'm jealous you get to spend so much time here with Sam and Lexa. I have friends in New York, but they're not like my TeamWork friends." Finished measuring coffee into the machine, Winnie put a carton of creamer on the table as well as a coffee mug, napkin, spoon and sweetener packets. "It's nice to be among friends, especially ones who take care of me, love and accept me for who and what I am to the point of knowing how I take my coffee."

"You've done the same for me many times," Winnie said. "Someone sounds philosophical today." Opening the lid of a plastic container on the counter, she pulled out an enormous muffin. She put it on a napkin and pushed a button on the microwave before leaning against the counter, facing her. "How about the TeamWork projects in New York and in your church? I'm sure you've met some wonderful people."

"Yes, but like I said, it's not the same. For one thing, my church is probably seventy percent over the age of sixty. I love those senior saints, but congregations in the city don't attract the younger couples. Most of them are in Connecticut and other bedroom communities. The last few times I've worked in the nursery, I've only had five or six babies, and it's a decent-sized congregation. I have friends at work, but the environment's so competitive, and I prefer to keep it separate from my personal life. And yes, there's some wonderful people on the TeamWork projects, but like I said, it's different." She paused, appreciating the aroma of the muffin as it filled the kitchen. Combined with the brewing coffee, it filled her with a sense of home. "You know what I think it is? We went through a lot together in the San Antonio work camp and then in Montana with Natalie and Marc. Those times bonded us together in a way that's unique and really special, you know?"

"I agree," Winnie said, her voice quiet. "Kind of like men in the trenches of war say they'll never forget their comrades. Not the same thing, I realize, but we're fighting spiritual warfare around us all the time, and that's very much a war, too."

"Or the war within ourselves," Amy said as Winnie put the muffin on the table and sat on a counter stool opposite her with a glass of water. After saying a brief prayer, she sampled the muffin. "Ah, this is delicious, not to mention big enough to feed half the state of Texas. Thanks."

"You seem awfully sentimental and reflective today, too." Winnie sipped her water. "Time to tell me your story because I can tell you've got a good one to share."

With a small half-laugh, half-sob, Amy leaned her elbow on the counter and rested a palm against her forehead. "I'm so ridiculously obvious, Winnie." She opened her eyes. "I was right about Cooper. He's Landon. One and the same."

Winnie's blue eyes widened but she didn't appear surprised or shocked. "Sweetie, I'm so sorry if I misled you before and after the wedding. I obviously heard his name wrong, and Lexa set me straight when we got back home. I felt bad when I realized I made you doubt him, but I guess I didn't expect a successful New York publisher to be at the same wedding in Baton Rouge with a Texas accent and—"

"It's okay. I understand why you felt that way, and I love you for your concern, but I should have trusted my first instincts."

Winnie's brows rose. "I've thought a lot about you since coming back home to Houston, and I've prayed for you and Landon." She took another quick sip of her water. "So, did you have a fun time together in Austin?"

What a loaded question. For the next twenty minutes, Winnie listened as she told her story. Nodding a few times, wide-eyed, compassion shone in her friend's expression when Amy told her about Landon's dad and the horrible confrontation on The Driskill balcony.

"So," Amy said as she finished, "if I'd simply asked the man flat out somewhere along the way if he was actually Landon, it would have saved a whole lot of time. He dropped some pretty broad hints, but I just chalked them up to coincidence—even though I hate to use that word—because I didn't know what else to call it. Any words of wisdom after hearing all that?"

"First of all, it sounds like you need some time to digest it all, sweetie," Winnie said. "Everything's happened so fast and you need to catch your breath and get back to your normal life. That'll help put the events of the last few days in perspective."

"I hope you're right," Amy said, knowing how wistful she sounded as she sipped her coffee.

"I want you to think about something." Winnie's eyes were warm, but her voice was firm.

"Ooo—kay." She'd heard that tone in her friend's voice before. *Here it comes.*

"You grew up around strong men, men of God who treated the women in their lives like royalty. In some ways, you could say they were . . . well, more or less perfect."

Amy frowned. "That's a bad thing?"

"Of course not." Winnie traced a circle in the sweat on her glass of water. "Most people never have that advantage. But, as a result, their expectations aren't quite so high either."

"Wait a minute. Are you saying I should *lower* my expectations?"

"No, I'm not saying that at all." Winnie frowned and her lips thinned. Classic signs of a pondering Winnie, and she found it so endearing. "What Landon did was wrong, but he explained his reasoning and came clean. It's difficult for a guy to admit when he's done something wrong, and an even stronger one who can humble himself and ask for forgiveness." Retrieving the coffee pot, she brought it over and filled Amy's mug before taking her seat again. "I also know a little something about keeping the truth from someone far too long. I should have come clean with Josh and told him about Chloe from the start. It was wrong, but I couldn't bring myself to do it."

"But that was completely different, Winnie. You didn't purposely misrepresent yourself."

"By telling Josh the truth about Chloe, I knew I'd be giving up the one thing in my life that was mine alone. From what you said, Landon's never had a woman love him for himself. They're always after his name, or his money or what he could offer them. Tell me this: until Mitch's phone call, you were having a great time with him on the road trip, weren't you?"

"Yes," Amy said. Winnie was right, so why deny it? "It ranked right up there as one of the best times of my life."

"Tell me why."

She nibbled another bite of her muffin and sipped her coffee before answering. "Landon sheltered me, he protected me, he fed me, he made me laugh and he made me feel more like a woman than I ever have before."

"And he's a gorgeous man." Catching her raised brow, Winnie smiled. "Doesn't hurt."

"I love his compassion and his kindness most of all," Amy said. "He was right beside me when I helped Tam and chased after Anson. Sure, he joked around a little, but he didn't question. He made sure I had a new jacket when I gave mine to Tam, a place to lay my head after the car broke down and then again for the next night in Austin, and he made sure I got here to Houston safe and sound like he promised."

"Sounds like a pretty decent guy to me," Winnie said.

Amy frowned. "He is, but now I need to somehow resolve the reasons why he lied and decide whether I can ever trust him again."

"Sounds to me like you trusted him before the big reveal, or whatever you want to call it."

"I did." Her brow furrowed and she gave her friend a helpless shrug.

"Honey, I know Landon's intense, but so are you."

Amy sputtered. "I am?"

She nodded. "It's all that creativity flowing through your veins. You look at people and situations differently than most of us, but you also see the inherent good." Her eyes misted. "As much as anyone I've ever met, you pour yourself into everything you do with your entire heart and soul. You feel things deeply, both good and bad. And, for what it's worth, you're also one of the most forgiving people I know."

"To be honest, Winnie, I don't want to tell Sam and Lexa, or Josh—or anyone else in TeamWork—about this whole thing. It's too embarrassing, for one thing, and rehashing it probably won't do me any good." She put her hand over Winnie's, squeezing her fingers. "Talking with you is all I needed. I'll pray and somehow figure all this out, but I think for my peace of mind, I need to avoid Landon for a while—no contact whatsoever. Nothing."

Her heart sank as she said the words. Glancing up at Winnie, she knew she wasn't fooling her for one millisecond.

~

Sharing dinner around Sam and Lexa's table kept Amy laughing while she devoured the delicious meal prepared by none other than Sam and Josh.

"We switch duties once a month for our weekly dinners with Winnie and Josh," Lexa told Amy as they cleaned up afterwards in the kitchen. "The guys cook and we do the dishes. Works out great and everybody's happy. Of course, sometimes we say 'forget it' and just go out to eat."

"Well, Sam's grilled chicken was the best I've ever had," Amy said, "and Josh's homemade macaroni and cheese was great. Next thing I know, Sam will be penning a cookbook for men."

Lexa and Winnie shared a smile.

"Please don't suggest it," Lexa said, shaking her head as she handed her another dish to dry.

Winnie finished putting everything away and excused herself to go check on the kids and Lexa gave her one of the knowing looks she'd perfected. Of course, living with Sam might have something to do with it.

"What's on your mind?" Amy asked.

"You fell in love with Landon these last few days, didn't you?"

She paused while drying the dish. Lexa always was a straight-shooter. "You got all that from a dance at the wedding?" When Lexa remained silent, focusing on scrubbing a pan, she blew out a breath. "Like I told Winnie, I'm way too obvious."

"I know what happened."

Amy's eyes widened. Setting the dried pan on the sink, she leaned against the counter, crossing her arms. Did Winnie tell everyone after she specifically asked her *not* to say anything? "I told Winnie—"

"Winnie didn't tell me. Sam did."

"Sam? How did he—" Why should she be surprised?

"Landon called while we were in our meeting downtown earlier today. I knew it was important when Sam excused himself and took the call."

Amy watched in silence as Lexa rinsed and laid the pan on the counter. After wiping her hands on a dish towel, she took her by the hand and led her to the breakfast nook. Sinking into a chair, Amy waited.

"Landon needed to tell someone and he and Sam have grown pretty close the last couple of years," Lexa said, sitting beside her.

"Sam and Landon?"

"Sam will explain when you interview him in the morning. Suffice it to say, Landon's been a part of TeamWork here in Texas the last few years, but he prefers to stay behind the scenes."

A vision of the television news story about TeamWork she'd seen in Austin fluttered into her mind. "The man likes to keep secrets, I guess. He's full of surprises, that's for sure."

"Not secrets, but he likes doing things anonymously. Apparently, he gets a lot of attention he doesn't want in New York, and when he comes back home to Texas—and being able to help out with TeamWork—he says he's able to relax and be himself."

"Interesting," Amy said, digesting this new bit of information.

Lexa nodded. "Sam and I both call him Landon, but Kevin and his friends from A&M always called him Cooper. At the wedding, none of us knew you'd met him as Landon in New York until we came back home and Winnie told me about the name confusion. Yes, Landon led you on, but I've gotten to know him well enough to know he didn't do it to be cruel or to play with your mind. I think—in his own way, crazy as it might seem—he enjoyed the opportunity to be the cowboy he really is, beneath the exterior of his publisher persona. Sam told me Landon confessed it all and asked him to pray. So they did, Sam in the hallway outside the conference room and Landon in Austin. From what Sam told me, the man's in love with you. Then again, I think I already knew."

"Lexa, I barely know the man and yet I know him so well."

"You've spent a lot of time with him and packed a lot of memories into only a few days. From what I know, you have a lot in common. Kindred spirits, I'd say." Lexa's aquamarine eyes were bright as she tossed her braid over one shoulder. "Oh," she said, putting one hand on her stomach.

"Something wrong?" Amy's pulse quickened and she inched closer to where Lexa sat facing her, inches away.

"No, no," Lexa said, rubbing her hand in small circles over her stomach. "I think one of the babies is showing her sister who's boss. A little rumble's going on in there right now."

Amy's eyes moved to Lexa's belly. "I can't imagine how . . . wonderful and life-affirming that must be."

Taking Amy's hand, Lexa placed it on her stomach. "Wait a minute and you'll feel it. I can't wait to finally meet our girls, and I'm sure it won't take long to figure out whether Leah or Hannah's the bossy one. Of course," she said, laughing, "Joe will claim his right to boss them both."

"I didn't know you'd given them names yet," Amy said. A giggle escaped when she felt a swift, hard kick beneath her hand. "I love them already."

"I know how committed you are to the pro-life movement in Manhattan, and I admire your strong stance. You do more than stand on the sidelines. If only more people were willing to put their faith into action, it might save a few more precious souls."

Tears filled Amy's eyes and she nodded, removing her hand. "What I just felt is something every scared pregnant girl should experience before she makes a decision to end the life growing inside her." In the next few minutes she shared how she'd met Angelina's taxi driver father and how Angelina sent her the two stories the night before leaving for the wedding.

"I think that was a God thing," Lexa said, still rubbing her belly. "No just maybe about it." She winked. "Interesting her name is Angelina." They shared a smile.

~

After she said her good-byes to Winnie and Chloe, promising to return to Houston for a weekend visit sometime in the spring, Josh pulled her aside. "Cut the guy some slack, Daydreamer. Landon's a great guy. His heart's in the right place."

Her mouth gaped. "Did Winnie tell you what happened?"

"Nope. She didn't have to. As soon as you got out of the car, I could tell something was up."

She shook her head. "Wow. I must be even more transparent than I thought. Josh, tell me something. Why would a guy pretend to be someone he's not?"

He frowned. "Only he can answer that, but maybe it's because he's not exactly sure who he wants to be. I have to get my girls home, but know we all love you and we'll be praying. Give us a call anytime you need to talk or want to come for a visit, okay? We're here for you." With that, he tweaked her chin and departed.

Watching them go, lost in thought, Amy waved from the doorway. When Sam asked if she wanted to tuck Joe into bed, she jumped at the chance. The little guy sat with her in the rocker, snuggling and burrowing into her. "But Jesus said, 'Let the children alone, and do not hinder them from coming to Me,'" she read from his toddler's Bible, "'for the kingdom of heaven belongs to such as these.'" Her eyes filled with tears and she hugged the little boy close to her heart, stroking his dark waves—so like his father's—and kissed the top of his head.

When a tear slipped down her cheek and landed on his hand, Joe—half groggy with sleep—touched her face, his big blue eyes searching hers, full of compassion well beyond his years.

"Oh, Joe," she whispered against his warm, soft skin as she picked him up and lowered him into his crib, "you are so blessed, little guy." Crossing her arms on the railing, she kissed her fingers and pressed them against his cheek as his eyes drifted closed. "So am I."

Chapter 40

THE NEXT MORNING, Amy settled in a living room chair across from Sam, prepared to start the interview. The spark in those clear, piercing blue eyes clued her in. *Time for a Papa Bear talk.* Lexa was in the kitchen with Joe, and Amy smiled as she heard them singing together.

"So, first things first, Sam," she said. "Landon's your publisher?"

"Yes. He's branching out into some different ventures and this is his first foray into book publishing."

"Quite an ambitious foray, but I know he's done a good job so far of marketing and promotion for you."

Sam nodded. "He knows the business and he's been great. Before we start the official interview, Amy, I want to talk with you. Off the record."

Why am I not surprised? Leaning back in the chair, she balanced her notepad and pen on her lap, drumming her fingers. A sudden case of nerves assailed her, and she struggled to keep her breathing steady. Hard to do when her heart was pounding out of control. "Lexa told me he called you. Did he ask you to plead his case?" Sarcasm slipped into her tone and her shoulders slumped.

"Landon called me, yes, but he didn't ask for anything more than for me to listen and pray with him. I'm going to tell you something I'd never share under normal circumstances. However, in your case, I think it's warranted. I know Lexa already told you he's been a part of TeamWork for a few years. What I'm about to tell you might help you better understand him."

Amy straightened in her chair. "I'm listening."

"Landon's personally flown TeamWork board members and directors—me included—to conferences, to scout out camp locations here in the U.S., and to deliver relief food supplies to storm-ravaged areas. Josh has flown on his plane a couple of times in recent months, sometimes with Landon at the controls, sometimes not. From what I've seen, the man's a confident, capable leader. He's also recruited several other pilots to help us out, and I'm very indebted to his dedication to TeamWork and for sharing his many gifts and resources." Sam settled his gaze on her. "Like you've poured a lot of *your* resources, including your money, into TeamWork and prefer to remain anonymous."

Amy sat back in her chair, her thoughts swirling. "I had no idea, and I wish everyone would stop calling it my money. It's my grandfather's."

"Earned by your grandfather, yes, but now you have control over where the funds he left to you are used. I've always admired you for your good business sense. You've got a solid sense of right and wrong, a strong work ethic and you love the Lord and put it into action. So does Landon. His relationship with his dad has a lot to do with the man he's become. I'm not sure how much he told you, but his dad was a self-made, wealthy man who squandered it all and ran his own company into the ground, but not before he left his wife and only child—Landon—feeling as though they somehow weren't worthy and didn't measure up. That kind of destructive thinking can destroy a man's psyche and self-esteem."

Leaning forward in his chair, Sam fixed his gaze on her. "Some men would allow it to beat them down, but Landon took the opposite approach. He's very protective of his mother and he's made a great success of his life, in part to prove his worth to himself and to her. But he's struggling in his relationship with his dad. As a Christian, he knows he needs to forgive, but he's finding it difficult to do."

Swallowing hard, she nodded. "He told me his dad's in jail for fraud. He went to see his dad yesterday morning and that's one reason why I was late coming to Houston."

The lines of tension on Sam's forehead eased. "Good. I knew it was something he'd been thinking of doing. When he can forgive his father for past transgressions—not just say the words, but in his heart—that's where Landon's going to find his peace." Sam sat back in his chair. "In some ways, he doesn't feel worthy of you and your love. It's those old feelings returning to attack him. In the past, he's protected his heart by not allowing himself to get too close to a woman. He was afraid a woman wouldn't accept him because of his father being in prison. On the other hand, I think there's been an underlying fear he might succumb to the same sin. When you thought he was someone else, he seized the opportunity to assume another identity for a couple of days, but trust me on this: the man with you on your trip to Austin would have been true to himself and his values. One of the reasons he didn't want to come to Houston with you is because he was concerned you didn't know he was my publisher—and you'd jump to the conclusion he wanted to beat you to the draw in interviewing me."

"Call me a naïve innocent, but I never thought of it." Amy's eyes met Sam's.

"You love him."

She nodded slowly, her eyes welling again. "I do. Problem is, I don't know what to do with his love."

"Pray about it and give it time," Sam said. "Know we'll be praying right along with you. I have no doubt you'll figure it out, but keep your heart open to the possibilities. We all make mistakes, including some of massive proportions. It's part of our humanity, but it's also our responsibility to forgive those who ask our forgiveness when we've been wronged."

"Forgiveness is the easy part, Sam."

His eyes met hers. "You don't *want* to forget it, Amy. From what I know, you'll take this experience and be all the stronger for it. I'm going to ask Lexa to come in and we'll pray together, and then we'll do the interview, but when you go back to New York, I'd ask you to pray for Landon, and especially his relationship with his father."

"Of course, I'll pray. Thank you for telling me all this, Sam."

"Remember this, Amy: Hurt builds up walls, but love tears them down."

~

Later that afternoon, Sam and Lexa drove her to the airport. She'd spent more than an hour with him during the interview and had a lot of great ideas for her article. Due on Friday morning, it didn't leave her much time and she needed to buckle down and focus on it. In some ways, having the deadline was a very good thing. She'd be too busy writing and editing and wouldn't have time to think about Landon or anything else if she wanted to keep her job.

Funny thing, though. Although she wasn't sure what had changed, the last week had shown her life wasn't about a job. A job could never give her the satisfaction she'd found in chasing a runaway dog and taking her back where she belonged. Or the rush of emotion she'd felt helping a misguided young waitress. Or the tenderness she'd glimpsed in a cowboy's eyes when he danced with her, kissed her and held her like the most precious jewel.

Hurt builds up walls, but love tears them down. Sitting in her seat on the airplane, Amy pondered Sam's words as the ground crew took their seats in preparation for takeoff. Her thoughts took her back to soaring high above Austin. Landon was right: it was a freedom she'd never before experienced. The much larger plane now gathered speed and left the Houston runway behind—taking her away from Texas and back to her life in Manhattan.

Resting her forehead against the window, she whispered a prayer. *Lord, I'm leaving a big part of my heart here. Help me find my way home. Help Landon, too, to draw closer to You and find* his *way home.*

Chapter 41

Wednesday, December 18, 2002 – Mid-Afternoon

LANDON SAT ALONE at a corner table of the small, quiet coffee shop, an open magazine beside him. He'd read the same paragraph five times. Rubbing a hand over his jaw, he grimaced. Besides not getting any sleep, he hadn't bothered to shave and his clothes were rumpled. Dona and the rest of the staff mumbled around him, ducked their heads when he passed in the hall and stopped their hushed conversations. He thought he'd heard the name "Scrooge" when he passed by the reception desk. What a mess he was, but he'd hand out their Christmas bonus checks a few days early and that might help. They deserved better than his bad attitude for all their dedication and hard work.

The bell on the front door jingled. Wearing a determined expression, Mitch strolled toward him with a purpose, peeling off his gloves as he crossed the small shop. The firm line of his lips and set of Mitch's jaw meant nothing good. He'd been expecting this visit from Amy's brother, and the man obviously had more than a friendly chat on his mind.

"Hey, Mitch." Standing, Landon extended his hand before being cut off by one hard blow to the right side of his face. Stunned, he staggered forward but managed to grab hold of the edge of the table. Righting himself, he clutched his jaw. "I assume that one was for Landon." He turned his head and offered the opposite side. "Might as well take a swipe at Cooper. Go ahead. I deserve it. Make it count."

Confusion crossed Mitch's face and he dropped his hand. "I think that'll do it. Unless you want a shiner to match."

The shop manager started toward their table. "We don't want any trouble here, guys."

"Sorry, Pete." Landon glanced at Mitch. "No trouble."

"Yeah, sorry," Mitch said, his voice resigned. "I'm done."

Landon pointed to a chair. "Sit down so we can talk about this. Please."

They stared at each other until Mitch relented. Landon pulled away his hand, relieved it hadn't drawn blood. If he'd aimed for his nose, it'd be broken. "You pack a good wallop, my friend. You're a worthy adversary and I appreciate your loyalty to Amy. If I had a sister, I'd do the same thing."

"Thanks, I guess. I don't know why I'm here considering what you did. I never expected you'd break her heart." Those gray-green eyes, so like Amy's, were on fire with righteous indignation. "Congratulations. I hope you're proud of yourself. You managed to dupe one very smart woman. Why you did it, I have no idea, but it was a lousy thing to do to a great person. Maybe I gave you more credit than you deserve for being a decent guy."

"Want something to drink?" Swallowing his frustration, Landon took another long sip of coffee bitter enough—even doctored with cream and sugar—to burn off his stomach lining. Disgusting thought, but fitting for his current mood.

Mitch shot him an incredulous look, one brow quirked. "This isn't a social call, Warnick."

Landon sat back in the chair, gathering his thoughts. "I take it she got back to New York safely?"

"She's on a plane now. She called me last night and told me the whole sordid story."

"What exactly did she tell you I did?"

Mitch met his gaze. "The way I understand it, you deceived and lied to her. *Big* time."

"I did, but it was more a mistaken identity thing, at least at first. I freely admit my mistake in carrying it too far. The whole thing was based on a miscommunication and a strange set of circumstances, but I never intended to hurt her, Mitch. You have to know that." He leaned forward, capturing the other man's eye contact and holding it steady. "If nothing else, understand this: I'm in love with your sister. She's the most compassionate, beautiful, generous, loving, infuriating, nutty, passionate, witty woman I've ever met. No woman has ever challenged me the way the way she does."

"Yeah, well, you have a strange way of showing it." With a look of disgust, Mitch raked one hand through his dark hair.

Landon slumped back in the chair and blew out his sigh. "I've apologized and asked her forgiveness. I pray in time she'll be able to get past it and move on."

"Seems to me your words got you in trouble," Mitch said. "It might take more than words to get her back, if that's what you want." He waved a hand. "Start talking."

As he began his story, Mitch listened, interrupting a few times to ask pointed questions worthy of a protective older brother. Excusing himself a half hour later, Mitch returned with a cup of coffee. "You want another one of whatever you're having?"

"I'm fine, thanks." The fact Mitch cared to ask was more than enough.

"Keep talking, then," he said, narrowing his eyes as he sipped his black coffee.

Another ten minutes passed before Landon finished his story. "I can't lose her."

The other man drummed his fingers on the table and pushed aside his empty cup. "Sounds like it was quite the adventure. After hearing all that, it's pretty obvious you love her. If our parents hadn't met and married so fast—and had such a great marriage for a lot of years—I'd laugh in your face and tell you it's impossible."

"That's because it hasn't happened to you yet."

"On the contrary. I've fallen in love lots of times. That's my big stumbling block. I dangle my affection on the line and pretty much nip at the first bait thrown my way. Back to you and my sister: for one thing, if we lived like a hundred years ago, I'd insist you marry her since you compromised her reputation."

"Nothing happened that shouldn't have. If you believe my word means anything, you can trust me on that one. I'd marry her in a heartbeat if I thought she'd be agreeable, but I don't think she'll even talk with me face-to-face right now."

Pinching his nose between two fingers, Mitch closed his eyes. "Okay, here's the problem as I see it," he said, his lids fluttering open, "Amy loves you, too."

Landon swallowed hard and his heart raced. "Has she told you this?"

"Not in so many words, but I can read between the lines. Ever since she met you, she's been more unfocused, scattered and forgetful. So, I guess the burning question here is: what do you plan to do about it?"

"I'd settle for a chance run-in with her at this point, but she's not ready. I don't want to embarrass her in front of her colleagues, not to mention her boss isn't my biggest fan. What I need is to get myself right with the Lord and then get some things straight in my life. And then accept what, if anything, Amy's willing to give me."

"These things you need to get straight—like what?" Mitch asked. "I know that's personal, but I have a burning need to know. Humor me."

Landon cupped his hands around his coffee mug as he gathered his thoughts. "I've been struggling with my future at the magazine. The board's headed in a direction I'm not willing to go."

Concern furrowed Mitch's brow. "I don't understand. Aren't you the one who started the magazine?"

"Yes, but I'm at the mercy of the ones bankrolling it. It's like I birthed the baby, but now others are calling the shots in how to raise him. Basically, I've been told to take my magazine in a much more liberal direction with no mention of spirituality, faith or quote-unquote religion." He sat back in the chair. "As a result, we're in a deadlock, but I'm not backing down. Nor am I giving into their demands."

"You know, Landon. Aside from this situation with my sister, you're a decent guy. Yeah, you made a massive error in judgment or whatever you choose to call it, but after hearing you out, I can sort of understand. It's good to hear it from your perspective. And in terms of the magazine, I admire your strong ethics." He darted his gaze to the table and finished his coffee.

"Thanks. Coming from you, that's high praise."

Mitch grunted. "Don't thank me too soon, but for what it's worth, I'm sorry about the magazine. That's tough. What can you do?"

"I'm resigning effective after the next issue hits the newsstands." Giving up the reins of the magazine wasn't a failure, but saying the words stung like nothing else ever had. The way he looked at it, it wasn't selling out nor giving in to pressure, but standing up for what was right in God's eyes. He'd prayed hard about it, knew it was the right course of action. No way could he continue to publish and edit the magazine by compromising his integrity and lowering his moral standards. *Denying his faith.* He wouldn't be able to look himself in the eye. As much as anything else, it was a matter of self-respect.

Mitch's shock was obvious. "I'm not sure what to say. I know *New York Scene* means everything to you."

"You know, Mitch, before I met Amy, I would have agreed, but spending time with her has changed my perspective. Keeping my nose stuck to the editorial grind eighteen hours a day isn't the way to spend my life. Where's the value or reward in that? I want a wife, a family and love instead of waking up one morning as an old man with nothing or no one." He leaned closer. "I *need* Amy beside me, and I hope I have your blessing."

Mitch met his steady gaze. "I came for an apology and an explanation. I didn't expect a proclamation of love, but why should I be surprised?"

"The truth?"

Mitch's eyes widened. "Nothing but."

He sat back. "If I stand at the door of Amy's heart and knock and she doesn't let me in, I'll accept it. But it'll be hardest thing I've ever done."

"I know I haven't held up my end of the bargain with God lately," Mitch said, "but I've been praying again. For you and Amy, believe it or not. Not that you should take credit for it. I want your word you'll never lie to Amy or deceive her again."

"You have my word and I hope you'll forgive me for hurting her. I'm sorry, Mitch. If she'll allow me, I'll spend the rest of my life making it up to her."

Mitch thumped the edge of the table with his palm. "In spite of her better judgment, she's probably already forgiven you. She's trying to . . . absorb it all."

A glimmer of hope surged inside him. "Any suggestions to get back in her good graces?"

"First, humble yourself. Two, beg her forgiveness but back off and give her the time she needs. If you ask me, that's what she needs as much as anything else."

"Already done, and I'm trying my best to be patient. What else you got?"

Mitch chuckled. "If and when she starts to come around and trust you again, kiss her stupid so she won't have any choice but to love you back, you idiot."

His brows rose. "Now you're calling me an idiot?"

"Sure am." Mitch shrugged. "Seems to fit."

"Well," Landon said, "there's a big difference between an idiot and a fool. Given the two, I'll take the former."

"Okay, I'll bite. What's the difference?"

"An idiot does something stupid, but a fool runs away. You won't catch me running away. I'm more determined than ever to get Amy back. She's worth fighting for and I intend to do it."

"Then it's a no-brainer the way I see it," Mitch said.

Landon's mind spun in a hundred different directions. "You gonna tell me?"

"What, has love blinded you?" Mitch shook his head. "That first night she met you, Amy told me how brilliant you are as a writer. She couldn't stop waxing poetic about you and used words like 'insightful' and 'thought-provoking.' Amy doesn't hand out praise like that lightly, especially when it comes to other writers, but don't get your head all puffed up about it." Mitch's shoulders hunched as he leaned across the table. "Time to do what you do best. Use your words."

Mitch's suggestion was better than anything he'd come up with on his own. Taking his advice sure couldn't hurt. No one knew Amy better than her brother. As if he needed a reminder, his jaw ached like he'd been pummeled by a middleweight boxer. The guy packed a hard punch and he'd have a decent bruise as a constant reminder over the next week or two, but he'd deserved it.

"Thanks, Mitch." Rising to his feet, he offered his hand. "Are we straight?"

"Yep, but if you ever do it again—"

"You don't have to worry about that. Pray I can go write the most brilliant and persuasive essay of my life."

Mitch stood beside the table and pumped his hand. "Don't worry about making it brilliant, make it *real*. Tell her what's on your heart. I'll give you one more key piece of advice."

Landon nodded. "Anything."

"We're going home to see our mom in Pennsylvania for Christmas and coming back on Friday the twenty-seventh. They're having a holiday in-between dinner and special end-of-the-year prayer meeting at Amy's church on that Saturday night. Seems to me she might be helping serve the dinner and then she'll probably attend the special prayer meeting." A wry grin creased his lips. "She'll be less inclined to rant or pound you if you talk to her in church."

Mitch was a good guy. Smart, too. "Thanks. I owe you one, but what's an in-between dinner?"

"In-between Christmas and New Year's." Hesitating, he turned back with a wry grin. "I understand you've got a Cessna."

Landon slapped a hand on his shoulder, allowing a small grin. "I'll consider letting you use it sometime. See you later, Mitch, and that's a promise."

"Sure thing. Merry Christmas."

Landon nodded, swallowing around the tight, hard knot in his throat. "Merry Christmas to you, too."

~

"Hear ye, hear ye. The Court is called to session, the Honorable Joshua Grant presiding."

Amy sat, wide-eyed and speechless, as Josh paraded into Sam's study wearing what resembled a black choir robe. Stealing a glance at Landon where he sat on the opposite side of the desk, she saw the corners of his mouth quirk and he shot her a quick wink before returning his full attention to Josh sitting in the massive black leather chair behind Sam's desk. Sam apparently had the good sense not to participate in this . . . whatever it was.

Josh lowered a heavy wooden gavel on the desktop with great care. "Court is now in session. Who is the defendant who comes to plead this case?" He nodded toward the back of the room where Winnie stood inside the door beside Lexa. Both avoided looking at her.

"Landon Cooper Jared Warnick comes before the Court, your Honor," Winnie said, infusing her voice with a kittenish tone. "Did I get all the names in the right order?" That question was directed at Landon, and he gave her a solemn nod.

Amy turned to look at Winnie, wide-eyed. *This is insane.*

Josh quirked a brow and laughed under his breath. "What is the charge against Mr. Warnick?"

After Lexa elbowed her, Winnie stepped forward. "Your Honor, Mr. Warnick is accused of fraudulent impersonation."

Josh directed a stern glance Landon's way. "Mr. Warnick, is this true?"

"Yes, your Honor, I'm afraid it is."

"Whom did you impersonate?"

"Myself, your Honor."

Josh scratched his head. "Oh. Okay. And how do you plead to this crime?"

"Unequivocally, undeniably, unrelentingly—"

"Spare me the adverbs. Journalists," Josh muttered, half under his breath. "A simple guilty plea will do, Mr. Warnick."

Landon sighed and his shoulders drooped. "Guilty as charged."

"And would you like to claim a defense?"

"Love, your Honor." Landon moved his hand over his heart. "I have no other plausible excuse for my behavior."

"Plus a little temporary insanity thrown in for good measure?" Josh inclined his head toward him with a raised brow.

"If it works for you. I'm sure the victim would agree."

"I see. Give me a moment." Swiveling in the chair, Josh turned around, but Amy could see his shoulders shaking.

"Does your Honor need to take a short break?" Lexa asked, her tone tinged with humor.

"No, no," Josh said, turning in the chair to face them again. "Your Honor was momentarily overcome by the magnitude of the heinous crime committed by this defendant. Now, then, let's proceed. Mr. Warnick, please start by telling the Court why you did what you did to this woman we all know and love." He ignored the snickers from the back of the room and his smile sobered as he fixed his eyes on Landon. "You don't mess with TeamWork, and the deliberate deception of a TeamWork volunteer is punishable to the highest extent of the law. No mercy is given—"

"All right, all right, that's enough! May I approach the bench, your Honor?" Amy jumped to her feet, unable to contain her exasperation with this ridiculous and unfounded proceeding. From the corner of her eye, she saw Landon straighten in his chair.

"Certainly. And you are?" The corners of Josh's mouth upturned.

"The aforementioned TeamWork volunteer you all know and love?" She gritted her teeth. "Your Highness."

Josh grinned. "Your Honor will suffice, but you sure are good for my ego."

"State your name for the official Court record." That request came from Winnie, but Amy kept her eyes trained on Josh. If she dared glance at her best friend, she'd probably fall to her knees and beg her to stop this madness.

"Amelia Madelyn Jacobsen, your Honor. The so-called 'victim' of Mr. Warnick's impersonation, deception or whatever it's officially called." She stared Winnie down. "For the record."

"Very well. What do you have to say to the Court, Miss Jacobsen?"

She took a few steps closer to the desk, fisting her hands and moving them down to rest on her hips. A quick perusal of the room revealed all eyes were focused on her. Lexa and Winnie both leaned forward, straining to hear her words, as did Josh and Landon.

A slow smile curved her lips. "Tell me something. Where's Sam Lewis when you *really* need him?"

~

"Okay, okay, I forgive you!" Amy woke up drenched in sweat. Based on the way her legs were tangled and wrapped in her sheets, she'd done a lot of thrashing about in the bed. Raising herself to a sitting position, she slapped a hand on her forehead.

Great. Now my daydreams are morphing into nightmares.

Chapter 42

Friday, December 20, 2002 – New York Scene Editorial Offices

LANDON CHUCKLED THE next morning when he heard a happy squeal "One, two, three . . ." he counted under his breath. Sure enough, the door opened and Dona rushed inside.

"Landon, look out, baby, I'm coming for you!" Dona moved faster than ever as she covered the office in seconds and reached the side of his desk. Flinging her arms around his neck, she planted a noisy smacker of a kiss on his cheek. "Hands down, you're the greatest boss in the world, but why'd you do this?" Out of breath, she fanned the airline tickets and DisneyWorld passes in front of her, staring at them in wonder.

"Merry Christmas to the best assistant on the planet. It's also a bonus for all your hard work this past year and always. I couldn't do it without you."

"I'd say it's too much, but you know it's my dream to go to DisneyWorld. Wait until I tell Pax. My hubby's not going to believe this! Ohhh, it's so exciting!"

"Wait a minute," he said as she started to depart. Walking over to a small closet in the corner of his office, he paused with one hand on the door. "I have something else for you, too. Close your eyes."

"Something else? Goodness, what more could there be? This is like my birthday, Christmas and anniversary all rolled into one!" Obediently, she closed her eyes as he reached into the closet. Her lips seemed creased in a permanent grin. "Should I hold out my hands?"

"Nope." He placed the black cap with mouse ears on her head. "Open, please."

Dona's green eyes opened, her lashes fluttering. Putting her hand on her head, she moved her fingers over the felt cap and found one oversized, round ear. Tugging the felt hat from her head, she ran a finger over the red cursive script spelling out her name. "You even had my name embroidered." A tear slipped down her cheek as she once more thrust herself into his embrace. "I don't know what to say, Landon."

Moving his arms around his dutiful assistant, he hugged her. "It's all worth it for the look on your face and the hug. They're open-ended passes, so go anytime. Go next week if you want."

"Honey," Dona said, planting a hand on her chest, still heaving a bit with excitement, "I might take you up on that offer. It might be twenty below zero and my bum's frozen solid here in New York, but Florida here we come! I don't know what to say except thank you forever."

"You and Pax are going to have a ball. Take the rest of the day off to make your plans."

"You sure?" She wiped away another tear and lifted eyes full of gratitude to his.

He waved his hand. "Go. I'm about to head out early myself."

She paused, and her smile sobered. "I hate to ask, but when's your last day in the office?"

"Officially, a week from today. I'm facing an uncertain future, but would you consider coming to work for a small, independent publisher?"

"Well, it's about time you asked me!" When her hand slid to her hip, he chuckled. "You know I will, boss. *New York Scene* without Landon Warnick at its hub makes no sense, and it's their loss. You know I stand behind you one hundred percent. That last piece you wrote is a great one, and I'm praying Miss Amy will see it and come running to your arms and never leave. I know that's what I'd do."

"Ah, Dona, you already have my heart."

She gave him an impish grin as she turned to go. "I know, but it never hurts to remind a man. We'll talk about the job and my salary when I get back. Toodles, love. You're the best!" After blowing him another kiss, she clutched the tickets to her chest and dashed from the office.

~

The days leading up to Christmas were a blur of last-minute shopping as Amy prepared for the trip home to Pennsylvania with Mitch. Purchasing a pretty necklace and earring set for her sister, Amy smiled, knowing it would please Celeste. From their several Saturday mornings browsing in an antique book shop in SoHo in recent months, Amy called the store, hoping they still had the signed, first edition of Mark Twain's *Innocents Abroad* she knew Mitch secretly coveted. He'd be so pleased and surprised. She splurged, thanking her grandfather for that one since she dipped into the trust fund. Her mother was always the hardest to shop for since she seemed to have everything she needed and never expressed a want to any of her three children. She picked out a new freshwater pearl necklace with matching earrings and bracelet, but as much as anything, she knew her mother wanted to spend quality time with her. Much to her chagrin, other than a short phone call the night of the wedding, she hadn't talked to her in ages.

On Christmas Eve night, after the service in their church, Amy sat beside her mother in the living room as they watched the fading embers in the fireplace. Mitch had retired to his room, presumably to call Felicity, Celeste to call her new boyfriend. While she relayed her story about Landon, her mother, Katherine, listened closely but thankfully didn't pass judgment or criticize his actions. When she finished, Amy eyed her carefully. "Mom, tell me something. Was Dad perfect?"

Katherine laughed. "Of course, not, honey. What makes you ask?"

"Winnie thinks maybe I expect too much of a man because all the men in my life have been perfect. For one, you and I both know that brother of mine isn't perfect."

"I heard that and will hold it against you for the rest of my natural born life," Mitch said, coming out of the kitchen with another slice of chocolate pecan pie and a glass of milk, headed for the stairs. She raised a brow when she saw he wore his old maroon Harvard Medical School sweats. He must have pulled those out of mothballs. "Night, ladies."

"I think everyone has a fatal flaw—men *and* women—if you want to call it that," Katherine said after they blew Mitch air kisses.

"What was Dad's?"

"Probably that he expected too much of people."

Amy smiled. "He did, didn't he? But I shouldn't think that's a fatal flaw."

"In a way it was because he expected the same of others as he did of himself, in terms of character. He was always disappointed."

"What else can you tell me about Dad?" Pulling the afghan up over their laps, Amy snuggled closer to her mother, leaning her head on her shoulder as she used to do as a child.

Katherine kissed her forehead. "He cheated at Monopoly once and it took years for him to finally admit it to me." She laughed when Amy mock-gasped. "He didn't enjoy grocery shopping but he'd tolerate it if I asked him to go. And don't tell anyone, but he didn't really like old Mr. Grainger. But your father rarely said an unkind word about anyone. He helped out around the house without my asking and massaged my feet after a long day, even when I knew he was too tired. And," she said, heaving a deep sigh, "when he knew he was dying, he held my hand and told me he'd miss meeting the wonderful mates you, Mitch and Celeste would marry, and all his grandchildren." Her eyes misted, and she gave her a tremulous smile. "That made him sad, but he was ready to meet his Savior and knew we'd all be together again one day."

Amy kissed her mother's soft cheek. "Please don't tell me he mentioned Felicity for Mitch," she said, shaking her head.

Her mother's laughter surprised her as they both wiped away a few sentimental tears. "No, he didn't." Katherine's smile sobered and she tipped Amy's chin. "As far as Landon, search your heart, honey, and pray. If he was here, your father would advise the same thing. Ask the Lord to give you the answer. He knows your heart like no one else."

~

Friday, December 27, 2002 – Manhattan – Amy's Townhouse

Feeling benevolent and in the spirit of Christmas cheer and giving, Amy decided to send Landon an e-mail. If nothing else, it would give her closure since she had some lingering questions.

Merry belated Christmas, Landon. Hope you're well. Question: what was your first big mistake?

Curious Amy

A response came within the hour—

Dear Curious Amy,

Great to hear from you, and I trust your time with your family in Pennsylvania was relaxing and everything you'd hoped. The first mistake as Cooper was when I said something about Landon being a magazine *publisher. You never said that specifically. Then I said asked you the question about liking me as* Cooper, *which sounds very strange, in retrospect. Scratching my head here. I honestly thought you'd figure it out, we'd have a good laugh and get on our way. Maybe I'm a better actor than I thought? Then I realized you'd never think I was the same guy because why would anyone deceive you like that in the first place? A thousand times, I wanted to tell you, but I kept getting in deeper and selfishly, I couldn't let it go. Couldn't let* you *go.*

I have no excuses except I thought if I told you I was Landon—after misleading you—you'd never go with me to Austin. I can't explain it except to say I needed you to go with me and, in spite of how it all turned out, I'm glad you did. I pray you don't regret the entire thing because it was the best two and a half days of my life, Amy. Believe that. I'll never forget it. Or you.

Fool for all time, LCJW

Two hours later, she was back in front of the computer again, unable to stop the stream of questions.

Dear Fool for all time,

I have another question, if you're willing to answer. What's the story with the scar? First of all, it is *real, isn't it? Do you keep it in a little box in your sock drawer with other trinkets and mementos? Something you take out and slap on whenever you feel like it?*

Reading through it, she winced and removed the last two lines since they sounded way too snarky. After writing *Fondly, Sincerely yours* and a few other sign-offs, she was at a loss and left it off entirely. She was curious and anxious to hear his explanation. Deciding at the last minute to add the sentences back in, she pushed SEND and moved away from the computer as she started to gather her laundry. Could anything be more pitiful than a woman who waited by the phone . . . or the computer? A few minutes later, tossing more dirty clothes in the basket on her bed, Amy's heart raced when she heard the telltale sound of an incoming e-mail. Throwing a blouse into the basket, she scurried over to the desk and slid into the chair.

Dear Miss Irresistible,

Wish I could say I know some people in the prop department of a TV show or that it's really nothing more than a slap-on decal that looks realistic as long as you don't get too close. Wish I could say I almost lost the dumb thing a few times when I was with you in Texas. Wish I could say it's gone now because I don't need the reminder of my foolishness.

But I can't say any of the above. The truth? The scar is all mine, and it's exactly what I told you in Texas. It's the result of being stupid when I was a teenager and deciding to do a flip on a motorbike. I'm thankful I didn't break my skull or worse. Perhaps more painful is telling you why you couldn't see my scar on our date in Manhattan. Right before you and I met for dinner that evening, I had a photo shoot. The makeup artist insisted on covering it up. So—and I hate like anything to admit this—I finally gave in to get the session over with or I'd have been late to meet you. She slathered heavy stage makeup over it so it was barely noticeable. If you've ever worn that stuff, you know how hard it is to remove. I kept combing a section of hair down over it because I wanted to cover up the makeup, not the scar. Any more questions? Feel free to ask. Anything. Anytime.

Yours always,
Vain I'm Not

Yours always? A dozen more questions flooded her mind, but she needed to assimilate them and put them on paper or into another e-mail. Pulling her notepad closer, she picked up her pen and jotted random thoughts. She stopped to throw clothes into the washer and fold clean towels before returning to her computer and composing another e-mail. Although she had other things to ask, she decided on one of the smaller questions. Typing it out, she sent it on its way before she could think about it. "Let's see what he says," she said with a little grin.

Me again.

Do you have two cells phones or one? One for Cooper and one for Landon? And you call me *the nutty one?*

Curious Amy

Eating a turkey pot pie, her all-time favorite comfort food, and listening to the evening news, she heard the telltale chime from the computer signaling an incoming message. "You're such a lovesick fool," she muttered, nearly falling over her feet as she stumbled to the chair and plopped down in it, staring at the e-mail inbox on the screen. Sure enough, he'd replied. Holding her breath, she stared at it for a few seconds, heart pounding, before reaching for the mouse and clicking on the message.

Dear Curious Amy,

Yes, I have two cell phones, one for Texas and one for New York, but I usually keep both with me. Call me strange, but it's easier and works better that way to keep the two parts of my life separate, ironically enough. You almost caught me after the incident with Anson when you asked to use my phone. I stink at role playing in more ways than one. Think about it. If I'd called you as Landon during your time with me as Cooper, that would make me even more of a fraud. Maybe I actually do deserve an ID bracelet and should check myself into a padded room. I worried I'd use the wrong phone at the wrong time, but in the end, I messed up in a much more spectacular way.

Missing you, LCJW

She needed one more.

Dear Missing You,

What's the card you always put down on the table with a tip?

Sort of Missing You Back

Dear Sort of Missing You Back,

It's a TeamWork card. You see, I'm a proud, card-carrying member, too. Sam has them printed up with a few Scripture verses, and the tag line, "Rebuilding lives worldwide and binding souls for Christ." If you don't have some, I can get some for you. Just let me know where and when and I'll be happy to deliver them in person.

Your Faithful Servant Always,
Landon

Printing out the string of e-mails, Amy carried them back to the table and picked up her fork. Funny how the pot pie lost its appeal as she read—and reread—Landon's e-mails, as if she'd discover some code message in between the lines.

The only "code" was that she missed him more than ever.

Chapter 43

Saturday, December 28, 2002 – Evening – Amy's Church

"AMY, CAN YOU serve the vegetables tonight?" Marcia Heilman asked as she headed into the kitchen of the large reception hall in the church basement.

"Sure. I'll be happy to." After storing her purse in a cabinet, she grabbed an apron from a drawer. Tying on the apron, she smiled and called out holiday greetings to a number of members and their guests as she positioned herself behind the warming trays of green beans, homemade mashed potatoes and a smaller pan of brown gravy. Picking up the large serving spoon, she stirred the beans.

As if he hadn't done enough, Landon had also managed to steal her appetite since their e-mail exchanges. If nothing else, the man was good for her waistline. Small consolation. Not to mention she'd already been to the gym twice today—working out like some type of fitness-obsessed fiend. Although she was bone-weary, she might get some decent sleep tonight, something hard to come by since her trip to Texas.

The members of the congregation slowly streamed through the serving line. Pasting on a smile, Amy poised her spoon. From the rather large group coming in the door, it appeared they'd have a good crowd. Maybe it was the cold weather that brought so many into the church, beckoning them with the promise of warmth, fellowship and good food. Could be the holiday spirit lingering in the air. Too bad she hadn't caught it. Even if her heart wasn't in it, she could still be polite and make small talk.

Watching the various members and their guests move through the line, she complimented the older ladies on their pretty brooches and colorful scarves, and smooth-talked the older gentlemen sporting their holiday shirts and ties. Not many couples with children came to their dinners or the mid-week prayer meetings, unfortunately—especially during the cold months—but she chatted with one mother as she assisted her three kids in the line. One of the girls needed help pouring the gravy, so Amy ladled it out for her. Taking a break twenty minutes later, she darted into the kitchen for a glass of ice water, downing it with a few quick gulps before returning. Stirring the green beans and noticing the man in line wasn't moving, she lifted her chin.

"Would you like . . ."

"Yes, I'd definitely like."

Landon stood in front of her and sported a rather large but fading bruise on his jaw. She tried not to notice how well his dark suit was tailored or how well the gorgeous blue silk tie matched his incredible eyes. Catching a whiff of his cologne, she coached herself not to breathe in more than necessary. "Green beans?" she snipped, keeping her voice steady.

"No, thanks."

"Mashed potatoes? Wouldn't you like some of those? They're homemade." She avoided his gaze and concentrated on staring at the spoon her in hand.

"No, but thank you. Amy."

The way he tacked on her name—the very *way* he said it in that deep, sexy voice—made her squirm, but she stood her ground. "Well, please move along then. There's obviously nothing here for you tonight. Bye-bye now. Thanks so much for coming. Have a wonderful evening and a nice life. God bless." She waved her hand in dismissal.

Landon grinned and ignored her glare as he moved along the line, taking only a chicken leg instead of ham and a dinner roll. Accepting a cup of iced tea from one of the ladies at another nearby table, he glanced her way and took a quick sip. Catching her stare, he winked.

The audacity of the man. Showing up here in my home church, of all things. Flirting. "Marcia," she called to where the other woman stood nearby, "do you mind if I go sit down for a bit? Most everyone's been through the line at least once."

"Oh, sure. Go ahead, honey, and grab yourself a plate. Thanks so much for helping tonight, as always."

Taking off the apron, Amy hung it on a hook in the kitchen. She nodded and smiled at some of the others through clenched teeth as she picked up her plate, napkin and silverware while trying to ignore Landon where he stood beside a table at the far end of the fellowship hall. Grabbing a plate and plopping mashed potatoes and green beans on it, Amy frowned when bean juice sloshed onto her shoes. Oh well, who cared if she'd smell like a green bean all night? Maybe it would have mattered a couple of weeks ago, but everything was different now. Perhaps God's intention was for her to spend the rest of her natural born life alone. *Maybe I should get a cat and take up knitting.*

"You're doing it again," a familiar voice said from behind her as she added a chicken leg to her plate. Her appetite migrated south, along with her mood.

"Doing what?" Turning slowly, she hoped her expression resembled disdain. Landon's apparent amusement made her want to slap him.

"Daydreaming. However, since the sun has set, perhaps it should be called something else after dark. Like night dreams or moon dreams. Moonbeams sounds pretty clever. You're a journalist. What do you suggest?"

"I suggest, Mr. Warnick, that you march yourself out the doors of this church and onto the street where you belong. This is *God's* house, and I don't think you'd be very welcome here tonight if these kind-hearted Christian people know the way you go around deceiving people for your own selfish purposes."

"Wow. That's quite a mouthful from a woman who hasn't taken her first bite of food."

"Stick around. There's plenty more where that came from." *I'm such a fool.* With the utterance of those words, she'd admitted to him that—beneath the sarcasm—she wanted him to stay. Glancing at the nearby tables, it was difficult to miss the interested stares directed at them. Nodding her head for him to follow, she led him in the direction of an empty table.

Landon made no move to sit down as they faced one another, still holding their partially-filled plates. "I do believe you're nuttier than before." He took a step closer. "And much more beautiful."

"That will be quite enough out of you." Her voice held a note of warning, and she turned to march away from him. The abrupt movement sent juice as well as a few beans flying off her plate. With a startled cry, Amy's eyes widened in horror as the mess splattered on Landon's starched shirt, and some of the juice stained his suit coat. She grimaced and gave him a sheepish shrug by way of apology as it made a slow trail down his jacket. "Here," she said, putting her plate down. She started to dab at the stain with a napkin until he took it from her and pressed it against the fabric.

"Go ahead. Throw things at me. Do whatever you need to do, Amy. If accosting me with green beans helps you in some small way, have at it. As a matter of fact, here, let me help you." Her eyes widened as Landon put his plate on the table. Using his fingers, he scooped a bit of mashed potatoes from her plate. With a grin, he smeared them over his tie, rubbing in circles, working them in good.

Staring aghast, she recovered her voice. "What are you doing now?" she hissed. "You're embarrassing yourself. Honestly, you should be ashamed. A world-class publisher standing here in my church, dribbling and smearing food on himself like an infant. Would you like a bib to go with your mess?" Laughter bubbled up inside her, and she bit her lip to keep from dissolving in giggles. "Not to mention the fact you've now had your way with my food, so I'm afraid now we both smell like green beans."

To his credit, Landon maintained his composure. "Perhaps I'm in the mood for some comfort food myself. Mashed potatoes and green beans fit the bill, wouldn't you say?"

"Are you speaking in terms of eating them or wearing them?"

"Maybe both." He took a step closer, staring her down. Amy met his gaze, determined to win this battle of wills and stay strong in her resolve to resist him. "As a matter of fact, I came here tonight at the suggestion of your brother."

Anger stirred within her. "Oh, now you've gone and done it. You've managed to drag Mitch into your shenanigans. What'd you do, dupe him, too? Honestly, does your shame stop at nothing?"

"As a matter of fact," he said, pointing to his jaw, "this bruise is compliments of Mitch in his avid desire to protect you from the likes of me. Imagine that."

"Mitch did that?"

"Yeah, and you don't have to sound so pleased about it. The guy packs a mean punch."

"Well," she said, inspecting it, "I suppose it's starting to heal. It's at that stage where it's a little red and . . . yellow." She stroked her fingers over the bruise with a light touch and turned his chin to one side to better inspect it. "A little blue and green, too. I think I'll call you rainbow man. That fits. Among several other names I could call you."

"That feels good. Do it again."

"Oh!" Amy released her fingers and gave him an icy glare. "Do you never stop? You might as well take your flirtations, and your green bean and mashed potato-covered self out the door right now, like I said before. Your kind is not needed—and certainly not *wanted*—here."

"Sure. I can do that." Grabbing a spare napkin from the table, he wiped potato residue from his hand. He frowned and shrugged before sticking a few fingers in his mouth and licking them clean, one-by-one.

Amy watched, incredulous. "I can't believe you're actually licking your fingers now."

He laughed. "Don't look so appalled. It's from the chicken leg, and you know what they say—"

Amy whirled on her heel. "Far be it from me to stop you. It's a free country. Lick your fingers all you want. Better yet, why not go get some dessert and smear it all over your pants since you like playing with your food so much? Do whatever you please, but leave me out of it. Tuck that accent under your Stetson and mosey on your way. I'm sure there's plenty of gullible women in Manhattan to fall for your overflowing charms." *Stop talking now.*

Landon's smile grew broader, annoying her. "You are adorable when you're all witty and *saucy* like this." Hearing spontaneous applause all around them, they both glanced up in surprise.

"Oh, Amy, thank you. That's the best skit we've had in months. Let's go in the kitchen and get your prize." With one arm around her waist, Lois Cannon guided her across the room. "You come, too, young man," Lois said, motioning for Landon to follow.

Amy paused, looking over her shoulder at Landon, who now wore confusion mixed with amusement on that way-too-handsome face. When Lois pulled her into the kitchen, Amy released her breath. "I really won a prize?" Surely this was a ruse to get them alone and render a serious tongue lashing. She couldn't blame Lois; their behavior was nothing less than shameless. Two adults acting like silly, flirty teenagers. Heat warmed her cheeks and she lowered her gaze like a child chastised after a prank.

"It's a prize for both of you. You really livened up our meal tonight. I can't tell you how entertaining it was. Thanks for inviting him to join you tonight, Amy."

"I didn't invite—" Amy closed her mouth. No sense in protesting, but she refused to glance his way. In that second, she'd rather spit nails.

Retrieving an envelope from a drawer, Lois checked it and then handed it to Landon. "Here you go. Dinner for two at the restaurant of your choice, complete with a carriage ride in Central Park." A wide smile crossed her face. "If I were you," she said with a knowing wink encompassing them both, "I'd save this for Valentine's Day."

"Thank you, ma'am," Landon said as Lois departed, leaving the lingering scent of her signature honeysuckle perfume. Slipping the envelope in his jacket pocket, he leaned against the counter, arms crossed. "I imagine she's old school and believes it's a man's place to take charge of romantic Valentine dinners. I happen to agree."

"I didn't say a word."

"You didn't have to. It's written all over your face. If you'd stop being so defensive and started trusting people more—meaning me in this case—you might be able to lighten up and enjoy the gifts right in front of your nose."

"I beg your pardon?" She'd played right into that one. Shifting from one foot to the other, she ran one hand back and forth along the smooth but cold stainless steel counter. "Just because we traded a few e-mails doesn't mean I'm inviting you back into my life."

With a frown, he pulled the envelope back out of his pocket and offered it to her. "Here then. You take this certificate. That performance out there was mostly you, anyway. You deserve it more than me."

She stared at him, not budging. "I doubt I'll need it. I'm sure you can find a willing woman—"

Walking over to her, he took her hand and gently pulled her fingers out of the curled fist. Opening her palm, he placed the envelope across it. "Can we at least be adults and talk about this?"

She blew out a sigh. "I don't even know where to begin, Landon. Or are you being Cooper tonight? Who *are* you? Have a new identity to add to your repertoire?"

"Stop it. Please. Although," he said, gentling his voice, "that was kind of fun tonight, don't you think? We should try role playing again sometime."

It took a moment before she recovered her voice sufficiently to speak. "Seems to me you've already done more than your share of that. I will not let you shut me up tonight. Those days are long gone. I can't believe you're joking about it considering what you did." She tried to ignore the hurt in his eyes. *When will I learn to curb my tongue?*

Others started coming into the kitchen laden with empty food trays and serving utensils. "I should go. I'm supposed to help. It's an important responsibility, and I take it seriously."

"Spoken like a fine schoolmarm. I'll help you."

She paused. "What do you mean?"

He slipped his arms free of the suit jacket and hung it on a hook. "Exactly what I said. I'm going to help out in the kitchen, and then I'm going to stay for the prayer meeting. We *need* to pray together."

"I meant the schoolmarm comment."

He leaned close, his warmth breath tickling her ear. "Beneath the prim and proper façade is the fun-loving, spontaneous Amy. She's dying to get out more. I know because I got pretty fond of her, nutty though she is, on a little jaunt through Louisiana and Texas." With a chuckle, he tapped her chin. "She's also incredibly witty and gorgeous, and I find it very difficult to resist her."

"I do—" No way would she admit how right he was since they both knew it to be true in terms of her social life. "As far as the prayer meeting, you're right. Trust me, I'll be doing some serious praying for your soul tonight."

"Great. Thanks." Rolling up his sleeves, Landon walked toward the men congregated by the sink. As she assisted the ladies in storing the leftovers, Amy twisted her mouth in an effort to hide her smile. He engaged the men with sports talk and listened to a few of them tell their war stories. Most of the regular members had heard the tales countless times, so they pounced on Landon like animals on fresh prey. He didn't seem to mind, and she admired the way he interacted well with all of them while he helped put away dishes and dry the pans.

"Landon looks so familiar to me." Lois handed Amy a foil-wrapped dish to load into the refrigerator.

"He's the publisher of *New York Scene.*"

Beside her, Marian King shoved something into the freezer, grimacing with the effort. "We need to schedule a time to clean out this monstrosity. Something's probably growing in here." Closing the door, she turned to her. "Don't let her fool you, Lois. Mr. Warnick's also one of Manhattan's most eligible bachelors. Read it in the *Times.*"

Don't believe everything you read. Amy concentrated on making space in the refrigerator for the next dish.

"I read an editorial Landon wrote in the *Post* a few months ago responding to an article about adoption dangers and pitfalls," Lois said, handing Marian a plastic bag with green beans to squeeze into the freezer. "My Kendra and her husband are considering adoption, and they said it was very helpful."

"I hope it didn't dissuade them from adopting," Amy said as she put the final container into the refrigerator. *That sounded pretty negative.* She needed to tone it down.

"Oh, no," Lois said. "The opposite. It's actually helped them know the right questions to ask to help weed through all the different agencies. They were very grateful I sent the article to them. I'll tell Landon myself when I get a chance. He might appreciate it since some people jumped down his throat, in a manner of speaking, after that piece was published." She turned bright eyes on her. "He's such a handsome man, Amy—tall, strong and such a gentleman.

Why, those blue eyes positively sparkle when he looks at you, honey. Are you two dating?"

It wasn't her imagination when it seemed every woman within range strained to hear her answer. "I, um . . ."

Someone slipped an arm around her shoulders. Closing her eyes for a brief second, she prayed for strength. She couldn't push him away in front of these well-meaning ladies. No, that would be rude. "I'm trying to convince Amy I'm not such a bad guy," Landon said. "Any help is appreciated, ladies."

He must have thought she needed rescuing. *Maybe he's right.*

The women all laughed—twittered was more like it—as though he'd said the wittiest thing they'd ever heard. *Oh, please.* Steeling herself not to roll her eyes, Amy grabbed another covered dish and hid her face in the refrigerator, hoping it would cool her flaming cheeks. When she pulled out and closed the door, she noticed Landon had resumed his dish duty on the opposite side of the kitchen and joined in another animated discussion of who-knows-what with the men.

A short time later, during the pastor's short devotional, they sat, heads bowed, side-by-side in a pew. Midway through the prayer time, Landon began to pray.

"Heavenly Father," he said, "help us to trust You in all things. Help us to know that You are the One in control, the only One who knows the true motivation of our hearts. Help us to love one another unconditionally, especially when we don't understand one another or why things happen the way they do. Help us to give up control and give our worries, concerns and apprehensions to You. Thank You for loving us beyond anything we could ever comprehend. In Jesus' name, Amen."

His prayer ended, they listened to the continuing prayers. Amy inched her hand toward his, giving it a nudge. He didn't disappoint. Tears stung her eyes. *I will be strong.* She startled, but didn't protest when he moved his arm along the back of the pew. Her pride had taken leave long ago and taken her common sense along for the ride. Sliding closer to him, she was filled with a sudden, unexpected happiness. Seemed she could be mad as spit at the man, but still crave his friendship and comfort.

After the prayer meeting, she made polite conversation with other members. From the corner of her eye, she saw Landon talking with one of the older couples. Why couldn't the man take his quiet leave? Part of her wished he'd go, but the other part wanted to fall into his arms. She was tired and wasn't sure she was up to another confrontation. Not tonight. Most of the congregants had already departed by the time she dropped onto a quiet bench in the outer vestibule. Kicking off her heels, Amy blew out a sigh. Pastor Thomas gave her a nod and told her to take her time and he'd lock up later.

After saying good night to the couple, Landon stopped in front of the bench. "Thanks for allowing me to sit with you in the prayer meeting."

"I'll do you one better." She patted the spot beside her. "Sit." With a small smile, he complied. "That was a very heartfelt prayer you prayed tonight," she said, massaging her forehead. "I hope you meant it."

"I did. Headache?"

"You could say that." Her shoulders slumped and her lips started to tremble.

"Amy, I hope my being here tonight hasn't made you mad or caused you more pain." His words were quiet.

"It's not that." Blinking hard, she willed the tears to keep at bay. *Do not cry.*

He nudged her shoulder. "Everyone I talked to tonight couldn't stop raving about you. I heard everything from how you saved the kids' Christmas program last year to how you stayed with Velma's grandkids for three nights straight so she and her daughter could be at the hospital when Velma's husband had emergency surgery. There was a whole lot more, but one thing was perfectly clear."

"All in the spirit of helping when and where I can. You'd do the same." That comment slipped out unaware, but it was the truth.

"I wanted you to know your efforts are appreciated." His gaze slid to where her hands rested on her lap. "How are things on the Amelia forgiveness barometer these days?"

Sitting up straighter, she cleared her throat. "The, um, atmospheric pressure is easing a bit, but it needs more time."

"I've missed my road trip partner." Gentle fingers tipped her chin. "And my dance buddy. The woman I've come to adore."

Her eyes were watery when she looked up at him. "I miss Cooper."

"He's right here." Landon's eyes were bright and they'd never looked bluer.

He hurts as much—if not more—than I do. She didn't protest when he drew her into his chest and wrapped her in his arms. Burrowing into him, Amy didn't stop her tears. Releasing the pent-up emotion that had been building throughout the evening—ever since she'd last seen him, really—she cried. He leaned his head against hers and captured her hand, holding it tight. "I'm always here for you, Amy." The words were whispered against her temple and he smoothed her hair away from her forehead.

"I'm sorry for making a mess of your jacket," she said, wiping her cheeks with the back of one hand. "Nice suit, by the way. It suits you. Sorry. Really bad pun."

He smiled. "That's what dry cleaners are for, along with removing green bean and mashed potato stains." With obvious reluctance, he released her. "Are there any tissues around here?"

"I'll get them." Padding in her stocking feet into the nearby ladies room, Amy grabbed the box. Back at the bench, she said, "Let me try and clean up your jacket." Plucking a tissue from the box, she dabbed it on the front of his jacket.

Putting his hand over hers again, he stilled her action. "Leave it. That's only making it worse."

"You don't get it," she said with another sniffle, "it's keeping my hands busy."

His warm smile thawed her evaporating resolve. "I'll keep them warm and protect them, if you'll allow me."

Slipping her hands from his grasp, she turned aside. "Like I said, I need to keep them busy, not warm. And I need time. This has all happened so fast."

He pulled her back around to face him. "I'm a very imperfect Christian, Amy, but I'm also saved by a perfect God. It doesn't mean I get a blank check for my bad behavior, but I've asked His forgiveness and now I'm asking for yours."

"I'm not looking for perfection, Landon." Dabbing the tissue beneath her eyes, she gave him a small smile as the conversations with Winnie and her mother floated through her mind. "I've missed you, too. More than I wanted."

Relief spread through his handsome features. "I've missed you my whole life. Now that I've found you, I don't want to lose you."

She shook her head and gave him a small smile. "I'm going to call you Cooper when you say things like that. Broad, sweeping, chivalrous statements."

"You love it."

"Didn't say I didn't. Landon, I have a question for you."

"Anything."

"Are you ashamed or embarrassed by your dad?"

He lowered his gaze before lifting it to hers again. "I used to be, and that was before he was incarcerated."

"What changed?"

"Meeting you and coming face-to-face with my shortcomings. I'm more like him than I realized. Someone I never thought I'd be, driven by ambition to get what I want."

"How long has your dad been in prison?"

"Almost four years. His sentence was longer, but he paid back some of the money he embezzled from his company. It took a long time to get through the court system and for him to be sentenced with all the red tape and bureaucracy, but he's been in a self-imposed prison for a lot longer. He gets out in February, but I'm not sure where he's going or what he'll do then."

"Have you forgiven him?"

He hesitated before nodding. "In my heart, yes, but I wasn't able to do it until after that last visit when you were in Austin. He seemed remorseful and was more honest than he's ever been. I guess I'm waiting for him to come around and ask the question." He looked away and rose to his feet. "It's hard to say until it actually happens."

Standing in front of him and putting one hand on the side of his jaw, Amy cupped it with her hand. Her eyes searched his.

"I'm asking you now, Amy. Will you forgive me? That's all I'm asking. I can't hope for any more than that." She caught the choke in his voice, the deep emotion behind it.

"Yes, Landon. I forgive you."

"Thank you." When he opened his arms again, she moved into them without hesitation.

They stood a long time, not speaking, holding one another. Finally, she eased out of his embrace. "I need to get home." Leading him to the coat rack, she pulled his black wool coat from the hook and handed it to him. She'd know it anywhere.

"Thank you." Taking it from her, his fingers brushed hers and then he helped her into her own coat. After slipping on her shoes and grabbing her purse, she walked outside with him into the brisk night air, inhaling deeply.

"My Range Rover's parked around the corner. Will you allow me to take you to supper since you didn't eat earlier or drive you home?"

She lowered her gaze. "Thank you, but I'm not hungry and I'd rather walk."

His eyes widened. "Please don't tell me you walk alone on a regular basis."

"Okay, I won't."

He shifted and looked away before returning his gaze to hers. "Does Mitch know about this?"

"No, but I carry mace and walk at a brisk pace."

"If you insist on walking, I'm going with you."

"Oh, I don't know," she said, glancing at his leather dress shoes. "Are you sure those shoes are appropriate for a long walk?"

He grinned. "If you won't allow me to take you, then I'm going to hail a taxi for you. No way are you walking home by yourself." Crossing the sidewalk to the curb, he looked both ways, but the street was quiet and deserted. "I'm afraid my record may not hold up tonight since there's not a cab in sight."

"Go for it." She knew her eyes held the challenge as much as her smile.

"Tell you what," he said, "if I can manage to hail a cab . . . here on this deserted street corner . . . in ten seconds or less, you agree to meet me for dinner on Valentine's Day. We can use that certificate you earned for us tonight. What do you say?"

Amy glanced up and down the street. "Seeing as how it's completely desolate on this street right now, I feel safe in saying you're not going to win."

"Just wait, my pretty. Oh, ye of little faith." Shaking his head, Landon stuck two fingers in his mouth and whistled. Amy clamped both hands over her ears. He did it again, and then a third time.

"You have five more seconds." She was really enjoying this. Although he didn't bat an eyelash, from the lights of the street lamps, she saw the muscles in his jaws work overtime. Her eyes widened a second later when a cab turned the corner and sped toward them. *Wouldn't you know it.* Her jaw dropped as the taxi made a smooth stop beside Landon. "You can take your fingers out of your mouth now. Your job is done."

With a wide grin, he opened the car door and bowed. "Your taxi awaits."

She leaned close as she passed by him. "Meet me at Kyle's at six o'clock on Valentine's Day. You owe me a dinner there, anyway."

"I hear they're booked way in advance for special occasions," he said. "It might be awfully hard to get in."

"I'm sure you'll think of something."

Chapter 44

Sunday, December 29, 2002

WORKING ON A new article, she heard her cell phone ring. Grimacing at the interruption, Amy crossed from the kitchen into the living room and retrieved the phone from her purse. Not recognizing the area code or phone number, she frowned as she walked back to her chair at the kitchen table. Normally, she wouldn't answer. She looked at the phone display again. Something registered in her brain. Texas.

"This is Amy."

"Amy?" The voice was female. Young.

"Yes? Tam, is that you?"

"Um, yeah. Look, I need some help and I didn't know who else to call. You were so nice to me and, um—"

"I'll be happy to help you if I can," Amy said. Leaning an elbow on the table, she rubbed her forehead while her mind spun in a hundred directions. Bad timing being only a few days before the New Year, but if it was important enough for Tam to call, the least she could do was listen. Tam probably had a fight with Andy, some other guy or her mom. She'd listen, give the best counsel she could and then get back to work. When she'd offered to help, she meant more as a sounding board.

You told her you'd help if she needed it. Hear her out. "Why don't you start by telling me what's going on." Leaning back in her chair, Amy closed her eyes, prepared to listen.

"Could you maybe come back down here?"

Amy's breath hitched. *Nothing this girl can say is going to get me to go running back down to Texas.*

"I think I'm pregnant and I'm not sure what to do."

Except that.

"Have you taken a pregnancy test?" Amy asked.

"Yeah. A week ago and again this morning. Both positive." Tam's voice broke.

Amy drummed her fingers on the table, and she started to say something before stopping herself. Now wasn't the time for *I told you so.* Tam sounded beside herself as it was. Inhaling a deep breath, she forced the question. "What are you thinking, Tam?"

"I'm thinking I should probably get an abortion. I can't keep *my* life straight, so why be saddled with a kid? My mom already signed a consent form since I'm underage. Says she can't raise no more kids and railed on me for being stupid enough to get pregnant even though she did the same thing when she was my age."

Amy clamped one hand over her mouth, stifling the sound of her gasp. Swallowing hard, she fought to control her breathing. Putting one hand over her stomach, she struggled out of the chair. With her eyes blurred by tears, she walked across the kitchen and leaned against the wall. Curling herself against it, she removed her hand from her mouth. She took a few quick breaths to try and control her voice. "Tam, please don't do anything rash. You need to think this through first. From what you're telling me, you're not sure of this decision, and that's why you called me." Try as she might, her voice trembled.

Tam didn't speak for several agonizing seconds. "I'm not asking you to tell me what to do."

Closing her eyes, Amy prayed. *Lord, give me Your words.*

The words whispered in her heart. *You are not alone, child.*

Her eyes fluttered open. "Tam, you're not alone."

"You'll come down to Texas?" The hope in her tone, the small sob punctuating the question, made her sound like a much younger child.

"Yes, of course. Tell me where you are."

"I'm in Asher, Texas. It's not far from the Louisiana line. The place where you met me before. Chances are, when you get here, I'll be working at Kleinman's. I'm pretty much always there."

"Is this the best phone number to reach you?" Scribbling down the information Tam relayed, Amy checked her watch. "I'm coming, Tam, but please promise me you won't do anything until I get there, okay?" She prayed under her breath and clenched and unclenched her fist.

"Promise." The word was quiet, and she had to trust the girl meant it.

Disconnecting the call, Amy groaned. Getting a plane reservation would be next-to-impossible with the holiday rush, and she didn't relish renting a car and driving alone to Texas. For one thing, her brother would never allow it. *Mitch.* With new resolve, she grabbed the phone again and punched the speed dial.

"Do you have any idea what time it is?" More than anything, Mitch hated being awakened from a sound sleep.

"Sorry, but it's important. We need to take a road trip to Texas."

"Funny," he said, exaggerating his loud yawn. "For a second there, I thought you said it's time for a road trip to Texas. I've never been there, so why would I want to go now? Am I dreaming?"

"Texas is great. Now's your chance."

"Tell you what. Let me go get something to drink and I'll call you back in ten minutes, then you can explain what this is all about."

A sense of relief swept over her. "Thanks. Make it something caffeinated and don't lay back down or you'll fall asleep again. I'll talk to you in a few."

"I'm not promising anything."

Once Mitch heard what it was about, he'd be halfway amenable, but it was still a long shot. Juliet wouldn't be pleased, and the thought of taking extra time off and driving through possible bad weather made her cringe. The saving grace was that because it was the end of the year, things were slower and more laid back at work. If she promised to keep up with her current projects, it might appease her boss and grant her enough favor to carry into the New Year.

For the next few minutes, she padded around her townhouse before washing up a few dishes. Of course, the phone rang when her hands were wet with suds. Grabbing a dish towel, she did the quick dry and put the phone to her ear.

"Tell me what this is all about." To his credit, Mitch didn't interrupt her spiel. She paused a couple of times for his assurances that he was awake and heard her. "Amy, you know I'd do anything for you," he said as she finished, "but I have two things this week I really can't get out of. If I drove with you to Texas, I wouldn't make it back in time. It's impossible, given the time and distance. I'm sorry, but I can't."

Tears stung the back of her eyes and she bit her lower lip. "What things?" She closed her eyes and regretted the question.

"Before you ask, nothing to do with Felicity. You might be pleased to know we're not seeing each other."

That statement stunned her. "Mitch, I'm sorry. Really." Tacking that last word on didn't help, but her heart was heavy for him. "You know I wasn't the biggest fan of that relationship, but I hate like anything to see you hurt."

"I'm man enough to admit when you're right, and you were. She's a nice woman, but it wasn't a healthy relationship. Not a solid basis for anything more than friendship."

She leaned against the kitchen counter and stared at the floor. "You should have told me. When did this happen?"

"Right after Christmas, but you had your own problems."

"That's borderline insulting. You know I'd drop everything for you if you needed me."

"I know you would." Mitch cleared his throat. "In answer to your question, I've been spending time at one of the children's hospitals, and I'm expected there in three days. They're doing a program for the kids. It's important or I'd consider the trip to Texas."

Tears sprang into her eyes. "I had no idea. That's great." He'd stayed far away from hospitals since he'd left Boston after the fiasco during his residency, and this was a huge step in his personal healing from the pain of the past. Mitch loved kids, and he was wonderful with them. With his sense of humor, he'd have them all laughing, and vice versa. Another answer to prayer.

"You can take my car, if you want. I don't want you to go by yourself. Surely you have a girlfriend or one of the ladies from *Habits* who doesn't already have plans for the New Year?"

She'd forgotten about his car. "At this time of year, I doubt it. Besides, I don't want to call anyone this late at night and beg them to go with me. I'm not sure if I'm up for another road trip, either, especially with someone I don't know well. That last one was enough to last a lifetime." She didn't realize she was smiling until she turned and caught her reflection in the oven door.

"There's a solution to your dilemma that makes perfect sense, you know."

She stopped pacing. "What's that?"

"Swallow your pride and stubbornness and call Landon. The man's got a plane, Amy. I'm sure he'd drop everything to fly you back down to Texas."

After signing off with her brother, she paced some more. "Oh, all right." Picking up her phone, she retrieved his number. Her heart pounded as she waited. He picked up on the third ring, but she spoke before he had the opportunity to say a word. "Landon, hi."

"Hey, Amy. What's up?" His tone was deceptively casual.

"I'm really sorry to call so late, but I have to go back down to Texas and I need your help. If you're willing." When he didn't speak, she thought better of it. "Never mind. Forget it—"

"You wouldn't have called if it wasn't important." She heard movement and a muffled yawn. "When do you need to leave?" She envisioned him in sweat pants and a T-shirt, sitting up on his bed. Her heart swelled with a rush of emotion. She could almost smell Irish Spring and minty mouthwash. *You are seriously delusional.*

She snapped back to attention. "As soon as possible. Tam called. Landon, she's pregnant and—to put it bluntly—she's thinking of terminating her pregnancy." She swallowed a small sob and brought her hand to her mouth, her fingers trembling. "I have to do what I can. She said she's in Asher, Texas, near the Louisiana state line"

"Hang on a minute." She could tell he was writing down the information. "Tam's underage, so I'm pretty sure she'd need permission from a parent."

"I know, but she told me her mother signed the consent form."

"I'll have the plane ready tomorrow morning." The confidence and strength in his voice assured her as much as anything else. "Nine o'clock is about the earliest I can get a pilot scheduled. I'll send a taxi to pick you up at seven-thirty. Can you be ready?"

"Of course. Thank you, Landon. I'll be forever grateful."

"Welcome."

Ask him. "You won't be flying the plane?"

He hesitated only a moment. "No. It's best if I don't come."

Her heart plummeted. "You can come if you want. This is too important. A child's life is at stake." She stopped short of saying she wanted—*needed*—him to come with her.

"You need to stay focused. Please let me know what happens and know I'll be praying for Tam. Just give me a call when you have any idea when you're ready to come back home."

She wiped away a tear. "I can find my way home." The words struck her as ironic as they slipped from her lips.

"I'm sure you can, Amelia. Still, I'd appreciate it if you'd please call me and let me know when you're ready."

"If you insist."

"I do. Go with my prayers. I admire you for doing this. As much as anyone I've ever met, you live your faith and convictions. That's a beautiful thing. Call if you need anything else, Daydreamer."

His tone sounded sad, resigned almost. So unlike him. No teasing, no flirting. Well, it was late. *Admit it, you miss him and want him to go with you.* "I will. Thanks again. For everything." Amy barely squeaked out the words before telling him a quick, rushed good-bye. Wiping away more tears, she headed into the laundry room. She had too much to do and couldn't waste valuable time stewing over missing Landon, or wondering why she had such a desperate, raw ache in her heart.

After leaving a message for Juliet telling her she'd be out of the office for a few days, Amy headed for the shower. By the time she was done, Landon had already called and left her a voice mail message. She smiled, listening to his voice. When he ended the message, she realized she hadn't heard a word. "Pay attention this time," she said, frowning. A taxi would pick her up in front of her townhouse and transport her to the plane at a small airport on the outskirts of the city. From there, a pilot named Frank Long would fly her directly into a private airport close to Asher where another driver would take her straight to the restaurant where Tam worked. Landon gave her every contact number available for him and said to call if she and Tam needed anything.

The next morning, she heard a tap of a horn. Peeking out her front window, she spied a waiting taxi, its door open while a burly man hurried up the front stairs. Her heart caught in her throat.

"Miss Jacobsen." Angelina's papa stood on the front stoop. Removing his cap, he stuffed it in one hand. His broad grin was the best sight she'd seen in days.

"Call me Amy," she said, offering her hand but feeling like wrapping her arms around him. *Oh, why not?*

He patted a beefy hand on her shoulder as she embraced him. "And I'm Luis Delgado, but call me Louie. I have to say, getting a big hug from such a pretty lady on a cold morning starts a man's day off right." Pulling out of the hug, he tugged his cap down over his head. "They're saying we might get a decent snowfall tonight." He hesitated. "You okay?"

The concern in his voice touched her. She nodded. "I'm fine." She brushed away a few tears. Seemed she'd been doing that a lot lately. "Just a little emotional."

"Yeah, well, the holidays will do that to you every time," he said, replacing his cap. "That man better be treating you right. He gave me his word."

"Things are a little strained right now, but I think everything will be okay in time."

"Ah, honey, you fell in love with the guy, didn't you? Listen, he's one of the good ones. Sure, he's smooth and all on the outside, but the man's got a good heart." He tapped a fist over his heart.

Amy tilted her head. "How do you know?"

"After that night when I dropped you off in Central Park, Mr. Warnick called my boss and asked for me special. He has me pick him up midtown on Saturday mornings, some Sundays. He's a Big Brother to some kid over in Queens. Been doin' it for years, I guess. Takes him everywhere and talks to him like he's a real person, you know? Not just some kid. Even took him to visit his daddy's grave last week."

"Thanks for telling me, Louie."

"Sure thing. You two make a real good couple. You both got real big hearts, the kind I don't see much anymore. Now, time is money. You got your bags ready to go?"

"Just one. It's right here." Stepping aside, she nodded to the overnight bag in the hallway.

"Listen, I want to thank you for encouraging Angelina," he said, grabbing her bag in one swoop. "Thanks to you, she got an extra nice Christmas present this year."

"What's that?" Slinging her purse over one shoulder, Amy followed him out the door.

"She got a phone call yesterday from a lady at one of those fancy teen magazines. Said you'd given her Angie's name and sent over her story. Now, my little girl's got a meeting to talk about some fancy internship this summer. You should have heard her jumping and hollering all around the house. She can't stop talking about it and didn't sleep a wink last night. I've never seen Angie so excited."

"Oh, Louie, that's such wonderful news." He couldn't know what a precious gift he'd given *her*. "Angelina's a talented writer, and the internship will be a great experience for her."

"Yeah. With a little guy to support now, she'll be needing a decent job. She's hoping she can turn this summer thing into a career. Go to night school while working at a magazine. Miss Amy, you've given her hope she can do more with her life, even though her mama and I have been telling her that all along. See," he said, that broad grin creasing his face again, "I knew there was something special about you."

That stopped her. *Angelina has a son.* With the key in the lock, Amy turned and met his eyes. "Thanks, Louie. I forgot something inside. You go on and I'll be right out."

"Sure thing." He started down the steps with her bag as she headed back into the townhouse.

Please let it be where I think it is. Crossing the living room, Amy pulled out her desk drawer, breathing a sigh of relief as she spied Angelina's stories. Pulling out "Just Maybe," she folded it and tucked it inside her purse. *Here we go, Lord.* Again.

Chapter 45

IN THE MID-AFTERNOON, Amy finally walked into Kleinman's, suitcase in hand. The flight had bounced through a number of air pockets. Combined with a lack of sleep, she felt tired and sluggish. Stopping by the hostess station, she looked around for Tam. The restaurant was busy with the usual clatter of silverware, conversations and piped-in country music. One guy eyed her with a "new-girl-in-town?" expression and a quirked brow, prompting the girl with him to sock his arm.

Coming out of the kitchen, a young man headed toward the host station. "Table for one or is someone else joining you?" he asked, his drawl exaggerated. He kept one eye on her as he retrieved a menu.

"Just one," she said, gripping the handle of her suitcase. Seemed to be a running theme these days.

"Table or booth?"

"Doesn't matter. You choose."

"This okay?" He stopped beside a small corner booth.

"Fine. Thanks." She noted his name on the tag hanging cockeyed on his shirt: DENTON.

Sliding into the booth, she yawned and rotated her shoulders. Opening the menu, she scanned it but couldn't keep her eyes focused. She wasn't hungry, but knew she should order something.

"You really came."

Amy glanced up with a tired smile. "How are you, Tam?"

"Still pregnant." Sitting down beside Amy in the booth, she blew out a breath. Other than faint circles beneath her eyes, she looked more her age without all the makeup. "I didn't think you'd really show up here. I mean, nobody's ever done anything like that for me before." Clasping her hands on the table top, she twisted them together. "This isn't about money, in case you're wondering. I got some saved up for . . . you know."

"I'm glad you called me."

Sliding back out of the booth, Tam pushed dark red hair away from her face. "I guess you'd better order something so I don't get in trouble." She pulled an order pad from the pocket of her uniform. "Seeing as how I'm taking off tomorrow, I can't afford to make my boss mad."

"Everyone's entitled to time off, especially for medical reasons." Besides the makeup, something was different about the girl. "Did you dye your hair recently?" It was difficult to keep the question casual.

"Yeah. Why?"

"Especially during the first trimester—the first three months—you have to be careful. Your baby is vulnerable right now. Do you know how far along you are?"

Putting one hand on her hip, Tam avoided her eyes and snorted. "Might not matter after tomorrow, anyway."

She refused to believe she really meant it. Flippancy was only a cover for sixteen-year-old insecurities. Otherwise, she wouldn't have called. When Tam started to leave, Amy put one hand on her arm. "How far along?" *Is it possible she doesn't know?*

Tam paused and sighed, but refused to meet her gaze. "About nine or ten weeks, I think."

"What time do you get off work?"

She shot a glance at the clock on the wall. "Two hours."

"Then I'll wait. Keep bringing me coffee and a sandwich or soup. Whatever. Order something for yourself if you can take a break and eat."

"Nah, I'll eat later. Grilled cheese and chicken and rice soup okay?" Tam's smile was genuine and transformed her face. "House special. Wheat bread?"

"Right." *Good memory.* "Sounds great. Throw in some crackers, too, please."

"That I can do." Tam started to leave but turned back. "So, where's that fine looking man you were with before?"

"Home in New York, I imagine." Amy lowered her eyes as she handed Tam the menu.

"New York? I thought he was from Texas. He sure looked the part. Aren't you and—"

"He's from Austin originally but lives in Manhattan now. And no, we're not a couple." She waved her hand. "It's complicated."

"That's what I hate about relationships," Tam said, shaking her head with all the wisdom of a teenager. "They're always complicated. Hope it works out, though."

As she watched her walk away, Amy breathed a sigh of relief she didn't sway her hips like before or flirt with anyone as she headed straight to the kitchen. Denton also watched Tam with what looked suspiciously like unrequited love shining in those hazel eyes. When his gaze moved to her, he ducked his head and fiddled with the children's menus before sorting through bins of crayons.

An older couple sat the next table over, the man shoveling in his food while the woman picked at her dinner. Neither one said a word. Were they so comfortable with each other that words weren't necessary? Or did they simply have nothing to say? The way they avoided conversation and eye contact, they might as well be strangers. The saddest part of it all was that she'd seen a *lot* of apathetic couples like this one. But it wasn't like she could march over to their table and ask, "What happened to the passion?" Well, she could, but why embarrass them—and herself? *Could anything be more sad?*

She pictured "Cooper" sitting across from her. Of course, he'd play devil's advocate and challenge her with something like, "Just because they're both wearing wedding rings doesn't mean they're married to each other. Maybe they're brother and sister, both widowed, and it's their weekly lunch date."

You're really going mental.

A young couple with twin boys sat at another nearby booth. The frazzled mother appeared irritated with her husband as he extracted one of the toddlers from his high chair and allowed him to run around the restaurant. Yawning, the woman leaned her chin on one hand, eyes half-closed.

Cooper came into her mind again. "Go away," she mumbled.

"Give the poor husband a break," he'd say. "He's doing his wife a favor by having the kid run around. It's depleting his energy and will help him sleep better."

Two women chatted at another nearby table. They shared an easy friendship, it seemed. "Reminds me of you and Winnie," Cooper would say. "Such deep friendship is a beautiful thing. Cherish it."

"You would be right," she breathed. *Now you're engaging in imaginary conversations with the man.* "Ah, then, I guess I'm crazy." Leaning against the back of the booth, Amy closed her eyes. *Lord, help me help Tam. You know her and her child. Use me as Your servant.*

"Are you okay?"

Startled, she opened her eyes as Tam lowered the bowl of soup to the table, followed by the plate with the grilled cheese. "Denton said you were over here laughing and talking to yourself. He thinks you're a little off-your-rocker and told me I shouldn't go anywhere with you."

"I'm okay, Tam. Tired and a little loopy, that's all."

"That's what I told him, but what were you doing with your eyes closed? Chanting or something?"

"Praying."

"Oh, right. You did that before. You do that a lot?"

"All the time."

"Why?"

"Because it helps calm me down and keeps me sane, no matter what it might look like to other people. Have a seat and I'll tell you about it."

"Okay, but only for a minute. You gonna pray again now, for your food?"

"I can pass on the prayer this time."

Tam raised a brow. "You're allowed? You don't get in trouble or nothing?"

Amy swallowed her smile. "Tell you a secret. Sometimes I skip church, and I'm a pastor's kid."

"Good to hear you're normal." Tam grinned, sliding into the booth.

"Jesus is my friend, and I talk to him all the time no matter where I am. He's always there, always listens. It's really a great relationship when you think about it."

"Yeah, He can't talk back like a man usually does, right?"

Amy hid her smile. "Oh, He answers, but not always in the way you think He might. For one thing, He loves me in spite of the fact that I sometimes say the first thing that pops into my head, do some really dumb things and don't always treat people with the respect they deserve."

"Yeah, right. Like Jesus is a regular guy and you're a bad person." She shook her head. "Don't believe either one."

"Are you saying you believe in Jesus?"

Tam tilted her head. "Maybe. I don't know much of anything."

Amy took a tentative sip of her soup. "I don't think you're as confused as you act."

"What's that mean?" The question sounded defensive.

"Think about it."

"Maybe I will." Tam slid out of the booth again without another word or backward glance.

Denton sauntered over to her table when she started on the second half of her grilled cheese. "Enjoying your sandwich?"

Amy wiped her mouth with her napkin. "Yes, it's very good. You can't go wrong with grilled cheese. That's my motto."

He dropped into the booth. "Are you staying here in town?"

"Have a seat, why don't you?" She needed to tamp down the sarcasm. "You know, that's a good question. Is there a hotel nearby?" This kid was up to something and she needed to find out if it was what she suspected.

He nodded. "There's a couple of motels down the road a mile or two. Not the best, but they'll do. I'll be happy to take you. You staying in town long?"

"Only planning on tonight and playing it by ear after that."

"Too bad. I thought you and me might go out on-the-town sometime and have a real good time, share some laughs. Sophisticated city woman like you, you could teach me—"

Is that all these kids do—flirt? "Cut the act, Denton."

His hazel eyes widened. "Whaaat?" He'd started to inch his hand near hers, but at her words, withdrew his hand.

"Admit it. You like Tamara and you're trying to make her jealous sitting here with me."

"I, uh," he said, his pale skin flushing beet red. Underneath his embarrassment and faux flirting, he seemed like a decent boy. "Real subtle," he muttered.

"Tam called me in New York last night. Did she tell you that?"

"No," he said, staring at her as if he couldn't fathom what would come out of her mouth next. That made two of them.

"She's got a big decision to make tomorrow morning. I guess you don't know that either?"

He shook his head and shifted on the seat. "No, ma'am."

"Well, she does, but please don't call me that."

"Madame?"

"No, that's worse. Call me Amy."

"Nice to make your acquaintance."

"You, too. So, here's the thing." He straightened in the seat again, appearing uncomfortable but attentive. "Tam could really use a good friend, a confidante. Tam called me because it seems she doesn't have many friends in this town." She almost slipped and called it a one-horse town. Even if it was true, saying such a thing wouldn't help her case, especially if Denton had been born and raised here, a likely assumption. She finished off another bite of her sandwich. "Do you want to help her?"

"Yep. Are you like a mind reader or something? One of those ladies with a crystal ball? I saw you talking to yourself over here. Most people don't do weird stuff like that."

"Sure they do. If you don't talk to yourself, you really should. It's quite normal, and I highly recommend it."

"How can I help Tam?"

Now he's on the right track. "First, be her friend. Second, pray for her if you're a praying man. At least you like each other and talk to each other about things, right?"

"Yeah. And I pray sometimes. I like to think He's up there listening." A frown surfaced. "Andy used her bad. I hate guys who do that." Seeing Tam nearby, his frown eased. "She's so pretty and a good person, but she's had it hard." When Denton lowered his eyes, she glimpsed his hurt. "She's done some things I know she's not proud of, but all she wants is to belong. Her mama threw her out of the house and her dad's a no-good excuse of a drunk who beats on her mom. He's in jail a lot, but that's a good thing."

Amy stopped chewing. "Does her dad beat—"

"I don't think so. At least I hope not. You ask me, getting out of the house is the best thing that could happen to her." Sitting back against the booth, he shrugged. "I guess she told you she's pregnant."

Her eyes widened. "Yes, but I wasn't sure you knew."

He laughed a little. "Kinda hard to miss. I mean, she don't look it or anything, but she's been throwing up a lot. She gets this look on her face and runs straight to the bathroom. She's not eating much and yells at me more than usual. My sister had a baby last year, so I sorta know what it's like. Babies are cool, though."

"I'm glad you're here for her."

"Yeah, but a whole lot of good it does when she doesn't see me as any more than a friend." His eyes met hers. "I hate Andy, but I can't ever hate a kid. It's not his fault."

"Do you think she wants to end her pregnancy?"

"She's scared. I told her we're all scared, just about different things." He shrugged. "I don't know what she'll do about the baby, but I want her to keep it. I told her that, too, but I don't know what good it did." His eyes met hers. "She called you, and that's a good thing."

Reaching across the table, Amy squeezed his warm hand. He looked up at her in surprise. "Denton, I think God's brought us both here to help Tam."

~

Two hours later, Tam approached the table wearing Amy's former jacket.

"That jacket looks a lot better on you than me."

"Yeah, thanks. Look, Amy," Tam said, still standing beside the table, "I know this jacket cost some money. I'm thinking I should probably give it back to you."

"As you can see, I have another one. I wouldn't think of taking it back now." Picking up the check she slid out of the booth. She grabbed her purse and the handle of her rolling suitcase. "Any suggestions where I can stay for the night?"

"There's a couple of motels nearby."

"How are things going at home for you? Have your parents—"

"I'm not living at home. I've been . . . hanging out with some people," Tam said with a shrug. "My car's parked out back. It's not much, but it gets me around."

Following her out of the restaurant after settling her bill and handing Tam the tip, she decided not to ask whether she had a valid driver's license. "Help me find a motel and we'll get a room for the night."

"What? You mean you and me?" Tam scoffed.

"Yes," Amy said. "Something wrong with that?" She wanted to make sure to keep an eye on her, and she wasn't about to let her out of her sight until they could have a sit-down, serious, heart-to-heart conversation.

"No," Tam said, stopping beside an old, rusty and dented blue Mustang. "I mean, I know you're not weird or anything. Some people . . . well, you gotta wonder about them. You know?"

"You can trust me. I'm here to help you. No hidden motives."

"The door's unlocked," Tam said as she tugged on the driver's door, grimacing with the effort.

The passenger door protested with a loud creak. Reaching around to unlock the back door, Amy opened it and wedged her small overnight bag inside. She tried not to breathe in when she spied dozens of bags of half-eaten fast food, empty soda cans and assorted but questionable trash.

"Sorry it's so messy in here," Tam said as Amy climbed into the seat beside her. "I keep thinking I'll clean it up, but never get around to it."

"How many hours a week are you working, Tam?"

She avoided her gaze and didn't speak for a few seconds. "I pretty much work a full shift."

"How many hours a day and days per week?"

"You're not my mom."

Amy shot her a look. "I'm here, so answer the question, please." If Tam wanted to play hardball, so could she.

"Um, almost every day and eight or nine hours." She shrugged. "Something like that. I fill in for people sometimes. Look," she said, "if you're thinking anybody cares about laws or rules around here, they don't, especially since I'm not in school anymore."

Amy settled back against the seat and closed her eyes. When Tam started the car, it rumbled, sputtered and shook before lurching forward with a hiss. She opened her eyes as Tam pulled the car out of the parking space. The smell of exhaust seeped through the slightly open window.

The ride was quiet and they stopped at a small roadside motel a few miles away. Climbing out of the car, Amy stretched, feeling a bit stiff. Glancing around at her surroundings, she tried to hide her shock at the rundown condition of the motel, if that's what it was—no parking lot to speak of with only gravel and large chunks of broken concrete, some windows broken out and cracked, and a sign hanging almost sideways outside a small building she assumed was the office. The place should be condemned. She'd thought the fleabag in Nowhereville was bad, but this was ten times worse. *Don't be such a snob. It's only for one night. Your Savior was born in a lowly manger and He turned out perfect.* Climbing out of the car, she spied a pillow and blanket in the backseat. *Lord, please don't tell me she's been sleeping in this car. Anything but that.* The heaviness in her heart told her otherwise.

"Sorry, but I can't do it," Amy said. "Let's go somewhere else."

Ten minutes later, after checking in at another, better hotel a few more miles down the road, she sat across from Tam in another coffee shop. "Can you tell me about your baby's father?" Amy asked. She didn't want to let on Denton already told her a little about Andy. Based on what she'd seen a few weeks ago, she was thankful Tam knew the identity of the baby's father.

Tam sighed. "He's twenty-four and works at the hardware store." She took another bite of her roasted chicken and mashed potatoes. At least her appetite seemed good.

"That's quite an age difference. I'm happy to hear he has a steady job."

Tam grinned. "Andy's okay. Really, he is," she said, defensiveness in her voice. "Problem is, he has another girlfriend. We had to see each other on the side because she was getting all jealous and started making stupid threats. Real nasty stuff, too. Things you probably never heard before."

"What kinds of threats?"

Tam frowned. "She kept telling Andy she was gonna tell . . ." Her sheepish glance was the first hint of shame or embarrassment she'd allowed. She drummed chipped nails painted red, white and green on the tabletop. "She was gonna tell his wife, okay?"

Quite a full card, Andy. As much as she tried to hide her shock, Amy wasn't sure she succeeded.

"Go ahead with the lecture. I can tell you want to give it to me. Might as well lay it on me." Tam sat back and crossed her arms, a sullen frown washing over her face.

"I don't want to lecture you, but you deserve better. Hanging out with a married man isn't what you need to be doing, especially at such a tender age."

"Tender?" Her tone was full of self-disdain far beyond her years. "I ain't tender nothing." Her glare was rough, hard-edged. "I'm just a girl who's halfway pretty and sleeps around, but I've been really good since you were here before. I've been trying to be discer . . . what's that word again?"

Amy's lips twitched. "Discerning?"

Tam snapped her fingers. "Yeah, that's the one. I looked it up. Basically, it means I should use my brain and try to make good decisions." Her lids fluttered. "Better decisions."

"Have you told Andy about the baby?"

Tam snapped her gaze away and took a long drink of her milk. "He knows."

"Please keep eating," Amy said, pushing the plate closer to her.

She nodded. "Okay." She took a hearty bite of broccoli and scooped up some mashed potatoes. "This is really good."

"Tam, I have to ask you a question."

"Okay," she said. "You bought me the best meal I've had in months, so you've earned the right. Hit me with it."

"Do you believe your baby is alive inside you?"

Tam stopped chewing. "You're talking about conception, aren't you? When it's made?"

"Yes, in a way." Amy nodded, ignoring the "it" part of her question. "Your baby's gender is already determined."

"Gender?"

"Whether the baby's a girl or boy. Did you know your child probably already has ten tiny fingers and toes?" She paused, pleased to see she'd captured the girl's attention. Finished with her chicken and vegetables, Tam put down her fork and leaned an elbow on the table, listening. "God knows every hair on your child's head, knows everything that's going to happen in his or her life, knows when he or she is going to start walking, talking, and everything else."

"Here's a question for you. How can you believe in something or someone you can't see?" Sitting back in her chair and crossing her arms, Tam fixed her brown eyes on her, as if defying her to answer.

"That's a question a lot of people ask. Are you talking about your baby or God?"

She appeared to consider the question. "Both, I guess. Do you have an answer? I mean, one that's not all religious and holier-than-thou like a preacher would give you?" She shook her head. "I've been to church sometimes, but I don't get much out of it, if you wanna know the truth."

Lord, it's You and me. "Let me give you an example. I love art, and I see the most natural form of art in the mountains, bodies of water, snowflakes, the moon, the stars, a blooming flower, a majestic tree, rock formations, rainbows, clouds, the sunset . . ."

"Okay okay," Tam said. "I get your point. But what does art have to do with God?"

"Everything. None of those things were formulated or concocted by some scientist in a laboratory somewhere. God's touch is everywhere around us. He's the original artist. Look around you at all the richness of color, texture, and the countless numbers of shades of one color. For instance, did you know the color blue actually has hundreds of shades? All blue, but different and every one incredibly beautiful and unique."

"No, but I'd say it's your favorite color."

"It is, but I can appreciate the variety of colors. What I'm trying to say, Tam, is that I know there's a God when I look at all the beautiful things He's created. He made them for us, for our enjoyment, and He wants us to appreciate them. But I know He's there in so many other ways, too."

"You're smart, so I want to hear what you have to say. Keep going."

"I don't have all the answers, and I can only tell you from my perspective, but God's there in the trust of a child when he takes your hand, counting on you to help him across the street or read him a bedtime story; when an older person needs help feeding themselves because they can't do it anymore, or when someone gives you a big smile and touches your heart in an unexpected way with his words or actions."

"You must be thinking of your friend. What's his name, anyway?"

"Cooper." She shook her head. "I mean Landon."

Tam shot her a curious glance. "Which one is it?"

"Trust me, it's a long story. He sometimes goes by Cooper, and it's his middle name, but his first name is Landon."

"Well, whatever it is, I wouldn't turn him down any day of the week," Tam said, draining her milk. "You two sleeping together?"

Amy's eyes widened as she signaled the waitress to refill Tam's milk. "No, we haven't slept together."

"Not even once?" When Amy shook her head, Tam scoffed. "Why not?"

Please let her try to understand. "I believe sharing yourself in a physical way should be saved for the person you believe God intends you to spend your life with in a committed marriage."

Tam cocked her head to one side, surveying her carefully. "Let me get this straight. You think there's only one person on the planet you're supposed to spend the rest of your life with? Only one?" She ran her hand over her face and yawned. "That's crazy. What's the fun in that? I thought you were smarter than that."

"I believe once you make a commitment to one person, you stick with it. When you share that part of yourself with someone, you lose a little bit of yourself each time. It isn't something to be taken lightly. When you do that, it takes away a large part of what makes it so precious. Our ability to love someone in a physical way is one of God's gifts, and He wants it to be special." She hesitated, trying to recapture Tam's eye contact. "Does that make sense to you?"

"But if it makes you feel special, what's so wrong with it?"

Her heart broke for this young girl. She might not ever have felt special to anyone. Sex equated with love.

"Answer a question for me as honestly as you can, okay?" Tam nodded, but the veil of suspicion clouded her features again. "After you're with Andy, how do you feel?"

"I'm not sure I know what you mean."

"Are you happy, angry, mad, sad?" When Tam shifted and lowered her gaze, Amy knew she'd touched a raw nerve.

"Sad." It was quiet, so quiet Amy leaned across the table to hear it.

Now we're getting somewhere. "Do you know why you feel sad?"

After hesitating a moment, Tam blew out a long breath. "Because it only lasts for a while and then he's gone. Again."

"And you'd like someone to stay around a long time, right? Someone who'll always be there? Tell me honestly, do you feel like if you have this baby you'll be all alone?" That was certainly a valid possibility, especially since her mom had thrown her out of the house and Andy had other . . . ties.

The teenager's shoulders shook with her sobs. Jumping up and scooting in beside her, Amy gathered her close and held her as she cried, smoothing her hair.

"I'm so . . . so . . . alone, Amy," Tam whispered. "I don't want to be alone."

"You're not alone, honey. God loves you and He loves your child. I don't have any children, but I have lots of friends who do, so I know how wonderful it can be. From what I hear, there's nothing quite like it, and it's different from the love of a man or the love of a parent. It's indescribable the feeling you get when you hold a newborn. They're precious and I think it's about as close to God as we can feel. There's nothing like the miracle of a baby."

"I don't know." Tam sobbed, taking a napkin and wiping her eyes. "Will God hate me if I don't keep my baby?"

Amy swallowed, hardly daring to breathe. "God will hate it if you steal away a life, but He won't hate you. That's not what He's about. He's about love," she said, smoothing her hair, "and goodness, and light." She cupped the girl's face between her palms. "He's about giving you hope."

Sniffling, Tam's watery eyes met hers and tears streamed from them, making a path down her puffy, blotchy cheeks. "I'm not the nicest person in the world and I've done a lot of bad things. No matter what happens, you promise God won't quit on me?"

When Amy opened her arms, Tam willingly fell into them. "God won't quit on you, and I won't either. I'll tell you something. None of us are good enough. Only one person was *ever* good enough and that was Jesus. He paid the price for all of us—and all our sins—when He died on the cross, but He didn't stay dead. He's alive today, for you and for me."

Tam's shoulders rocked with quiet sobs for a minute or two. Sitting back, she wiped the napkin over her eyes and took a deep breath. "That's a lot to think about, but it sounds like you know God pretty well. I mean, you talk to Him and everything. But," she said, heaving a deep sigh, "I guess we'd better get going."

"Do you want me to order something for you for later tonight if you get hungry again?"

She shook her head. "No, I'm done," she said. "I'm really tired and need some sleep."

"Let's go." Amy paid the bill and a few minutes later, they pulled into the hotel parking lot. "Do you have anything to sleep in?"

"I have some long T-shirts in the car," Tam said. "Let me get them."

Waiting while Tam retrieved the shirt, a change of clothes and some toiletries from a small case, Amy glanced up at the moon and whispered another prayer for Tam and for wisdom to know what to say in the morning.

Oh, Lord, please hear my prayer.

Chapter 46

WAKING EARLY THE next morning, Amy rubbed her eyes and glanced over at Tam's bed. Empty. Jumping out of bed and running over to the bathroom and not seeing her there, she ran to the front window. Parting the curtains, she spied Tam in the parking lot, engaged in a heated discussion with a beefy-looking, bearded man.

This must be Andy.

Grabbing her house slippers, Amy pulled them on and threw her robe around her shoulders, shrugging into it. She tied the belt in a loose knot as she hurried out into the cold, foggy morning. Belatedly, she realized she should have taken the time to dress in her street clothes. Andy did a thorough job of looking her up and down, much more than Landon had done, and he'd done a decent job of it without actually leering.

"Hello, gorgeous," he said, the closer she came. The staring transitioned into a full-on, invasive gawk. This boy needed to be taught some manners. "Where'd you come from, this vision walking toward me out of nowhere?"

Amy avoided glancing at Tam, not wanting to see the fire her eyes. *Not a good start to the morning.* She couldn't risk this man saying or doing anything that would anger Tam to the point of stomping to the free clinic and ending her pregnancy. It probably wouldn't take much, and it was obvious he wouldn't be going with her to the clinic for support. He needed to leave *now.*

"Stop it. She's not your type," Tam snapped.

Amy could feel the force of her glare, but it wasn't aimed so much at her as the surly man standing in front of her.

"Yeah, she looks too nice," Andy said, his voice dripping with sarcasm. He moved his gaze back to Tam, full of disdain. "You stopped being nice a long time ago."

Tam let out a stream of profanity that made Amy cringe. When Andy raised a hand to strike her, Amy rushed forward, pushing her out of the way. As a reward for her efforts, she ended up on the receiving end of Andy's large, rough hand striking her cheek. Tears stung her eyes, but she refused to cry out or give him the satisfaction of letting him know how bad it hurt.

Putting a hand on her cheek, she backed away from Andy. Fear didn't enter the equation, but anger simmered beneath the surface.

"Please leave," Amy said through clenched teeth. "You have no business being here. Tam doesn't want to see you."

"Why don't you let her tell me that for herself?" His eyes bright with anger, Andy looked over at Tam as if daring her to say otherwise.

"Just go away, Andy."

"Come on, baby. You know I love you," he said, his voice placating.

"You don't love me and you never did, and now I've gotta figure out what to do about the little gift you left me."

Amy's heart slid down to her feet. *Please, Lord. Help us.* She marched over to stand between them. "You've caused enough trouble, Andy. Please go now."

He stared at her for a long moment before shaking his head and looking at Tam. "I need a word alone."

"Anything you say to me you can say in front of Amy," Tam said.

The tires of an approaching vehicle crunched in the parking lot, and all three turned. The fog still rolled in, but Amy's heart quickened as a vintage, red and white truck came into view. "Matilda," she murmured, moving her hand over her heart. With her cowboy behind the wheel.

The truck pulled up to where the trio stood. Amy's gaze widened as the driver's door opened. Her heart in her throat, she spied the familiar, well-worn boots followed by the broad shoulders filling out that great suede jacket. When her eyes fell on the face of the most handsome, incredible man in the world, a small cry escaped. Putting on his Stetson, Landon gave her a wink as he walked around the front of the truck and pulled open the door. Chloe—all bouncy blonde curls and a sleepy smile—scampered out followed a second later by Winnie.

"Buttercup!" Amy opened her arms for Chloe's hug and she peppered her cheeks with kisses. Picking up the child, she squeezed Winnie's hand. "I can't believe you're here."

"As soon as Landon called, I knew the Lord needed us here with you."

Amy nodded, speechless. *Thank you, Lord.* He'd answered her prayer in a way over and above what she could ever imagine. *Your ways* are *perfect.* Not that she'd ever doubted it. She slanted a glance at Landon, and he tipped his hat, those blue eyes inviting. The warmth in them chased away all the chill of the morning fog.

"We don't need no audience people," Andy said, pulling her back to reality. "This is private between me and my girl. It ain't no three-ring circus."

Amy tilted her head toward the open motel room. Picking up on her cue, Winnie took Chloe by the hand and led her inside and closed the door.

"I'm not your girl, Andy, and I never was," Tam said, spinning on her heel to head back into the room. Reaching out and clamping her arm, Andy pulled her backward. Crying out in pain, she wrenched her arm away from his grasp.

"I'd keep my hands to myself if I were you." Landon—towering at least six inches taller than Andy—stared him down. "I think that's what got Tam into this situation in the first place. Move along, buddy."

Andy snarled and turned back to Tam. "What'd you do, tell the whole world how loose you are, girl?" he said, his voice tinged with contempt.

Stepping close, Landon trailed a gentle finger across Amy's cheek. The sting of Andy's hand was all but forgotten, but seeing the compassion in his expression brought it all back full-force. "Did he hit you?" His eyes lit with anger.

"It doesn't matter now."

"Amy took it for me," Tam said.

Landon turned and headed for Andy, but he squealed like a little girl and sprinted toward his sorry-looking truck. Without another glance, he tore out of the parking lot, the wheels of the truck spewing gravel.

"Good riddance," Tam said, heading back to the room.

"Give us a few minutes to get dressed," Amy said, turning to follow.

"Amy." Landon's voice was husky and deeper than usual. Gathering her into his chest, he hugged her like he never wanted to let go. His warm lips found her cheek. "Are you okay? I'm so sorry he did that to you, honey."

"Better me than Tam," she said, swiping one hand across her moist eyes. *He called me honey.* "I'm fine. It's only a surface wound. She said she might be getting 'rid of it' this morning. I can't let that happen. I *can't.*"

He dropped a light kiss on the top of her head. "No matter what happens, the Lord will honor your efforts and devotion to this girl. Let's pray for her. Right here, right now." And so they did. He kept her warm in his embrace as they asked the Lord for His grace and mercy on behalf of an unborn child with no name on Earth, but a place reserved in God's Heaven.

"Thanks for coming. You're my hero," she said, finally pulling out of his arms. "Give us a few minutes to get dressed."

He smiled. "I'll wait in the truck and keep it warmed up."

As she entered the room, Winnie caught her attention and put a finger over her lips. Following her cue, Amy saw Chloe sitting beside Tam on her bed.

"Did God give you a baby?" Chloe asked.

Tam laughed a little. "Maybe He did, Chloe."

"That's what He did for Mary," the little girl said. "Babies are great. Mommy's friend Lexa has two baby girls in her tummy and my mommy has my new brother or sister in her tummy."

Tam looked over at Winnie. "That's great, Chloe. You're going to be a great big sister."

"What are you going to call your baby?"

"Chloe, honey, it's time to let Tam and Amy get ready to go," Winnie said, walking toward her daughter with her hand outstretched. "We'll wait outside with Landon in the truck."

"Chloe?" Tam rose from the bed.

Winnie and Chloe turned from the doorway as she approached. Crouching down, she held out her arms. "Can I get a hug?"

Without hesitating, Chloe moved forward and put her arms around Tam. "Thank you," the teenager said, releasing her a moment later. "I hope I have a child someday who's as special as you." When Chloe kissed her cheek, Tam hurried into the bathroom, closing the door.

"Is she okay, Mommy?"

"I think she's going to be just fine, sweetie."

Chapter 47

FOR THE NEXT hour, they sat in a nearby restaurant. Tam declined to eat and only drank water, saying she wasn't sure if she should eat anything. After hearing that, Amy couldn't think of eating. When Tam assured her she didn't mind, Winnie ordered tea and a bran muffin. In the booth behind them, Landon ate breakfast with Chloe and helped her color a Christmas scene on the placemat. From the giggles coming from the little girl, Amy could tell they were having a grand time while she and Winnie talked quietly with Tam. She knew she was waffling over her decision. Winnie told the teenager about giving birth to Chloe as a single mom. Although she listened, Tam's expression was difficult to read.

After dropping Winnie and Chloe off at the town library, Amy scooted closer to Landon on the front seat of Matilda. "Hero or not, this doesn't mean I'm ready to let you back into my life, so don't get any big ideas," she said.

"Okay, I'll stick with the small ideas and hope they snowball."

"Tam's mother threw her out of the house and I think she's been sleeping in her car. I've got to figure out some way to help her."

"*We've* got to figure something out. You always want to take on the world by yourself. That's exhausting. Even superheroes need a little help every now and then, you know. I'm here, so let me help." He glanced in the rearview mirror, apparently satisfied Tam wasn't listening to their conversation. Matilda's engine was running a bit rough, and she knew it bothered him. Landon lowered his voice. "We can't leave ourselves open to any legal action her mother might file if we take Tam anywhere else. Even if she doesn't want Tam in her home, I don't think it's a stretch of the imagination to think her mother could do it, but that doesn't leave us a lot of other options since she's underage."

"Tam mentioned an older woman who works with her at the restaurant," Amy said. "I think she said her name's"—she thought for a moment—"Kaye. Her kids are grown but live nearby. Maybe if we talk with her, she can take Tam in and watch over her, at least until the baby's born. By that time, hopefully we'll figure out something else. I think we're almost there, if I understood Tam's directions."

As Landon pulled into the parking lot of the small clinic, Amy twisted around in her seat. Her head throbbed and she feared she might be sick. Tam chewed on a fingernail and stared out the side window. *She looks so scared.* "Do you have an appointment?"

"No."

Opening the back door, Amy held out one hand. "I'll go with you to meet with the doctor, if you want. We're here to do whatever you need. Anything."

"Come inside with me if you want, but I can meet with the doctor by myself."

Amy squeezed her hand. "You're braver than a lot of people I know. Please tell me what you're planning to do. If you're thinking of ending your pregnancy, I want you to tell me."

Tam shrugged and gave her a helpless look, indecision written in her expression. "I don't know. I wish I did, but I don't. You won't hate me if . . ."

"No, of course not. I could never hate you." Amy wrapped her arms around the thin girl, stroking her hair and kissing the side of her head. "And remember, God won't hate you. But He might cry, and so will I."

Wiping her eyes, Tam pulled out of her embrace. "God would cry over me? Why would He do that, and how do you know?"

"I don't, really, but what I know is He loves you and your baby. His heart is grieved when a child is . . . when a child dies, no matter the reason. But that child will rest in Jesus's arms forever." Unable to say more, Amy turned and tried to regain her composure. *Lord, what more can I say?* Should she offer to take this girl's child and raise the baby as her own? Is that why she was here? *Is that what You want?*

She startled when she felt a hand on her shoulder. "Thanks for caring about me, Amy. I don't know why you do, but no matter what happens," she said, sniffling and moving tear-filled eyes to the sky, "I want you to know you're the best." Tam released a shuddering breath and dropped her arms. "I'd better go inside now and get this over with."

Still unable to speak, Amy draped her arm around Tam's shoulders, thankful she allowed it. Perhaps as much as she did, Amy needed the contact. Standing nearby, Landon's eyes were bright, mirroring hers. He shuffled his boots on the ground and turned aside.

"Tam, please. I'm begging you," Amy said, her voice breaking. She had no other recourse, and she didn't care that she appeared totally broken before this young girl. Maybe that's what she needed to see so she'd know how deeply affected she was by the possibility she'd end the young life growing within her. Reaching out, she was relieved when Tam moved into the waiting circle of her arms. Cradling her head, Amy pressed her lips against her hair. "Remember, God knows your baby. If you decide to keep this child, He'll bless that decision. Like I told you before, you're capable of doing so much with your life. Having a child is a beautiful thing. Don't let it slow you down for following your dreams for your life. If anything, you can make this child part of living your dream."

As Landon held the door open, Amy walked inside the clinic, one arm still around Tam's shoulders. After signing in at the small window, they settled in a row of chairs. Three other patients waited in the small waiting room. Landon took both their jackets and hung them on pegs mounted on the wall.

"Just Maybe." Amy opened her purse and dug through it, pulling out the pages. "Tam, I'd like you to read this. It won't take long."

"Okay." Taking it from her, she stuffed it in her pocket. Catching Amy's intense gaze, she sighed. "You mean now?"

Amy nodded. "It's written by a girl in New York who had a baby when she was about your age."

Maybe it was the urgency in her tone, but Tam stared at her for a few seconds before unfolding the pages. None of them said anything, and the only sound was the occasional scooting of a chair, the ticking of the large clock on the wall, a cough here and there and the flipping of magazine pages. Amy prayed Tam's name wouldn't be called until she'd had a chance to read through Angelina's story. Maybe it wouldn't make a difference, but then again, it might. At this point, she was willing to try anything.

Needing his touch, Amy captured Landon's hand, threading her fingers through his. She dared not look directly into those blue eyes or she'd break down. At least until Tam disappeared behind the door, she had to maintain the appearance of confidence, although she was crumbling inside.

"Tamara Coughlin," the nurse called, holding a clipboard. She seemed matter-of-fact and none-too-friendly looking. Tam shot a frightened glance at Amy.

"Let me come with you."

"No," she said, taking a deep breath. Folding the paper, she handed it back to her. "Nice story, and I know what you're trying to tell me, but I got myself into this mess, and now it's time to take care of it." Her determined expression and firmness of voice sent chills up and down Amy's spine and she shivered.

"Remember what I said." Amy squeezed Tam's hand as the nurse grunted and stood aside for Tam to pass through the doorway. As soon as the door closed, Amy pivoted and marched out the front door of the clinic, rounding the corner to the side of the building. Leaning against the concrete wall, she lifted her head and prayed for all she was worth. Tears streamed down her cheeks, her voice broke on her sobs.

Strong arms moved around her in a comforting embrace. She didn't need to open her eyes to know it was Landon. When she started to fall, he leaned against the wall, pulling her with him. If it weren't for his arms, she would have hit the ground. He burrowed his head against her shoulder, absorbing her quivering body, stroking her hair.

"My heart is breaking," she whispered against his cheek. She moved her shaking fingers over the rough stubble of his morning beard.

"I know." His cheek was damp, and she knew it wasn't only from her tears. "You want to save the world and fix everything. You can't and that frustrates you, but you try." Cupping her face between his hands, he looked deep into her eyes. "You have such a beautiful soul and a heart filled with pure grace."

Amy's eyes overflowed as he brushed the pads of his thumbs over her cheeks as new tears fell. When she leaned against him, he curled her into his chest in the way she loved, and it brought her a measure of comfort.

"Let it out, sweetheart," he said.

Putting one hand on his chest, she felt his strong heartbeat which made her cry that much harder.

"I knew you two couldn't stay away from each other." Arms crossed, shaking her head, Tam eyed them with a raised brow. Denton stood beside her.

"Tam! Denton!" Disentangling herself from Landon's embrace, Amy cried out and almost tripped over his feet. Accepting his hand to steady her, she hurried over to Tam. "What happened?"

"I couldn't do it. Any of it."

"You didn't meet with the doctor?" Landon asked.

"Oh, I stayed long enough to find out I'm ten weeks along, but then I told them I had to leave. Walked right out of there."

Amy choked out the words. "What changed your mind?"

Tam stared at her boots for a few seconds before raising wet eyes to Amy's. "A bunch of things kinda added up when I was sitting in there. There was this other girl and you should have seen her. I mean, she gave me this scared look like 'What have I done?' I figured if you took a chance by flying all the way back down here to help me, then why shouldn't I give my baby a chance? You, Landon—Cooper or whatever your name is," she said, giving him a small smile, "Winnie, Chloe and Denton . . . you're all my angels."

"She called me when she in the examining room, waiting for the doctor," Denton said, moving his arm around Tam. Amy watched in wide-eyed wonder as Tam didn't push him away and leaned against him. "I high-tailed it over here."

"You should have seen him," Tam said, half-laughing, half-crying. "Marched right in there and told them he was taking me home."

Denton's cheeks colored and he shuffled his boots on the pavement. "I told her I'd help take care of her and her kid, if she'd let me."

Tears blurring her eyes, Amy flew to Tam and pulled her into the circle of her arms, holding her close. Landon put his arm around Denton's shoulders and they walked toward the parking lot.

"I've got a card with a schedule of appointments they gave me," Tam said. "I have to come back and they wanna run some tests. And I need to find a regular gyno doctor . . . whatever they're called."

"I'll find someone to help you, Tam. I promise you that."

"Actually, Denton said his sister can help me, and he talked with Kaye. She wants me to live with her for now, anyway."

Amy smiled and the huge weight on her heart lifted. *Thank you, Lord.*

"You don't know happy I am you have people willing to help you. Lean on them and they can help you, but trust in God, too, and He'll help you every step of the way."

Tam gave her a half smile. "I'll keep in touch and you can tell me more about this God stuff. Seems to work for you and Mr. Handsome, so why not?"

They shared a grin. "By the way, did somebody slug him or something? That bruise on his face looks like it was pretty fierce."

Amy tried not to laugh. "Something like that."

"Well, you know what I want right now?"

"What's that?" Amy hooked her arm through Tam's as they walked toward Matilda.

"A grilled cheese sandwich and soup. Good comfort food."

Chapter 48

Tuesday, December 31, 2002

HOW PITIFUL AM I? In the middle of the afternoon on New Year's Eve, she sat in her office while most of her coworkers made plans to leave and start celebrating. All that awaited her was a bowl of chip and dip and watching the ball drop in Times Square. Why should this year be any different than the last decade? A part of her hoped Landon would call—even last minute, but in her heart, she knew he wouldn't. She'd told him she needed more time, and he was still honoring that wish. "Sometimes you don't have to be so honorable," she muttered.

Tossing down her pencil, she knew trying to work was a lost cause. She swiveled in her chair and stared out her office window, not really focusing on anything, doing what she seemed to do best these days—endless daydreaming. She'd spent a lot of face time with this window. At least it was quiet around the office, the calm in the sea of deadlines before the inevitable storm that would blow into the *Habits* offices in the next few weeks.

The intercom buzzed. "Amy, you have a visitor."

Turning back to face her desk, she frowned. Who would be here today of all days? She pushed the button. "Who is it, Lana?"

Marcheline breezed around the corner. "Mr. Warnick to see you, Amy," she announced, standing aside as Landon entered her office carrying a bulky, square but rather flat package. "I'll close the door and give you two some privacy," she said, giving her a wink.

Before she could protest, the intercom buzzed again. "Amy?" *Oh no. Juliet.* With her finger poised on the intercom, Amy bit her lip. She couldn't very well disconnect her boss, but this couldn't be good. "Juliet, I have company at the moment."

"I know that. Landon, what are you doing in my offices? Trying to steal another one of my employees before the New Year?"

To Amy's surprise, Landon chuckled. "Nothing sinister, I assure you. Happy New Year, Juliet. What do you say we bury the hatchet for 2003?"

Amy hid her smile when her boss snorted. She pressed the intercom button. "Landon's only here for a minute and then he's on his way."

"I'll bet," Juliet said. "If he's here with a job offer for some new business endeavor, throw him out. But first find out what he's offering."

"Will do," Amy said, trying not to laugh.

Releasing the intercom, Amy willed her heart to slow. "Now see what you've done? My job could be in serious jeopardy."

Landon's eyes lit with warmth, and he looked not unlike a small boy at Christmas. It was the same look he had in Macy's. How she loved that smile, infectious and inviting.

"I highly doubt that. After all, Juliet keeping you means I can't have you, and that seems paramount in her mind." He winced. "Sorry, that came out wrong."

"I know what you meant, but whatever this is, you shouldn't have."

"I didn't. Cooper did." His grin was irresistible. "Never can control what that guy does."

She laughed. "You're deranged."

"You love it."

Her eyes met his. "Never said I didn't. I didn't get anything for you."

"I didn't expect anything, but this is something you need. Trust me."

"Please stop buying me things."

Landon held up his hand. "The element of surprise is much sweeter if you play along. Humor me. Close your eyes."

"So bossy," she said, unable to resist his enthusiasm. Closing her eyes, she put her hands over them to reassure him she wouldn't peek. "I feel like a kid playing a game."

"Okay, you may open your eyes now." He stood beside her desk, holding the package.

"This must have been hard to wrap."

"I wouldn't know. I bribed Dona to do it for me a few weeks ago."

"That woman's a saint for putting up with you. I hope you gave her an insanely expensive Christmas bonus."

"I take excellent care of my employees . . . when I have them, that is." He angled his head to the door and raised his voice. "Hear that, Juliet?"

"Shh," she said, putting a finger over her lips.

"Open it already. It's getting heavy."

"Yes, sir." Giving him a skeptical glance, Amy tore off a large section of paper and gasped. As she continued to tear off more paper, her fingers shook when she unveiled the Jackson Hawley painting. "*Finding Amelia*? How . . . how? Even for you, this is too extravagant."

"I knew you wouldn't buy it for yourself, and I know how much you liked it."

Seeing the look on his face, she couldn't disappoint him. "I'll treasure it. Thank you, Landon." Words seemed so inadequate for such a thoughtful, valuable gift. Taking the painting from him, she lowered it to the floor. Beckoning him with one finger, she kissed his cheek.

"I won't wash this cheek ever again," he said, and she relished his grin.

"You're mocking me?"

"No, I can't resist teasing you."

"Your dutiful assistant e-mailed me a couple of weeks ago, you know."

Crossing his arms, he leaned against the edge on the side of her desk. "Go on."

"The intriguing subject line was 'Ten Reasons to Forgive Him.' I particularly liked reasons number four and eight."

"Out with it. You've got me curious, but I pray this isn't painful."

"Let's start with reason number eight: you visited a Christian Academy for their 'Walk Through the Bible' Day and got a little too animated."

Landon groaned and massaged his forehead. "She didn't."

Amy giggled. "Such an adorable story. Seems you split your dress pants right up the back with your exaggerated interpretation of the Creation split. Apparently, it was the highlight of the whole event for the kids. Dona said you covered your backside with a file folder and waited in the nurse's office while the school librarian did a quick mend, then you rejoined the fun and carried on with your head held high."

"See why I like wearing jeans?" His lips twisted. "What was the other one? It can't be any more humiliating."

"Reason number four." Her smile sobered. "You've been a Big Brother to a boy in Queens for over four years and spend almost every Saturday with him—taking him to baseball games, arcades, the movies and to visit his dad's grave. I saw our friend Louie the taxi driver the other day and he told me the same thing." She paused, taking a deep breath. "You inspire great loyalty from your friends and family, and they all seem to agree on one thing."

"That you should throw yourself in my arms this minute, kiss me until tomorrow and forgive me for all the stupid things I've done and am destined to do the rest of my life?"

"No," she said, her eyes misting. *Tempting as it is.* She was afraid he'd take a step closer or pull her into his arms. She wasn't ready. Not yet. The most difficult thing was the disappointment shining in his eyes.

"Then what, Amy? Tell me. I need to know."

"They told me how passionate you are about everything you do in life, and they know how much you care about me."

"All true." He slid his hands in both pockets. "I more than care about you, Amy, and I think you know that, too. I lo—"

Moving quickly, she put two fingers over his lips. "I still need time, Landon."

He nodded, the muscles in his jaw flexing. "Understood. Take all the time you need. What was number one on Dona's list, if I may ask?"

"In due time. As someone once told me, I'll tell you when the time is right. Mitch told me you're resigning from *New York Scene.* I know how much it must hurt you to give it up."

The look in his eyes confirmed her words. "I hope you don't believe I'm selling out."

"Why would I ever think that?" she asked. "If anything, it's the opposite. You're standing up for your principles, and that's never wrong."

"Not to change the subject, but your *Habits* article on Sam's book was great," he said. "The advance preorder numbers are very encouraging, and I'm sure your article helped contribute to that to a large degree. 'Hurt builds up walls, but love tears them down.' Brilliant concept. Wish I'd thought of it so I could use it as a tagline for the book."

She smiled. "Sam came up with it, but he was actually talking about our situation at the time."

His eyes bore into hers. "Sam's one of the wisest men I know. Very knowledgeable about love, marriage and God's word. A powerful combination, if ever there was one. I can learn a lot from him. I've already offered him a contract for a follow-up book."

"Sam knows about a lot about things," Amy said, turning to face the window, unable to see the opposite office building through the thick fog blanketing the city. "His book is a terrific first project for your new company."

He stepped beside her. "That's only the beginning. There's a number of other exciting things on the horizon. I'm happy to say Dona's already on the payroll." He ran his hand over his jaw. "I've got a lot of things to figure out, though. It's a daunting challenge, full of uncertainty."

"I'm sure you'll be successful." She tilted her head. "I have a few more questions if you don't mind."

"Ask away." Crossing the room, he dropped into a chair and Amy followed, sitting in the opposite chair.

"Is it true about the rental car, the motel, the one room, the one bed . . ."

"All true. If you ask me, it was part of God's plan to bring us together."

"Now you're making the Almighty part of this?"

Landon's gaze pierced through her. "You can't tell me you don't think He is, Amy."

"Like I told Tam, if we trust Him, He's with us every step of the way."

"So you agree?"

She sidestepped that one. "What's the story about the writer Juliet believes you stole from *Habits*?"

His brow creased. "Ah, yes. She never forgave me for that one. In fact, Lenora asked *me* if she could work for my magazine. She's a talented writer, but she moved on to another publication more than a year ago." He leaned forward, arms resting on his thighs. "I never had a relationship with Lenora apart from work."

"I didn't say a word."

"She's nowhere near as talented—nor as beautiful—as you."

Amy needed to speak now or she'd throw herself in the man's arms. "Who was the man in The Driskill lobby?"

He rubbed a hand over his brow. "Man in the lobby?"

"You shook hands and enjoyed a rousing conversation. Right before the Macy's excursion."

"Oh, yes. That's Tom Lawler. He's a business acquaintance and lives in San Antonio. If you'd walked over to us, you probably would have discovered my true identity right then and there."

"One more question." He waited, silent. "When you sent me back down to Texas on Madelyn, how did you get there? Thank you again. It was very generous."

Landon straightened in his chair. "Welcome. I'm glad you called me. Since you asked . . . men with private planes . . . well, we know other men with private planes."

She laughed. "Oh, yes, of course. Let me guess, the Howard Hughes Aviation Club?"

He chuckled. "Before I left New York, I called Josh, and he drove Winnie and Chloe to meet up with me to drive into Asher. It saved a lot of time. He's a great guy."

"I'll agree with you there. TeamWork has some of the best people you'll ever meet. But then, I guess you know all about that. That's another thing. Why didn't you tell me you're part of TeamWork?"

He appeared slightly uncomfortable. "I prefer to keep it behind the scenes. Enough of my life is laid out for public scrutiny and consumption."

"I know." Blowing out a breath, she rose and walked back over to the window. "I've been doing some thinking."

"As a wise woman once told me, that's always a good thing."

Facing him, she ached for his strong, protective arms to hold her close. "You were right. A part of me—subconscious or not—didn't want to know you were Landon although I think in the back of my mind, I must have known all along. I wasn't sure of you, but for some reason, I instinctively trusted Cooper. Explain that one."

Crossing the room, he stood beside her. "Maybe it's because Landon is running from the past, but Cooper's more comfortable in his own skin." He caught her look. "Okay, I realize I'm talking in third person again and I sound a little nuts, but hear me out. Until I met you, I couldn't see it. You've opened my eyes to so many things, Amy, and for that, I'll always thank you. Like I told Mitch, there are some things I need to settle and get straight in my life." Taking both her hands, he laced his fingers through hers. She didn't stop him, didn't want to stop him. "And then I'm coming for you. I only pray you'll still be waiting."

He didn't give her the opportunity to answer as he withdrew his hands and left the room, not looking back.

"Happy New Year," she whispered.

Chapter 49

Mid-January 2003

"AMY, IF YOU haven't seen it yet, you need to run—don't walk—to the newsstand and get the Valentine issue of *New York Scene.* It's Landon's swan song." Mitch's message got her heart pumping. She was already in her pajamas. At seven o'clock. *What an old maid.* Next she'd be visiting the animal shelter on adoption day. After the last episode with Tam, she'd made a personal vow: no more running outside in sleepwear under any circumstances. Grunting, she ran into her bedroom and pulled on sweats and a T-shirt. Shoving her arms into her jacket, she grabbed a twenty from her purse. Locking her door and pocketing the keys, she scrambled down the front steps of the townhouse and hurried down to the corner, hoping the cranky old guy who operated the newsstand hadn't already closed up shop for the night.

"Wait! Please!" she called, raising her arm in the air as she ran.

"Gimme a break, lady." He pulled down the screen to cover the newsstand. "I open again at seven in the morning."

"Please," she said. "Look, this really is one of those things that could change the course of my life." Maybe. Dramatic yes, but true all the same. *I need to find out.*

He looked at her like she was delusional, but he stopped and gawked at her. "You mean to tell me something in one of these papers or magazines is gonna change your life? Yeah, right." He snorted and continued on with his task. "Did I tell you I'm meeting with the Queen tomorrow? We're having high tea at The Ritz-Carlton."

"Fine. I'll see you at seven." Shoulders slumping, she turned to go. Hearing a car horn, she jumped and put a hand on her chest.

"Miss Amy!"

That friendly voice made her pivot. "Louie!" When he stopped the cab in the street, she ran over to the side of the taxi. "What brings you to my neighborhood?"

"Took on an extra shift. Hey, Mel," he said, nodding to the newsstand operator. "You know my friend here?"

Mel waved back. "You mean Miss I-gotta-buy-this-now-'cause-it'll-change-my-life?"

Louie surprised her by bursting into laughter. "Give her what she wants and put it on my tab."

"Oh no, Louie. I've got money," Amy said, starting to offer the twenty curled in her palm, feeling like a street urchin.

With a grunt, the man reversed the screen. "All right. Make it quick. Which one?"

"*New York Scene*, please. Thanks, Mel. I really appreciate it."

"Yeah, yeah. Save it." Pulling out the magazine, he thrust it in her hands and refused to take her money.

"That your boyfriend's magazine?" Louie asked, humor infusing his voice.

She glanced at the issue in her hands with its cover story, *What the Eyes Conceal, the Heart Reveals*, by outgoing editor, Landon C. J. Warnick. "Could be," she said with a wistful smile. "Thanks, Louie. Tell Angelina hi for me. One of these days I want to meet her. Tell her I'll call her and we'll go to lunch."

"Make it high tea and I'll bring Queenie along," Mel said.

Amy laughed and Mel waved her off.

"Thanks, Louie! See you soon."

She couldn't get back home fast enough. Securing the door, she tossed her jacket on the sofa and ran into the bedroom, diving on her bed, prepared to read.

~

Before turning off her light to go to sleep, Amy had to read the beautifully written piece one more time. Her lids growing heavy, she read some key passages of his article again.

I was a groomsman in a wedding in Louisiana recently. After meeting a lovely young woman and falling a bit in love with her during the course of only a few hours spent together here in New York, I discovered she was a bridesmaid in the very same wedding. When I first saw her coming down the aisle in the wedding, my journalistic instincts kicked into high gear. I'd always thought of doing an exposé on the life of identical twins, and the advantages and disadvantages. Could this be my chance? She knew me as the New York publisher, but could I make her believe I was an urban Texas cowboy? Knowing she could have no idea of my connection to the groom, the irresistible lure of combining the wedding with my article proved too potent. It was my opportunity to live out the fantasy of being two distinct individuals identical in looks yet different in personality.

I've heard it said how powerful a kiss can be, but I'd always discounted it as the illusion of romantic fools. I've also heard how love can make a person do crazy, irrational things. Not me—a completely sane, rational, logical person. A man too proud to admit he needed love, a man afraid *of loving because of past hurts and failures. A man who kissed this woman for the first time and knew he loved her. I barely knew her, yet knew her so well. Was it because of the romance in the air at the wedding reception or something from my wildest imagination or sweetest dream?*

I quickly dismissed the idea of writing the story about identical twins. However, in a strange twist of irony, the joke was on me. She had the mistaken impression I was, in fact, someone else—an urban cowboy, no less. We'd arranged to go to Austin together after the wedding so I could show her my hometown before I was to take her to Houston. Against my better judgment and my conscience, I played along with the mistaken identity ruse, becoming the exact type of romantic fool I'd always scorned. Through all our adventures, I began to see the true beauty and honesty in this woman. She's so trusting with her heart. She touched me deeply and I callously toyed with her affections, although that was never my intention. I've seen her grace when she hugs a child, her compassion when she takes action when so many stand on the sidelines, her fierce loyalty to her friends and family, and her spirit and unflagging devotion to a moral cause near and dear to her heart. This incredible, beautiful woman has touched many lives, and none more so than mine.

I soon realized I could no longer keep up the deception. I had to somehow reveal my true identity to her. Although only one man, I'm both a Texas cowboy with a ready wink and flirtatious smile and also the publisher of this New York magazine. Two entirely different identities, but with one heart beating between them. A heart that beat faster whenever she was in my presence. A heart that hurt knowing how I'd failed and disappointed her. A heart that bled with the realization I'd pushed her away because of my unjustified loyalty to a nonexistent story. No story is worth losing someone, no deception worth losing your soul. What started out as a mere story idea quickly became my albatross, and the sharp arrow that ultimately pierced straight through her precious heart, wounding her deeply, and I will forever be ashamed.

She skimmed down the page and continued to read.

My plan worked, but it also misfired in colossal fashion. Instead of having the effect I intended, this woman I'd grown to love felt deceived, hurt, angry and unbelievably betrayed. Looking back, I can see why, and I can only hope she'll forgive me in time for breaking her trust in me. I love her, and I hope she'll accept my heartfelt apology for hurting her. With God's help, I'll spend the rest of my life proving to her she's the only one who makes my heart beat faster. I have been truly blessed and abundantly graced by her presence in my life. If she reads this, I only pray that, at the very least, she'll give me the opportunity to one day prove to her the depths of my adoration, affection and boundless love for her.

Amy didn't know how Landon was able to sneak the words "pray" and "with God's help" past the powers that be, but he'd managed to do it. Closing the magazine, she switched off the bedside lamp, and fell asleep with a smile.

Chapter 50

Friday, February 14, 2003 – Valentine's Day

THE PHONE RINGING woke her up at five in the morning. "Amy, have you heard?" *Winnie.* The perkiness in her voice—at this insanely early hour—assured her nothing was wrong.

Rubbing her eyes, glancing at the clock, Amy yawned. "I guess I haven't since I don't know what you're talking about."

"Lexa had the twins shortly after midnight. Hannah Grace and Leah Rachel arrived safely and all is well. Sam's beside himself and loves holding a little girl in each arm."

"I'm so thrilled for them all," she said, covering her mouth to stifle another loud yawn. "Let me know when you find out which twin is the bossy one."

"What?" Winnie asked, laughing.

"Something Lexa said when I was in Houston."

"Things going okay with you and Landon?"

"We're making progress. I think everything's going to be fine." Her heart swelled with the words. A new peace had settled in her heart in the last week alone.

"He's got it bad for you, sweetie. On our trip to Asher, he gripped the steering wheel so hard, I thought the thing would break off in his hands. The whole way, he asked questions about you. He tried to be subtle, but he was pretty obvious."

"I hope you gave him the good stuff."

Winnie giggled. "Trust me, sweetie, I sold you good. You came out smelling like a Texas rose. Don't mind saying I even fell in love with you all over again. He barged into that restaurant like a police officer. Sounded like one, too, the way he grilled the employees. He's a great guy, Amy, and he loves you. Know we're praying for you and hope it works out. Promise you'll fly down to Houston again soon, okay?"

"Sure thing, and you'll have to schedule a trip here, hopefully in the spring since you'll be paying a visit to the maternity ward yourself soon enough. Bring Chloe and we can make a weekend of it."

"Sounds great and we'll talk soon."

"Hey, Daydreamer." She smiled at the sound of Josh's sleepy voice.

"Tell Josh hi, give Chloe a hug for me and thanks for calling." Hanging up the phone, Amy hugged her pillow. She startled when the phone rang not ten minutes later. *What's up with all the early morning calls today?* Glancing at the phone, she recognized the area code as Texas, but couldn't place it. *Here we go again.*

Knowing it probably wasn't a random phone call or wrong number, she picked it up. Hopefully, everything was okay with Tam. Last they'd talked, she was feeling good, working at the diner, living with Kaye, getting help from Denton and his sister, only "just friends" with Denton, and expecting a little boy in the fall.

"Hello?"

"Is this Amy Jacobsen?" The woman's voice had a distinct southern drawl, warm and pleasant.

"Yes." She waited, not knowing what else to say until the woman identified herself.

"This is Madelyn Resnick."

The name registered and her breath caught. "Mama Warnick?"

The woman laughed, soft and gentle. "Call me Madelyn, and yes, I'm Landon's mother. Resnick is my married name."

"Of course." Her heart thudded. Why would Landon's mother be calling her at five in the morning? "Is everything okay with Landon?"

"Yes, and I'm sorry if I alarmed you. I don't make it a habit to call someone I don't know this early, but I wanted to let you know that Landon won't be able to make his dinner date with you tonight at Kyle's. He'll call you later, and I know how much he regrets it. It's all my son's talked about since the New Year."

"It's okay," Amy said, swallowing her disappointment. "I'm sure he has good reason."

"Landon's father was due to be released from prison earlier this week, but it was delayed. We found out he's had a heart attack and he's in an Austin hospital."

"Is he . . ."—Amy gulped—"going to be okay?"

"We don't have any details yet but he's holding his own at this point. I wanted you to know that Landon's getting ready to fly down to see him. I know he'd love it—"

"Is he taking Madelyn, I mean, his plane?"

"Yes." She gave Amy the name of the airport—the same one she flew out of when he sent her to Texas to see Tam—and what time he planned on leaving.

"If I hurry, I can make it. Thanks for calling, Mrs. Resnick, but I have to go now."

"Call me Madelyn, please. I'll have Landon bring you to see us while you're here, Amy. I need to meet the woman who's completely captured my son's heart."

"I'll look forward to meeting you, too."

Dialing Juliet's line, thankful for the answering service, she left another hasty excuse. At least it was a Friday and no articles were due. She hoped her boss wouldn't think this was becoming a habit with her, but this was too important. Important enough for Landon's mother to call. She loved her already.

~

Two Hours Later

"Wait! Stop!" Of all the days to wear her ridiculous new high-heeled designer shoes in an effort to look pretty.

Landon's dark head was visible through one of the plane's small windows. His head was bowed, most likely in prayer. Hurrying as fast as she could, sliding when she hit a patch of ice, Amy kept going, praying under her breath somehow the pilot—or his passenger—would hear or see her. It was a miracle she didn't twist an ankle or worse. Finally, she stopped. It was hopeless. "Landon!" Her cry was lost in a bitter gust of cold wind; her tears froze as soon as they hit the tarmac.

I'm too late.

Her heart heavy with an unbearable sadness, she slumped to the ground as his plane soared overhead. Crossing her arms across her mid-section, she rocked back and forth a few times. *This isn't the best idea.* It was too cold and she was already partially frozen. Feeling like she'd never be warm again, she hauled herself to her feet and walked back to where she'd dropped her suitcase. Numbness—emotional as well as physical—overwhelmed her as she headed toward the small terminal. If only she'd been a few minutes earlier, she might have had a chance. She brushed away a few more tears and gave into the sob hovering around the edges of her heart, her soul, her mind. *Lord, I tried.* Problem was, she wanted Landon to know. *Needed* him to know.

Hearing a noise behind her, she stopped. If she wasn't mistaken, it was the sound of an engine. She turned as it grew louder. A small cry escaped and her mouth dropped open as a small plane landed on the runway. She blinked hard. Could it be? Surely not; she'd watched his plane lift off the runway, heard it fly overhead. Many of the smaller planes looked very similar, but something kept her rooted to the spot. Sure enough, when the plane pulled closer, her eyes widened as she spied the numbers identifying the plane as Landon's. "Madelyn." When she saw Landon rise from his seat and peer out the window—a wide grin on his face—she half-laughed, half-cried.

Immobilized, she stared as the door opened and he jumped onto the tarmac, sprinting toward her. He was the most welcome sight she'd ever seen in his jeans, black wool coat, Stetson and boots. He stopped a heartbeat away, slightly out of breath, staring at her as though she was a figment of his imagination.

"Don't just stand there," she said. "It's cold out here. Aren't you going to invite me in?"

The lines of worry eased and Landon unbuttoned his coat and opened his arms. She felt his smile as he wrapped her in the cocoon of his warmth, pulling his coat around her and tucking her into his chest. Where she always wanted to be, where she belonged.

"You're the best sight I've seen in a forever of Fridays," he said. "Tell me, what brings you here to my desolate stretch of runway on such a harsh, bitter winter day?"

"Mama Warnick—Resnick," she self-corrected, "called me this morning. I'm so sorry about your dad. Have you heard any more?"

"He's doing better, but I need to see him. Whether or not he asks the question, I need to let him know he's forgiven, and then ask him to forgive me. We have a lot to discuss."

"You're a good man. Do you have room for one more?" Tugging on the lapels of his coat, Amy moved her gaze upward to meet his.

"Depends on who's asking." A smile upturned his lips.

"Me." She rested her gloved hand on his cheek, her eyes filling with tears. How she loved this man. "I'm not only talking about today."

His eyes softened and he nodded. "I know. I'll always have room for you, Amelia. Come with me." Scooping her in his arms as if she weighed nothing, he hurried with her back to the plane.

"Wait! My suitcase!" She waved her hand toward the bag on the ground. He sighed, turned and marched back toward the small terminal, lowering her so she could retrieve it. "That's a Louis Vuitton. You can't leave something that valuable sitting on a runway." Curling her fingers around the handle of the case, Amy held onto her hat with her other hand as Landon hurried with her back to the waiting plane.

"Funny thing," he said, amusement coloring his voice. "I was thinking the same thing about you." He ducked as he stepped onboard with her in his arms. Lowering her, he secured the door and then helped her out of her coat, hat and gloves.

Unable to resist, she gave him an impish grin and raised her brows. "Hoping to see me again, were you?"

"Not at all," he said, tossing his coat and hat aside. "Hoping to do this again." In a split second, his arms circled her waist and he captured her lips in a hard, passionate kiss of pure possession. When he pulled back, his eyes were damp. "You don't know how much I've missed you."

Smoothing his brow, Amy pulled his head down and planted a gentle kiss on his scar. "I kind of missed you, too." She cried out as the plane lurched forward.

Scrambling into the nearest seat, Landon tugged her down beside him. "Never had a woman chase my plane down a runway before. Pretty heady stuff." He helped her buckle in before doing the same.

"I've never done it before, and I never plan on doing it again."

"No need," he said, settling back in his seat. "You've already caught me." Lifting her hand, he traced a line across her ring finger. "So, let's get back to that question from a long time ago. You wanna go steady?"

Amy laughed. "I'm thinking we should date for a while first. Get to know each other better."

"As long as you don't believe in long periods of courtship or engagement." Leaning close, he captured her lips again as the plane taxied down the runway.

She pushed herself up straighter and tried to concentrate on anything but how his kisses affected her. "You drive a hard bargain. Answer a couple more questions first."

Collapsing against the seat, he laughed. "Talk about driving a hard bargain. If you must, go ahead. Then back to the passionate kissing. I have one question first: did you read my article?"

"I did. It was beautifully written. Very persuasive. You once mentioned one thing a woman can't say no to. What's that?"

His smile was blinding. Leaning over, his lips warm against hers, he whispered, "Will you marry me?"

Closing her eyes, she shook her head.

"Please don't say that's a no. I have your mother's permission."

"You what?" Her eyes fluttered open.

"She gave it to me when I visited her last month and asked permission to marry you. She's lovely, Amy, as I knew she would be. I thought I might have an uphill battle, considering my unseemly behavior, but I groveled and she gave us her blessing."

"And Mitch?"

"He couldn't be happier. Of course, he only wants to borrow the plane. This is only the beginning, sweetheart. I want you to wear my Stetson. I want to buy you cowboy boots and sexy lingerie, make up bad country songs and sing them to you, maybe get a puppy and teach you to cook. Bring you daffodils in winter. But most of all," he said, pulling her closer, planting a kiss on one cheek and then the other, "I want to snuggle in bed with you every night, talk Texan with you—fun and kinda naughty Texan," he said, his low, husky voice making her heart soar—"and make at least two or three stubborn, intelligent and very articulate children with you."

"I like the way you think," Amy said, flushed with joy, "but who told you I can't cook?"

"Mitch, of course."

She laughed. "First rule of business, you need to stop listening to my brother. I want to fix him up with Cassie one of these days and then he can worry about his own love life, not mine." With a small smile, she tugged on his red sweater. Bringing him closer, she gave him a long, deep kiss guaranteed to make him forget his name.

"So, I take it that's a yes to my offer of marriage?"

"That would be a definitive yes. Of course, I know you're only marrying me for my money."

His eyes danced. "Right. And you're only marrying me for my mind."

"No, I'm only marrying you because you'll be handy around the house and can screw in a light bulb or two. I predict we'll be doing the Sunday crossword together within a year."

"Are you kidding? Six months, tops." Landon nuzzled her nose and cheeks, those lips soft and warm before he nibbled her lower lip, stealing all rational thought.

"What made you change your mind?" he asked a few glorious minutes later.

Her smile was wistful. "Prayer, friends, your TeamWork involvement, your Boys Club work, the fact you flew me back down to Texas on your plane and then followed with Winnie and Chloe, you comforted me when Tam was inside the clinic . . ." She ran her finger along his jaw, and he leaned into it, kissing the side of her hand. "Your mama raised you right."

She watched, wide-eyed, as he unbuckled his seat belt and reached across the aisle for his coat. Pulling a small velvet box from the outside pocket, he handed it to her.

With a catch in her throat, Amy looked at him with wide eyes. "You've already—"

"Open it."

Doing as he asked, she smiled. "The locket. You just happened to have this in your coat?"

"What can I say? I prayed you'd come back to me one day, and I wanted to have it ready when you did."

"May I?" Taking it out of the box, Landon fastened it around her neck. "Back where it belongs. I love you, my beautiful Daydreamer. Like I said in the article, with God's help, I'll spend the rest of my life making you happy."

"You do, and I kind of like you, too. As in I love you like crazy, and I plan on doing it the rest of my life." His gorgeous smile reached the remaining places in her heart not already overflowing with love for this man. "Can I call you Cooper every now and then? Just for fun?"

"You can call me whatever you like, sweetheart, as long as it's flattering."

"Be good and it will be."

He laughed. "Are you going to tell me now what was number one on Dona's list of ten reasons why you should forgive me?"

"Number one—" she laced her fingers through his— "because Landon Cooper Jared Warnick is the husband of God's choosing for Amelia Madelyn Jacobsen."

"I'm so glad I hired that woman. And so thankful God gave me *you*."

With a smile that promised a thousand tomorrows, Landon kissed her soundly before clasping their joined hands over his chest, above his heart.

"Let the adventure begin."

About the Author

Daydreams is JoAnn's fourth published novel in ***The Lewis Legacy Series***, following the popular ***Awakening*, *Second Time Around*** and ***Twin Hearts***. Get ready for romance, adventure, friendship, faith and family in each installment of the series with Sam and Lexa Lewis and their lively TeamWork Missions volunteers.

JoAnn lives with her husband, Jim, and their three children in southern Indiana and works as a full-time estate administration paralegal in Louisville, Kentucky. She's a member of the American Christian Fiction Writers and the Louisville Christian Writers.

Please visit her at **www.joanndurgin.com** or at Author JoAnn Durgin on Facebook.

The *Lewis Legacy Series*

by JoAnn Durgin

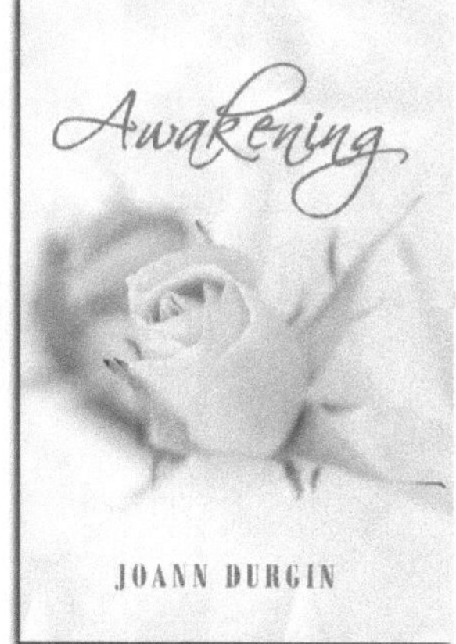

A God-fearing man. A God-seeking woman. For Sam Lewis and Lexa Clarke, it proves a combustible combination. You'll keep turning the pages of this sweeping romantic adventure. With great characters, plenty of humor, enough emotion to make you shed a tear or two, and an ending that'll have you cheering, *Awakening* will leave you breathless. Hold on tight.

Paperback ISBN 978-0-9912252-0-0

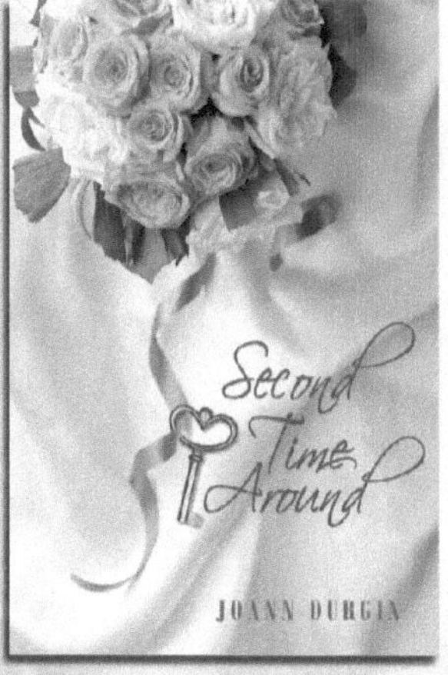

Newlyweds Marc and Natalie Thompson have it all, but two months after the wedding, Natalie suffers a horrible fall. Not only does she not remember their life together, but now Marc has a personal timeline to reconnect with her—seven months. You'll root for them as they fight against the odds to find their way back to one another... the second time around.

Paperback ISBN 978-0-9912252-2-4

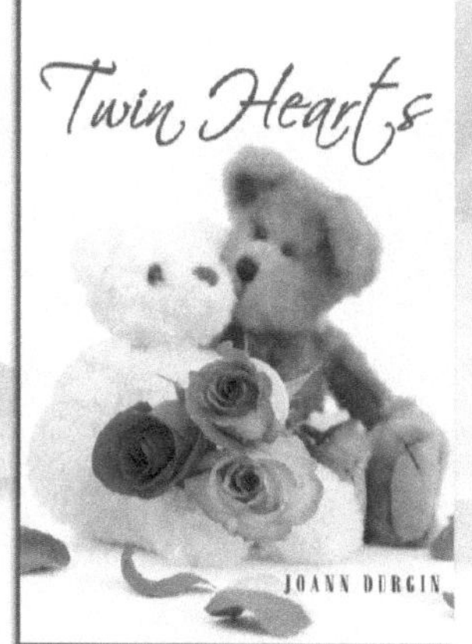

It's been more than four years since Josh was thrown out of the TeamWork missions camp, and he's still haunted by the bittersweet memory of his final meeting with another volunteer. When he also seeks her forgiveness, he gets the shock of his life. Could turning his deepest sin into his greatest blessing be God's answer for his hurting heart?

Paperback ISBN 978-0-9912252-4-8

The ***Lewis Legacy Series*** is available in paperback and eBook

www.ingramcontent.com/pod-product-compliance
Lightning Source LLC
Chambersburg PA
CBHW020237180626
46810CB00006B/2234
9780991225262